I fell in love
with hope

I fell in love with hope

with hope

A Novel

Lancali

EMILY BESTLER BOOKS
—
ATRIA
New York • London • Toronto • Sydney • New Delhi

An Imprint of Simon & Schuster, Inc.
1230 Avenue of the Americas
New York, NY 10020

This Emily Bestler Books/Atria Paperback edition June 2023

EMILY BESTLER BOOKS/ATRIA PAPERBACK and colophon are trademarks of Simon & Schuster, Inc.

For information about special discounts for bulk purchases, please contact Simon & Schuster Special Sales at 1-866-506-1949 or business@simonandschuster.com.

The Simon & Schuster Speakers Bureau can bring authors to your live event. For more information or to book an event, contact the Simon & Schuster Speakers Bureau at 1-866-248-3049 or visit our website at www.simonspeakers.com.

Interior design by Dana Sloan

Manufactured in the United States of America

1 3 5 7 9 10 8 6 4 2

ISBN 978-1-6680-3453-8
ISBN 978-1-6680-3454-5 (ebook)

To my Sam,
and to everyone in the world who
needs to feel a little less alone

Foreword

THIS STORY TAKES pieces of my heart and spreads them thin on paper. Told from the perspective of an all-knowing narrator, it is an exploration of friendship, sin, illness, love, and all things that make us human.

These pages are full of real memories given the shape of different characters, similar places, and the same ideas. It's important to mention that many of the technicalities of disease are portrayed fictitiously in this novel and should not be analyzed as medically reviewed cases.

This story contains domestic abuse, eating disorders, intense physical bullying, self-harm, suicide, rape, depression, anxiety, and gory descriptions of disease.

Autoimmune disorders are a tricky thing from an outsider's perspective and even more so from an insider's experience. It's a wide spectrum, a pendulum that swings from chronic to terminal. A large majority of people with autoimmune diseases can expect to live normal lives. A small minority can't.

This story is for both. It is for all who know loneliness and for all who search for themselves.

I hope you find a piece of you in Sam, Hikari, Neo, Sony, and Coeur as I did.

before

THE LOVE OF my life wants to die.

That's a tragic thing to say out loud. No. Maybe not tragic. Maybe just unfair. But as you begin this story, I think you'll find that tragedies and injustices usually stand under the same umbrella.

Before the love of my life decided he didn't want to live anymore, he told me the stars belonged to us. We spent every night together, our bodies softly intertwined on harsh roof tiles, memorizing the patterns in the sky. So even as he withered, as his body became less body and more corpse, I believed our stars would give him faith. I believed they would keep him alive so long as he could look up and see they hadn't fallen.

Tonight, he and I stand on a bridge as the river rushes black and streetlamps cast a golden halo on our winter-numbed fingers.

"Are you angry at me?" I ask, because tonight, I tell him the truth. I tell him the truth about me, the truth I say to no one, the secret that makes me different from everyone he knows. I throw it like a lasso around his neck, a lifeline, something to keep him from taking that final step into the dark.

He shakes his head, grasping the railing. "I'm just curious." The yellow-flared eyes I've always fallen into find mine. "What does it feel like? To be you?"

"It feels like I've stolen," I say. "Like this body isn't really mine."

Confessions can be brusque and surrendering, but mine are gentle. The truth of who I am doesn't make sense, but it doesn't have to. He knows that. He's been sick since he was born. Being sick teaches you that reasons are just poor attempts at justifying misfortune. They give you an illusion of *why*, but *why* is a loud question, and death is quiet.

"Do you believe me?" I ask.

He nods.

"Do you still love me?"

"Of course I still love you." He sighs, palm cupping my face, thumb trailing my cheek.

I smile.

Love is our staple. Love made us pretenders.

As children, we pretended the hospital was a castle, and we were its knights. We used to play cards on patrol, and he let me win every time. We ate on the ground floor as he made up stories about the commoners in gowns that walked past. We slept in the same bed as he whispered about the adventures waiting for us outside the palace walls. Then he kissed me because we were alone and each other's and everything was all right.

We had to pretend.

The air was just thin. That's why his lungs failed to draw breath. He was just sad that day. That's why his heart couldn't beat on its own. We were just tired. That's why his muscles gave out, and he collapsed in my arms.

We spent our whole lives together pretending, but if you pretend for too long, reality reminds you one way or another that it doesn't like being insulted.

Tonight, we argued. We fought like we never have before,

and he came to this bridge alone to get away from me, I think. I'm not sure. Now that my secret is free, now that he knows who I am, *what* I am, the anger we shared dissipates, like it was housed in a sore muscle starting to heal.

He puts his coat on my shoulders when I shiver. His arms slip beneath mine, and he pulls me against him. I lean into his warmth, our silhouette interrupted by specks of white sinking into the scene.

"Are the stars falling?" I ask.

"It's snow," he whispers. He runs his touch up my spine, reverberating with chuckles. "It's only snow."

Cool and delicate, *snow* falls to my lips.

"Is snow ours too?" I ask.

"Yes," he says, his mouth against my neck. "Everything is ours."

"Thank you." My fingers tangle in his hair. "For the everything."

"Thank *you*." Hurt etches his throat. He presses himself against me even harder, like he could disappear into me if he tried. "For making me want to chase it."

He tries to laugh again, but it's not the same laugh I've always cherished. The laughs I cherish echo. I roused them from his chest when he lay with needles in his veins. When he squeezed my hand, desperate to hold on to something real. Now his laughter falls flat. It ends abruptly rather than fades.

"My love," I say, my voice half-lost. "Why did you come to this bridge?"

The streetlamp flickers. The stars start to fall with urgency. The dark creeps into the scene, gripping the edges of the halo.

He bites down. His eyes squint shut as snow beckons his tears.

"I'm sorry, my sweet Sam," he says, his breath catching, his fingers wrinkling the coat like sheets on my back. "I wish I could keep pretending with you."

Our castle stands behind us, listening. As he cries into my shoulder, I only feel every moment he ever opened his eyes when I thought he wouldn't. I feel the smiles we shared when death decided to give him back to me, over and over again.

So I can only whisper, "I don't understand."

He presses his forehead to mine, streams burning trails down the frosted edges of his cheekbones, and a fear I used to know too well takes the place of his embrace.

"I'm happy you told me your secret," he says, tears catching on the curve of his smile. "I'm happy that you'll keep living even when I'm gone."

He kisses me, snow and salt between our lips.

He kisses me like it's the last time he'll ever have the chance.

"Remember me," he says. "Remember that just because the stars fell doesn't mean they weren't worth wishing on."

"I don't understand," I say, but the kiss is over.

His touch has already fallen from my face. He's already turned around and walked away. I reach for him again, to interlace our fingers, to pull him back as I always have, but death takes his hand instead.

"Wait." His footprints fade beneath the white, erased. "Wait!"

He doesn't hear me. He only hears the night calling from the other side of the bridge with the promise of peace.

"Wait—please—" My tears find fruition because no matter how hard I try, I can't follow him.

The shape of our memories thins, disappearing from the streetlamp's glow and off into the shadows.

"No, you can't—you haven't"—I shake my head—"you can't go yet—you can't leave—you—"

You.

My light, my love, my reason.

"You'll die."

The fear digs between my ribs. It breaks my body, my lungs, and my heart.

When the dark swallows the last of him, reality comes to reap, and pain lies heavy in its hand like a scythe.

The snow turns into a storm. I try to gather the dancing flickers in my hands and somehow send them back to their sky. My knees fall to the earth, burning from the cold. My castle watches me with pity. My tears rain into the river, my whimpers turn to sobs, and my memories turn to nothing.

My stars are falling.

And I can't save them.

1
yellow-flared eyes

WHEN HE DIED, I became someone else.

I used to dream of us, thinking that within his yellow-flared eyes there was a future I could count on. Futures are never certain. Nothing will teach you that better than watching someone you love walk away.

Nothing will teach you that better than growing up in a hospital.

The steady white noise keeps you sane. Stretchers pass and staff walk in their assigned lanes like they're on some kind of medical highway. Apart from that, there is bland, tasteless food and bland, tasteless decor to accompany your sentence. That's all a hospital is, really. Not a place to get better or a place to be treated, but a place to wait.

Imagine a bomb chained to your wrist. It makes sounds. Like a heart monitor. Day and night. A countdown. A countdown, by the way, that you can't see. Look at your bomb, hold it up like a watch. All that'll stare back at you is a blinking red light with

9

that barking beep. Reminders that this bomb *will* go off. You just don't know when.

That's what waiting to die is like.

A bomb drifts through your veins by the name of illness.

You cannot defuse it. You cannot destroy it. You cannot run from it.

Time, disease, and death are rueful mechanics that way. They enjoy crafting nooses out of fear, and they love playing games. Shadows are their tools, curving over your shoulders with eerie fingers, coaxing you into the dark, taking your body, your mind, and anything they please with it.

Time, disease, and death are the greatest thieves in the world.

Or they were.

Until we came along. Four friends who do not believe in bombs.

———

Sony barged into my life not lying on a hospital bed but kicking a vending machine that had robbed her of her chocolate. The second she saw me her frustration melted away, and we shared crappy chocolate and spoke of far-fetched dreams sitting on a cold hallway floor. Though I didn't know it at the time, she had survived a loss far greater than one of her lungs. With hair the color of fire and an air of freedom, she is a gladiator, the bravest thief I know.

Coeur is a much calmer being. He's our muscle, our ever-guilty muscle. His mother is French, his father Haitian, both pretentious namers. *Coeur* means *heart*, though the heart in C's body is broken. Literally. But the heart in his soul is the biggest among us. He is the lover in the bunch and the worst thief among us.

Neo is a writer, a bitter poet. Unlike Sony, he is silent, and unlike C, he is remorseless. His spine is fragile, but his words make up for it. He's bony and short, so small we call him Baby, although, for a baby, he sure has a temper. I'm fairly certain he's never worn a smile in his life. I've known him the longest, and though he's scowly and mean, it's all a mask, his protection. He's also the smartest person I know—observant, creative, resilient— the one who plans and records our great feats of thievery. He claims that Sony and I are extroverts who've kidnapped him and coerced him into being our friend, but I know he secretly enjoys the company. Hospitals are lonely until you find your people.

It's been years since Neo, Sony, and C have been in and out of the hospital.

Now, when they go home, they don't go home for long. Disease is greedy. It takes pieces of you until you no longer recognize yourself, and Neo, C, and Sony don't recognize themselves outside this place anymore.

Whether you're sick or not, the night creates mirrors out of windows. In the past, it showed my friends images of corpses in the glass: skeletons with bones unwrapped by flesh, organs falling through the rib cage, blood seeping from the mouth. They trembled at the foretelling, their fingertips grazing the surface that entranced them. Diagnoses, pills, needles, and so many new mirrors they never meant to find encroached on their lives. Their reflections became their realities.

So rather than meet the new versions of themselves made vulnerable by the beds they slept in and the gowns they wore, my friends turned off the lights. They climbed a staircase and met on a rooftop. They let their fingertips graze the sky with no barrier to stop them from touching the stars.

Defiant.

We should just steal everything, Sony said. Even with a low-burning flame, she was brave. *Let's steal everything we can before we go.*

Everything? C asked.

Everything.

Everything's a long list, Neo said.

Your lives were stolen, I said. *Why don't you steal some of it back?*

That was the day our hit list was born. But so far, everything isn't ours yet.

Stealing is an art form, and we've yet to become artists. But it doesn't stop us from trying.

On a cloudless afternoon we slip out of the hospital. Sony leads the charge, C pushing Neo in a wheelchair across the boulevard. We make our way down the sidewalk and inside a minimart. Sony sidles up to a kiosk filled with sunglasses and dons a pair of aviators, scopes out the place, and nods her head.

"Now," she says, the price tag dangling from her temple.

C makes his way toward the refrigerated section.

"Now?" Neo looks up, caressing the book that never leaves his side. His copy of *Great Expectations*. It's a constant, like a beauty mark or the shape of his nose. And it's bent at the spine, just like him.

"Now," Sony commands, chest high.

"Won't we get caught?" I whisper, looking around the gas station mart. Three people roam the aisles; the cashier flips through a magazine.

"We're definitely getting caught," Neo says.

Sony smirks down at him through the periphery of her soon-to-be-stolen sunglasses.

"Why would we get caught?" she teases.

Neo snorts. "We *always* get caught."

"Today is different. Today is on our side," Sony proclaims, taking a breath, deep and dramatic. "Can't you taste it, Neo? How sweet the air is?"

"We're in a candy aisle, you idiot!" Neo's wheelchair creaks when he throws his head back to look at me. "Sam. Tell her she's an idiot."

I would, but I value my life.

"Sony, you're an idiot," Neo says, grabbing a pen and notebook wedged in his chair and slamming the book open, and scribbles, *4:05 p.m.: Sony is an idiot.*

Neo is our scribe—the one who records our great deeds. Granted, he didn't exactly *agree* to the job. He didn't even agree to come along on this mission. But when your spine is hook-shaped, you can't escape the shackles of friendship. The wheelchair groans as I pull it just out of Sony's reach.

"It's a wonder you need back surgery at all, Baby." Sony doesn't have a job per se. She's the giver of jobs, doubling as the devil on my shoulder with toothy, shameless grins. "That stick up your ass could surely serve as a spine, no?"

"You talk a lot of shit for someone who can't go up a flight of stairs," Neo growls. I pull his wheelchair a little farther back.

"It's a gift." Sony sighs, her one lung filled with ambition. "Now watch me work, and don't break my concentration."

Neo and I watch as Sony marches to the front counter, her dirty white sneakers squeaking against the tiles. The devil doesn't forget to sneak a lollipop into her back pocket on the way.

Neo grumbles, "Klepto."

"Excuse me . . ." Sony waves her arms over her head to catch the cashier's attention. His sidelong glance becomes a double take. Sony's pretty. The kind of pretty that's brutal, bright-eyed, and heavy-handed. But I'm guessing his stares have more to do with the breathing tubes trailing the space under her nose and around her cheeks.

The cigarettes she points to behind the counter dig her grave.

"Just those, please," Sony says.

"Miss, I . . ." the gas station attendant interrupts himself, looking at the cigarettes and then back at her. "Are you sure? I don't think I could give these to you in good conscience."

"He's staring at her chest in good conscience," Neo bites out, like he's about to chew on the fist holding his head up.

"Oh no, sir, they're not for me—um . . ." Sony recoils, dipping her head. "My friends and I, we . . ."

The devil is quick to tears. She presses a hand to her lips. "We don't know how much time we have left. Neo, the boy there. He has to get surgery tomorrow. Cancer."

She points over her shoulder to Neo and me, the attendant making eye contact with us. Neo and I instantly look away. Neo goes so far as to pretend he's browsing for chewing gum by looking at the ingredients on the back.

Sony sniffles dry air and wipes at tears that haven't fallen. "We just wanted to go to the roof like old times, rebel a little," she says, shrugging her shoulders, laughing at herself. "I don't know what I'll do if he doesn't make it. He's such a good soul. He lost his parents in a fire, you know, *and* his puppy! I—"

"Okay, okay!" The cashier grabs a pack. "Just take them. Go on."

"Why, thank you," Sony chirps, taking them without a second thought, and prances out the door.

Shocked that even worked, Neo and I chase after her. He manages to swipe a bag of gummy bears, tucking it between his leg and the armrest. Once we're out and the door shuts behind us, we both exhale our jitters while Sony takes a few giddy steps and stops.

"Write it down," Sony commands, pointing at Neo's book.

Neo does as he's bid, writing in the notebook, *4:07 p.m.: The idiot has successfully conned a boob looker into giving her free cigarettes.*

Sony flips the pack in the air and snags it with one hand.

"I don't have cancer," Neo says.

"No, you don't. But cancer just saved us ten bucks, which is the only good thing it'll be doing anytime soon."

"Sony," I whine.

"What? The cancer kids love me. They always laugh when I run after them and keel over from lack of air. Quid pro quo, yeah?"

"You sure they weren't crying?" Neo says.

"Quid. Pro. Quo?" I ask.

I'm not well versed in commonalities, things everybody knows. Sarcasm, irony, idioms, sports. It all eludes me till Neo explains.

"It means 'something for something' in Latin," he says. Neo knows everything.

"Yeah!" Sony chimes in. "Like when you kill somebody, so they kill you. Like karma! That's how quid pro quo works."

I look at Neo. "Is it?"

"It isn't. Is there a reason *I* had to be here for this?" he asks, his wheelchair suddenly creaking, the weight disturbed by something slipped into the cubby beneath it. Neo's brow crinkles. He turns as much as his back will allow and sees a six-pack being placed beneath his seat.

Our mission's brawn has arrived. C looks more man than boy, tall and beautiful. With his hands tucked in his pockets, he gently shoves the beer farther into its hiding place with his foot.

"How'd it go?" C asks.

Sony's quick to show off her spoils.

"I saved ten bucks with cancer!"

C cocks his head to the side. "On cigarettes?"

"And gummy bears," I say. Neo tosses the bag over his shoulder into C's chest.

"C'mon, C." Sony puts her hands on her hips. "What would we be without irony but boring clichés, yeah?"

"Not using a wheelchair patient as a mule?" Neo tries to roll himself away, but C holds on to the back like you'd hold a shirt collar.

Neo rolls his eyes. He takes out another notebook from the side pocket, this one with the front torn off. As we start making our way across the street, back home, he adds today's conquests to our hit list.

> Cigarettes (the cool ones in Bond movies)
> Beer
> A lollipop
> Crappy sunglasses
> Gummy bears
> An afternoon outside
> A heaping pile of jitters

Hospitals are bland, tasteless places. But even if I do not dream as I used to, there is no more thrilling company than the company of thieves.

"Baby, you are a pillar," Sony says, pride and camaraderie lighting up her face. "Without you, the mission would fall apart. Who else would keep track of our glorious histories?"

"Plus you make an excellent shopping cart," C adds, petting the top of his head.

"Look, C, traffic," Neo says, pointing at the road. "Push me into it."

C shoves a handful of candy into Neo's mouth instead as we make our way back.

Sony jumps the white lines of the crosswalk like skipping stones over a stream. C pushes Neo right behind her, two ducklings following in a row. I'm the tail end, the narrator. They always reach the finish line before I do.

Neo carries our hit list in his lap, a glint of light catching on the notebook's metal spirals, fleeting like the sun decided to tease it. I look up to find it, staring beyond the line of cars that branch off after the intersection.

My heart drops.

Just past the cars, a river cuts the city in two. Its bridge is all that connects either side. A bridge I've known my entire life that creates an ache in my chest. Instead of laughing strangers and children throwing coins into the water, I see snow across the railing. I see the dark.

I start to look away, leave the past on its own, but something else emerges behind it.

Yellow.

Just a glimpse of it.

The gray cowers, strands of color carried by the river's breeze. Did the sun descend to Earth and decide to spend a day among its subjects?

I crane my neck to get a better look, but there are too many people on the bridge; the couples, the tourists, and the children block my view, and cities are impatient. A honk pulls me back to where I stand, my friends waiting for me just ahead.

"Sam?" C calls.

"Sorry." I scurry the rest of the way back. As we step inside the hospital together, my chin catches on my shoulder, the bridge too far to hurt me. I keep looking back till my reflection ghosts across the glass doors.

"Well, well," Sony says, lollipop between her teeth. "The smuggler crew returns from a day at sea." She tucks the cigarettes in her sleeve once we reach the atrium.

It's old and falsely joyful, as most children's hospitals are. Fancy balloons and faded colored tiles attempt to brighten a space where many enter and leave, feeling dimmed. There are posters and banners on the walls about treatments and real-life survivor stories, but those are old too, nurses and doctors clocking in and out to complete the scene. "Now, quick!" Sony says. "Let's get everything upstairs before— Eric!"

Our floor's most notorious jailer (nurse), Eric, has a keen sense of timing. He raises a brow at Sony's tone, his foot tapping away at the ground. His bullshit detector is a honed weapon, and when he gets mad, I wouldn't wish his wrath upon actual prisoners.

"And right under the idiot smuggler's nose, history repeats itself," Neo narrates. "Should I say *I told you so* or rat you out for kidnapping me . . ." C stuffs more candy into his mouth while I open the book from the side pocket and put it in his face.

"Where were you?" Eric asks. His under-eye bags and dark hair match in color, his arms crossed on his chest. He's worried about us, otherwise, he wouldn't have made the trip all the way down here to wrangle us home.

"Eric, Eric—first of all—are those new scrubs?" Sony asks, pointing smoothly up and down. "They really bring color to your face—"

"Not you." Eric puts his hand up, silencing her. Then he looks right at me.

I wish I were invisible.

"Just getting some fresh air," I say, looking at the ground and scratching the back of my neck.

"Fresh air, huh?" Eric scowls, unconvinced. "Did you forget we have an entire floor dedicated to that?" He's referring to the garden on the sixth floor.

When Neo's back still functioned, the four of us would hide in the bushes up there. We made a plan to live our entire lives in the garden and pretend we were woodspeople living off wild berries. It worked for about three hours, but then we got hungry and cold, and C was close to tears at being unable to charge his phone to listen to music. We came back covered in mulch and smelling of soil.

Ever since then, Eric hasn't been too keen on letting us out of his sight.

"Well!" Sony is undaunted. "Excuse us for needing a change of scenery."

"Enough." Eric swipes his arms through the air, the four of us huddling closer together. "I shouldn't have to tell you not to be reckless."

He points at Neo—"You have surgery tomorrow"—and to C—"and you have an echo appointment"—then to Sony—"and you aren't even supposed to be out of bed. Now get upstairs!"

C hurls Neo's chair forward as we trot to the elevators. Sony presses the button with the sole of her shoe. Once we reach the top floor, C picks up Neo from his chair, cradling his skinny frame, careful of his spine. From here, we have to travel upstairs to get to the roof. I grab the wheelchair while Sony skips up the steps.

Halfway through, Sony and C need a break.

Sony closes her eyes and leans against the railing. Half her chest rises, deep and quick, but she refuses to open her mouth to breathe. Such an admission of defeat is not a satisfaction she would ever give to a mere rise in altitude.

C leans against the rail too, Neo's ear pressed flat to the center of his chest.

"Does it sound like music?" he asks, his voice nearly gone.

"No," Neo says. "It sounds like thunder."

"Thunder's nice."

"Not when there's a storm between your ribs." Neo taps the scars of blood vessels climbing C's collarbones. "Your veins brew lightning. It's trying to escape."

C smiles. "You really *are* a writer."

"Yeah." Neo shifts for balance, ear called back to the beating. "Breathe, Coeur."

This is ritualistic too. A moment of silence for half a pair of lungs and half a heart.

Sony is the first to open her eyes and start up again. She kicks the door to the rooftop wide open, arms stretched, reaching for the horizons on either end. She whistles the tune of an unconvicted criminal by a few giddy foot taps.

"We made it!"

"We made it," I whisper, putting Neo's chair back down and adjusting the breathing tubes at Sony's ear. C gently sets Neo down, handing him some pieces of paper he's pulled from his back pocket.

"You liked it?" Neo asks.

"Yeah, I did." Neo and C are creating a novel together. Neo is the writer. C is the inspiration, the reader, the muse, the one with ideas he can't always put into words.

"But I was wondering," C says, still reviewing the chapter in his head, "why do they just give up at the end?"

"What do you mean?" Neo peers over at the pages.

"You know, the main character. After they find out their lover has been lying all this time, they don't yell or get angry or throw things like you want them to. They just . . . stay."

"That's the point," Neo says. "Love is hard to walk away from, even if it hurts." He absentmindedly caresses the bandage on the inside of his elbow, the cotton still guarding a fresh needle prick. "Try walking away from someone who knows you so well they ruin you. You'll find yourself wondering how you could ever love anyone else. And anyway, if I gave you the ending you wanted, you wouldn't remember it."

Neo doesn't just write stories, he becomes them. Most of the little things he writes ring true, give a certain chill, but then again, most little things he writes get erased or tossed away. That's how it's always been.

Sony places a cigarette between Neo's lips, then another in mine. Gripping it firmly in his mouth, Neo cups a hand, a shield from the breeze. The lighter flickers till the embers catch Sony's fire.

Neo doesn't inhale. Instead, he observes, as I do, lets the scent tingle his nostrils, and watches the smoke rise, becoming one with the clouds. C and Sony don't sip the brew bubbling beneath bottle caps. They lick the foam, tongues slapping the roofs of their mouths.

We're greedy creatures, but not ungrateful. You don't have to partake in destruction to admire the weapons.

"Do you think people will remember *us*?" Sony asks, staring at the sky, toying with her collar. C caresses his scars and the lightning in them. Neo shifts protruding bones against his seat.

Injustice or tragedy, my friends are going to die.

So what is there left to do but pretend?

"I don't know."

They all look at me.

"Our ending doesn't belong to us."

Sony smiles. "Let's steal our endings back, then."

"That's why we came up here, right?" C piles on. "We said we'd plan it today. Our great escape from the hospital." Neo glances his way. The possibility of today, but grander, stirs between us. C shrugs. "What's stopping us?"

Suddenly, the door creaks open.

"Here we are. You're not supposed to come up here, but sometimes the kids like to . . ." Eric's voice startles us. C nearly breaks his bottle by stepping on it, while Neo and I toss our cigarettes so fast we almost set each other's hands on fire.

The second we're on our feet and turned around, Eric is already seething, but amidst the chaos, time slows. A familiar melody strikes a single note, turning all heads in the orchestra.

I go silent.

Yellow light emerges from behind Eric's frame.

And a sun hides behind him in the shape of a girl with yellow-flared eyes.

2
sunrise

I STILL SEE HIM sometimes.

He frolics, a boy who doesn't feel the weight of the place where he lives. His hands toy with mine. He doesn't hold things—*holding* is the wrong word.

Can hands kiss? he asks. Questions are his favorite form of play.

I don't know.

I think they can. His laughter rings in beats of three, all the way down to his fingers. *Our hands are kissing.*

He settles in his bed during the painful hours. Needles protrude from his body, tubes and machines with names too difficult to pronounce attached. He's a machine of his own. A broken one that engineers, deemed doctors, take a crack at.

His nerves protest, sharp, like a jab in the ribs. I see their symptoms in his twitching face, the shifts, and subtle groans. None inhibit his curiosity. His mind, while his body cannot, frolics all the same. He continues to play with my hands in any way he can. He laughs when his ribs allow it.

Needles are swords, he says. Pretending. His most glorious of games. *Pills are gems.*

What are gems? I ask.

They're stones, he says. *Very pretty stones. Some even shine. Like the sun.*

Aren't all stones pretty?

No, he says. His voice shifts with his body, into a territory where playing takes too much energy. He empties, little by little. The disease drains him and weighs him down.

I feel like a stone, he says, sinking into the bed.

I interlace our fingers and move along the joints so that he knows I'm still there. Our hands kiss.

You're a gem, then, I say. *Like the sun.*

He likes touching in the same way he likes pretending, asking, talking, even when he has nothing to say. It makes him feel like he has a greater purpose than just to be kept from death.

He smiles for me, but his face twitches. He shifts, rustling the sheets, looking out his window.

The sun rises every day, he says, light from between the blinds affectionately caressing his skin. *Do you think it rises because it fell?*

He didn't understand that I never could've answered him at the time.

I never knew any more than what he taught me. I knew that hands could kiss, and that I wanted to caress his face as the light did.

He was my light. He was my sunset. Violent with color. Submerged peacefully by the dark.

That was a long time ago.

He lives in my memory now. Buried. Rebellious, as he was before. He emerges, sometimes, in the corner of my eye, his laughter lost in a crowd, remnants of his questions still waiting for answers in the night.

The truth is, I don't fear the night at all.

I live in it. Your eyes adjust, your hands become used to not being kissed, and your heart settles in the numb. The night isn't the enemy I make it out to be. It's the natural state of things when your sun burns out.

So color me surprised when, years after mine has long set, a beam of yellow rises from the stairwell and eclipses the gray . . .

Yellow.

Her hair is yellow. Not blonde or flaxen, *yellow*. Like dandelions and lemons. The color crowds dark roots just enough that you know it's a choice, framing her face with the glasses perched on her nose. The eyes behind them flicker, and I can hardly breathe when they land on me.

"Eric!" Sony spreads her arms and legs out as if it's possible to conceal foaming beer bottles and cigarette stench by puffing her feathers. "Would it help if I told you your shoes are just stunning?"

While still holding the door open, Eric makes a throat-cutting motion across his neck. Sony promptly shuts up.

"Hikari"—Eric sighs—"this is Neo, Sony, C, and Sam."

Hikari.

Does Hikari know she has suns in her eyes?

"Hey there!" Sony yells, waving with an open mouth, while C waves more subtly and Neo just nods his chin.

"Hi," Hikari says. Her voice is liquid, streaming, sultry and cool like shade spooling over the edge of her mouth on a hot day.

"Wow," Sony says, making her way into Hikari's personal space. "You're pretty."

"Sony," Eric scolds.

"It's fine," Hikari says, like she's amused, enchanted even, by Sony's enchantment with her.

"Are you fun?" Sony asks. "You seem fun."

"I like to think so."

"Hikari," Neo says, pensive over the syllables as he rolls his chair deliberately in front of Sony. "Are you from Japan?"

"My parents are," Hikari says. "I'm from the suburbs."

"I'm from the suburbs too," Sony coos.

Neo rolls his eyes. "Didn't know the suburbs were in Hell." He deservedly gets flicked on the temple for that statement. "Hey!"

"That's Neo," Sony says, patting his head. "He's our baby."

"Your captive is what I am!" Neo smacks her hand off. "Hikari, you've got legs. Run for it."

"Oh dear God." Eric sighs into his hands, and I now wonder if they teach babysitting in nursing school.

"That's C." Sony points. "His name is big and French like him, so we just call him C."

"Hi, Hikari. Do you need any help to get settled?" C leans over Neo's handles, propping his upper body weight on them. The wheelchair tips back, Neo nearly falling out of it. He hits C's arm with his notebook till the wheels reconcile with the ground.

"I'll help!" Sony offers.

"No, you will not." Eric grabs her and C by the sleeves, using his foot to keep Neo in line.

"But—"

"I don't wanna hear it. And cigarettes? Really? Have some class." He starts pulling them toward the door held open by a cinder block. "Go to your rooms."

"But Erriiiiic," Sony whines, trying in vain to return to her newcomer. "What about initiation? I haven't even told her my jokes—"

"Get downstairs—Hikari!" Eric's face changes instantly, chin hooked on his shoulder, welcoming grin beaming. "Sam will show you back to your room. If you need anything, don't hesitate to ask."

"Bye, Hikari!" Sony says, waving her arm straight out over her head. "We'll find you when we escape!"

"Keep walking!"

The door shuts, locking my friends' and their captor's voices behind its creak. Hikari stays put, only turning once there's nothing else to face but me.

I can't move. Because for the split second that she turns her head, I catch someone else's shadow in her place, someone else's expression, someone with the same eyes and the same voice from a different lifetime.

"You're Sam," Hikari says, half a question balanced on her lips.

"Yes," I breathe, half-enthralled, half-stunned, fully terrified.

Hikari cocks her head to the side, gaze traveling about me as if I'm wearing a map for clothes and she's reading the landmarks. She smiles with a crooked edge. "Are you shy, Sam?"

"I—uh." My voice stutters—treacherous thing. "I'm not shy—I don't think. I'm just bad at existing."

"What does that mean?"

"It's just—I guess this body never felt like mine."

Hikari's smile stretches rather than fades, that earlier amusement playing with her features.

"Did you steal it?"

Hikari is a patient, and from the glossy white band on her wrist, she's going to be here for a while. This can only go one way: We keep exchanging these pleasantries. I offer to help however she may need. She accepts a bit and declines most. Then we part ways and become backgrounds to each other. That's how it always goes. That's how the part of me that's terrified of her needs it to go.

"Would you like me to show you around?" I ask, recoiling, trying to stare at the ground instead of at her. "I could show you the cafeteria or the gardens?"

Hikari laughs, three beats' worth, roaming the roof with a slow, coquettish step.

"No," she says.

"No?"

"No, I'm not a fan of tours," she says. Her baggy white T-shirt doesn't quite fit, and the skirt that bares her legs flows with the wind as her hair trickles like liquid gold down to her forearms. There, bandages conceal her from wrist to elbow, and though I want to ask what led her to the hospital, Hikari has other plans.

"I have an agenda," she says. "Not to mention, I like exploring one thing at a time."

"You're exploring the roof?"

"I'm exploring you." Hikari hooks her chin on her shoulder, her mischief grinning back at me. "Didn't you know, Sam? People have stories written on them, around them, in their past, in their futures. I like to unravel them."

As invasive as that sounds, the wind catches her scent, sweet yet forceful, and distracts me with it. I almost lean into it before catching myself, but Hikari notices. She smirks, and I'm starting to realize, as she eyes me like a book she wants to tear off a shelf, that she may be more of a troublemaker than any of my thieves.

"Sam," she says, not to me, to the sky, testing my name, like a lyric she can't place. "It's funny. I feel like we've met before."

My heart leaps into my throat. I swallow, unable to speak in anything past a whisper. "Maybe in a past life."

The wind disturbs us, knocking the glass bottles into one another. Hikari's gaze drifts to the ash marks and spilled alcohol at my feet.

"You stole those cigarettes and beers, right?"

"Technically, Sony and C stole the cigarettes and beers."

"So you're just an accomplice," she says, her suave attitude replaced by a long sigh. "Well, it looks like you'll have to do."

Without another word, Hikari flips her hair into a ponytail and heads for the door.

"Wh-where are you going?"

"I've got something to steal. And you're going to help me."

"I—but—" I stutter, but ultimately the gravity of my infatuation is stronger than that pesky shadow on my shoulder telling me this is a bad idea, so what can I do but follow her? "Where did you say you were from?"

"An infernal little town in the middle of nowhere."

"Nowhere?"

"The kind of place everyone wants to know everyone else's secrets."

"Well, that sounds like everywhere."

"Where are *you* from, Sam?"

That's a question I often find difficult to answer. Not to mention, while following Hikari down the stairs and waiting for an elevator, I can't do anything but look at her, and every time I look at her, my thoughts no longer begin or end. Instead, they jumble together until I'm an incoherent, flustered mess. My cheeks flush and butterflies make a fun house of my stomach.

I clear my throat. The elevator arrives, and Hikari leads the way into it, pressing the button for the ground floor.

"I'm from here," I say.

"The city?"

"The hospital."

A less-amused expression finds Hikari. She holds on to the back railing as I do. So little distance remains between my hand and hers that I wonder what it would feel like if they kissed.

"Sam."

"Hm?"

"What do you have?" Hikari asks, and for such a serious question, it is so softly said.

This is a scripted moment between sick people. A rule of sorts. It states that when you meet someone within these walls, you are to ask one thing. *What do you have? Who is your killer?* It's a different way of asking, but it's the same question. What she's asking is why I've been confined to the hospital for so long that I view myself as an extension of it. She wants to know to what degree I'm dying.

Looking at her bandages and the otherwise healthy nature of her being, I want to ask her the same, but—

"You're not supposed to ask that," I lie. And rather than nod or say she understands, Hikari has another easy fit of laughter that shakes her chest. Three beats again. As if her heart is laughing with her.

"What, like prison? What are you in for, Sam?"

"Apparently, I'm an accomplice to petty larceny."

"Good," she says, the word paired with flirtatious endnotes. "Then this won't be your first time helping someone steal."

The elevator doors open, but neither Hikari nor I make a move.

I told you I like to watch people, but sometimes I struggle talking to them. When you've lived in the same place as long as I have, you find that people don't know what to say to someone they think is dying. People feel awkward around the sick, so they pretend the sickness is invisible. They avoid the elephant in the room so blatantly that you can tell it's all they're thinking about. They create distance without even meaning to because distance is comfortable.

But not everyone gets stuck in that pattern. Hikari thinks I'm dying. I know she is. Otherwise, she wouldn't be here needing a tour guide who's been convinced to help her commit a crime instead. Yet somehow, whatever distance I create, Hikari wants to close it—with her curiosity, her teasing tone, her pretty looks, and her even prettier language.

"You're not very skilled at conversation, are you, Sam?"

Crap. I was staring again.

"Um—I—sorry."

"Why are you sorry?" she asks.

We step out of the elevator's mouth onto the ground floor. She stops to sightsee the atrium, the light pooling through the windowed ceiling. When she looks at me again, that playful manner returns to ghost over her smile. "I'm plenty good at it for both of us, and it's actually kind of cute how nervous you are."

My face heats, and suddenly I can't form a single syllable, let alone a sentence to respond.

Hikari smirks. "There's a library here, right?"

I nod, and because I know I won't get any answers from her before I do, I lead her there. The library is different from the atrium, more secluded, less central and medical. It's where patients can come to read in the plush chairs and find little worlds to escape into.

"Excuse me, ma'am? I can't seem to find this book," Hikari says to the volunteer behind the counter. She says a random title and author so out there I'm not certain either exists. "Do you think you could help me?"

The volunteer nods curtly and says she'll look in the back.

"I don't think checking out a book is stealing unless you intend never to give it back," I whisper.

Hikari quirks a brow. "Why do you steal, Sam? You and your thieves?"

"Don't ask why."

"Why not?"

"I don't believe in reasons."

"Why not?"

I narrow my eyes at her inability to suppress her teasing.

"We made a hit list," I say. "We steal to fill it."

Hikari catches me glancing over her shoulder.

"Coast is clear?"

"Huh?"

It dawns on me that a book is not what Hikari set her sights on. She doesn't waste a second hopping up and over the counter to the other side. My jaw drops, neck craning side to side frantically to make sure no one is looking.

"What are you—"

Without a care, Hikari undoes the electric pencil sharpener on the front desk and uses a pen to dislodge the sharpener part. I cringe as it makes a noise like breaking glass. Hikari holds it up to the light, testing the authenticity of the blade before frowning when she realizes bolts still bind it to some of the plastic.

"She's coming back," I whisper, and Hikari doesn't bother looking. She takes a few pieces of paper and a pencil, concealing her spoils beneath them. Then she hops back over the counter, grabbing me by the sleeve of my shirt.

I panic. Every nerve in my body pulls taut. The finite distance left between her skin and mine is so slight that I can practically feel the heat radiating beneath her bandages.

"Hurry." Hikari laughs, letting me go and winking as she starts running away with me in her shadow.

I gaze at the papers she holds tightly without crumpling. "Are you an artist?"

"Of sorts," she says, looking over her shoulder and giggling as the volunteer looks around to see where we've gone. She storms an empty elevator, using her foot to keep it open so I can catch up to her. Once the doors close, she throws her head back, exposing the column of her throat. A scar I can't help but admire peeks from her collar as she searches for her breath.

"A hit list?"

"Hm?"

"You said you made a hit list," Hikari repeats, her eyes softer now, diluted in the darker color, as if a wave of something comfortable and tired just hit her.

"To kill our enemies," I say.

"How poetic."

"You condone stealing because it's poetic?"

Hikari smiles. A contagious smile. It doesn't catch my lips, but its crook certainly tries.

"There's nothing more human than sin," she says, shrugging. "Now, where might I find a screwdriver, my dear accomplice?"

Being called anything of hers brings back that warmth to my face, making me stutter. "Why do you need a screwdriver?"

"I thought you didn't believe in reasons."

I can't help the laughing breath that escapes me. I shake my head to scare the smile away. I rarely smile, even for my thieves, but even this fear I can't explain has no power compared to her.

We reach the floor where her room is. The whole path, our distance, becomes a plaything.

Out of the multiple maintenance employees, there is one who always leaves his supply bag unattended, and though he's taken numerous falls from a faulty stepladder, he has not learned his lesson. Hikari and I peek into the supply closet I knew he'd be in. He's fixing a lightbulb, his back to us, wobbling as the stepladder threatens to give out again.

I put a finger to my lips. Hikari nods and watches me carefully step into the closet. Tools spill out of the bag, a screwdriver in the corner. I grab it as quickly as possible, but then the stepladder buckles. The maintenance employee falls to the floor, almost onto me.

"Hey!" he yells. I jump over him as Hikari shrieks and shuts the door behind me, the two of us making yet another run for it.

"You were holding out on me." Hikari laughs.

"I never do this."

"You never steal?"

"I never run."

"Well," Hikari breathes, "you ran for me."

Under the hall light, a pack of doctors storms through, interrupting us. They rush by, residents, the tadpoles of the training pool, following an attending. Hikari and I step back against the wall like cars pulling over for an ambulance. The doctors' white coats wave past, two nurses in tow, one with a stethoscope around her neck, another looking at her beeper. Their expressions are unreadable—part of their training.

Hikari follows the responders with her gaze, worry there. I don't waste time. The patient they tend to is in his own limbo. Our wondering will do nothing for him.

Hikari doesn't relax even once they're out of sight. The way I resume our escape like nothing happened strikes her more than it should.

"You've lived here all your life, haven't you?" Another half question. This time the assumption speaks for itself. I told you that I see the same things day after day. Apathy is a symptom of repetition. I pay running doctors the mind you would pay a breeze.

"*Life*," I say, "may not be the right word for what you're thinking of."

It finally dawns on her. That I may not be exactly like other patients or other people she's met. Narrators are a natural part of the picture until you take a second glance at them.

"Who *are* you, Sam?" she asks, and when she does, yellow flares dance in her eyes. "Something tells me you're more than just a familiar stranger."

Look into a person and see someone you used to know and ask yourself if you believe in reincarnation. If you believe a soul is never truly dead, only passed on to another body, another mind, another life, another reality. If you do, I must ask, what do you think makes someone real?

Is it the ability to touch them? To feel the palpable nature of their heat, the texture of their skin, the pulse thrumming in their veins? Or is someone real simply when their name is said aloud? When you breathe it into otherwise empty air, and it fills with the notion of them?

Hikari moves closer, and an old fear I know all too well wraps its claws around my shoulders.

It may not make sense to you, but I've only ever known one person who could compare to the light she emits. You may think she looks like *him*, acts like *him*, and that's why I'm so enthralled.

He's dead. He's a ghost, and so is what we shared, so I don't compare the two. I compare only what they are. And sometimes suns are so bright that you're forced to look away.

The fear takes over as it did when I caught her color on that bridge and whispers its rules:

If she is what I think she is, I must not, for any reason, fabricated or not, say her name. And I must not let us close that distance for any custom, invitation, or temptation. I must not let her be real.

"I'm—"

"Hikari!" Hikari's face falls. An older couple, each wearing visitor badges, calls for her, stomping down the hall.

"Sorry, stranger." She sighs. "Fun's over."

"Give it to me," I say. Hikari looks at my outreached palms, confused. "I'll tell them it was my fault. That I stole them," I say. "I'm an accomplice either way. You might as well let me take the blame."

"Trying to be a knight in shining armor, are you?" Hikari slips the stolen artifacts into her pocket, save the papers, which she uses to hide the bulge of the screwdriver and sharpener. "Don't worry. One day you'll have the chance to steal for me again."

"Hikari!" her mother begins, worry winding her face tight, her words coming out as scoldings in a language I don't understand. Hikari doesn't say anything. She doesn't even seem to care that she's getting yelled at.

Although when her mother turns to me, frowning harder, and starts to say something, Hikari stands in front of me. She talks back to her mother with crossed arms, coming to my defense. I wish I could follow her when she gets taken away by the hand.

All I can think of the farther she gets taken from me is that the more Hikari gets to know this place and the more it becomes a part of her, the more she'll come to realize the truths only our killers can teach her: No matter what you steal, the nights are long, and *one day* is as much an illusion as reason.

"Sam!"

Sony doesn't always need her oxygen therapy. Her single lung fluctuates in efficiency, but she certainly isn't supposed to run. Not ever. So when she and C come storming down the hall without a wheelchair following them, my stomach drops.

"Why aren't you in your rooms?"

"It's Neo," Sony says. "He's going into surgery early."

"What?"

"His parents are here," C adds, and all three of us know that if we aren't quick enough, it'll mean disaster.

3
resilience

three years ago

THE HOSPITAL ADMITTED a mean, skinny boy today. Pink shades flood his face in a butterfly rash, its wings kissing his nose.

He cradles a cardboard box in his arms, stalling at the door of his new room. It used to belong to someone else. Not knowing what state that someone else left in makes his step hesitant.

Eventually, he settles on the bed, the way you do on a bed that isn't yours yet. His legs hang off the edge, shoes weighing down his ankles like cinder blocks welded to sticks.

"You should try to make some friends, Neo." Neo's mother fumbles with the cross around her neck. She stands as far into the corner as she can. Her stress runs rampant, a kind of untouchable worry for her child that makes her grow distant.

"C'mon, son." His father is a taller man, big-armed, big-voiced, the opposite of Neo. He looks like he calls coffee *joe* and complains about the government. "Just because you have to stay here for a while doesn't mean you can't meet some new people.

Once you're back in school, you'll have a fresh perspective. Get your head out of those books, yeah?"

"This is a hospital, Dad," Neo says. "The only people I'll meet won't be here long."

I don't hear any more than that.

My post is at the nurses' station today, which happens to be right across from his room. Since he's new, the blinds aren't closed, and the door is propped open. My curiosity gets the better of me when it's given such a chance.

Eric notices.

"Have you met him?" he asks, going over charts, checking boxes, doing whatever it is Eric does. I shake my head no. "Why don't you bring him his dinner tray?" He points at the cart. "Strike up a conversation."

"Conversation?"

"Conversation."

"I don't know how those work."

"He probably does. Bring him his tray."

"Are you trying to get rid of me?"

"Yes. I have work to do, and you haven't moved in hours. So get." Eric's pen is a mighty weapon. It pokes my forehead relentlessly, but Eric isn't wrong about my not moving.

Doctors, patients, nurses, and techs walk through this hall all day. I watch them from behind the desk like a barnacle stuck to a ship's hull. My life is spent people-watching from different hulls throughout the hospital. Most moments I witness are fleeting, a few seconds' worth of emotion to feed off of until the patients or visitors or strangers depart. Those moments sate my curiosity while I wait for the next one.

But there's something different about Neo. He's quiet. Silence starves my curiosity. So, around seven, when his parents are gone, I bring Neo his dinner.

He's alone now.

As it turns out, alone, Neo has a lot more noise to him.

On the other side of the door, the cardboard box keeps watch, now empty. Papers are spread about Neo's bed, the sheets submerged in a sea of inked lines.

He is a boat, writing manically, without pause, pen dancing across the waves. A book rests in his lap. It ties the room together, a splash of color. The title, bold-lettered, atop a cover withered at the edges, reads *Great Expectations*.

Neo doesn't notice me gawking at first. He only glances in my direction, then, realizing I don't have the look of a staff member, he glances a second time.

Suspicion laces his tone. "What are you doing?"

"Eric told me to bring your tray."

Neo thins his eyes, flicking them to the tray and then back to me. "Did my parents send you?"

Ah. For a moment I thought he was worried I had plans to poison him. From his tone, I gather my being sent by his parents would be much worse.

"No, Eric did." I motion to the food, offering it. "Your tray."

Neo doesn't say anything to me after that. He just puts the tray on the bedside table and returns to his ocean. Before I leave, I catch a sliver of a line at the top of the page.

Humans have a knack for self-destruction. Only those of us who love broken things will ever know why.

Neo quickly shuffles the piece of paper beneath the others and shoots me a look. My curiosity isn't welcome. I bow my head in apology and turn around, leaving Neo to his words and his books.

Despite his attitude, I leave pleased.

Because Neo isn't quiet at all.

Neo is a writer.

————

For the next week of nights, I bring Neo his food. Every time, I steal a detail. He doesn't brush his hair. His hands are impeccably clean, his fingers lean and long. His clothes are a size too large, baggy around his arms, never so much as a shade livelier than gray. He likes apples. He always eats his apples.

He spits out his pills. When his father visits, he is anxious. He flinches at little movements. When his mother visits, he is calm. When his parents visit together, he is sad.

Neo sometimes drops the pen. His hand wanders to his arm, thumb and forefinger overlapping around his wrist like a noose. He squeezes till his knuckles go white. As if the bone could be made smaller.

As the nights go on, I grow bolder. I begin stealing his work.

You see, Neo and I never exchange any greetings. He never says *thank you*, and I never say *you're welcome*. Our communication is a transfer of sustenance and a peek at a sentence or two.

Destruction is addictive, he writes. *The more I am, the less I want to be. The less I am, the lesser I want to become.*

That particular line plays with my head. It takes up space.

In a neighboring hall, I pace and ponder it.

Just as I turn on my heel to pace in the other direction, someone knocks into me. Our chests collide, and a tray falls from the person's hands, clattering to the floor. It's a familiar tray. One full of food I left in Neo's room a half hour ago.

Neo stands there for a moment. The plate's been knocked up-side down, Jell-O cup split, and water spilled. He sighs at the mess.

It's odd seeing him here. I don't know what to make of him not sitting in a bed surrounded by literature.

"Just leave it," he says, dropping to his knees, his pants wrinkling around sickly, thin thighs. I wonder how they can even hold him upright.

I follow him to the floor and help him tidy up.

Neo scoffs. "You got that much of a savior complex?"

"No," I say. "But I think you have an eating disorder."

Neo's face pales, snapping up, staring at me.

His body turns to stone.

I blink at the silence and the shred of space between us. I've never noticed how his cheekbones protrude until now, nor how intense his eyes become when a sliver of emotion passes through.

"Whenever I bring your tray and come back to get it, only half the food is gone, and the plastic wrap is missing," I explain, putting the empty water cup on the left and the Jell-O cup on the right. "I assume you wrap the food in it and then flush it down the toilet. If you were purging, your doctors would've noticed by now."

Once the plate is at the center, napkins soaking up the liquid, I finally meet Neo's gaze. He still stares. Only it just now occurs to me that it isn't confusion looking back at me.

It's panic.

I pick up the tray, awkwardly holding it out to him, trying to return some familiarity to our relationship, before asking, "Are you okay?"

Neo doesn't answer. He doesn't take my offering either. His face contorts, teeth tight against each other like grinding stones.

He grabs the corner of the tray and flips it over, its contents clattering against the tiles again. Then he marches off, leaving me to clean a second time, now on my own.

————

That night, despite our encounter, I bring Neo his dinner.

He's not writing. His anger has subsided. Instead, he bites his nails, twirls his pen, and taps his fingers like his mother does.

"Did you tell anyone?" he asks.

I put his tray down on the bedside table and shake my head.

He thins his eyes. "Why not? What do you want?"

"I'm not sure what it is I want," I say. "But I'm not good at talking, so no, I haven't told anyone."

"Are you autistic or something?"

"No."

"So you're just weird?"

"Yes, I've been called weird before. But you're not good at talking either." Neo scowls, waiting. Insults come in two parts. "You're mean," I explain. "I don't like what you say."

"Get out, weirdo," he mutters. He uncaps the pen with his teeth and lays it in his ocean. He doesn't pay any mind to the plate of food.

I pay mind to his body. His clothes are loose, but they don't conceal as much as he thinks they do. His skin is grayer, his neck and ankles considerably thinner than they used to be. He hasn't left because he isn't getting better. He's getting worse.

It occurs to me that no one but Neo and I know about this part of him.

It's a secret.

Secrets make people vulnerable. Vulnerability is an isolating force. It pushes people away.

"I like what you write," I say, hand on the doorknob. Neo

glances at me, and for a moment, I think, finally letting his guard down. "Your writing sounds like music."

———————

The next day, when I put Neo's tray down, he doesn't look up. Instead, he holds out something for me.

"A book?" I ask, looking at the cover. It's rich with blues and gold, a pair of eyes looking back at me, and *The Great Gatsby* written in thin, elegant letters.

"Yes," Neo says. "Read it."

"Okay."

I walk to the corner of the room and sit in the chair, opening the book to page one.

"Wha—not here!"

Neo doesn't like company—I forgot. His vulnerability flinches at it. So I read on my own. In the hall. In waiting areas. In doctors' lounges. In the gardens. I read anywhere I can till the pages I have left become fewer than the pages I've consumed.

"You almost done?" Neo asks, passing the nurses' station.

"Mhm." I nod from behind the desk, enthralled by Gatsby's torrid affairs.

Neo doesn't say anything else. He places another book in front of me. This one is *Lord of the Flies*. It's a bit smaller, a pig bleeding from the eyes on the cover. It takes me a day to read. I bring both books back to him that night.

"I didn't like this one," I tell him.

Neo quirks a brow, an apple in his hand. "Why not?"

"I don't like violence."

"It's not real violence," he says, tucking the books back in that box.

"It feels real."

"Weirdo," Neo grumbles. He grabs another book and hands it to me. This one is called *Wuthering Heights*. The cover has an old house on it, a woman and a man in the foreground beneath dreary skies.

There are so many books to read. My curiosity turns absolutely fatal. It wonders about all those beautiful things Neo writes and what stories his mind could possibly conjure up.

"Could I read something of yours?" I ask.

"No. Go away."

And so I'm off to read *Wuthering Heights*.

The next morning, I run, beyond eager to tell Neo how wonderful this story is. That it's my favorite yet. That there isn't a single word I could stop at. That despite the violence, this is a masterpiece. I sprint to his room, no tray in hand.

"I thought we were past this!"

I skid to a halt before I even reach the door. It's shut, but through the wall, voices bleed.

"Honey." Neo's mother. Through the blinds, I see her tight hands soften on her husband's elbow. "Calm down."

"Don't defend him," Neo's father says, only it's not said, it's bitten out. Papers crumple in his fist, papers I recognize. Neo's mother holds the cross around her neck. Then his father starts to tear Neo's stories to shreds. Slowly. In full view of his son.

"It's fine. You're just confused. You're young. I can't blame you," he says, creeping closer to the bed, his quiet footsteps threatening. He lifts the papers, tossing their remnants at Neo's feet. "But don't let me find this filth again, you understand?"

I don't hear any more. I just see Neo staring out the window, his face blank of anything. Only his thumb and forefinger move, tightening the loop around his wrist.

———

That night, I don't bring *Wuthering Heights* when I arrive with Neo's food. I set the tray down on the side table and observe the carnage. The cardboard box is knocked over on the floor. The books are gone, all but *Great Expectations*, cradled in Neo's arms.

"It's not Monday," Neo says. His voice is drained, wet at the back of his throat. He picks up the apple off the plate.

Mondays are apple days.

"I think apples grow any day they want."

"Thank you," Neo says, but he doesn't take a bite.

I don't ask him about the shredded pieces of paper on the floor or the broken pen oozing ink. I don't ask where his books have gone, and he doesn't ask me about *Wuthering Heights*.

"Are there TVs in this place?"

I nod. "Do you want to watch something?"

Neo shrugs. "Okay."

TV rights are an expensive commodity. Sick kids get the perks when no one else is around. Eric's generosity (and desperate attempts to get us to leave him alone) wins us the remote.

Neo and I watch movies all night. During, Neo chews on his apple and spits it into the trash when he thinks I'm not looking. Out of the room, distracted, he seems more at ease. If there's one nice thing about books and movies, it's that they can make you forget for a while.

Forgetting is an essential part of grief.

When I see Neo the next morning, I put a copy of *The Great Gatsby* in his cardboard box and kick it under his bed.

That ever-suspicious brow of his rises. "I didn't give you that."

"I took it from the library."

"You stole it?"

"I suppose."

"Weirdo."

"Can I read your stories now?"

"I don't write stories."

My head snaps in his direction. Never has one of Neo's sentences quite broken my heart till that one.

My own grief morphs into tightness in my gut. Neo's writing is something precious, even if it isn't mine. It's another secret we share. I read once, on the very corner of one of his pages, *Paper is my heart. Pens are my veins. They return words I stole, blood to paint a scene.*

If that's true, a cemetery is all that remains of Neo's heart. It lies in a pile of rubble on his bedroom floor like the outline of a dead body. He hasn't bothered to pick up the pieces. He knows his heart will only shatter again if he does.

Neo's father is a taker, and he has no material left to steal. When it's only he who visits, Neo is never unscathed. The first time, it's a bruise, bottle green and patchy purple. When Eric asks what happened, Neo says he fell in the bathroom. The second time, it's blood, the back of Neo's head stained with splatter spots. Some of his hair has fallen out or, more likely, been pulled.

There are other incidents, but we never talk about them.

So, every day, I bring Neo apples. Every day, he eats them to the core. We watch movies at night. We go to the library in the afternoons. He says he's learning French, so I help him when time allows.

There are days we can do none of those things. There are days pain lashes at Neo without warning as his body rejects itself, an aggressive civil war.

There are days I think I'll lose him. The worst days.

In a particularly bad fit, his skin becomes waxy, sweat lacing the sheets. Neo clenches his fists, lying supine, roughing out his breaths.

I scoot my chair closer to his bed during the worst days. My hand sneaks beside his. I press the backs of my fingers to his knuckles. I can't do much for him, but I can be another body, another soul, so that he knows he isn't alone.

The worst of the worst days comes when Neo was supposedly well enough to go home for a few weeks. He returns through the ER. His face is bruised from forehead to chin, all down one side, as if he's been shoved into something. Both bones in his wrist are cracked down the middle, and he can't move his spine for the larger part of a month.

"Neo," I whisper. "Have you told anyone?"

"It wasn't him," he says.

"Your wrist is broken, and your back—"

"It wasn't him," he snaps at me, reverting to his silence. "Just leave me alone."

I don't leave. I just join him in silence. But the tear that rolls down his face isn't lost on me.

The worst days subside eventually. Neo finds the means to sit back up when the weather warms. He doesn't spit out his pills as frequently. He starts to eat more. And it takes a few months, but Neo finally considers writing again.

I am determined. I steal pens from Eric's station and ask for notebooks. Eric obliges since I won't stop bothering him. He returns with fifty-cent composition books made of cardboard and thin, lined sheets. I toss them, loud enough for Neo to hear, into the cardboard box. As we mull over books, I make noise with it. My foot nudges the box. I innocently pull it out from under the bed and let it slowly slide back. Neo never misses my attempts to draw attention to the tools. Actually, he goes to great lengths to ignore them. It isn't until I put one of the notebooks directly in his lap that he considers it.

It's difficult to ignore what you love, even when its existence is as conditional as what you hate.

Neo brushes the edge cautiously, as if a palpable heat rises from within. The blank pages daunt him. It's been a while. Once he lets the pen's weight settle in his palm and summons the courage to lay it on paper, Neo, drop by drop, re-creates his ocean.

He writes every day now, at random times, on random surfaces. He and I watch movies on Eric's tablet at night and read during the day. He takes notes in the margins of the books and pauses the movie to grab a page when an idea strikes.

We take walks when Neo has the strength. We lie in the gardens for air when it's cool. He writes on my shirtsleeve on a particularly sore morning, on his pant leg too. Together, we hide his stories. I bring him food, and when his parents arrive, he hands me the box. I swear, at times when I return with it, that he breaks into a smile.

———

Tonight, something changes.

Tonight, our routine breaks. Tonight, dinner tray in hand, I slip an apple from the basket in the cafeteria on the way to his room. But alas, when I open the door, Neo isn't alone.

"You get results like this again, we're taking you home. I don't care if I have to force it down your throat—"

Neo's father stops talking the moment I walk in. He stands over his son's bed, papers clutched in his fist, this time in the shape of bloodwork. It looms over Neo, although he doesn't flinch. He lets his head hang like whatever comes his way will come, and that is that.

"I'm sorry, I should've knocked," I mumble, tucking my chin to my chest. Neo sits, the lower half of his body under the covers, his face downcast same as mine. Hair covers his eyes, his thumb and forefinger clenched around his wrist.

"It's fine," his father says politely. He ushers me forward with a wave. "Bring it in."

That man doesn't frighten me, but one of my rules is never to interfere. I can't break it. There are many moments I wish I could, but this moment may be the greatest of them.

Neo's father either doesn't notice or doesn't care about the pain whimpering through Neo's lips when I lay that tray down. He stares at him, not with hate or anything so grotesque. He looks at Neo with expectation, a nod of encouragement his final say.

He's going to watch Neo eat. Because eating disorders aren't about vanity. They're about control. And he wants to take whatever his son has left of it.

When the door shuts behind me, I can't bear to leave. I barnacle myself to the nurses' station and wait. I wait for over an hour. I wait and wait, the clocks mocking me, slowing in time's favor. I wait till Neo's father finally leaves. I wait till he slips his coat on, disappears down the hall, and into the elevator.

Then I sprint.

I slam the door open. Neo isn't in his bed. The room is bare in darkness, sheets undone, cast aside. There are no torn books or pages. Only the tray I've come to memorize the weight of sits upside down on the tiles, discarded, like the day Neo flipped it over in his anger. Only now, it's empty.

Light peeks under the bathroom door, accompanied by retching. I go to it, dread in my throat. On the other side, a boy sits, a fraction of himself.

Neo's back slams against the wall, vomit staining the edge of his mouth. Tears fall from bloodshot eyes, the realization dropping in his chest, sending spasms through his chest; it was never supposed to go this far.

He pulls at his hair. The heels of his palms cover his eyes. He bangs his head and pushes himself into the wall like he wants to become a part of it. Like he wants to disappear.

Vulnerability craves isolation. Desperation weeps in it.

He fights at first. When I kneel to his level, he pushes me away with clenched fists, whining. I don't say anything. I give him my arms and my quiet and hope that's enough to coax his fear away. I hope it's enough as he collapses and cries into my shoulder.

"I hate him. I hate him so much," he says, heaving for air. My palm drags over his spine, drawing slow rhythms to guide his breaths.

"He loves me because he has to," Neo cries. "That's worse than hating someone. He knows I'll never be who he wants me to be. He knows I'd rather die here than be who he wants me to be. I'm no one in that house. I have nothing there!"

His voice is a chorus of rough notes, his anger cracking. Even before he was sick, Neo's life wasn't his. It was never his. Wet sobs unravel a hurt beneath the surface as he comes to terms with the fact that it may never be.

"I *am* nothing," he says, without air, like a ghost. Like it's true.

"You're not nothing."

"I'd rather be nothing than hate myself."

Neo's shredded poems and pages ache like phantom limbs. He bites his lip to hold in a whimper, a grieving cry for them. He cries for them and the boy his father will never let him be.

"You know, I used to believe in God," he says. "He makes me hate God."

Love and hate aren't interchangeable. They don't mean the same thing, but they are not opposites. If it were a doctor or a nurse forcing this pain onto Neo, this humiliation, he wouldn't care. He doesn't. They have no place in his life past fleeting moments. His father is a powerful animal in that regard. He loves

Neo, and Neo loves him too. Even if it's because they must. Love gives people the power to be treacherous. Being hurt by someone you share such a thing with is draining—a needle under the skin or a knife in the rib.

Hate is a choice. Love is not.

There's nothing so out of our control as that.

"You don't owe him anything," I whisper. "You're allowed to love books and broken things."

————

Neo's dad doesn't come back for a long time. Business trips, Neo tells me. His mother comes instead. What she lacks in warmth, she makes up for in patience. It doesn't matter how long it takes for Neo to make eye contact or pick up a fork. She waits. Sort of like me. I think that makes Neo feel safe. *Great Expectations* never leaves his possession, but at least the loop around his wrist loosens with time.

One day, I stop bringing Neo his trays. Instead, I just bring apples, and he gives me books. The cycle of exchange continues until one day, as he writes and I read next to him . . .

"What's your name?"

"I'm Sam."

"You like love stories, right, Sam?"

"Mhm."

"Have you ever been in love?"

An uncomfortable question. One that brings up vulnerabilities I don't know how to share.

I shrug, looking at the ground. "I don't remember."

"Then you haven't," Neo says. "You'd remember."

My fingers stiffen around the book in my hands.

"Maybe I don't want to remember."

Neo's never experienced my pain. Only his. But he has no

cages for pity in his soul—only blunt remarks, wit, and, at times, a little softness.

"Sorry," he says. Softly.

"Do you have a love story for me?" I ask.

"No." Neo reads over the last few lines he's written. Then he picks up the small stack of papers filled to the brim with ink, making sure they're even. "But I didn't add any violence."

Then the extraordinary happens.

Neo offers me a treasure from the sea.

He frowns at my awe. "What the hell are you smiling for? Take it."

I do. I take it like it's the most fragile thing in the world. Because when a writer gives you a gift as precious as their work, they give you their trust, their control, their heart put to paper.

Before I leave, Neo calls for me.

"Sam," he says. I glance at him over my shoulder, and he glances back. "What are we watching tonight?"

I don't make it a habit to converse with patients. But when I look at Neo, at the weeks I've spent getting to know him, I realize between our silences that this is not the start of a conversation.

It's the beginning of a friendship.

4
soliloquies

THERE'S SOMETHING WORLDLY about her. She's not elegant or dainty. She's raw, unapologetic, with a type of beauty only confidence can carry off. Anywhere she goes, anyone she encounters, Hikari is a universal puzzle piece. She belongs wherever she sets foot.

Tonight, Hikari is unguarded, even in the dark. Her hair is straight, thin, a bit frizzy near the top of her head. She wears a nightgown that reaches just past her knees, little yellow flowers spread about the fabric. From afar, you could mistake it for a hospital gown. It sways around her legs as she roams the halls, looking into rooms, into people, exploring past curfew.

The windows welcome her in sequence. They do, as the night does, create those dreadful mirrors. Hikari doesn't look long. She tucks her hair behind her ears, adjusts her glasses, fixes herself. She doesn't glare at the bandages on her arms or the scar on her neck. What the mirror dares to show of her illness, she claims power over.

She ignores it.

"Sam?" I should mention that I'm hiding around a hall corner, suspiciously peeking out by a hair right now. I jump, turning around to find Eric right next to me with his hands on his hips. "What are you doing?"

Due to our criminal acts, Sony and C have been confined to their rooms, and though I wouldn't mind joining them on a normal day, I'm currently suffering from my curiosity's ceaseless desire to follow the sun that's lit up my home.

"Absolutely nothing."

I try to smile, but Eric finds it off-putting.

"Go do absolutely nothing somewhere else."

"Okay."

I go back to following Hikari as inconspicuously as possible.

Also, I have a job to do.

Neo's in surgery for his back. His parents wait in his room, where there will be no evidence of their son to rip apart. Tonight, his heart is mine to protect. It makes for hefty luggage when following a girl.

Hikari reaches the elevators a few minutes later, sketching on those papers she stole earlier. It's a short hall, so I have to wait on the other side to avoid being found. Although when I peek, she's already disappeared.

There's only one place she could've gone from here, and my curiosity and I both know it.

The door to the roof creaks when I open it, the wind that goes feral at night flurrying into the stairwell. The only luminescence is that of sleepless city dwellers who keep the lights on and the stars sifting through clear skies.

That and the yellow with whom the night flirts. Only now, the yellow isn't exploring the roof. It's on the ledge, the silhouette of a girl standing against the moon.

My stomach drops. The box falls from my hands, announcing my presence far more abruptly than the door did.

"Oh," Hikari says, like I'm a pleasant surprise on an otherwise uneventful evening. "Hi, Sam."

"What are you doing up there?!"

"It's quite the view. I thought I'd see what it has to offer at night."

"We have windows for that, you know!"

"Don't be silly. How can I befriend a breeze behind a window?"

"The breeze is going to push you over the edge, please. I—"

"Look at the stars, Sam." Hikari upturns her chin to the sky, wonder aplenty in her eyes. As if the wind isn't playing with the material of her nightgown and caressing her hair in an almost threatening way. "They're so faint tonight." A sigh works through her. "Don't you wish you could brighten them?"

"I don't understand."

"Stars aren't eternal. They should burn and shine with everything they have while they can," she says. "Those five right there. You see them?" She leans back and points up at flickering specks of white against the black. "You can almost draw a five-point star between them."

Hikari looks back at me again. When her body weight shifts back on her heels, I shiver. Every movement she makes is like a finger hooked on a grenade pin. My lungs cease when her hand so much as reaches for the pencil at her ear, and adds a detail to her drawing.

I realize then that she's doing the same thing we were when watching smoke rise from cigarettes and foam bubble in beer bottles. Admiring a weapon.

Truth is, I've been thinking about her. What else would I think about? When I grabbed Neo's box, and he lay drugged in his bed, I thought about how Hikari would give him something to smile about before the strenuous journey. While roaming,

I thought of every word she said. I thought of her yellow, her voice so flirtatious and playful, her conspicuous bandages, and that scar. I wondered if she was sad about her parents and what she would do with her sharpener and screwdriver. I wondered if she thought about me. Every time I pictured her and listened to her in my head, all I thought about was this urge I haven't felt in years—this urge to want.

"Please," I beg, and from the breath alone, Hikari finally notices my panic. "You're scaring me. Can you please get down?"

Hikari's glasses reflect me in a much kinder way than the night would. Her contagious smile curves to one side, and under different circumstances, it may have reached me.

"Since you said *please*," she whispers, sitting on the ledge, shifting on her seat, and hopping back onto the safe side like you'd hop from a swing. "You followed me."

"Yes, I'm sorry."

"Why?" she asks. "I would've been disappointed if you didn't."

Flipping the pencil in her hand, Hikari eyes me up and down. I am drawn to her wrist, the white band around it, glossy and reflective with her bandages to match. One of them seems fresher than the other, specks soaked red at the seams.

"Why did you steal that sharpener and screwdriver?" I ask.

Hikari shrugs, circling me. "Why does anyone steal anything?"

"To sin?"

"To be human?" She smirks, reminding me that to her, I'm merely an instrument of amusement, a puzzle she wants to solve because she doesn't know how she fits with it quite yet. "Although you aren't very good at being human, are you?"

"I feel like I'm supposed to be offended by that."

"You probably aren't very good at being offended either. You're quite awkward."

"I'm starting to think you're quite mean."

"Give me your story, Sam," she demands. "Sate my quite mean curiosity, and maybe I'll tell you why I stole what I stole."

"Something tells me your curiosity is quite greedy."

"Tell me about the hit list," she says, and her scent and voice surround me like a whirlwind, obscuring everything else until I'm sure I'd tell her anything she wanted to hear. "What's it for, other than thievery? Who are you killing?"

"Time," I say.

"Ooh," she mocks. "Crafty enemy."

"Disease."

"Cruel enemy."

"Death."

I don't notice I am stepping backward till my heel knocks into Neo's box, the cardboard and contents jostling like a sound of pain. I pick it back up, dusting it in apology.

"How do you kill time, disease, and death?" Hikari asks.

"You steal what they stole."

"Cigarettes and beer?"

"Moments," I correct. "Childhoods. Lives."

Hikari stops her circling. She looks at me for a long while. I should tell her more. I should tell her of our great plans to escape this place, to go to the ends of the world and back. It's C's plan, Sony's plan, Neo's plan. It's our plan to reach a place we don't have to steal at all.

"You really think I'm mean?" Hikari asks after a while.

I shrug. "A little."

"Mm."

"Neo's mean too."

"Is he?"

"Constantly." I hold his box closer to my chest. "But he needs me."

Neo barely cleared the requirements for his surgery. His doctors have wanted to operate for years. His spine is beginning to displace his organs, organs weak enough from malnutrition. They had no choice but to risk it. It's scaring me more than I care to admit. That his heart, after tonight, may only be mine.

It helps to just focus on a mean girl and her pretty words.

"He's well-read," she says, eyeing the titles of the scattered paperbacks in the box. "*Hamlet, Lord of the Flies, Slaughterhouse-Five, Wuthering Heights.*"

"*Wuthering Heights* is my favorite," I say, inclined to impress her.

"'You said I killed you—haunt me, then,'" she says, the way she introduced my name to the sky. A lyric. A line from a poem. Prose. It stills in me. Clears my vision, drops my jaw, till I pick it back up, swallowing down my wonder.

"A stupid wish," I mumble.

"Is it?"

"The dead do not haunt, no matter how much you beg them to."

"Sam?"

"Yes?"

"Why are you wandering the night with Neo's books?"

"It's complicated," I say. "Neo never asks for anything. Salvaging his stories is the least I can do." Hikari asks with her eyes that I say more. "His parents are here for his surgery. They don't like his books. Or his stories," I explain. "They love him, I think, but—"

"But sometimes parents love the idea of their child more than the person they are."

A harsher edge of Hikari's puzzle piece emerges. She stares at the books, her fingers toying with the nightgown, bunching the material near her thigh. "That kind of love is suffocating." Like fingers closing around a wrist.

"Why are you wandering the night on ledges?" *Hikari*. "Aren't you afraid you'll fall?"

"Of course I am," she says. "But fear is just a large shadow with a little spine."

My own fear snarls at that. It resents her, tugs me further by the rope, possessive, but I pay it no mind. Her gravity is stronger.

"You're a writer," I breathe like I've found another treasure of the world.

"More of a reader," she says. "*Hamlet* was my worst influence."

"Does reading make you happy?" I ask. I want to know all things that bring her joy.

"Reading makes me feel," she says.

Feel.

Emotions and I don't have the best relationship. It's a distant, bitter affair—a divorce. Emotions are disgusted by me. They're a gust of wind on the other side of that ledge, and even if they toy with my hair or stroke my skin, I ignore them. Emotions are with the ghosts I buried, husks of what they were, hollow hauntings. But who knows? Maybe Shakespeare can dig them up.

"I haven't read *Hamlet* yet," I say, peering at the cover.

Hikari looks at me like she has a devious idea, and you already know I'm done in by it.

———

We read on the rooftop for an hour. The breeze, though, is an intruding, whorish bastard who can never stop copping a feel. I ask if we can go inside and read in the warmth. It's a lie. Hikari keeps the roof plenty warm. I just want to get away from the wind. I'm jealous of how free it is to touch her.

Hikari agrees, and we settle in the crook of a hall I know where very few pass. It used to be an extension of the cardiology department, but now it's more of a dead-end spot where doctors come to take a phone call or have midshift breakdowns. Either way, I like it. There's no wind. It's a place where hearts were once healed.

Hikari and I sit against the wall. I'm the one who holds the book. She's the one who assigns theatrics. She claims certain characters, gives me the role of others, and we read aloud. It's less passive than I'm used to, with lots of existing involved, but I like it. I like hearing her voice travel, the dramatic pauses, and the dedication she takes to her audience of one.

Sometimes, she scoots closer to me. A funny feeling tingles in my chest when she does. I think she likes hearing my voice too but in a different way. She likes the stuttering when I peek at her, the nervous swallows, the guttural clearings. She likes my reaction, not to *Hamlet*, but to her.

She keeps enough distance. We share it. We play with it like an extra pair of hands.

Hours pass. Hours I don't notice. We aren't around windows anymore. It may as well be morning. Hikari's patience thins with daybreak. As we reach certain scenes, ones she says are pinnacle, she becomes less an actor and more a stage director.

"Sam, you're doing it all wrong." Hikari slaps her hands on her hips. "Stand up."

"I am standing."

"That's not standing, that's *hunching*."

I look down at myself, puzzled.

"Hunching?"

"Hunching. Do you even have arms?"

"My arms are right here." I extend them from my body as far as they'll go, the book still propped open at the heels of my hands.

"Those aren't arms," Hikari says. "They're appendages at best."

"You're starting to hurt my feelings."

"Sam, come here."

"What about *Hamlet*?"

"I'm Hamlet." Yes, she claimed the character. However, those words don't fit right in her mouth. "What?" Hikari catches my distaste, the way my nose crinkles. "Am I a poor actress?"

"No. You just have nothing in common with Hamlet."

"Because I'm not bitter?"

"Because he's not a sun."

Hamlet is earthly.

"You think I'm a sun?" Hikari asks, head tilted.

"You're bright," I say. I put my hand out, fingers apart, mimicking a reach. Hamlet rests at my side in the other. "I feel like if we touch, I'll burn away like paper." The picture of her sifts over the hills of my knuckles. She stands there, listening. The kind of listening you can tell only belongs to me.

I retreat, catching myself. "Sorry."

"Don't be." Hikari's shoulders bounce once. Her amusement pinches her lips, half-pursed, half-curved. "You actually remind me of a moon."

"A moon?"

"Yes. Gray, subtle, only brave in the night. Maybe those were our past lives."

Maybe they were our first.

Hikari raises her hand. Her palm faces me like the pretense of a wave. She takes a step, our distance tightening. Alarm flinches through me, translated into a violent step back. Hikari halts at the little noise my body makes—the shuffle of my clothes, the screech of the floor beneath my shoe. Like I'm prey and her hand is an open maw. Her eyes travel to my face.

"I won't burn you. I promise," she whispers, but it doesn't matter.

I can't touch her. Touching her would mean admitting that she's more than a ghost of my imagination. It would be admitting she was real.

I *want* her to be real. That's probably the worst part.

"It's all right," she says.

Coaxing the hesitance away, I raise my hand the way she did. I let it draw parallel, a sliver of space between our palms.

"Good," Hikari says, the word just barely skidding past her teeth. "Now pretend I'm your mirror."

Her fingers trail left, palm following. I do the same, right, following her. Then, she moves the opposite way, so I do too. She draws up. She draws down. She makes patterns in the air. I do the same as if strings tie us together.

"Are you teasing me?" I ask.

"I'm teaching you."

"How to be human?"

"You're so caught up in trying not to exist, Sam," she whispers. "If you'd only let yourself go, you'd see how easy it is. Haven't you ever dreamt of dancing?"

"I don't dream."

"Never?"

"Not anymore."

"Why?" she asks, and I can't help but indulge the tragedy in her voice.

"It's not a part of me."

"Who stole it?" I almost want to smile at the way her wit survives even the sad moments. "There must be something you want."

"I want answers," I say.

"Answers?"

"Reasons."

"I thought reasons didn't exist."

"I wish one did."

"And what one reason do you wish for?"

Our words fold over one another, dance together as our hands mimic them, act them out, that comfortable, ruinous distance the only thing keeping her mine, ghostly, unreal. But her questions, her voice, her scent, they feel so palpable I want to bottle them.

"I want to know why people die," I say, but asking why people die is the same as asking the dead to haunt. There's no one there to answer you. I shake my head. "I know it's stupid—"

"How long do you have?" Hikari asks, somber.

"What?"

"Are you dying?"

I scoff. "We're all dying."

"I don't see it that way."

"No matter how you see it, everyone you know is eventually going to die."

"Is that why?"

"Why what?"

"Why you're so afraid to be close to someone?"

Neo's box of books has eyes. It looks back and forth between us like it's waiting for a victor.

In Hikari, it sees plentiful dreams. It sees them flooding behind her eyes, heavy on her body. She wears her dreams in yellow, in flowers on her nightgown, and in her trusting nature. She is a feeler. She's married to feelings. It's addictive to witness.

Whatever she feels next, I know I'll see it written on her, hanging on her mannerisms.

That's what *he* used to do. He used to carry himself without shields. He used to tell the world, even without speaking, everything he ever wanted with a look on his face.

I don't remember his face. I barely remember him. There are only slivers left, escaped details from the coffin frames. I choose to not remember, just like I choose not to wonder too much or feel or dream.

"Sam." Hikari doesn't realize that my name from her lips has a power. Little-shadowed and large-spined. So for all I say of needing to walk away, you know I won't.

"Yes?"

"We're going to meet here every night."

I blink. "Huh?"

"Since we're all inevitably doomed to die, I will be Hamlet, and you will be Yorick, and this shall be our grave." She looks around at the empty hall like it's a house yet to be a home and smiles back at me with ambition in the curve. "I'm not sure what you are. All I know is you're a beautiful set of bones and some curiosity tied together by gray, and I want to bring you to life. I think *that* would make me happy." The more my jaw loosens on its hinges, the more everything in me relaxes in awe of her.

"I want to see you," she whispers. Hikari slips a piece of paper no larger than the size of my palm from a fold in the bandage on her elbow. She smooths down the crease at the center and hands me a drawing of a figure holding a box of books with stars circling her like dancers.

"You think I'm beautiful?" I breathe.

"All readers are," Hikari says. "Good night, stranger."

And when I look back up, she's gone.

5
Hee

THE HIT LIST, in and of itself, is a heist. Heists have three stages.
  Planning.

Execution.

Escape.

When we first agreed to become thieves, Sony was all about the second stage. Her excitement outran her. That night on the roof, she pointed across the city, to the sweets shop, the bookstore, and the street vendors. She was never about the tangibility of stealing but about the act itself. She wanted the rush, the nerves, the racing.

Neo preferred the planning, the hypotheticals, the logistics. He walked (this was pre-wheelchair era) to his room, rummaged through his cardboard box, and found an old notebook with a metal spiral spine, one he used to rip pages out of when he was dissatisfied. He held it up over his head on the roof, then dropped it onto the concrete beneath the night sky.

He took everything into account. He was the one who coined the term *hit list*. Because we weren't just stealing, we were killing. Our targets lay on the first pages in smudged black ink:

Time. Time must always be the first.

Disease. Not pathogens, not titles derived from Latin, the essence of illness. The name of suffering.

Death. Death must always be the last.

There are more. We have endless names to take, to steal from.

The next page was the declaration. Dramatic, I know, but challenging such things requires it.

To all who stole from us, we defy you. You tempt the world and lay waste to it, but try and lay waste to us. Our minds are stronger than our bodies, and our bodies are not yours to call weak. We will kill you in every way we know. That way, when we must go, the playing field is even.

Time will end. Disease will fester. Death will die.

C wrote that. Neo took the pen and wrote it, but C crafted it himself, like a song. All except the final line. That one belongs to Neo. C was never about planning or execution. He was about being present for it all, not in the grip of elsewhere. He wrote what we all thought but didn't know how to say.

The following pages were the results of our execution. What we wanted and what we would steal. Things, yes, but also feelings, desires, chances—anything our three enemies run away with.

However, we were never doing this just for a thrill. That's why, in the end, we will escape with all we took.

Our escape is a collection of yet-to-be-filled pages. They lie at the latter end of the hit list, waiting for the day we summon the courage to leave—a place where we will be unbound from our lives, happy and together and unafraid.

We call it Heaven.

By the time we were done writing, our seat bones ached.

Dawn hit the skyline and illuminated the notebook, now given a soul. Sony held her ankles, rocking back and forth, throwing out every idea in her head. C lay down, listening to me read aloud Neo's words.

It's a part of our lives.

The hospital has plenty of boredom to go around. Wake up, eat, take medications, undergo treatments, the ministrations that don't belong to us. They belong to time, disease, and death.

But the hit list moments?

They're ours.

———

Neo is in a state between conscious and unconscious. C and I sit at his bedside, waiting for him to reenter the world of the waking. It's been over twenty-four hours since we saw him, and no one is more worried about Neo than C.

He tries to distract himself, flipping through a magazine he isn't even reading. Seeing Neo this way after surgery is hard enough. The fact that Neo has a bruise trailing down his neck to his shoulder makes C's jaw grind. He starts the magazine over once he's reached the end, a nervous tic, like tapping your foot.

"C," I call.

"Yeah?"

"What does it mean to be beautiful?"

"Beautiful, how?" he asks. "Like a flower? Like girls?"

"Like Yorick's skull in *Hamlet*."

"Like whose what in what?"

"I think that's what I was in her metaphor. Or was it bones?"

"Whose metaphor?"

"I guess they're the same thing." Bones and skulls. It's all hollowness.

"Are you talking about Hikari?" It dawns on me we're not having the same conversation.

"She called me beautiful."

C's eyes flick from my feet to my head.

"You are beautiful," he says.

"But she says I don't have arms." I extend them for emphasis.

"You have delightful arms."

"She says I hunch."

"You do hunch. You belong at Notre Dame." He says that last part in French, so I don't know what it means, but given that it's probably offensive, I don't ask.

"Do you know how to dream?"

"Sure."

"She said I need to dream."

"You seem pretty preoccupied with what this new girl thinks about you," C says, like I'm a child with a crush at recess. "I like her. I had breakfast with her and Sony. She actually reminds me of you in that strange yet likable way, only less awkward."

"Less awkward?"

"Well, she probably knows how to dream. And stand up straight. And read sarcasm."

"She knows how to read everything," I say, pouting.

C chuckles. "Are you jealous?"

"I'm suffering."

"Sure sounds like it."

"She's making me suffer."

"That's what girls do."

This girl. Yellow and amorous. She's a story. A novel I've already read, but in a foreign language.

"She scares me, C," I say, and it's starting to taste like a stale truth.

"Why?" C asks softly, closing the magazine.

There isn't a way to answer him. When you meet someone infatuating, someone you can stare at and listen to and talk to without taking notice of time, someone you think of constantly, there comes the question of blooming addiction. Nothing addictive is ever good for you. Not Hikari and especially not Hamlet.

C drags a hand across my back, patting it. "Don't overthink it. You always overthink. That's why you have no arms."

Coughing fills the room, an easy kind. C perks up. He's quick to give Neo attention.

"Hey," he whispers, moving the hair out of Neo's eyes. "How are you feeling?"

Neo's eyes flutter open, a darker color surrounding them. "As good as I probably look."

"Mm," C hums, patting down the sheets around him, making sure his back brace doesn't pinch his skin. "Drink your juice."

"Urgh," Neo sounds, as the straw is forcibly placed against his lips.

"Now, please," C says.

"I should've asked for more sedatives."

"You're finally up, huh?" Eric enters, tapping the monitor by the bed. He gently takes Neo's arm to change his IV.

"Haven't I been roughed around by medical professionals enough?" Neo groans, to which Eric flicks the inside of his elbow. "Ow."

Our nurse feigns innocence. "I'm just looking for a vein."

C sighs, his worry audible.

"Neo," he whispers, caressing the purpling blotch of skin just beside his collar.

"Don't say anything," Neo says, hissing at the pain.

"I know it's not from the surgery."

"It sounds like you're saying something."

C doesn't have the chance to retaliate. A loud pair of tiptoeing shoes trail past the scenery and kick the door open—dirty white sneakers.

"Hello, heathens!" Sony spreads her arms wide open, carrying a full tote bag on her arm that seems to have something inside jostling around. "Eric! I didn't see you there."

"Why is your bag moving?" Eric asks, narrowing his eyes at her.

Sony grasps the bag closer to her body. "I have no idea what you're talking about."

"Did you steal a baby or something?" C asks.

"Steal? C, how dare you accuse me of such fiendish activities? Hikari, come defend my honor."

Walking in behind the devil, my sun from last night emerges. Easy and warm with the morning. She and Sony seem to have gotten close in all of a day. I guess flames tend to take to each other no matter where their light is from.

Hikari laughs at Sony. She says hello to Neo in that soft voice, touching his brace, saying more, asking things. Neo doesn't seem to mind. He's there with her, despite the drugs, listening, responding, not looking out the window he likes so much. She can read anything, I forgot. Even someone so hell-bent on hiding his pages.

"Oh. Flowers," Sony says, her nose wrinkling in distaste.

Beside me on the windowsill, bouquets lie next to unread cards wishing recovery in messy cursive. I haven't always understood irony, but I like this particular piece. For someone you wish to live, give them something that is dying.

"What do you have against flowers?" Hikari asks, touching the wax paper and the petals.

I've been staring at her face for so long that I didn't see the little clay pot in her hands. Two little clay pots. They can't be larger than juice cups, plants surfacing an inch's worth from the soil, still in infancy. She sets one down next to the bouquets, her offering, sans card, and alive.

"I have nothing against flowers," Sony says, taking a single stem and motioning with it. "I have everything against flower corpses."

Adjusting the little pot under the light, Hikari caresses the barely there leaves, dusting them, positioning them, so they're kissed by light between the blinds.

"Did you sleep well, Sam?" she asks, leaning back on the heels of her palms, her leg crossed one over the other, chin propped on her shoulder. It's a mandatory question. A flower of conversation. She says it with satire. She's teasing me. She's acting.

"No," I say. "The sun was out."

"Ah," Hikari breathes. "It kept you up?"

"Actually, Hamlet did."

She fakes a gasp. "How dare he?"

"It's all right." I'm inclined to tease her back. "Hamlet is beautiful."

"So it's his beauty you like."

"And his meanness."

"It's just as well. I like Yorick's arms." Teasing. Teasing. Teasing. "Here," she says. She places the second tiny pot, which fits in the circle of her thumb and forefinger, between us.

"What is this?" I ask, picking it up. Her warmth leaves residue on the clay, the idea like a shock of static to my fingertips.

"A little gesture." I didn't go through surgery. What have I been through to deserve a heartfelt offering? Or is this for my crippling case of armlessness?

"What do I do with it?"

Hikari shrugs.

"What does one do with plants but watch them live?"

"Have I graduated from being a skull to a cactus?" I ask.

"That's a succulent," Hikari corrects.

"All right. You're all set, Shakespeare. Take it easy," Eric says, patting Neo's head and double-checking the vitals on his chart. "You be gentle with him," he warns, pointing at all of us.

Sony presses a hand to her chest in offense. "Why are you looking at me?" Although the moment Eric leaves the room, she changes her tune.

The door clicks shut, and Sony's tote bag rustles. She spreads the straps, and from it, a creature pokes its head out. Matted fur and dull green eyes, with a scarred triangle nose and a thin mouth to add.

"Aw, a kitty," C coos. The cat makes itself at home, unfazed by its limited residence inside a carry-on. Sony sets the bag on the ground. It waddles out, one of its ears missing a half, its black coat showing an ashy finish.

Neo raises a brow. "What's wrong with its leg?"

"What leg?" Sony asks.

"Exactly."

The three-limbed cat makes its way onto Neo's bed, sniffing his face.

"Hikari and I chased him down the street. We saved him from getting hit by a truck." Of course they did.

"She's a girl, idiot," Neo says, tilting his chin away from her.

"So? He acts masculine." I'll just say the cat's name is Hee to make things less complicated.

"Hello, Hee," Hikari says, voice gone tender. The feline hops from Neo's bed to her feet and plays with her shoelace. She (or

Hee) looks up at me, a kindred thing. It looks like it wants to tell me something. It sits in the small crevice between my feet and rubs its head against my leg.

"C'mon, Hee." Sony bends down and scoops her up. "Warm up Neo's lap."

"My lap is fine."

The cat doesn't protest as Neo does. Her adventure in the city and under Sony's reign has tuckered her out. She curls into a ball against Neo's stomach as C pets her head.

Sony plops down on the bed too. A chill shivers through Neo, so she takes off her sweatshirt and puts it on his legs. As she does, she glances at Neo's neck, stilling at the bruise that peeks over his shoulder.

She doesn't say anything. She never does, but I see it lingering in her mind even as she removes the hit list from the box under the bed and sighs away the tension.

"The next part of our everything," Sony breathes, pen gliding across the sixth page filled to the brim with our stolen treasures. Her tongue sticks out between her teeth when she writes. "Hee. Taken—from—death." Her words are spoken both in speech and paper. "Baby's—new—best—friend."

"Don't push it," Neo grumbles.

"The infamous hit list," Hikari says.

Sony giggles. "I've got to add you to it."

"Me?"

"We stole you. Or Sam did, I guess."

Hikari smiles at me. "It's a pleasure to be stolen by you, Sam."

I blush so intensely that C can't help smirking into his hand.

Sony unfolds the hit list, where brushstrokes paint our vigilantism in the margins.

Tangible things taken. *Apples,* The Great Gatsby, *six beers, a pack of cigarettes, a coffee mug with a chipped lid, an abandoned teddy bear, a cat.*

Intangible things taken. *A look at the park, a day laughing till our ribs hurt, a full flight of stairs in one go, an afternoon in the library from which we're banned.*

Everything we could ever want to steal.

"That has such a nice ring to it," Hikari says. "Everything." The word comes out in a breath, a faraway concept washed into shore.

"Will you help us, Hikari?" Sony asks, but she looks at me until the last word. Then her legs shuffle, and her fluttering, toothy grin faces the girl next to me. "*Everything* could always use another pair of hands."

"You just have to add something. Something that you want. To the list," C says, tossing her the pen. "That's how you get initiated."

"What if I want to steal something for someone else?" she asks.

"We could do it together," I say. Hikari looks at me when I speak. "I—I mean, we could all write something down again and promise to steal something for one another."

Sony bounces to her feet.

"I like that!"

"We can tear out an empty page from the hit list and tear it into five. We'll write to one person in this room, one piece of everything, on one piece of paper what we intend to steal for them." Hikari pauses, the five of us in a constellation reflected in her glasses. "Like a thieving five-point star."

"I like that." We turn to Sony, but to our surprise, it wasn't her. Neo shifts as much as the brace allows, petting Hee's head, lost in the thoughts Hikari lent. He looks at her with a side-eye, unable to rotate his head. "Can I steal it?"

"For your writing?" she asks.

"Yeah."

"Sure," Hikari agrees, amused, flattered, still mostly grateful.

"Hikari, you'll steal for Sam." Sony hands her one of the pieces of paper. "Sam, you'll steal for me."

"I'm honored," I say. Sony ruffles my hair in response, pecking my forehead.

"I'll steal for Neo."

"Great." Baby doesn't even try to fake his enthusiasm.

"Neo will steal for C, and C will steal for Hikari."

Sony is the first to write the note for Neo. She giggles as she does. Neo goes next. He doesn't even have to think about it.

C leans closer to him. "You can just get me gummy bears again."

"Shut up." Neo hands the pen to him, the paper too. C reads it almost as impatiently as Neo wrote it, a little exhale and happy tone born from it.

"You're adorable," he whispers.

"And you're still talking," Neo says, rolling his eyes.

C writes his note next, putting a little thought into it first. He twirls the pen around and eventually decides on something before handing it to Hikari.

She takes her time. She waits as Sony and Neo bicker and C turns on some music. She waits, watching them interact with each other and with me.

She already knows what she wants to steal. She only starts to write when she knows I do too. Using her knee as a desk, the object of her thievery, whatever it is in this world she swears to steal for me, becomes immortal in ink. Then Hikari lifts my plant, sliding the paper underneath without a word.

"All right, you guys. As soon as Baby's got leg power again, we're coming back with a vengeance," Sony says, hit list in hand. "You ready, Hikari? Sam?"

"Mhm."

"Of course I am."

"Boys?" Sony calls.

"Yes." C gives her a thumbs-up.

"Whatever gets you to stop annoying me," Neo says. Sony pokes his ankle with the tip of the pen.

"This is the last thing we need before we have everything. Our great escape," Sony says, setting the notebook horizontally on her lap so we can all see the great big plan that comes before the empty pages waiting to be filled. "Our Heaven."

The piece of paper tucked beneath the succulent stares back at me. I pick up the pot with both hands and keep it close to me. Then I read Hikari's letter. Three beats' worth, a poem dedicated to me.

> *For Sam,*
> *I'll give you*
> *A dream*

If only the day we shared together didn't feel like one.

————

This is a darker place than Neo's room. The blinds are drawn, and a blue tint settles like we're underwater. One of Sony's doctors carries a chart, a resident behind him.

Sony sits at the foot of the bed, caressing the sheet as if Hee were there purring beneath her palm. Only she isn't. Her cat is with Hikari. Hikari is with C and Neo. Only she and I are here to bask in the sadness.

"Sony?" Her doctor clears his throat. "Did you hear what I just said?"

He's a nice man. Some doctors fall victim to ego or lack of

dedication, but he's been taking care of Sony almost as long as Eric. That's why it's hard for him to deliver what is, to be blunt, a death sentence.

I've tried to spare you the ugliness.

I gave you four children, all on the later edge of their adolescence. I gave you glimpses of their struggles, but I haven't given you many moments of truth.

I haven't told you that Sony's skin is near translucent. It's thin, past fits of hypoxia rendering some of her tissues feeble. Her throat is scarred from infections, making her voice crack at the ends. There are days she can't get out of bed. You can tell she's sick. You can tell she's getting sicker. Even if she's overcome it before, there are only so many battles one can win.

"Yeah, I heard you," Sony says.

The nice doctor sighs. He pushes up his glasses by the frame.

"There's always a chance your lung could survive," he says. "Probably around five or ten percent—"

"Chances don't interest me. You know that." Sony acts coy, holding back an awkward laugh. She caresses the space just beneath her collarbone like she did the sheet. She feels the rising and falling of her lung.

"So," she whispers. "How much time do I have?"

6
passion

two years ago

NEO FALLS ASLEEP teaching me about sarcasm. He explains the use of irony in literature is often to show that surface appearance can directly oppose actual meaning. Sarcasm is a way of using irony to hurt my feelings. I'm paraphrasing, but by the second hour of me still being unable to pick out a sarcastic remark, Neo gives up and goes to bed.

I asked if it was ironic that we call fallen angels *devils*. He said he'd tell me once he went to Hell.

Nightmares sometimes visit him in the early stages of sleep, so I remain, an afterthought in my chair across the room. Unwanted guests in Neo's mind make him squirm, the sheets rustling. He moves like he's being restrained, his body tied down by an invisible weight. Every time that happens, I bring my chair to his bedside and hold his hand. A tether to something real, even in sleep, calms his breathing.

I may not know much about irony, but I do know a lot about sick people. I know when they need more care than they let on.

Ever since the day Neo cried on his bathroom floor in my arms, I haven't let that slip my mind.

Once the first hour of his sleep has passed, I leave Neo to better dreams.

My people-watching hulls have been neglected lately. However, fate has other plans. When the elevator doors open to the ground floor, the last thing I expect to walk in on is a wild girl mercilessly kicking a vending machine.

"Urgh!" A bright, fuzzy sock leading to a dirty white sneaker slams against the glass. The girl huffs from the effort, hospital gown swaying around her bare legs. Her fists clench at her sides, clutching some of the material. She stares down the machine like she could kill it.

I really need to pay attention to what floor I get off on more often. Rectifying my mistake isn't an option when the elevator doors shut behind me.

Patient Kicker snaps her neck in my direction at the sound. Her hair swings with her movements, red, tinted like fire. She stares like she could kill *me*.

I blink, my wish to exist less drifting into the territory of wishing I didn't exist at all.

"You want my picture?" she bites out.

"Uh—I—I don't have a camera."

"What happened to you, anyway?" She looks me up and down, frowning. "You get hit by a bus or something?"

"Uh—"

"Urgh!" she sounds, interrupting me. Another swift kick is delivered to the machine.

"You have to push the button longer and reach your hand into the compartment," I tell her.

A bit of nostalgia pricks my curiosity, disturbing its slumber.

Putting my hands up in surrender, I step forward, press the button beneath the keypad, and reach my arm into the mouth. The display beeps, the inside clicks, and two bars thump to the bottom. I take them out and offer both the way you would a dinner tray.

"They all do that?" the girl asks, far calmer now that there's food in front of her.

"Just this one."

Amusement blooms on her face as she takes my offering. Her features come to light, chapped lips curving, stretching fresh cuts on her cheek.

"What is it?" I ask.

"Nothing." Her fingers trail the glass scuffed from her kicks like an apology. "Just that broken things seem to like you."

Broken things. How endeared she seems by those two words, just as Neo is.

"Are you alone?" I ask.

"My mom's asleep in the room," she says, sinking to the ground beside the vending machine, enemy-turned-friend. "Here." She holds out one of her bars. "Sit with me."

Honestly, a bit afraid to refuse her, I take it. She unwraps hers with impatience, sitting cross-legged, head thrown back. I settle next to her, about a foot away.

"You never seen a chocolate bar before?" she asks. Before I can answer, she reaches into my lap, bites the corner of the wrapper, and skins it with her teeth. Then it's handed back to me, less like an offering, more like a handshake. "I'm Sony."

Sony.

All of Sony's acts are full-bodied, I notice. There's aggression to her, like Neo's too-candid words. At the same time, youth peeks through her manner. Her eyes and hair are bright, a middle-of-the-night excitement only a child could wear.

"I'm Sam," I say.

She smirks, knocking our chocolate together like champagne glasses. "You look like hell, Sam."

"You don't look that great either."

"Yeah." Her chewing slows. "It wasn't a good day."

"Did you get hit by a bus too?" I joke. Neo says I'm awful at it. Every time I attempt one around him, he throws a book at my head. Not Sony. Sony likes my joke. She even laughs, nudging my shoulder with such harshness I almost fall over.

"Do you like hiking, Sam?"

"Hiking?"

"I went hiking yesterday. I think it's my favorite thing in the world."

I swallow. Bruises climb her arm, a similar age to the scratches on her face.

"Is that why you're here?" I ask. "Did you get hurt?"

Sony stops chewing altogether, bright eyes dulled behind a veil of something that brings her pain. They are drawn to her lap much like her hand draws to her stomach, as if observing a memory.

"Yeah," she says, but it's a lie. "Have you ever been hiking?"

"No."

"Oh, it's amazing, Sam. You have to try it." She pokes me for emphasis. "I was so close to the top of a mountain, you know. I could see the ocean from up there and everything." Her voice gains a wondrous quality, like rather than a drearily lit hall and a trio of steel elevator doors, the sea folds out before us.

"I wish I had wings," she says, like a fallen angel who used to have them on her back. "I could've flown free over the water forever."

I find this intimate. Listening to someone get lost like that. It's akin to reading Neo's words, which he lets too few people see.

Sony grins, chocolate staining her teeth. "You should come hiking with me one day."

Sony and I talk most of the night. I discover hiking and chocolate for the first time. Chocolate, as Sony and my taste buds teach me, is one of the greatest things in the world, right up there with *Wuthering Heights*. Sony says she doesn't read much. I tell her about Neo. At first, she doesn't believe that he's a real person. She tells me about her mother, a mild woman who raised a beastly thing. Sony laughs at herself some more. When she grows restless, I show her around the hospital. By the time dawn stretches through the windows, Sony returns to her room and presses endless kisses to her mother's face.

After that night, Sony is discharged. I don't see her for some time. That vending machine misses our conversation. I let myself trail the scuff marks in her memory. I even show Neo chocolate. He tells me chocolate isn't a discovery and that I'm dumb. I ignore him, and we share candy bars while watching movies.

A few months later, while I sit barnacled to a bench on the third floor, reading through *Lord of the Flies*, a familiar fire crackles.

"Where's Sam?"

I look up, red hair and a backpack colored with markers standing at a decentralized unit.

The nurse working at said station, *not* in charge of Sony or me, cocks her head to the side. "I'm sorry?"

"The person is yea high, sort of weird-looking," Sony says, motioning with her hands. "C'mon, you can't miss 'em. I mean, the kid's never seen chocolate before."

"Sony?" I call.

She turns around.

"Sammy!" A cheery giggle shakes through her chest at the sight of me. "Hah. That's a nice smile you've got."

"You look good," I say. The cuts on her face have healed, and freckles dance across her nose.

She winks as she whispers, "Bus just missed me."

Swinging her backpack off one shoulder, Sony rummages through trinkets, clothes, and whatever else is crammed in there, pulling out a chocolate bar. "I got you this just in case you were still here." She pats my head like a puppy.

"Sony." A woman appears behind her, one with matching freckles. "We need to go see the doctor now, honey."

"Bleh." Sony's mother rolls her eyes, wrapping an arm around her daughter. Sony melts into the touch. "I've gotta do boring crap now. But I'll find you afterward. Let's have fun!" She unfolds my palm with force, writing her room number with a pen from the bottomless backpack. Her tongue sticks out between her teeth, her handwriting crooked, unsteady, like a toddler's.

My neck cranes to read it, Sony's fingers smoothing over the numbers.

"Don't leave, okay?" she whispers. An oxygen therapy tube sits around her neck, and her voice is frailer than it was the night we met. But Sony's joy doesn't falter even when her breathing hollows.

As she goes to follow her mother, I squeeze her hand and then watch her disappear down the hall.

Two nights later, Sony has surgery. It takes six hours, so for six hours, I sit outside Sony's room with her mother. She asks if I'm Sony's friend. I nod and tell her Sony gives me chocolate. A pleased expression takes her, the one mothers wear when they remember their children's idiosyncrasies. The memories soothe her for a moment, but the thought of those memories being all she has makes her foot tap, her heartbeat quicken, and her teeth chew her lip. I ask Sony's mother if she'd like to walk with me. She nods. I take her to our vending machine.

Six hours later, Sony wakes in her bed, silly from the anesthetics. Her mother doesn't wait for the doctors' approvals. She goes to her daughter's side, pressing kisses to her face. She tells her she's proud of her and that she can have all the chocolate she wants. Sony hums, hooked up to so many machines, her body exhausted from merely being awake.

I'm not sure what Sony has exactly. So many different illnesses target respiration. Suffocation is one of death's favorite methods. Sony's disease ravaged her lung and left her with infection after infection that her body couldn't handle on its own.

But Sony isn't the kind to submit to anything.

She still has wings to grow.

"Sammy!" A smile greets me as I walk into her room and round her bedside. Sony takes my hand, the same one with her room number, and presses it to her chest. "Feel! Oh, sorry, that's my boob. But look!"

The breaths beneath my touch are hollow, Sony's mouth open to take them.

"That side's empty now," she whispers. "Only one lung left."

Drugs lull her eyes closed with every word. For a creature so full of life, half of Sony's adventures have been taken.

She lets out a dry chuckle. "I don't think I'll be doing much hiking anymore." Her head turns limp on her pillow. "But at least I can breathe."

"Let's just breathe, then," I whisper.

"That sounds good."

But it fades all too quickly. The air and fluid filling the empty space in her rib cage object to her joy. They rein in her leashless energy and her bouts of laughter. At least, despite the pain, they leave her strength intact, the flame I met kicking in the night far from being snuffed out.

Sony squeezes my hand. "Don't leave, okay, Sam?"

I sit beside her.

"Okay . . ."

Sony's recovery is quick. She eats like an animal, always in need of a napkin. She tries to run before she can stand, shoelaces untied. The times she almost falls flat on her face from trying to skate on her IV pole exasperate both her mother *and* me.

Sony teaches me about racing. She wants to race absolutely everywhere, at any time. Down the hall, up stairs she can barely climb, to the elevators, to the bathroom, to her room, everywhere. She likes games too. Board games I've never heard of, puzzles she's too impatient to finish, and Red Light, Green Light (which is essentially a race).

The day she says she wants to read, I bring her to Neo.

————

"Wow, you're tiny. Damn, you've got a lot of books."

I didn't take Sony's lack of boundaries into account before opening Neo's door without warning. She walks in, her focus split between the boy in the bed, the stacks of papers, and the books on the floor. Even her attention span likes to race.

"Hi, Neo." I greet him with last week's chapter in hand, setting it on the side table. "Do you have the next part for me?"

"Who the hell is that?" His pen points at the girl flipping through one of his books.

"Your name's Neo? Neo like *neonate*?" Sony asks, trotting to his bed. "You kind of do look like a baby."

"Neo like Neo. Don't touch that." Neo, like Neo, swipes the book from her hands. Sony jumps like she's been barked at.

"Grumpy baby."

"Saaamm." Neo drags out the syllable in my name, his eyes wide, begging for an answer to his earlier question.

"Neo, this is Sony," I say, prideful like I've found a delightful pet and brought it home. "She gives me chocolate."

Neo raises his lip, annoyed. "What are you, a dog? You can't just follow people around because they give you things."

"That's what I did with you," I mutter, turning my chin away.

"Ooh, pretty," Sony sounds, hands behind her back as she ogles the papers on Neo's lap. "Can I read it?"

"No! One weirdo is enough. Shoo."

"This *is* the next chapter," I say, bending to Sony's level and trying to catch whatever words I can through the gaps.

Neo groans. "I need to start locking my door."

But he never does. Neo spends the whole day with Sony and me. First, we stake out the cafeteria, waiting for the perfect opening to steal some apples. Neo calls Sony a klepto for spiriting lollipops out of the bin. Our spoils of thievery taste even sweeter in the garden, where we commandeer a bench near the middle. Overhead, the cool autumn breeze spreads clouds against the blue.

"Neo, let's play a game," Sony says.

"No."

"Okay, so, you have to pick a cloud and figure out what shape it is. You go first. What does that one look like to you?" Sony points straight up, her finger following the moving shapes across the sky.

"A cloud." Neo chews, not even looking.

Sony flicks his forehead.

"Hey!"

"That one looks like a bird! You see the wings?" Sony pulls

me by the shirt collar so I can see from her vantage point. Our baby grumbles, crammed between us. Watching more clouds go by with the time, Sony swings her legs back and forth, as enamored with the sky as she is with the sea. With wonder, she whispers, "I've always wanted wings."

At first, Neo scowls every time Sony and I walk through his door. He complains when she talks too much and turns away when she wants to play games. He goes so far as to try to escape us, practically running. He's yet to learn of Sony's love for racing.

After a time, Neo begins doing what writers do. He listens to Sony. Sony says senseless things, childish things, no matter the audience. She observes, she questions. She's unafraid to exist to her fullest. Her fire burns hot, and Neo is small. He gets cold easily.

When I bring apples, Sony brings a child's imagination. She reads his stories with audible gasps, tangible tears, and snorting humor. Those reactions let Neo look at her. Not with a scowl. With a kind of gratitude that only writers understand.

Sony asks me why Neo's books and stories are mine to hide during parental visits. When I tell her, sadness plagues her eyes.

That night, once Neo's parents are gone, silence sits in her mouth. We walk into his room together. Sony sits on the bed and wraps her arms around him.

"You okay?" Neo asks.

Sony rests her head on his shoulder.

"Yeah," she whispers. "I just missed you, silly baby."

———————

The weather starts to bite in the last week of November. Our visits to the garden become less and less frequent. We blame it on the wind instead of Sony's lung. Her smiles have started to thin.

Her laughter is becoming rare. The freckles on her nose are pale. Neo and I don't race her anymore. We take the elevator rather than the stairs. Soon enough, Sony can barely walk without collapsing.

Her heart monitor beeps throughout autumn's end like a metronome. I keep my own count, holding her hand as my finger trails the pulse in her wrist.

"Neo," Sony says, her voice a raspy thing.

"Yes."

"Why do we *have* diseases?" she asks, looking at the ceiling as if she could look through it and see the clouds passing by.

Neo sighs, playing with Sony's other hand, fidgeting with her knuckles. He's wearing her sweatshirt, a neon one with *smile* written in a curve at the center.

"Illness is temporary," he explains. "Injuries borrow our blood, infections use our cells, but our illnesses are different. In a way, they're self-inflicted. An error in the code. This kind— well—it owns us, it hurts us, because it just doesn't understand."

Language is flawed. That's what he means.

We don't have diseases.

They have us.

They found a home in us.

"Why can't we make it understand?" Sony asks, fear trembling from her throat.

Neo bites his lower lip to keep it from shaking. He's grown attached to Sony. So much that he tucks red strands behind her ear and pretends he isn't holding back tears.

"We have soldiers in our blood," he whispers, like the start of a bedtime story. "They're ruthless and unbiased. To them, there's no difference between who they're meant to protect and an enemy."

The metronome slows. Sony's lung matches the beat of her heart.

"They're blind. You can't convince them of their wrongdoings," Neo says. He continues to pet Sony's hair. "The irony is lost on them."

Like an apology for the sins of our sickness, Neo drops his head to her shoulder and holds Sony till she falls asleep.

————

Winter arrives. When it does, death no longer waits for Sony.

Little by little, the fight tilts in her favor. The inflammation in her lung goes down with every step she climbs and every laugh she manages. One day, she puts on her dirty white sneakers and steals apples in the early morning. Neo and I wake to the sound of her chewing and her chuckles as she watches cartoons.

"Neo, let's do a puzzle," she says.

"I hate puzzles."

"You adore puzzles. And it'd be great if we actually finished one."

"Fine. But only because you're disabled."

Sony snorts. "Your back's screwed. Soon you'll be disabled like me."

"Yeah, yeah. You got any corner pieces?"

————

"Sam." Someone whispers my name. I wake to Sony's head in my lap. "Look, Sam," she says, holding up *Lord of the Flies* with the giddiest grin. "I read a whole book. See? I can't wait to tell Mom."

The wild children in it, the ones who held on to their humanity past their hardships, remind me of her. My devil searching for her wings. I fix the breathing tube over her lip and tell her I'm proud while she flips through the page she's conquered.

Sony gets discharged in February. Every checkup she has, she practically rams into Neo and me with hugs and thousands of kisses. She even starts coming to the hospital for visits. We have puzzle nights once a week.

———————

One day, Sony comes to the hospital without calling first. Neo and I are watching movies in an empty waiting room, Eric's shift allowing us to sprawl out on the chairs past our bedtime.

Sony walks through the door like a lost soul. She wears nothing but pajamas and those dirty white sneakers. Her eyes stray, from the ground to us to her hand squeezing her arm.

Neo and I sit up, making room for her between us.

"Are you okay, Sony?" I ask. She looks at her shoes, tapping the soles together.

"Yeah," she says, her voice a distant thing. Concern crinkles Neo's forehead. Sony sniffles, her jaw locking, unlocking. "I'm a little cold, I guess."

"I can get you chocolate if you want," I say. Sony scoffs, her hand ruffling through my hair as she pulls me in, nuzzling against me. Silence envelops her like a fog. "Was today not a good day?"

My quiet is a constant, a formulation of my curiosity's wish to listen. Neo's quiet is verbal. On paper, he's as loud as they come. Sony's quiet is made of sorrow. It aches in her chest beside her heart like she could breathe from it. Tonight, it brings her here. It steals from her fire and her full-bodied movements. It tears her down, half of herself left to live.

"No," Sony breathes. "It wasn't a good day."

"Sony." Neo beckons her gaze. He crouches in front of her,

reading her pain like lines in his stories ready to be erased. "What happened?"

Sony's jaw quivers with her lips. A smile forged like a shield spreads across her face, if only to convince her she isn't trying not to cry. Her eyes shut to the question. Then it comes from her, like a confession. A sin. An irony.

"My mom died."

Neo doesn't move. He simply looks up at her, his hands on her knees.

Blue and red touch Sony's face, the ambulance that brought her here tonight still fresh in her mind. She tries to laugh, a dry sound, the kind I never want to hear again. It's an insult to her true laughter.

"She wasn't sick," she says, like the greatest tragedy of her life is a sick joke of its own. "She just died in her sleep."

Sony is a gladiator. She was born to conquer mountains and race the gods. She even raced death and won, crossing the finish line, her body broken, but her soul still childish and alive. Shame cowers in fear of her, and defeat never knew her name till now.

I think of Sony's mother that day, sleeping in her daughter's room. She never looked twice at Neo and me. She never let discomfort through as she brought us gifts and treats. She always asked about our days rather than our health. Her warmth, like her daughter's, knew no bounds. Sony's mother was one of those people who would give anything just to see her child happy. Not in her expectations, not in a vicarious future, but wearing her own joy, climbing her own mountains. It's a rarer thing to find in parents than you may think. Having to lose her and not knowing why brings Sony to the edge.

Reasons are illusions. Their absence is common. If only it weren't their presence that keeps people sane.

Sony starts to cry, holding her chest as if her lung could fall from her ribs. Neo takes her by the shoulders. He holds her upright.

"Is someone coming for you?" he asks.

"No." Sony shakes her head. "It was just me and her." The last words come out in whimpers. Tears spill from her eyes. Neo wraps his arms around her, hand in her hair, the other gripping the shirt at her back.

"I didn't get to say goodbye," she says, sinking into him as she once did with her mother. I kiss her temple as she sobs with her whole body. I hold her from the side, my arms overlapping Neo's.

"I wish I had wings," she cries.

"It's okay, Sony," Neo whispers, caressing red strands of fire lost in rain. He holds her tight, taking my hand in the process. "We're not gonna let you fall."

Sony learns something that day.

She learns that death isn't playful.

Death is sudden.

It has no taste for irony or reason.

It doesn't wait for another tick of the metronome.

It doesn't wait for goodbyes.

Death is a taker, plain, direct, no tricks up its sleeve. And it will give you nothing in return but a last endless kiss for those you leave behind.

———

Sony's mother had a lot of money. Like a child, Sony places no value on it. Lawyers meet with her about inheritance, wills, and many other things Sony doesn't want to talk about while planning to spread her mother's ashes.

Sony's estranged family tries to contact her, but she never

calls them back. Money's gravity is stronger than tragedy's. Sony knows that.

Eric sets up a ventilator in his apartment's second bedroom. He knew Sony's mother for a long time and therefore, Sony. She stays with him for some time. When she spreads her mother's ashes in the sea, he goes with her.

Sony finds joy again. She doesn't seek it out. It lies waiting in unfinished puzzles and adventures she's yet to have.

Children filled the space her mother left behind. Eric takes her to the oncology wing, where her dramatic readings of bedtime stories and notorious games of hide-and-seek are great successes.

She finds peace in letting Neo steal her hoodies and in stealing forbidden fruit for herself. She and I carry the story box to the gardens and play the sky games when Neo's parents visit him.

Sony's lung, sadly, doesn't live well on its own. The hospital keeps a steady hold on her, only relinquishing its grip when that single organ missing its other half finds the strength.

Years later, when our lives fall into steady rhythms, no met-ronomes to be found, Sony's fire learns to burn on its own. I give her a piece of paper, a mock puzzle piece, telling her to chase the half that's been stolen.

For Sony,
I'll steal you a pair of wings.

7

quid pro quo

OUR ESCAPE PLAN is simple. It's a heist, like all our missions. Only this time, we are the objects of thievery. Remember that our diseases own us. We are theirs. But we can take ourselves back from them. Now that we've practiced stealing both tangible and intangible desires, it's time we slip through the iron bars.

There are multiple steps to think of. A five-point star isn't exactly inconspicuous walking out of a hospital. The plan is top secret. Need-to-know basis. The first step is getting Neo to walk again.

He stands, his weight uneasy, imbalanced. His doctor said he had to practice. Having to practice standing is a bit dehumanizing. I think, though, that Neo is less bothered by the vulnerability than he is by my hands holding him upright.

"Why are you so cold?" he grumbles, his fingers curled like claws around my arms.

"Neo, what do you dream of?" I ask, chewing on the chocolate Sony gave me. Neo shook his head when she offered some earlier. Now he just sucks on a single square, letting it dissolve in his mouth.

"Lately?" he asks, moving the chocolate with his teeth. "Annoying cats and C's shitty music."

"That's not what I meant."

"I know what you meant."

"Do you dream of publishing your stories?"

"I don't know. If I ever write for money, it would be just so I can keep writing."

"Isn't that why all writers write?"

"No." Neo shifts on his feet. His muscles haven't been used in a while. They're learning to work around an unbent spine. "Some people write so their name will be bigger than the title," he says.

Neo is a good writer, even if he doesn't believe it. He makes me feel despite the fact that I don't remember how. Even Shakespeare doesn't have that power. I know his stories can do that for people who need it. *One day.*

Neo's weight shifts away from me. He stands on the balls and heels of his feet, upright. A breath shakes through him from ankles to neck. He is able to stand, no butterfly rash or swelling to be seen.

"You're getting better," I say.

Neo stiffens. He leans his weight back onto my arms, clutching them. "I'm not leaving, Sam."

"I know. That's not what I meant."

"I know what you meant."

His fingers detach from me mechanically. He settles back on his unmade bed.

"Are you mad at me?" I ask. His face is scrunched up, more than usual.

"No." He grabs the papers on his side table, his pen too. "I have to fix Sony's escape plan. It's straight out of an action movie."

When he says Sony's name, his eyes wander to the neon sleeves pulled over his knuckles. She isn't with us now. She can't be. Some burdens of one-lungedness have to be handled alone. Maybe not alone. Maybe just with a cat.

Neo puts his hand on his chest and breathes in a little deeper to feel it rise and fall.

"Is she okay?" he asks. "I know you were with her yesterday."

Yesterday, I got on my knees the way Neo would have if he were submerged in Sony's blue. I held Sony once the doctor left. She didn't cry, but she needed to be held. She needed to not be alone. Eric came in at the end of his shift and took her for ice cream. She accidentally let it slip that there was a cat in her room. It had bladder-control problems. Eric pinched the bridge of his nose and told her that if she cleaned up after it, he would just pretend it didn't exist. He bought her a litter box and a food and water bowl. Later, when Sony had little strength left, he took her back to her room and spoke to her for hours, telling her about all the kids she hasn't been able to play tag with lately. The mask didn't hide her smiles. The ventilator was nowhere near as loud as her snorty laughs and teasing. When she fell asleep, Eric ran his hands through his hair. He cried. Silently. So that he wouldn't wake her. His sobs were all breath. He covered his mouth till the dread he couldn't carry left his body. Then, he wiped his face, stood, and checked every vital sign, screen, and machine connected to Sony. Before he left, he kissed her forehead and whispered something I couldn't hear.

It's unfair. That those you take care of usually end up being the ones you care about. I should know. It's what Eric and I have in common. We aren't supposed to love them. Narrators and nurses mustn't get attached. We are tied to this place, and they are tied to a pendulum swinging to either side of the ledge.

"Don't tell me, actually," Neo says, wiping his nose. "It's better if I don't know." He scatters his papers above the sheets, re-creating his sea so that there's noise to fill the quiet. "Why are you still standing there? Go see Hikari or something."

When he says *her* name, my eyes don't wander. They unfocus. All my senses rush to my hands, the ones that mirror hers. I reach into both my pockets.

"I shouldn't."

Between my thumb and forefinger, my succulent peeks, only its container concealed. In the other pocket, Hikari's note sits folded in my palm. Last night, I was supposed to meet her in our old cardiology wing, but I couldn't summon the courage.

"Why?" Neo asks.

"She's scary."

"Aren't I scary?"

"No. You're small."

He grumbles. "She doesn't want to bite you. What the hell are you worried about?"

"I don't know what she wants."

"I've never understood what it is *you* want."

"Wanting is useless for someone like me."

Neo looks up from his writing, waiting for me to look at him too.

"Someone like *us*, you mean," he says, his voice gaining an edge.

"Sorry."

"Sony wants to play with her kids and have the freedom to do whatever and go wherever she pleases," he goes on, bypassing the awkward pause that would've been. "I want at least a part of me to be immortal, and Coeur wants—well—"

"Shitty music?"

"Probably."

With a sigh, Neo glances toward the windowsill where the bouquets lay. In the middle, under just the right amount of light, my succulent's sibling sunbathes.

"From the looks of it," Neo says, admiring it, "Hikari wants the same thing you do."

"I thought you didn't understand what I want."

"I don't," he admits. "But it doesn't have to make sense."

He goes back to work, the origins of our relationship making my hands feel weightless. As he writes, I reach under his bed and grab *Hamlet*, *Wuthering Heights*, and the hit list from the cardboard box before pushing it back under.

Last night, I didn't go see Hikari as I promised. I didn't even go to her room to tell her I wasn't going to go either. It was rude of me, but after what happened with Sony I couldn't risk it. When you're empty, the wind can toss you side to side with ease. The sun can shine right through you. Last night was a night I felt emptier than most.

"I'll let you write," I say.

"Sam," Neo calls after me. He catches sight of the books in my hands, the little clay pot and succulent peeking from my pocket. "Don't let those things you don't want to remember ruin this for you, okay?"

I nod, even if I don't mean it, before shutting the door.

C is with his family tonight. They took him to dinner.

They're rather nice. His father always slaps me on the back and laughs loudly when I don't understand a joke. His mother is strict, much more strained than her husband. She tells me to stand up straight and fixes Neo's hair without asking. She's fond of Neo. People with harsh faces are always fond of each other. C's brothers—he has many, five, I believe—are more like their father: bellowish, large, talkative. C is a black sheep in the herd. Whenever they visit, he doesn't take the time to be in the room with them as he does with us. He keeps his earbuds in and reads some of his and Neo's book, ignoring the mass of conversation.

I wonder what he thinks about. I wonder if tonight, he thinks of Neo's back, Sony's lung, and Hikari's blood. I wonder if, instead, he thinks of our soon-to-be escape and the adventures that lie in wait. I wonder if he's holding the promise Neo gave him the way I hold the promise Hikari gave me.

It's only a thin, torn piece of paper with a dream in its lines, right? But it has her on it. Like *Wuthering Heights*, *Hamlet*, the hit list, my succulent, and her drawing, she is embedded in the matter. Anything she's touched, either with skin or words, I hoard. I may as well be a smoker clutching nicotine patches.

I press my forehead into the stack of books, walking, walking, walking, till the hum of chatter fades in. The cafeteria is busy for this time of night. Those in scrubs stir black coffee. Others, some waiting for results, some waiting for loved ones, mull over food going uneaten.

At the near center, a couple sits across from a girl.

They're arguing. I can tell that much. The woman has her head in her hands, frustration flaring. The man has his arms crossed, his eyes downcast, his head shaking now and then.

Hikari's back is to me, yellow hair tied back in a ponytail.

I can't see her face. All I can see is her body. Her legs don't rock. Her arms stay tame at her sides. I don't move until Hikari stands and leaves her parents at the table. Quickly hiding in a corner on the other side of the entrance, I wait for her to walk past.

I can't say her name, but I want her to turn around. I want to see her and make sure she's okay. I want, and the anxiety of that crawls like spiders up my stomach.

"Hamlet," I call.

Hikari turns around, no tears staining her cheeks, no sadness in her eyes. A rush of relief escapes my chest.

"Yorick." She smiles, but it doesn't reach her eyes. It doesn't reach me. "Is that your succulent?" she asks as it waves from my pocket.

"Oh. Yes," I say, looking down at its withered leaves. "It's wounded. I didn't want to leave it by itself."

Hikari snorts, sticking her hands in her own pockets. She wears shorts, her legs bare. They look smooth beneath the light, unbruised and unblemished except for goose bumps and a few Band-Aids.

"Are you okay, Sam?" she asks. My eyes snap up, cheeks reddening.

"Um—yes—I—I just called you, because—well—"

"Because you saw my parents scolding me?" The books in my arms tighten against me. She has the same look as Neo when I brought up wanting, a sort of muted disappointment.

"What's wrong?" she asks when my gaze draws to the ground, and my chin falls on my stack of books.

"I made everyone mad today," I murmur.

"No one's mad at you," Hikari says.

"You should be."

"Why? Because a skull stood me up?"

There it is.

"I'm sorry."

"It's okay." Hikari laughs. It's dry, no discernible beats to count.

"You can talk to me about it if you'd like," I say, nodding my

head in her parents' direction. "About what happened. Or if you
need me to carry a box around, I can do that too."

"You really want to know?"

"Yes." I swallow, eyes flicking side to side, foraging for some
courage. "I'm exploring you."

She's been tying her hair up more often nowadays. Whenever
we stand or sit this close, little details like that become appar-
ent. She's colder when she's upset. And if I say something out of
character, she *searches*. She reads lines in me she's already read
as if she misunderstood them the first time. And if you give her a
chance, she's forgiving.

"Okay." She nods. Then she turns on her heel, hair swinging
with her, striding away from the weary cafeteria. "But you owe
me a night. So c'mon."

———

"So why did you stand me up, Yorick?" she asks.

"I was scared."

"Scared?"

"Neo says you won't bite me, but I don't believe him."

"You should listen. Neo knows everything."

Her room is full of plants, some wounded and others healing
like mine. Her clothes are piled rather than folded, avalanching
out of a suitcase in the far corner. Her bed is unmade, her medication thoughtlessly strewn about.

"You're messy," I say, smiling as I put the books down. It's
endearing. The comfort she has with the space. She's adopted the
room, given it a personality.

Hikari narrows her eyes at me, faking a bite, her teeth clicking
together. We both laugh.

Once my arms are free, Hikari breaks into a run, out of her

room, into the hall, a chorus of nurses yelling at her to slow down in the distance. She doesn't even explain what we're doing. She trusts I'll follow, and I do.

"Where are we going?" I ask.

Hikari just chuckles, her steps unbreaking. She shrieks when we both almost run into a group of doctors, quickly ducking her head and taking another turn. Her laughter rings, keeping me close even when I'm several strides behind.

She only stops when we reach the gardens, panting, the cool night making steam of her breaths like the cafeteria makes of coffee. The stars are dull once more, but nonetheless, she looks up, taking them in like it's the first time.

"How about now, Sam?" She caresses the dark shrubbery and sits down on a patch of grass. "Do you feel alive yet?"

"We stole a race," I realize, wiping my mouth.

"For Sony." Hikari holds her knees in the crooks of her elbows. She knows. That Sony isn't doing well right now. She knows it pains me as much as it pains her.

"Can I ask you something?" she asks.

"Yes."

"What is a life to you?"

"There is a medical definition," I say. "Neo says there are too many philosophical ones."

"I didn't ask for a definition. I asked what it is to *you*."

What if I told you that I am not meant to be alive? What if I told her? Do you think she'd understand?

Hikari's earlier coldness resurfaces. "My parents think I'm throwing my life away," she says. "They say I don't want anything worthwhile, and when I bring up the fact that they've never *asked* what it is I want, they call me childish. My parents are logical. Their faith is expensive. It has to be earned. They believe scans, bloodwork, doctors, but whatever I'm feeling? Whatever I say?" As if her parents are sitting across from her, a barrier a table thick between them, she sighs. "It's difficult to feel heard by people who have no faith in your words."

"They don't believe you're suffering?" I ask.

"It's not that."

Hikari's fingers caress the scar from the crook of her shoulder to her chest. There is another scar just adjacent, younger than its predecessor. She bares them to me as if baring secrets.

"I was so happy as a kid," she says. "They don't understand how all of a sudden things changed. Although it wasn't sudden really, it was more like the older I grew, the clearer my vision became. My imagination thinned like fog, and the world I saw was so gray in comparison." The touch at the column of her throat falls to the bandages around her forearms. She trembles, but I think she trusts me enough to undo them. Beneath, little white scars form lines like a ladder up her arm.

"It started with loneliness," she says. "I could eat and not taste a thing, cry and not feel sad, sleep and still feel tired. I didn't like what I used to like or want what I used to want. I thinned until I felt like a blur. A little piece of the background no one would notice had gone missing. And even if I'd never felt emptier, every time I tried to get out of bed, I felt like I was sinking. I'd stare at my clock and watch it tick, wishing I could break it." She closes her hand around the cuts. It looks like she wants to cry but doesn't remember how. "Thank God you all hate time too, Sam. I've been wishing it dead for as long as I can remember."

She's still a teenager. Teenagers aren't as malleable as children. They have a sense of self, aspiration, *dreams*. Sometimes, parents feel threatened by that autonomy. They cling to the idea of their child, the idea of who they are. Anything off script feels like disobedience. So when that child would rather read and write than follow in his father's footsteps, violence ensues. When that child is trapped in her own mind, her mother and father negate the pain as nothing but a symptom of age.

"Hamlet was always my worst influence," Hikari whispers, the breath ghostlike.

People glorify youth. Maybe that's why she strays from hers. They see it as a period of freedom, sex, and stupid decisions. *These are the best years of your life. Enjoy them. You'll be grateful you did.* Say that to a child and watch them be reduced to a fruit, ripe and ready for harvest. *You'll be grateful you did*—that is a regretful argument made by those who look in the mirrors and see rot. This is what comes of it. People who *don't believe* one could be so numb that even their disease doesn't hurt enough.

"You're depressed," I say. A new truth. One that tastes sour in the mouth.

"No, not depressed. They ruined that word for me." Hikari shifts, tucking her hair behind her ears. She makes a disbelieving sort of noise. "I think the worst feeling in the world is telling someone you're in pain and hearing them say there's no wound."

"You need a wound," I say, the urge to defend her trembling through my fingers. "Depression—I don't care if you hate the word—depression is a better thief than you or I ever will be. It steals moments that should be yours. That's why you walk ledges and run and draw and rob and read, and . . ." I stop myself, remembering the pencil sharpener she stole and took apart, tucking the blade into her pocket.

"Depression is exactly like fear," I say. "It's all shadow and no body, but it's real."

That shadow looms over Hikari as mine does. It holds a noose just as tight around her neck. At night it's harder to see, but there's no mistaking it. The stars cast their dull light on her, and when one of them decides to flare, her shadow flinches.

"It has you too," she says. "That's why you're bad at existing."

"No." I shake my head, not taking my eyes off her. "I chose this. My depression is consensual."

She can't help the laugh.

"You like the numbness?" she asks.

"It's better than the pain."

She opens her mouth like she wants to refute me, but no words come to fruition. She wants to tell me that pain is temporary, but she isn't so sure now that she has to say it aloud. She shuts her mouth again, her jaw grinding as she refocuses on the dewdrops.

Fear's shackles dig into my throat as I almost say her name.

"My Hamlet," I say. It doesn't matter. Right now, she's all that matters. "I may just be a cowardly skull, but I'm here," I say, my hand closing around the grass just beside the hit list as I think about the shape of hers. "I'm always listening, and I'll always believe you."

The hit list and my succulent sit between us as a marker of distance. The warmth we share disobeys. I lean into it. I haven't said her name. I haven't touched her. She isn't real. I'm just a skull in the cup of her palm, so what does it really matter if I fly too close to the sun?

"Do you believe that I'm alive yet?" I ask.

"No." Hikari shakes her head, but her smile lingers. "I still have to make you dream."

"What do you dream of?" I ask.

Hikari sighs, staring through the stars that have yet to shine for her. "I dream of . . . annihilating that loneliness." She hooks her teeth on her bottom lip, shrugging. "And maybe a grand romantic gesture."

"Like in the movies?" I ask, remembering the ones Sony made Neo and I watch that ended up being renditions of my favorite love stories.

"Yeah." Hikari laughs. "Like in the movies."

We exchange something pure then, something wordless, a flirtation that goes past teasing.

"Then I'll steal that for you too," I whisper.

Of course, the garden can only keep us away from reality for so long. Hikari's phone buzzes, and when she takes it out of her pocket and reads the message, her face falls.

"It's C," she says. "He had an accident."

8
countdown

C HAS NEVER SAID the word *heart*.
 Losing something unsaid is simpler than losing something you loved enough to name.

A year ago, during a swimming competition, his was on its last legs. It gave out just as C's dive broke the water. He was plucked from the pool by his coach, his father, and two other swimmers, limp and barely conscious.

A cardiovascular disease, they said. Caught early enough to salvage C's body but caught too late to salvage what's left of his swollen heart.

C tells the story differently. He says all he remembers of that day is floating. The stifled thrashing of competitors and faded cheers of the crowds above. The blurry blue and every muscle in his body gone flaccid. He says that *thing* between his lungs was pounding without rhythm like a crying set of drums. He says, even as he felt it fighting for its life, that it was peaceful. He says down there, underwater, he didn't have to listen to anyone or anything.

It was just him and his heart.

Everything else became a faint notion lost to the surface.

When you're underwater there's nothing to think about except your own body. There are voices, but you can't make out what they're saying. There is a barrier, crystal clear, between you and the people you used to know. And they *are* people you used to know. The moment someone realizes you're going to die, they will not treat you the same way as if you were going to live.

Of course, there are exceptions.

"Why the hell were you on a stepladder?" Eric asks, dabbing the cut on my forearm with hydrogen peroxide.

"That clock is broken." I point to the space above the doorway. Just below, a corpse of a stepladder lies on its side, a soldier fallen in battle. Granted, I should've probably had someone hold it for me, but I'm short-staffed in the non-physically-impaired-friends department. "I was stealing it."

Eric pulls my arm farther over the counter to get a better look. "Why?"

"For my Hamlet."

"I'm not even going to ask what that means. And haven't you little pests stolen enough? Your rooms might as well be storage facilities for broken crap."

"It's the only way to kill our enemies," I remind him.

He flicks my forehead. "Save it. That dramatic shit doesn't work with me."

"I'm not dramatic."

"You're all dramatic. Especially you."

"Me?"

Eric rolls a bandage around my wound. "You're paraphrasing Shakespeare."

"Neo paraphrases Shakespeare."

"To insult people."

"Isn't that dramatic?"

"That's my point. Now get." He slaps the uninjured side of my arm, rubbing a disinfectant wipe over his hands. "And make sure Sony doesn't go chasing cats. She rests, or I take that flea magnet to the pound."

"Please don't take Hee."

"What?"

"You said you'd take Hee."

"Who's Hee?"

"The flea magnet."

"Go away, Sam."

"All right."

Eric turns his back to me, putting a stethoscope around his neck and gesturing to another nurse so they can get back to work.

I flex the muscles in my forearm. It doesn't hurt. Pain and I have a reasonable agreement. Pain is jealous. As long as I don't feel anything else, it's content staying at bay.

That means I don't get punished for objectively stupid actions. Hopping on a stepladder to steal a useless clock from a wall would be one of them. I look down at the stepladder, then the clock. Would Eric's fury and a possible head wound be worth the smile on Hikari's face when I present her with tangibly killed time right before our great escape?

"Sam?" Someone pops out, too tall not to block my way.

"C?"

C passed out a few nights ago. He had been discharged and was having dinner with his family. A few minutes after they were seated, C's eyes rolled back into his head, and he collapsed from his chair. He woke up a few seconds later, but the event was enough to startle his doctors *and* us.

C's eyes flick to my bandages, while mine flick to the black-and-purple splotch spreading from his cheek to his brow.

"What happened to your face?"

"My brother hit me," he says. "What happened to your arm?"

"I don't have arms. Why'd your brother hit you?"

"Eh. You know."

"I don't know."

"Ever since I got back, the doctors have been making me do all these tests, and my parents won't stop arguing with me about the"—he taps his chest twice—"situation, so having heard it all before, I put my earbuds in. My brother, who I was ignoring, got frustrated, and frustration is an excellent excuse for punching, so—"

"Oh."

C's teeth show in delight as if the bruise is something to be flaunted.

"You have no idea how nice it was to finally have him do that, Sam," he says, like a spectator rather than a victim. "My brother and I used to roughhouse when we were little. He'd pick on me, make bad jokes, prank me. After last year, he changed. He became polite and pleasant; I hated it." C chuckles. "Guess he finally snapped, though. He got a nice swing too—good momentum, see?"

He leans down a bit to show off the bruise.

I sigh.

C doesn't like when we talk about our diseases, let alone his. To him, the illness is of conditional existence. It's only real when his muscles strain at the last stairstep or when its name is ushered from someone's lips.

"What did your parents say?" I ask. What I really ask, subtly, is, *Are you okay?*

C shrugs. "It's not important. I want to see everyone. Headquarters?"

Headquarters. Neo's room.

"You literally could not be more wrong!" C and I open the door to a less than quiet scene.

Three sit on the bed, Neo leaning on his pillow, sans back brace, Sony with her back to the door, avec oxygen tank, and Hikari across from her, gaze jerking back and forth between them.

"There's no such thing as more or less wrong," Sony says. "Either I'm wrong, or I'm right."

"You're wrong," Neo says vehemently.

"I'm right. I could not be more right."

"There's not enough oxygen in your brain for you to be right!"

"There's not enough food in your body to feed your brain, ego, you cannot be one hundred percent sure that I'm right or wrong."

"It's *ergo*, you idiot!"

"Baby, don't start another argument. If I keep winning, you're just gonna boost my ergo."

"What are you two fighting about?" C asks, peering over the board game laden with stray pieces.

"It started with Monopoly," Hikari says. "Now they've de-clared war."

"I'm still right about Monopoly," Sony says, flipping her hair.

"You landed on my property and didn't pay. That's the whole point of the game!"

"Okay, but you're in jail. Was I supposed to give money to a criminal, Baby? That's just not right."

Neo leans forward, another comeback on the tip of his tongue. It never leaves his mouth. His breath hitches, his teeth grit together, his eyes shut tight, body paralyzed in an instant.

"Neo? You okay?" Hikari touches both his shoulders, steady-ing him.

His back seizes up, throat laboring as he fists the bedsheets. "I—I need to stand."

Neo and pain have a far different arrangement. C doesn't stand still when it takes pleasure in lighting his nerves on fire. He runs his palm under Neo's back and carefully pivots him out of bed, Sony moving aside to make room.

"Hold on to me," C says. Neo's fists curl around the fabric of his shirt, beads of sweat catching on his hairline.

"What happened to your eye?" Neo asks, hissing.

"Hush," C scolds. "Just breathe."

He drags his touch down Neo's arm, confused when he flinches. He pulls back the sleeve, Neo protesting with a hum. C pulls it back anyway. A bruise taints Neo too, drawn from the crook of his elbow, spiraling up his bicep in the shape of a hand.

C goes taut, staring at the cloud of beady purple and black. Neo's father visited last night. He puts it together quick enough for a vein to show on his forehead.

"Don't say anything." Neo pulls his wrist away. "And don't be angry."

"I'm not angry," he says, his nails forming crescent shapes in Neo's sweatshirt.

Neo eases back into comfort as the minutes pass, listening to C's heart thrum against his ear. "Tell that to the thunder between your ribs."

Nights till the escape: 5

Eric has a watch. It has a red leather band, old-fashioned, like he is. He still has a flip phone and refuses to own anything else digital.

His watch stopped working the night he cried at Sony's bedside. Eric keeps flicking the glass, but the arrow won't tick on.

He gets a new one, but he keeps the old one too. When I ask him why, he says he can't bear to toss old things away. I ask him if I could steal it. He takes it out of his pocket and considers it for a moment.

When our eyes meet, he doesn't look for a reason because we've known each other long enough for him to know that I don't lie.

Hikari and I have been exploring. The hospital, the skies, each other. Nurses are so used to us running past that they don't even yell at us anymore. We've become background noise gone unquestioned.

We read *Hamlet* together, singing and dancing as she likes.

We steal moments by people-watching. She has horrible people-watching skills. Her impatience is dreadful, like a reader who can't wait to get to the good part. It's always worth it, though—her little reactions when a couple reunites in an embrace or a parent kisses their child just released.

Today, she draws while I read in the library, but we become restless fast. She hides from me, smirking when I catch glimpses of her between the aisles. She entices me, makes me give in to the chase.

"What's this?" she whispers once I corner her against an arm-chair.

"A gift." Red-banded leather and motionless arrows. I lay the watch in her hand, careful not to let my fingers graze her palm. Hikari blinks at it in the easy light, a wave of silence humming between us. "I—I thought about getting you a fake skull, but I would've felt replaced."

"It's perfect," she says, clutching the watch against her heart. A bashful line tints her cheeks, as she stares up at me through her lashes. "You want to know something?"

"Mhm."

"This is my favorite gift I've ever gotten." She bites her lip, thumb gliding over the crystal. Then she points at my lips with the watch still in her hand. "Second to that smile."

Charmed, I point back at the smile worn on her own lips, wondering how I ever thought she could become background noise when she's so obviously a chorus.

"I stole it from you."

Nights till the escape: 4

C is a philosopher without a mouth. He thinks. Constantly. But he never shares a single thought.

He and I wend down the halls to his echo appointment. Earlier, he said his chest felt funny. He kept on scraping his sternum, gliding his tongue over sore gums.

"It sounds like the effects in space movies," Neo says as he, Sony, Hikari, and I sit along the wall inside an exam room. C lies on his side, arm over his head, skin soaked with ultrasound gel as Eric swipes the transducer over his chest.

"If you're lucky, some space movie director will buy the tapes," Sony says, eyes glued to the screen. "You get enough echoes done for all nine *Star Wars* movies and the stand-alones."

"I didn't peg you for a space nerd, Sony." C smirks.

"So what if I am?"

"You getting modest on me?"

"Modest?! Eric, shove that thing down his throat at once."

Eric clicks a few keys on the computer. "I assume I would get a better image, but let's not risk it."

C rolls his eyes, appreciating the distraction as he looks up at the ultrasound for himself. It's humbling to witness your own organs. It's chilling to witness their demise. Neo stares at C's reaction over the top of his notebook, then back at their story, writing, writing, writing.

"How long does it take to get pictures of his heart? Isn't only half of it in there anyway?"

"Sony," we all scold.

"Hey. I've got half my lungs, he's got half his heart. Together, we'd make a fully functional human."

An hour later, C's parents intercept us in the waiting area. They take him back to his room and ask for privacy. I sit outside, rereading Hamlet's lines till Neo joins me.

It's odd glancing up from the ground and seeing legs rather than wheels now. Bundled in Hikari's sweater and Sony's sweatpants, he settles next to me without a word.

C doesn't make an appearance till midnight. When he does, he wipes his cheeks with his sleeve and crouches to our level.

"You didn't have to wait for me," he whispers.

Neo fell asleep against my side, papers lazing on his lap. His eyes flutter open to the sound of C's voice. He takes a waking inhale, shaking himself upright.

"C'mon." C moves the hair from his eyes. "You need to go to bed—"

"What were your ultrasound results?" Neo murmurs with gravel in his throat. "What did your parents say?"

"It's not important," C says. His knuckles press against his chest. The petechial spots climbing up his collar catch the light. C is a large vessel, and his engine is tired. His heart is too weak to carry him through any more of his life.

"I"—C roughs his hand over his face—"I need a transplant."

Empathy flashes across Neo's face. He cups C's jaw, wiping a tear.

"Coeur—"

"Let's just go," C says. "Let's go right now. Tonight. Just the five of us."

"I can barely walk."

C grasps Neo's hands. "I'll carry you."

Neo tilts forward till their noses brush.

"Just wait. A few more days. That's all." Under the soft weight of his voice, C's shoulders slack. The tension he carries washes away with Neo's touch. "Then we'll go get our Heaven."

Nights till the escape: 3

Hikari and I go to the roof tonight.

We laugh over chocolate pastries because she talked the bakery owner down the street into giving them away. Crumbs soil our clothes, but the taste dances on our tongues.

Hikari asks me why I like *Wuthering Heights* so much. I tell her it is truthful, that I can see myself in it somehow.

I ask why she likes *Hamlet*. She laughs and tells me she doesn't.

We read our play's lines together. Hikari interrupts herself in the middle of monologues, edging closer when she does. Her teasing enchants me, and we make a game out of testing the limits of our distance.

"Do you believe in God, Sam?" she asks, putting the book down.

The smudged corner of her glasses reflects the stories we see dimly lit in apartment windows. She reads them like she reads our play, her arms folded over the stone ledge.

"I don't know," I say, overwhelmed by her scent, how sweet it is, her skin, how it's only a succulent's distance from my own. "Do you?"

Her lips twitch with wonder.

"I believe in artists."

"Artists?"

"Some paint the sky and the sea. Others sculpt mountains. The delicate sow flowers and stitch the bark along trees. Some sketch people and the lives they live." Her eyes meet mine. "Your artist isn't done yet," she whispers with a smile. Crooked smile. "He's indecisive."

"You sound angry at him."

"How dare he not give you arms?"

"Do you believe in Heaven?" I ask.

"I don't think so. Heaven is a perfect place. Perfection isn't real. A perfect place in death sounds a lot like something to bait you into behaving. Or into dying. Behaving and dying are poor endings for thieves."

"Neo's dad says that he wants his son to go to Heaven," I say. "He says that's why he does what he does and says what he says."

"Do you believe him?"

"I think Neo believes him."

"Is that why he doesn't take his medicine?" Hikari asks. "Is that why he doesn't eat?"

Neo took to Hikari the day he met her. He said she was a genuine kind of girl. He never put a guard up around her. That means it's not difficult for her to notice things: the pills he tucks behind his gums and the bathroom trips he takes to spit them out—the sweaters, no matter how thick, that can't hide the sinking skin beneath his cheeks or the wobbly nature of his legs.

"You know how Neo writes?" I ask. Hikari nods. "He wrote once that 'clothes are a strange and clever hiding place. Bruises, scars, insecurities—we hide them all if we choose to, the essential parts of us kept only for the gazes of mirrors and lovers.'"

"That's nice," she says, toying with the band on her wrist. "Even if it's sad."

"Everything Neo writes makes me happy. Even if it's sad."

"Because he's your friend."

"Because he's at peace when he's writing."

"He's at peace when he's with you." Hikari smiles. A smile that always finds a way of tilting the glass till it looks half-full.

"We can make our own Heaven," she says. Her fingers glide over the slightly protruding rawness on her neck and the scars on her arms. She touches them like paint, as if it could rub off on her, were she not careful. "You know, Sam, loneliness has no kindness to offer, so . . . thank you for giving me yours."

Nights till the escape: 2

I help C up the stairs. He pants with an open mouth till we reach the roof. Hikari sits against the stone wall, a little black ball of fur in her arms. Sony's cat climbs onto C's stomach, purring as she scratches her head against the stubble on his chin.

C doesn't talk much today. Blood pools beneath his eyes in purple, a pale shade on his lips. Hikari brings up blankets for us to cuddle under while we contemplate the gray skies and relish his music.

Neo and Sony come up later, stolen beer and candy in their arms. We lap at the foam and smell the fetid liquid. C shows the bottle's rim to Hee, earning a gag and a sneeze from the feline. We all chuckle, chewing on tart, sour, and sugary gas station sweets.

"We're escaping soon," C says, his voice too rough to be his.

Neo cuddles him, nuzzled into his chest, legs tucked. He burrows under the blanket, face squished. Old albums stream from C's phone while Sony slow dances with Hee.

"We still have to decide where we want to go," Neo says.

"Everywhere." Sony laughs. "Let's go everywhere."

"You have an *every* addiction, Sony," Hikari says.

"I want to see everything before I die," Sony whispers, leaning down and pressing her forehead to Hikari's.

"You will." Hikari tucks bright red strands behind Sony's ear.

"Neo." Sony releases the cat back to C's care. She reaches for the little writer, only just peeking out. "Dance with me."

Neo crawls farther into the blanket. "I don't dance."

"You dance all the time." Sony rips the blanket off and snatches Neo by the wrists. "Physical therapy time."

"Just throw me off the roof."

"Don't tempt me. I have good aim."

Neo's lips curl. He hides them in Sony's neck as the two prance around with no skill or pattern. Caught by their snickering and lack of rhythm, C rises to shaky ankles. He outwaits his blurry vision and poor hearing, then takes Hee with him to join the dancers.

We used to think the roof was a radical rebellion. This is where there aren't any mirrors. It's chilly, and the ground is coarse. The sky is always gray, and the only color is us. This is our swimming pool, the deepest part, where those who dwell above the surface cannot see.

C takes Sony into his arms, hugging her tight, swaying side to side. Neo scratches Hee's head as he moves with the music.

The roof was never a place to steal but a place to elude time entirely. Here, I watch my friends dance and drink to their hearts' content, whatever hearts they may have. I race up the stairs with Sony and listen to old songs with C and read Neo's stories and forget for a long while.

Sony lies back down when the sky grows dark. Neo clings to

one side of her, C to the other. She chuckles and calls them monkeys. They talk about the everywhere they're going to see, the everything they're going to steal. They fall asleep fast despite the nipping weather, a thin layer of clouds concealing the stars soon after time strikes midnight and tomorrow turns to today.

I savor the moment.

Hikari shifts below her blanket, a little yellow hill. She groans when she stretches, but her movements are cautious of those around her. I can't help the tug at my lips when she wakes. Her eyes are half-lidded, a bit of spittle on her chin.

"Sam?" she whispers, rubbing under her glasses. "You're still awake. Are you cold?"

"No." I lie down parallel to her. "Are you?"

Her face scrunches up. "A little."

"Do you want me to walk you back inside?" I ask.

"Not yet." Hikari yawns, closing her eyes. "I like when we're all together this way."

When she falls back asleep, I reach across the distance. I want to tuck the blanket higher on her shoulders, run my palm up and down her spine, hold her against me the way C does Neo. My hand halts once her heat is close enough to burn and my touch recoils.

But I don't want it to.

My hand creeps closer to her again like it's fighting a current.

"*Hi . . .*" When I try to say her name, my memories shake, graves screaming beneath the snow. "*Hi-ka . . .*"

Hikari, Hikari, Hikari.

She can't hear me. She can't feel the blanket I move over her wrist or my fingertips slipping over the material. Beneath the blanket, her joints lead to her wrist like a spiderweb, our watch taking shape like a tiny bridge. I close my touch around them.

I am not touching her. There is still a barrier. She is not real.

Hikari, I say, not enough courage to voice it out loud. *I wish we'd met anywhere else in the world. I wish I were not me. I wish I could touch you and be with you and treat you as you deserve. I wish, more than anything, that I were brave enough to love you again.*

Nights till the escape: 1

Hikari wakes in the early hours of the morning. It's still dark out, our escape not due for a few hours. She and I walk back inside and find a stretcher in an unoccupied hall; above it, solemn windows, black and reflective.

I tell her that sometimes stretchers are left scattered about and reorganized come morning. She caresses the straps and cushioned edges like she feels sorry for all lonesome carriers of grim cargo. Then she tells me to sit and wait for her.

I do.

She returns, running, with our copy of *Hamlet*.

"Let's finish it," she says.

"Now?" I ask.

"Now."

———————

"What happened? I don't . . ." Confusion plagues me. I hold in my hands what people call a masterpiece, absolutely dumbfounded. "What is it even supposed to mean?"

I hold up the last few pages for Hikari to see. She sits crosslegged, fidgeting with the stretcher's straps, amused by my reactions.

"It means a lot of things," she says. "Mostly, I think it's about an annoying narcissist who's obsessed with death till it actually knocks on his door, but—"

"He—he lost everything in the end, and—and he *did* die."

"That's why it's a tragedy." No. I refuse. That is a horrid ending. "Sam, are you pouting?"

"I don't like it," I say, frowning, flipping through to make sure there isn't another act we missed. I fail, shutting the book with fury. "And on top of it all, it's violent." At least *Wuthering Heights* had good qualities to compensate for that particular flaw.

"You don't like violence either, I take it?"

"No. And why does Hamlet not like Yorick's skull in the end?" I scowl at her like it's her fault.

"Oh my God." Hikari puts a hand to her mouth. "You're offended."

"Don't laugh at me. This is serious. You don't like me in the end, and you die because of a stupid vengeful plot that I told you from the beginning wouldn't work."

"I'm sorry. Next time, I'll be a far less impulsive and self-obsessed character. How about Romeo?"

"Ophelia would've never treated my skull this way. Next book, I want a happy ending, and you have to like me."

"Everyone likes you, Sam. A lot of people better than Hamlet."

There it is again. She doesn't think I catch her turning the other cheek to compliments. She doesn't think I notice her interruptions, our moments cut in half by her lip chewing and pulling away. She doesn't think I care that she's in pain or that she cuts herself, and she doesn't think she's made me happier than I've been in a long time.

Suns can't see their own light.

I put the book down and stand up off the stretcher. Facing her directly, I shove the distance aside and press my hands down on either side of her legs. I become her field of vision, all she can see.

"You're not Hamlet," I say. "You're *my* Hamlet."

She looks me up and down and thinks I'm kidding.

"I mean it." My voice echoes. "He's not like you. He wouldn't get up early just so Sony would have someone to wake up to. He wouldn't make Neo laugh. He wouldn't listen to C's monologues about music. He wouldn't believe in artists, draw endless universes, or raise little plants. He's not like you."

Under my voice, Hikari's face blanks. The shape of her hand beneath that blanket ingrains itself into my wanting. I want to touch her again. For real this time. I want to draw to the surface of the water and breathe again if it means I can breathe her. Reality be damned.

"I never feel anything," I whisper. "But every time I remember how little you think of yourself, I feel angry. I feel like banishing anyone and everyone who ever made you believe you deserve to be alone. Because that kind of pain, it—it can ruin people; it can make them lose faith in everything, just like Hamlet did, but *you*? You look at me more than anyone ever has, and no one ever looks twice at me. I'm a skull in a graveyard. I'm empty."

Hikari's breath shakes in her mouth as she leans forward. "You're not empty, Sam."

"I am." That is an undeniable truth, not a stale one. "Yet somehow you find a way to see something in me in a way no one ever has."

"Sam."

"Yes?"

I lean to meet her on the very edge of this verging distance we are but a moment away from obliterating. And then she asks, "Can I kiss you?"

9
kind

one year ago

SONY WANTS TO race today. Since she barely has the strength to pace without getting light-headed, she and I came up with a set of rules. I walk a loop around the atrium, twice around, *to make up for my two-lungedness*, she says, while she only does one. Whoever crosses the finish line first wins.

A few steps from a corner, I look back over my shoulder to see how much Sony has to catch up. And whoever I knock into this time isn't as small as Neo.

My front meets with a body as I turn the corner. Seconds later, my shoes slip out from under me and my back meets the floor. A noise I don't make often rises flatly to my lips.

"Ow."

"Oh my God! I'm so sorry!" A man bends to my level. His voice is deep but not heavy, light enough to pull you back to where you are. "Are you okay?"

"Sam!" Sony scurries to my side, skidding to her knees like a superhero, sound effects and all. She removes her backpack, pretending to rummage through it.

"Don't worry," she says, planting a hand on my chest. "I'm a first-class medic!" She is not.

Making all sorts of phony medical machine sounds, Sony tickles my sides up and down, rousing squirmy, unwilling giggles. "Get up at once, you scoundrel. We have worlds to conquer—"

Sony stops when she notices the man standing at our level. She blinks, looking him up and down. "Wow. You're big. I'm Sony!" Her hand almost hits him in his face as she reaches to shake his hand. It's when I notice he's not a man at all.

He's a boy.

"I'm Coeur."

Coeur's hair is curly, eyes big and brown, his most pronounced features. His lips are full, a nose above them with a gentle, broad slope. His skin is dark, paint-splattered, petechial spots and veins spread about his arms.

Sony cocks her head like a puppy with its ears flipped.

"Co-what?"

"Coeur?" Neo rounds the corner behind us. He always follows Sony on races, a single crutch his companion for a spine gradually curling like a fist. About two weeks ago, he got in an accident. He fractured his wrist, among other injuries, and though he assures me it wasn't his dad, he doesn't want to talk about it.

As soon as he sees Coeur, his expression falls, his shoulders slack, eyes a little wider than usual.

"Neo." Coeur breathes out his name, standing up straight as Sony helps me back to my feet. "Hey." His lips curve, slowly, kindly. They share a wondrous tone only people who've met before can share.

"What are you doing here?"

"Oh." Coeur feigns a scratch at the back of his head, looking at the ground and then back up. "It's no big deal, I just—uh—almost drowned."

Neo steps forward. A solid annoyance weighs down his face.

"You look fine to me," he says through his teeth.

"Neo." I frown, pulling at his sleeve, but he ignores me.

Coeur must not have caught Neo's tone, because he just laughs, relief in its wake.

"*Neo*," he says again, enamored with his presence. "I can't tell you how happy I am to see you." The longer Coeur remains lighthearted, the more Neo's anger grows. Coeur turns to Sony and me to explain: "We have literature together. Our teacher can't get enough of him; he's a genius—"

Coeur doesn't get to say anything else. Cutting him off, Neo pushes right past him and storms down the hall.

———

The last time Neo had an outburst like that was when he flipped the food tray over in my arms. I open the door to his room warily.

"Neo?"

"I wanna be alone, Sam." Pulling himself back into bed, he submerges himself until he's surrounded by pen, pages, and the safety of his paper-and-ink sea.

"Will you come to dinner with us later, then?" I ask. "I already stole you an apple."

"Is *he* gonna be there?" Distaste sours his tongue. He avoids eye contact, rummaging through pages he isn't actually reading with more force than necessary.

"You don't like Coeur."

"What makes you think that?"

"You were rude."

"Sam."

"Sorry." I catch myself. "How do you know him?"

Neo throws his pen down, jaw tight. He doesn't lean back against the wall, he thumps against it, crossing his arms.

"People call him C," he says. "He's been on the swim team since middle school. Everyone adores him because he's good-looking and an idiot. Everyone but teachers, at least. He spends all of class listening to music and staring out windows. His grades probably don't matter because of his star athlete gig. Girls practically cling to him in the halls like popularity leeches. His taste in friends is just impeccable too. I should know. They beat me up while he watched."

Neo's eyes lock with mine. Neo's father inflicts pain, but there's distance between them, a distance that nurtures indifference. There's nothing *indifferent* about Neo now.

He's not telling me the full story. If Coeur were just a passerby, someone who ignored his assault, Neo wouldn't care. He doesn't push past his mother, trembling with rage, and she is the greatest bystander in his life. There's something else I'm missing between the lines.

Neo makes an ugly face at me when I don't respond. "Anything else you wanna know?"

I blink, my hands flat on my knees.

"What are leeches?"

"Get out, Sam."

I do. I just feel like a blind bystander turning the doorknob.

Back where I left them, Sony and Coeur are gathered around our old vending machine.

"No, no. You're doing it all wrong. You gotta crane kick it first. Like this." Sony raises both arms over her head, lifting one leg and flicking her foot forward so hard that her shoe almost flies off. She doesn't even strike the glass, slipping over her feet and falling backward. Coeur catches her.

Sony blows the hair out of her face and points at the vending machine.

"See, Coor?"

"You can just call me C."

"All right. See, C? Wait."

Sony forgets her qualms over the consonant when she sees me.

"Sam!" she yells, scrambling upright. "Where's Baby?"

C looks over at me too, expectantly, in a polite way. I don't like that he's polite. I don't like that all I see looking at his face is it turning the other away as my friend gets beaten.

"You let people hurt Neo?" I ask, but it's more of an accusation.

Sony's chin draws back. "What?"

"What?" C asks the same question.

"You and your friends beat him up."

"I—I never beat anyone up," he says. My brows knit together, but C keeps defending himself. "I'm his partner in class for reading—"

"Neo doesn't lie." I remember the ache in Neo's face when he saw C standing in the hall, so oblivious.

Neo is in and out of this place constantly. One day, not long ago, he came in with bruises all down his shoulder blades, a black eye, and the wrist he likes to squeeze broken. That day, he wouldn't talk to anyone, even me. We lay together in the dark. A single tear rolled down his temple. I thought it was his father at first. But now I'm not so sure. "You hurt him."

"Yikes. Sorry, dude." Sony plants her hand on his shoulder, tsking. "I can't be buddies with a bully. Maybe in your next life, you'll be likable. See ya!"

"Wait!" C calls out to both of us before we walk away. He

swallows a lump in his throat, confusion and memory morphing into a realization. "Can I talk to him?"

C, I quickly find, is not unlike Neo. Whatever he's thinking, it isn't said aloud. When someone talks to him, only half his attention is on the words. The other half is lost, glazed over behind his eyes.

I don't think it's intentional ignorance. I think, like when he knocked me to the floor and missed Neo's clenching teeth and fists, he simply doesn't notice.

I lead him to Neo's room, not only for Neo but also to feed that selfish curiosity. I want to know what Neo didn't say. I want to help them. And something tells me the rest of the story lies in C's side of it.

He opens the door.

"Sam, I said . . ." Neo stills the moment he sees C. There's no anger in him. Just surprise. It makes him look young, almost his age.

"Hi, Neo," C says. He tries to close the door behind him. Sony sneaks her foot into the crevice so that it remains just barely open.

I poke her. "Sony, we should—"

"Hush!" she whispers, putting her finger on my lips and pressing her ear to the opening. "I'm eavesdropping."

"Can I sit down?" C asks, motioning to the chair at Neo's bedside. Sony and I peek through the door. Neo eyes the chair, then C, then the chair again.

"No," Neo says. He snaps back to his sea, pretending the boy still standing awkwardly at his door doesn't exist.

"Listen, I just came to talk."

"What's there to talk about?"

"I'm sorry," C says.

Neo writes with more pressure than needed, swiping his pen

across the paper to accentuate the silence. C goes on. "I'm sorry for, you know—what my friends did. I didn't know they were—"

"Ramming me against lockers and calling me a faggot?" Neo's tone is as flat as his features. For the first time, he looks C in the face. "You were there. You knew exactly what they were doing, and you just walked away."

"I'm sorry. I should've stopped them."

"You didn't."

"I'm sorry."

"Stop apologizing. I—" Neo stops again, interrupted by his own observation. Since I can't see C's face, it takes a sniffle and squint from Neo for me to understand what's happening. "Are you crying?"

"A little." It sounds like more than a little.

"Why?"

"Don't you remember? You're my English partner."

"*That's* why you're crying?"

"You're so mean, Neo." I won't argue with that statement. "But we both know I wouldn't have passed last semester without you."

Neo may be mean, but he isn't past recognizing someone genuine. Weakness and gratitude with it pour from C like a dripping faucet.

"I'm sorry I didn't do anything. I swear I don't even really know those guys. They're just on my team, and I didn't want to—"

"It's fine." Neo drops his head.

"No. It's not fine," C says.

"No, it's not, but what the hell do you want me to do?" Neo's wound-up energy from the moment he laid eyes on C locks his muscles. The past dances across his eyes, but it's not the same past C recollects. It's half of the bigger picture.

"Just go to your room, Coeur." Neo sighs. "Go hang out with

Sam and Sony. I don't care. Once you're healthy again, you can go back to your life and pretend we never saw each other."

C lingers even once Neo returns to his writing. His lips remain slightly parted, shelving things he wishes he could say. When Neo's pen hits the page, the barrier is put back up, and C has no choice but to walk away as I did.

"Well." Sony crosses her arms, the two of us greeting him back into the hall. "You're obviously sorry."

C only stares at the ground.

"I'm such a coward." The proclamation sounds comfortable coming from his mouth, as if he's said that before.

When C knocked into me, the first thing I noticed was his size. The second things I noticed were all the signs of cardio-vascular disease. He says he almost drowned, but his body temperature is rather cold, and the clothes he wears are too heavy for summer. Skin flakes at his lips and fingers. When he walks, he sometimes falters. His brain needs added time to process the movement. He even leans forward when people speak to him and sometimes doesn't respond as if he can't hear.

C *did* almost drown, although that's not why he's in the hospital now. Whatever his killer is, he's been sick for a long time.

"It's not always easy to do the right thing," I say. More souls than those lost to this place taught me that. "If you can look back and see the mistake you made, you're not a coward."

I nod to the stairwell. C may not have books or chocolate bars to give, but at the very least, he's got an interesting story to tell and manners to pair with it.

I take him and Sony to the garden.

Sony and I settle on our usual cloud-watching bench. C follows. His mind is still on his wrongs, still on the other side of the doors lingering outside Neo's room.

"Can I ask you something?" He sits, still towering over us. "How did you two become friends with Neo?"

"I wore him down," Sony says, unwrapping the candies Eric bought her.

"I used to bring him his food trays," I say.

"He likes food?" C asks like he wants to take notes.

Sony shakes her head. "He hates food."

"He likes apples," I say. "I wore him down with apples."

"Apples?"

"He likes books too," Sony says. "And being an ass."

"An ass?"

"A lovable ass. A lovable writer too." Sony pops a sour candy in her mouth and lifts one to mine. "He's my favorite writer in the world."

Asking how you become friends with someone is like asking how the world came to be. It's a process. It's neither linear nor cyclic. Not unlike the world, people aren't always as complicated as we make them out to be. Sometimes you just have to offer a little bit of yourself, a little bit of your time, and, as C will soon find, a little bit of your kindness.

————

C is a poor thief. Not only is he too noticeable, but his aversion to being rude means trying to take something without permission goes against his nature. He's already apologized to the cafeteria attendants three times for *my* thievery. When I ask him where this compulsion comes from, he says his parents never stood for it and would "beat his ass." I tell him that misbehaving is a part of being human. He tells me this particular part of being human makes him want to vomit with guilt.

I end up stealing most of the apples for him. C never eats them. Instead, he brings them to Neo, my and Sony's advice in mind.

———

The first day:

"Hi." He shuffles into Neo's room like a parent trying not to disturb a child doing homework. "I brought you an apple."

He sets it on the side table.

"Thanks?" Neo says, picking it up warily.

C smiles curtly, hands folded in front of him.

"Can I sit?"

"Uh—no," Neo says, like his answer is more than obvious.

C is unfazed by it. He nods and exits with his resolution intact.

"I'll see you tomorrow, then."

———

The second day:

C opens the door, puts the apple on the side table, stands with his hands folded in front of him and that same eager smile.

"Hi," he says.

Neo squints his eyes. "Coeur."

"Neo."

"I forgive you, okay?" Neo takes the apple and plants it on his lap. "Now will you leave me alone?"

"No." C opens the door. "I'll be back tomorrow."

———

The third day:

C opens the door. The apple finds its spot on the side table. C takes his stance, hands folded, smile dimply and fresh.

"Hi."

Neo slams his pen onto his papers.

"I don't remember you being this stubborn!"

C's smile doesn't waver. "I learned it from you," he says.

Neo scowls. "What do you want?"

"To be friends."

Neo shakes his head like he's been smacked. "What?"

"I've wanted to be friends ever since you started helping me in Lit," C says. "But you went back to the hospital before I could ask."

"My bad—"

"Shut up. Be my friend."

"We can't be friends."

"Do you like music?"

"No."

"Oh, c'mon. Everybody likes music." C takes out his phone from his back pocket along with a tangled pair of earbuds. "Here. I'll make you a playlist."

"You'll make nothing," Neo scolds, although having to point a finger *up* at the scoldee doesn't make for a very intimidating warning.

"How do you feel about Coldplay, Bach, and Taylor Swift for an opening trio?" C's thumbs tap away at the screen.

"Am I going through a seventeenth-century breakup with a beach?" Neo asks, tone monotonous.

"That'd make a cool music video, actually." C looks up, considering it. "We'll start with classic rock. You can't go wrong with classic rock."

"Coeur!" Neo yells. C jumps, startled, catching the pain in Neo's voice. "I forgive you, but we are *not* going to be friends."

Neo bites down on his lower lip to keep it from shaking, and C hears the idea of threading a connection with a few apples and some music fade out like the end of a melody. Suddenly, the space between them seems a lot larger than it did before.

Neo wipes his eyes. "Just leave, please."

And C does after he lingers. The sound of Neo's pen carves

at his efforts. It tells him that half of an apology and half of an attempt are not enough to stitch the injury he caused, but I don't think that's all there is to it. I do think Neo doesn't want to be friends with C. I think, from the sheer sadness that swims in his eyes whenever C tries to apologize, that he wants something more.

The following week, C doesn't go to Neo's room. Instead, he spends time with Sony. She's a delightful companion during dreary times. For all her unintentional insensitivity, she's understanding. C enjoys her energy. He buys her chocolate and races her all she wants.

I join them sometimes. I listen to C and watch him. He's simple, but even if he is half there, what is there is kind.

He listens. He watches. He tells a nurse how much he likes the new color in her hair, discusses sports with his doctor. With Sony, he visits the oncology unit, plays with the kids, and helps however he can, wherever he can, in a way that shows he really wants to.

He thinks of Neo every day. When we walk past his room, the other half of him is still outside the door, trying to find a way in.

One night, it preys on him more than the rest.

In the cafeteria, he and Sony sit at an empty table. She sleeps soundly, head in her arms, her mouth open. He lazes, eyes half-closed, chin propped on crossed arms. A single earbud plays tunes in his ear, the other in Sony's.

"You want one?" he asks, fingering the wire connected to his phone as I sit beside him.

"No, thank you. Let her keep it."

"I was gonna give you mine," he says.

"No luck with Neo?" I ask. C shakes his head. "How's your heart, then?"

His face scrunches up when I use that word.

"Beating." He presses a single hand to his chest. "I mean, I think it is. It hurts right now."

"C," I say. "Can you tell me what really happened between you and Neo?"

He looks at me, considering the past behind the question, because, I think, he's never been asked.

"I don't know," he says. "I mean—I'm not smart. I'm not good at anything. Except swimming, I guess. That's all I've ever been good at." The hand on his chest bunches his shirt. "But a few years ago, my chest started to ache."

"You never told anyone?"

"My parents would've made me stop swimming. I wasn't anything else but a swimmer, and I didn't want to be nothing," he says. "After I noticed something was wrong, I started to listen to music all the time, watch movies, stare out windows, just so I could—"

"Exist less?"

C and I exchange a glance.

It's not easy to acknowledge that something is out of your control. One day, your skin turns to a rash, and your bones start to bend. Your lungs give out, and your mother is no longer there. Your heart hurts and in the depths of a silent, lonely place it stops beating.

It's sudden. Sometimes too sudden to accept.

"Sorry, I'm not good with words," C says. He exhales choppily, releasing his shirt.

"Neo was never *nice* to me like most people are," he says. "But he looked at me longer than everyone else did. He asked questions. He taught me things with every conversation. There's something rugged but at the same time elegant about him that I've always been drawn to, something curious."

"It's why he likes reading," I whisper, fond memories behind it.

C chuckles a dry laugh. "I never liked reading. Neo made me want to read even though I couldn't and—I don't know. Everybody liked me because of my looks, the swimming, the shallow stuff. Neo waded through all that and looked for me in the deep end." C stutters when he talks. Like he's searching through a maze for the answers and suddenly hits a dead end every sentence.

"I like him," he whispers. "I guess I thought he liked me too."

The picture comes together behind the fog of their history. This goes further than an altercation in a hallway against lockers and foul-mouthed bullies. There are words and moments that came before that.

Neo's single tear didn't belong to those boys, his father, or broken bones.

It belonged to C.

"You're compassionate," I say. "That's why *I* like you. Neo likes you too. More than you think." I stand up and push in my chair.

"Wait," C calls. "How do you know? Did he tell you that?"

I imagine how hard Neo must've fallen for someone who cares so much. I imagine how smitten he must've been as C tried to read despite not being good at it. I imagine, from the hope in C's eyes, that he didn't fall quite so soon, but when he did, he fell so much harder.

I offer him a curt smile.

"No." The last arrow of advice in my quiver from all the years I've spent watching escapes like a loose end, a finish to the melody. "But he wouldn't be so hurt if he didn't care about the person who hurt him."

———

On one of his worse days, Neo tells me about the first time he met C. His body is sore and heavy beneath his sea. His medicine renders him drowsy and pale.

He eats less than enough to sustain his body weight. The toll it takes on his nerves is palpable.

In his daze, Neo tells me that he met C long before C met him.

He wrote a story, he says. About a boy in a rowboat, searching for land to no avail. He says that's how it began.

Neo isn't tall enough to reach the textbook cubbies in most classrooms. In his first year of high school, when he was already out sick half the time, he'd hear snickers behind his back. He'd get shoved aside. The chair he stood on to gather books would get kicked out from under him.

It was crowdsourced bullying. When you're small and a little different, you're expected to be the punch line. Nobody protects you from a few faceless flicks and bad jokes.

Neo is rude, standoffish, a little pretentious, but he isn't hateful. He wishes no harm to anyone. His worst bullies didn't care. A group of boys from the swim team in Neo's grade looked for reasons to bully him. They spat slurs at him in the halls and subtly pushed him so he'd trip.

Neo says it wasn't till the whole school found out he was sick that teachers finally decided to speak up, and the population of his attackers thinned. Not even the swimmers targeted him much anymore.

Still, Neo couldn't reach those cubbies.

Then, one day, someone new joined the class. A boy from the swim team Neo had never seen before, who sat in the back row and stared out the windows.

When the teacher instructed that everyone go get a textbook row by row, rather than watch Neo grab a chair, the new boy reached over Neo's head and grabbed two books. He handed Neo one of them and went back to his seat without a word.

"He never paid attention, so he had no idea who I was," Neo says, clutching my hand as more spasms of pain travel through his muscles. "He didn't know I was sick either."

Neo noticed early on that C had trouble. When the class read excerpts, C dragged his finger across the lines and stalled. Some words were bumpy. He couldn't just glide across them as effortlessly as everyone else.

The teacher called on C for answers, and he would freeze up. He was paying attention, or at least trying to, but words he couldn't read sat in the back of his throat without a voice. It happened a few times. The teacher stared at C over the line of his glasses, and C could only sit there in the awkward intermission between question and inevitable embarrassment. C didn't realize that he wasn't alone in the pool of the silently pitied. The boy next to him swam the same waters.

The next time the teacher called on C for an answer, he, of course, didn't know what to say. He and the teacher looked at one another. He curled his lips back in apology and waited.

The sound of a piece of paper sliding across his desk interrupted the silence. C looked down to see a yellow note written in Neo's handwriting.

The theme is love, it said. *Love and loss.*

C's attention flickered to Neo, whose eyes were steady on the board. C swallowed and read the answer Neo wrote for him. Surprised, the teacher nodded and went on with the lecture.

C said thank you. Neo never answered him.

Over the course of that year, even if Neo was out half the week, the two fell into a routine. C grabbed their textbooks every day, and when C had to answer a question, Neo would give him hints and lead him in the right direction.

Neo got curious the closer he and C got. He asked where C's name came from. C said he was the youngest child, his mother's last, and she wanted to name him after her heart. C asked where Neo's name comes from. Neo said his parents were religious, and they named things for reasons he didn't care to understand.

C asked Neo why he had so many books. Neo said books were an infinite source of escapism. C asked if Neo had any friends. Neo said he had two weirdos. Neo asked if C had any friends. C said sure. Neo asked if C had any *real* friends. C was silent for a while, then he asked Neo if he could borrow a book.

That's when Neo began to fantasize. He couldn't wait for class anymore without smiling to himself. He'd let his touch linger over C when he handed him a textbook. And it didn't skate by him that C sometimes got flustered when he caught himself leaning too close, or when Neo fixed his hair.

They got in trouble often. Their teacher would scold them for talking too much. According to Neo, the detentions were worth it. During, they played Rock, Paper, Scissors from across the room.

Neo was happy. The smile that touches his lips when he says that makes my chest cave. But Neo's happiness ended there.

The rowboat felt empty, he said. So he added another character to keep the other company. The story itself was harmless enough. Just two boys lost in the endlessness of the sea. Neo left the story on his desk in English class by accident when packing his bag.

When he got to school the next morning, he found a group of boys from the swim team waiting for C. They were reading through the papers, passing them back and forth, spitting wisecracks.

Neo stopped at the door. When they caught sight of him, he didn't even bother running.

They asked if he wrote the story for his boyfriend. They asked if he did the teacher favors for the grade, that maybe that was who the story was about. Between insults, they pushed Neo harder and harder.

The first boy tugged on his hair and ripped his papers to shreds. The second slammed him against the lockers. He grabbed Neo's thigh and asked if he was into things like that. The third tugged Neo's belt and threatened to rape him, saying it would be charity to rid him of his perversions. The rest laughed in a chorus.

Neo is familiar with cruelty.

His father's cruelty is hungry. It always has been. It taught him to dissociate from his body.

When C walked in on the scene, he had his earbuds in.

He was heading to first period, hair still wet from his morning practice. He looked at Neo, at the boys, who'd stilled their aggressions to make it seem like nothing was out of the ordinary. A pack of wolves caging a bloodied lamb, waiting for the shepherd to walk away before mauling the rest of it.

"I didn't even feel those bruises, Sam," Neo says. "I didn't care that they punched me or broke my wrist or said they'd tell my parents how disgusting I was or any of it."

He struggles for his next breath.

"No one ever liked me. No one ever thought anything of me. So, the whole time, all I saw was the back of Coeur's head when he left me there. I thought *he* was the one I could sail with. I thought that maybe instead of rowing to the end of the sea, I could row to Heaven. Because even if it was just one person, I finally had someone." Neo's breath hitches. "I thought I finally had someone."

Neo doesn't cry. His jaw aches with how hard he represses it. I kiss him and hug him. He hugs me back till the medicine lulls him to sleep.

I understand why it hurts.

I understand the loneliness of not being seen.

I understand, most of all, from years of watching, that ignorance is worse than cruelty.

In time, C finally steals without fear. It's not very skillful. Like I said, he's too big, too noticeable. He steals an apple and a book from the library and, more determined than ever, he goes to Neo's room. Without so much as knocking, he opens the door full force and shuts it behind him.

Neo glances up from his writing, legs beneath the sheets, Sony's stained sweatshirt on his shoulders, and the hood on his head. C waits for his full attention before talking.

"I'm sorry I wasn't there when you needed me. Denial is my life's work, and I'll be damned if I let it ruin this." He motions between Neo and him. "Every day since the day those guys hurt you, I missed you so much it ached and I miss you now. I miss you because even if you're a stubborn pain in the ass, you're the only person I've ever wanted. So I'm sorry and you don't have to forgive me, *ever*, but you're going to get used to me being around, because I am *not* leaving you again." C runs out of breath, holding the edge of Neo's bed to regain his balance. "And most of all, I'm sorry I treated you like the shallow end of a pool."

Neo's stunned expression shakes till he forces it into a frown. "What does that even mean?"

"I don't know!" C waves his hand through the air. "But I'm trying here. Because I like you. I *really* like you. So am I going to

---

148   *Lancali*

have to go steal our old textbooks and a pack of sticky notes from school? Or are you finally going to accept that you like me back?"

Neo stays quiet. So does C. It's not comfortable, but at the very least, it's not a quiet that stems from a grudge.

Neo looks at the book in his arms, squinting.

"Seriously? Jane Austen?"

"The theme is love. Love and loss," C says, twirling his wrist to show off the cover. He lays it on Neo's lap. "I like love stories."

Neo raises the corner of his lip in disgust.

"Not another one."

"Will you read it to me? Like you used to?"

"I've already read it." Neo picks up the book as if he's ignoring it, ready to hand it back and reject it yet again. The familiar tone hits C in the face. Like when his teacher would dismiss his inability to understand. He wallows in the embarrassment and perhaps starts to accept that Neo may never truly forgive him.

"Okay," he whispers, turning around and grabbing the doorknob.

"Where are you going?"

C halts. He turns back around. The book isn't thrown aside or abandoned. Neo slides his hand across the first page, tucking his knees to rest the weight against. He takes off the hood and nods at the chair by his bed. "Sit down and be quiet."

———

Neo reads to C in a different way than I read to him. There's no monotone drawl over every passage. He works across the chapters with smoothness, sure to side-eye C when he flips a page to make sure he's paying attention. He is. He props his chin on his arms, and every time Neo picks up the story again, C admires him.

They make it a habit to read every day. They exchange numbers. They text each other after hours when they should be sleeping. C sometimes sneaks into Neo's room, and they listen to music while laughing over the nurses they tricked. When C gets discharged a week later, he messages Neo every single day and visits us every afternoon. He doesn't swim anymore, he says, so he has no responsibilities anyway.

A month passes like this, but one day, we don't hear from C anymore.

Sony and I worry. We ask Neo if he's messaged him. Neo shakes his head, his thumb dragging over the edge of his phone.

Two days pass. Neo doesn't get out of bed, a familiar disappointment settling in his gut. Sony and I stay with him to alleviate it. It isn't till the sun is about to set on the third night that we hear a voice floating down the hall, fading in like music.

"Neo! Neo! Neo!" C comes running, almost falling over when he opens the door. He enters breathless, some sort of school assignment in his hands. He's wearing a hospital gown, and what made him trip wasn't the door but an IV strapped to a pole and connected to his arm under a thin piece of tape.

Neo looks him up and down with horror in his eyes.

C's fingers shake, and with every breath he takes, he winces.

"Neo, look," he says, no preface, limping over to his bedside and sitting down next to him. "Look, I got an A." C shows Neo the paper, pointing at the red letter near the top. There's a giddy smile on his lips.

"What happened?" Neo breathes, touching C's face with the most delicate reach. He moves aside the gown's collar, tracing scars atop his veins.

"Nothing, I'm fine." C takes Neo's hand. He kisses his fingertips. "Look," he says. "Read my paper. I wrote it all by my-self."

Neo, with the greatest reluctance, obeys.

C smiles at Sony and me and asks us how we're doing. We both say we're doing okay. Neo reads C's paper, half his attention on the words, half of it lost.

Cardiovascular issues are points on a broad spectrum of severity. What's nice about the heart is that in most cases, if you catch the problem early, it's salvageable. What's more difficult about the heart is that it's essential, and if you *aren't* fast enough . . .

––––––––

When the night casts a muted blanket, Sony and I go to the gardens. Neo and C sleep inside, tangled like little kids beneath the covers, while she and I lean against the great barrier and look at our city. Out there, people always look twice at people like us. They glance at the hospital on their way to work or from their office building, and they see doctors and blood and gray. They don't see our books or our broken things. They don't see a disabled poet and brokenhearted composer making promises in the night.

They don't know what it's like to drown or to be cut from gardens. It's uncomfortable for them to witness it. Sick people attract and repulse. Dying is a fascinating idea and a terrifying reality.

"We're gonna die, aren't we?" Sony says. Faraway stars reflect her gaze, drawing string lights across her freckles.

A sigh works through me.

Like I said, I rarely feel anything.

When I do, it's muted, purposefully, like the dark.

Hearts are essential, though, aren't they? Everything has a

heart. Even books, broken things, and me. Mine is locked away, frozen by the night in the snow. At least, that's what I'd like to believe.

But love is not a choice.

"Without you, we would all be alone right now, Sam. You know that, right?" Sony says. "We love you." She takes my hand across the railing. "Don't ever forget that."

10
the bridge

OUR HEIST BEGINS when the broken clock should've struck noon.

A few flights of stairs. That's all we have to conquer. Just a few flights and we'll be free. Neo and C cling to the railing, looking down the seemingly infinite spiraling steps. Their feet shuffle, anticipating.

Sony is waiting for us downstairs. She's the oldest on paper, making her the only one who can actually leave without arousing suspicion. Neo and C are known for wreaking havoc *and* not being legally allowed to. Sure, we've slipped off to the gas station across the street, but that's different. We've only actually pulled that off a few times, and Eric was waiting in the lobby with his arms crossed and his foot tapping both times.

Today is different. I remind myself of that every time the urge to run back into our rooms and hide pokes at the back of my mind.

"We're gonna get caught."

C chews on his nails.

"We're not gonna get caught," Neo says through his teeth.

"We *always* get caught."

"Oh, for God's sake. Just pretend we're going to the roof."

"We're not, though. We're running away. We aren't allowed to run away."

"We aren't allowed on the roof either, you idiot."

C makes a face of realization, twice as anxious from that revelation.

"Think of it this way, C," Hikari speaks. "Our artists already drew our paths. So, no matter what, our fates are already decided. Worrying won't change a thing. And if that doesn't help"— Hikari holds her hands behind her back, grinning—"just hold Neo's hand."

Neo makes a face. "What?"

Hikari laughs at them. At Neo's flustered expression and the heated, rosy trail across his face. At C's obliviousness, the confused-puppy tilt of his head.

Her laughter makes my head dip. It isn't meant for me. I can't sink into it as I could before. Its edges keep me out.

Neo and C are focused on the mission at hand, but their bodies converse. Even if they *don't* hold hands, there's always a sense of connection. Their fingers brush. Their walking pace equalizes despite C's long legs and Neo's skinny ones. They are never too far in front or too far behind each other.

I think of that as I look at Hikari across Neo and C's hands on the railing. The watch I gave her hugs her wrist, snug with the white band over her scars.

Hikari and I had that connection. That binding distance Neo and C share. That was before this morning. That was before the sun rose, and I drew a line Hikari wasn't ready for.

———

"Can I kiss you?" she asks. Her voice is permeable. It bleeds into my heart and coaxes me closer. Her seat shifts on the lonely stretcher as she leans just enough to tease.

Our lips chose each other the night they first sang Shakespeare. Our hands chose each other then too, mimicking dances and postures, creating mirrors in pairs. They don't dare to meet, they don't dare to touch, but they wonder. They remain in this one intermediate moment of *what if*.

What if I do touch her? What if I caress the stray yellow strands on her cheek and drag my fingers over the pulse in her neck? What if I do kiss her? What if I start with the cupid's bow perched just beneath her nose and work my way down, worshiping her with every breath?

I wonder, would she be real then? If I closed my eyes and leaned into the sun, would it set me afire, or would I finally feel the light on my face?

I shake, unable to decide. Hikari's mouth is just barely open. Her eyes are half-lidded. Her head tilts so that if we took that final step, we'd fit together.

I want her to see herself as I do. She wants me to see the world as she does.

Every time Sony failed to draw breath, or Neo collapsed over his own feet, or C couldn't hear a word, I used to accept it and look the other way, but it's not like that anymore. It hasn't been for a while. Now, with every reminder that my friends are going to die, there she is.

She is not a recycled version of someone I once loved. She is a rhyming line in the poem of my history.

We stare at each other's lips. We mirror each other the way our hands practiced.

She is what begs the question, what if I'm wrong? What if

they live? The yellow lights a path to memories I've yet to make: my friends in their old age sipping beer foam, leaving cigarettes lit and unsmoked, laughing in the city, in the countryside, anywhere and everywhere they've ever dreamt of going as they tell stories of a rebellious era, marked by suffering and the joy that defeated it back when they were prisoners.

I lean closer to Hikari over the stretcher. My hand draws up to cup her face. Just another barely there line to cross, and I can touch her. Just a minuscule little push, and I can feel her. Just a moment, a breath, a kiss, and she'll be real . . .

But what if I'm right?

What if this dream I deny having, of Hikari in my arms and a future where we all smile together, is a test? What if this rhyming line ends the same way the last one did? What if I'm left staring into the dark as the stars fall?

My eyes open, and in the black window's reflection, time smirks. It laughs over Hikari's shoulder, the past dangling in its hands like keys on a chain.

My noose snaps. The pressure chokes me. Before I can make contact with Hikari, my hands flinch down to my sides. My breath hitches in my throat. Gravity falters, throws me off my path, and fear throws me against the wall.

Hikari sits there, still holding the edge of the stretcher. I don't know if she can see how afraid I am. I don't know if she realizes what I'm afraid of. Either way, I don't miss the confusion in her eyes that slowly turns to the same darkness she wore when she gave me her memories of pain.

"I'm sorry."

That is all I have to say. At this moment, that is all I know how to say before I run.

I'm sorry.

––––––––––

The stairwell is dead silent. Neo is iron. His jitters are already gone. C swallows on a dry throat, biting his lip. Hikari keeps a lookout, ears perked, listening for Sony's signal.

Hikari hasn't looked at me since the five of us gathered. After our almost kiss, I thought about our almost everythings. The times I almost held her hand, almost said her name. Every chance I've been given has turned into an almost.

I said hello this morning. I had to say something. Hikari smiled a hollow smile, one that didn't reach her eyes. Then everyone got caught up in the excitement. There wasn't a chance to explain myself. Even if there were, I don't know how I would. I don't know what to say to her. It would just turn into another almost.

Eric clocked out five minutes ago. Once he's gone, there are so few leashes that can tie us down. He usually says goodbye to Sony before leaving. She said she'd meet him outside, on the street in front of the hospital's main entrance. He was suspicious, I think, but Sony goes off on her own no matter the state of her lung. When we return, Sony promises to recount all our adventures to her cat and kids alike.

The service stairwell is one of the only ways you can get in and out without too much traffic. The only thing we lack is an ID card to access it. Eric always has a spare in his pocket. I may be a poor liar, a poor criminal all in all, but even when my arm is being tended to from a stepladder injury, my sleight of hand has never failed me.

I hold the card tight in my palm, flipping it around. The plastic clinks against the metal, another metronome, another countdown. We hold our breaths.

Then—*ding*.

Neo practically hurls his phone upward, almost dropping it over the edge of the railing.

Coast is clear, losers! :D

C and Neo shriek, stumbling. Hikari follows as they start running down the stairs.

A rush of air floods the stale, clean stairwell with a taste of the city. Cars and pedestrians fly by, startling compared to the medical staff and carts passing tame hall lanes. There are no walls, no locked doors, just the sky and the great expanse of roads that lead anywhere but dead ends.

Sony speeds from the street corner, where she waved goodbye to Eric's bus. Her backpack bounces with her, smile catching on her breathing tubes. My gut twists in a bittersweet tangle. She struggles to take those final steps, but at the same time, she's never looked happier.

"Today's here!" Sony yells, jumping into us full force. She hugs and kisses us manically without a care for anyone else. "It's today! Let's go!"

"Where do you want to go first, Sony?" Hikari asks, holding her face as they touch noses.

"Let's get tattoos. No! Let's go star watching! No! Let's go to the beach! To the sea! I adore the sea!"

"We're gonna need a bus for that," Neo says, pointing with his thumb over his shoulder.

C looks at the postings on the bus stop schedule.

"There's one that comes in twenty minutes."

"Why don't we walk a little through the city while we wait, hm?" Hikari suggests, taking Sony's hand so she can lean on her. "We have all the time in the world."

"You're right," Sony says, inhaling deeply, relaxing into Hikari's side. She gives her body a moment of silence, its customary intermission.

"Let's go," Hikari says after a while, mimicking Sony's excitement, keeping it alive. "Let's go get your everything."

The crosswalk, our stepping-stones over the river, welcomes us back beneath the shadow of the hospital building. C and Neo take the lead in a pair.

At this time of day, people flood the streets like schools of fish. We become the few among the many, following their lead. There's freedom in that anonymity. In being a stranger. At the latter end of the crosswalk, the crowd gets thicker, faster too, in a rush to beat the light. Neo reaches for C's hand without much thought behind it. C interlaces their fingers, keeping him close.

Sony and Hikari are right behind. Sony hangs on Hikari's arm. Hikari hangs on Sony's every word. Sony marvels at the city as if she's looking at it through an entirely new lens. I can tell from here that she's talking about her kids. She tells Hikari about the seashells she'll bring back to them, the tattoo she'll show off, adding to her list of crazy stories that they can't get enough of.

Sony's fire is eternal. If I reach, I can see her passing it on to children of her own, maybe a classroom full. She'll brag about her famous writer friend and her tall, pretty friend and her funny thief friend. She'll tell them all her adventures at the hospital, and they won't realize it was a hospital at all.

Sony's step falters for a moment when we reach the sidewalk on the other side. She catches her breath again, adjusting the backpack.

"Sorry." She tries to laugh it off. "Needed a second there."

"I'm sure your cat will forgive us if we're late getting home," Hikari says. She holds Sony steady, pretending the falter was just a clumsy trip.

"You like Hee, right, Hikari?"

"Of course."

"Good, good. I'm gonna need somebody to take care of her."

"What do you mean?" Hikari asks. When Sony doesn't answer for a moment, Hikari frowns, slowing their pace. "Sony, don't talk like that." She caresses the red framing Sony's face. "You're gonna make it."

Neo and C glance back at the conversation. It's a half second, a few words, but it's enough to cause a shift among them. One of our unsaid rules is not broken, but poked at.

"You're such a kid," Sony says, nudging Hikari along.

It's when we near a place I'm too familiar with that I start to slow down.

The river surges beneath the bridge. It dares me to look. It takes a shovel to my memories. My friends walk along its edge. I recoil, close my fists, try to take up less room, hide away.

I don't want to exist here. We're about to pass the bridge, walk right past its glaring eyes, but I can't. I stop before we get close enough for me to look.

I refuse to look. Everything starts to hurt. I refuse to see him, but no matter how tight I shut my eyes, he's there. He puts his coat on my shoulders. The air is tight-knit, cold. White blankets the ground, a streetlamp spotlighting dancing snowflakes, the rest of the world dark and alone. He kisses me hard. Then he fades. I try to go after him, but the dark rejects me. My tears take the rhythm of the water. My sobs choke me. Everything hurts. My memories crawl out of the ground like monsters swimming back up the river.

"Sam?" I look up. Hikari stands in front of me, pale-faced. Neo, Sony, and C are ahead of us, closer to the bridge, walking still. "Sam, are you okay?"

"I can't do this," I whisper.

"What do you mean? What's wrong?"

"I can't come with you," I say, shaking my head. I feel exposed, endangered. "I can't—" The words get lodged in my throat, afraid to be spoken into existence.

"It's okay," Hikari says. She comes closer, putting her hand up. She doesn't touch me with it. She doesn't tug me aside for the next school of fish passing. Her palm rests in the air, waiting for mine to mirror it.

"Sing, Yorick," she orders gently, moving her forefinger as I mimic.

"The last time I was on that bridge, the stars fell," I say. I'm not sure she understands, but "I can't cross it again."

"It's okay," Hikari says again, and in her tone of voice, it's almost believable. "It's okay. I'll stay with you."

"No, you—"

"I'm not leaving you, Sam." She speaks with conviction. She still cares about me. Even when I couldn't give her what she wanted. Her palm stays parallel to mine.

I think I could've caught my breath. I could've found the strength to stand up straight and keep on going if our dancing obscured everything else.

Only it doesn't. Over her shoulder, time is still there. It looms over my friends, casting a shadow with my past twirling on its finger.

Neo and C hold Sony's hands as they all turn onto the bridge.

My heart drops in my chest.

"Wait," I say, a barely there noise, a question no one could answer. "Why are they—"

I don't finish the question. I walk past Hikari.

"Wait," I say again.

They walk farther onto the bridge. I push through people surrounding me on the sidewalk. I go after them. I need to go after them. They aren't supposed to cross it. It's too early. They aren't meant to go yet!

Sony faltered once before. If she falls or hurts a rib, her lung could collapse in an instant. Neo is still too thin. His bones have no protection, and his body is too frail to run or withstand anything more than a push. C's heart is damaged to the point of no return. He needs another. He won't live without another.

I'm a fool. I let myself remember. My memories unveil themselves. Of Neo, my poet bruised by people meant to protect him, my poor little boy who should've spent his years growing under the sun rather than under exam lights. Of Sony. My flame so determined to burn, whose mother was taken too soon and whose childhood should've gone on forever. Of C. My heartbroken bear of a boy, so aloof yet so gentle, so willing to be kind.

I let myself fall back on the past. And it's thrown me a future that doesn't exist.

No matter how much I try to claim that my memories are buried, they are out of my control. They come on suddenly. They remind me that denial is not as strong as reality.

My reality has been the same since I was born.

My friends are going to die.

"Wait!" The crowd envelops them. "No, you can't go, you haven't—you can't—

"C!" I yell. "Sony!" I can't see them anymore. "Neo!" I run, push through people, and try to get to them before they cross. They can't hear me. No one can. I beg endlessly. To be heard. To be allowed to follow where they disappear. I call for them again, but it's as if I have no voice at all.

Before I can even reach the bridge, a force pushes me backward. I stumble, the railing slipping from beneath my fingers. Gravity pulls me down from the sidewalk into the road. A honk amplifies, getting closer. People start screaming.

The last thing I hear is my name as the sun curves over the hood of a car.

11
empty

YEARS AGO, I fell into the road.

Friction shredded my legs, dirt soaking up my blood like cotton. Tears stung. The soil mingled with open wounds. I hovered my fingers over the tear in my pants.

That whole day was a tumble. My stomach twisted up. The desire to vomit, to claw at myself was overwhelming.

I had just watched someone die.

I had to listen to her mother scream. I had to see the life fade from her eyes. She had yet to take her first steps. She was in an era of her life without language. She held her mother's fingers in her fists and became enamored with anything that caught the light.

She was the first baby I ever held, and I had to watch her die.

The sadness was sudden. It was forceful, a propulsion. I wanted to open myself up and let it escape like steam.

I ran away from the hospital grounds. I ran away, and I fell. The cuts hurt, but they alleviated some of the inner pain. It was as if my body felt the damage my heart had taken and wanted to share some of the burden.

"Sam!" I heard my name as I sat defeated on the road. The sun gleamed off the hood of a car. "Sam!"

There was a noise, wheels swerving. I turned to look. A large metal thing hurled in my direction. Then I was whiplashed. Someone grabbed ahold of my wrist and hoisted me out of the way.

I was on the side of the road, a body on top of mine, shielding me. He was out of breath, his head in the crook of my neck and shoulder, one of his knees between my legs like he'd fallen, getting me out of the way.

"My sweet Sam," he panted, raising his face to look down at me. He dried my tears, his still fresh, burning as they dripped onto my cheeks. "I've got you," he said, shushing me as I began to cry. "You're okay. I've got you."

"Why did she die?" I sobbed. He pulled me up into his arms. I kept crying till night came, and he was all I had left to hold. "Why did she have to die?" I asked again, over and over. "Why does everyone die?"

He never answered me.

The emptiness that question left behind still sits like a hollow place where my heart should lie.

————

The memory flashes by in a second. That's all it takes. The same force that pushed me down back then does it again. Only this time, it's not on a dirt road. It's one made of asphalt and concrete, busy as the sidewalk traffic. The sun flashes, a car honks. My eyes shut tight, ready for the impact.

"Sam!"

But the car never hits me. Instead, I feel a warmth like no

other tense around my wrist. My breath hitches. It's as though I'm breaking the water's surface, being pulled from the bottom of a pool. The road fades out behind me, becoming an echo of gasps and angry drivers. I land with my feet on the pavement, my body stumbling into another.

Hikari's face comes into view, as close to mine as it was last night. She is as breathless as I am. She was running behind me. I fell into the road, but she caught me. She saw the car, she reached for me, she saved me.

The crowd goes on around us as if nothing's happened. The traffic resumes behind us.

She saved me.

Her pulse races beneath my palm. Her nose brushes mine, wisps of her hair like fingers caressing my temples.

I feel her. Skin, rougher than I imagined, hilled and scarred, hot beneath the surface. She touched me. The illusion is destroyed. The glass wall made of our almosts is shattered.

She's real, tangible, right there in front of me.

It makes me shudder.

"You're okay," Hikari says. "I've got you."

"Let me go." The words leave me before I can think of them. They're not spoken, they're spat, bitten, aggressive. Hikari opens her eyes, confusion strewn about the flares. I look at my feet, unable to look at her.

"Let me go!" I yell, and this time, she does.

"Sam!" Sony. She sounds like she's running. No, she can't be running. C is right behind her, Neo limping along with him. "Sam, are you okay?!"

Hikari rushes backward when they arrive, like a wave that collides with a cliff and recedes back into the sea.

"Sam," Neo says softly. He checks my back for scuff marks, my neck and head for blood. Sony stands next to him, her oxygen tank still on her back, her freckles still dancing on her nose. C can see the dread in my eyes. His forehead wrinkles, but he doesn't reach to touch me.

"I'm sorry," I say. That's all I have to say. At this moment, it's all I know how to say.

My friends are okay. They didn't cross the bridge. They came back. Yet this urge to hide and run away doesn't dissipate. It grows. I put my hand to my mouth like I'm about to be sick.

"I'm sorry," I say again, but before they can say anything else, I run back to the crosswalk and into the safety of my hospital.

———

Her touch is like a burn. The mark radiates heat. I walked into the lobby, staring at it. I bypassed the elevators entirely, climbing the stairs up to the roof.

The roof is cool and quiet, and my mind is anything but. In my mind, Sony has blood on her tongue and sleeve, Neo thins away into nothing, and C's heart ceases between his ribs. Blue settles over the building, drowning everyone in it.

Hikari's touch lingers. Reverting to old habits, I pace. I hover over the spot on my wrist as if Hikari left paint there and it would rub off on my fingers. Every time I replay the moment she pulled me back into reality, I feel the sunlight on my face. My fear burns into ash, and I see all the lies I fooled myself into believing:

Neo and C together in school, writing their book together. Neo is bruise-less, the torments of his father no more. C's skin is scarless, stormless. He takes Neo to the beach for swims on the weekends and brings Sony along. Sony has her children in her arms, a husband or wife, or anyone in the world she desires.

She carries them across the sand into the water, making grimaces and kissing them as the waves gently wash in. Their disease, their stolen time, their deaths are all things of the past. They survive, and they are happy, and they live.

But it's a lie. It's all a lie, and Hikari made me believe it could be true. With her *one day* and her constant game of pretend that she plays with the future as if it's set in stone. She made them all think it could be true.

"Sam?"

I flinch. Hikari stands in the doorway, alone. My anger rises like smoke from the place she touched.

"Are you okay?" Her voice is edgeless. She's worried about me. "I'm sorry I grabbed you like that." She walks to me without caution as my jaw works on its hinges. "I just couldn't let you fall—"

"Why did you say that to Sony?" I ask. My fists clench at my sides.

Hikari halts, our distance the same as the day we met.

"What?"

"You said, *you're going to make it*. Why did you say that to her?"

Hikari shakes her head like she's been hit.

"I don't understand."

"You're acting like a motivational poster. Like those tapes they remake every ten years telling sick kids to keep fighting as if any of it is in their control."

"Because it is—"

"Sony's body eats away at the very thing that breathes for it, and no one in their right mind will give her a pair of lungs she's only going to destroy. She *will* die. It's not a matter of if, it's a matter of when. Do you have any idea what it's going to do to Neo and C if they start thinking she's actually going to live?"

"You don't know that she isn't."

"Yes, I do." The more I speak, the more Hikari's expression falls. "You make fun of me because I draw lines—"

"I never made fun of you—"

"You think I'm wrong!" I yell. I remember when she told Neo the whole world would read his stories, that C would be there with him, that Sony would get to run races again. I would look the other way like I did when I saw death pulling at their necks.

I can't anymore. "You dangle futures that don't exist in front of them like bait. You're making their pain inevitable."

"They're already in pain," she says, and the truth of that stings more than it should. "They deserve to have hope for each other."

"Hope is useless." My voice drops. The mere word crawls beneath my skin, makes me wince at the sound. "It's nearsighted and blind to the fact that it *always* fails."

Hope is the name that should be at the top of the hit list. It's worse than our enemies. Our enemies are thieves, but they come as advertised. Hope is ignorance, a liar, an accidental creature made of fear. And it failed my first love just as it failed me.

"You lost someone," Hikari says, her voice traveling to realization.

When I face her to meet it, I don't see her at all.

I see him. It's only for a moment, but there he is, standing atop the stone, reaching for me, dark-haired and golden-eyed. It's colder than it is now. The past is always colder. Suddenly, he's crying, telling me that he's sorry. He gets on his knees, his head against my stomach, begging me to forgive him, begging me to just hold on, to *hope*.

He falls apart into ashes. I wave him away like fog.

"I'm not going to pretend I can change the past," I say. "*Or* the future."

"Hoping for a future is *not* pretending."

"It is. That's all hope is. It's a lie we tell ourselves so that we can break watches and pretend time is dead."

"Is that why you gave me this?" Hikari fingers the glass, the arrow that doesn't tick. She laughs at my audacity. It isn't a laugh I once cherished. It's dry and hurt and disappointed. "To mock me?"

"No."

"'I'm here,'" she says. "'I'm always listening. And I'll always believe you.' You said that. Do you remember? Was it a lie?"

"No!" I shake my head, remembering the joy on her face. "No, I care about you. I just wanted to make you happy."

"Why? Because you think I'm going to die?" she asks. She grips her wrist like Neo does. She tightens the loop with her thumb and forefinger as if she could squeeze the watch off her wrist. "Or because you love me?"

She looks the same as she did sitting on the stretcher when I pulled away from our kiss. The question weaves into the wound on her neck and the illness in her blood. Her voice turns faint, weaker with every breath.

"Do you love me?" She motions to the hospital below us. "Do you love any of them? Any of the people you claim to watch over?"

"I'm not supposed to love," I say. "I'm not supposed to even exist."

"Are you that afraid?" she asks, only now it's a dare. A push. "Are you that afraid to lose again?"

"I already lost everything. I will always lose everything. No matter how many times I try to steal it back."

Hikari cups her hands around her nose and chin in the form of a prayer. Horror works across her face. She looks down as if three graves sit between us. She looks at me as if I'm holding our friends' hands as they lie down inside them.

"That's why you spend so much time with them," she says. "That's why you do so much for them."

I already know what she's thinking.

"No. No, that's not true."

Hikari adopts my anger and takes it as her own. "What are they to you, exactly? Lonely dogs in the back of a pound whose days are numbered?" Disgust works through her tone, thinning her eyes heavy with judgment. "You're just as bad as people who look at sick kids and see lost causes only alive thanks to pity."

"You don't understand!" I yell. "You don't understand because you haven't only existed in a world where people rely on hope like crutches to keep them upright. You've never held a boy who was just skin and bones crying for any god to see him for who he is. You've never had someone die right in front of you as you try to push the blood back into their body. You've never watched those you care about wither day by day. You've never lost anything, so don't pretend to know what it feels like."

I lose my breath. I feel like I'm running across that bridge, only it's endless. I'm running after my friends, after our enemies who lead them into the dark. I'm running after him, away from him. Only I'm standing still on a rooftop, just praying that the stars won't fall from the sky if I look up.

"I've been here my entire life," I breathe, looking back to Hikari. "Never once has *hope* saved anyone."

"Hope isn't meant to save people," she says, reticent now.

A wall rises, made of glass. Her color dims behind it, and the burning sensation on my wrist fades to nothing. She isn't angry when she speaks, but she can't look me in the eye anymore. "And just because it failed you doesn't mean the rest of us have to give it up."

The reason I'm afraid of her comes to fruition. It brings all the things I promised never to feel again to life. Hikari knows, I think. She knows what I really think. She knows why I can't bear to touch her.

I am not afraid of her. I am afraid of loving her.

Because I wouldn't just have to admit she was real.

I would have to admit that I'm going to lose her too.

Hikari wipes her nose. She runs her hands up and down her arms from the cold.

"You want to pretend you know me?" she asks. "Because we've spent the past month flirting on rooftops and exchanging secrets? Here's a secret for you, Yorick. Hope did fail me once." She traces the wound between her collarbones all the way down to the scars on her wrists. "You don't realize how powerful loneliness can be till even hurting yourself isn't painful enough to sate it."

The gray skies form thunderclouds and lay her past out before us like a screen. The sensations of her memories play across her body, her mind, her eyes, till the words fall from her mouth like stones.

"I had a plan and everything," she says. "After my parents left for work, I was going to walk down the road and swim into the lake. The water is practically black. It reflects everything. I was just gonna"—she stops, finding the right words—"let the dark swallow me."

I remember the day we met more clearly now. Something had happened, something her killer wasn't responsible for, I was sure of it. I remember how she tucked that screwdriver and sharpener into her pocket. I remember the bandages on her arms. I remember everything she tried to hide.

Her injuries aren't from her disease. They're all her own.

When our eyes meet again, I can hardly breathe. Because how could I have missed it till now?

Hikari beams. She brings things to life, plants, broken things, and sick people who need a contagious smile to catch their lips. She gives people life only to deny it for herself.

"Hika . . ." I start to say her name, reach out, walk across the distance, but I can't. She doesn't want me to anymore.

"You might have seen more, suffered more, but don't tell me I have no clue what loss feels like," she says. The watch unclips from her wrist and falls onto the concrete. Thrown across the line she draws. "I've had enough people tell me it's all in my head."

She smiles. An empty smile with tears trailing down to the corners of her mouth. Then she turns around, back from where she came, another sun setting, my fingers caught in the cold air.

The pain is sudden. It's forceful, a propulsion. I want to open myself up and let it escape like steam. I fall into the concrete, letting my knees scrape against the ground.

My ghosts escape their caskets.

My memories come flooding down the river.

And I feel so empty I could die.

12
hope

before

M Y NAME WASN'T always Sam.

When I came into existence I had no name, no memories, nothing. There is a belief that all intentions have a soul. That every wish, every dream, can come to life if it is willing.

Blood is my first memory.

It stained the room, a large fleshy circle where a man's leg should have been. He was screaming, the man. Women in white gowns dabbed his face with cloth and leather strapped his remaining limbs to the bed. Another walked in, wiping off a metal saw slick with that same shade of red. She threw the thing down aimlessly, wiping her arms on her legs so the blood was on her once-white dress and not her hands. She grabbed a needle and injected the screaming man with clear liquid. He struggled against the bonds and the women. It took a while for the screaming to die down. It morphed into a rhythmic moan till the man's consciousness faded.

I should've been scared. I think a part of me was. Another

was curious. About the blood. Blood is accusatory. It spreads, and it stains, and its reach is infinite.

I wanted to know why.

My first memory makes hospitals seem like a violent place. Hospitals are not violent. Hospitals diffuse violence and cure its victims.

My second memory is less gruesome. More sudden. Just as sad.

There was another soldier. This one was silent. You might've thought there was no life behind his eyes till he blinked. He took breath after breath, one hand on his chest. Then his hand fell. His eyes closed. He stopped breathing. Red pooled from the spot he'd held and dripped from his fingers.

When the one-legged man woke, he started to scream again.

He crawled out of the cot, dragging himself across the floor. Screaming, crying, screaming some more. He grabbed the other soldier's bloody hand hanging off the bed and wailed into it. The nurses had to pry him off.

Until he fainted, the soldier stared at the dead man. He cursed the war. He cursed the nurses and doctors and hospital alike. He cursed death most of all.

My second memory makes hospitals seem like a field. A place of harvest for death to collect. I don't argue with that. I challenge it silently as the soldier silently waits to die. Same as him, I don't believe it. I accept it. I have to.

Death is not a being. It is a state of being. We humanize it, demonize it, give it a soul because it is easier to condemn something with a face. Disease is in the same boat, only it's a lot easier to convict it. Disease has *reason*. Virus, bacteria, defective cells. Those already have a face.

Time doesn't need a face at all.

Time steals openly.

Such carelessness on its part is enough to be found guilty.

Guilty of what, though? Time, disease, and death don't hate us. The world and its many shadows are not capable of hate. They simply don't care about us. They don't need us. They never made and, as such, never broke any promises. We are mediums through which they play.

I call them shadows. Sometimes enemies, although that may be a bit hypocritical. They are mediums through which we play too.

Disease is weaponized. It's profited off of. Humans rarely search to *cure* diseases. There's more value in treating someone for the rest of their life than in healing them once. Death is no different. It's a means to an end, a tool, a toy. With it, the people at the top of the pyramid decide how many will be sacrificed at the bottom.

No one is better at killing people than people.

Time is different. Chase it, gamble with it. No matter the game, time likes to play because it always wins. But unlike its partners, time can be kind. Or maybe that is an illusion too. Maybe time has teeth only to grin and a voice only for the last laugh.

I don't understand it enough for a concrete answer.

I don't understand a great many things. I give them all souls too. Blood has a soul. Books have souls. Broken things have souls—especially broken things. Even the hospital has a soul traipsing through the halls, watching, like an onlooker inside its own bones.

Souls are susceptible to suffering.

That's why I bury memories.

Living them once was enough. Reliving them is a destructive habit.

But my memories of *him* are ones I have buried inside a glass coffin.

He is the one who broke a pattern in the red.

He was a little boy who rose with the sun when the night was all I knew.

————

There is never any wasted time with him. He plays with life to every extent.

"Hello, wall," he says, dragging pudgy hands across the ashy, poor paint. "Hello, floor." The uneven tiles clack against his feet. "Good morning, sir," he says to a passing doctor. "Good morning, sky," he says to a passing window with a crack in the checkered glass.

The boy gives souls to all. He calls them his friends.

Even his disease has a soul. It's an all-encompassing kind. His medication, his exams, his treatments are all to be administered exactly on time. Little does it know, time has a challenger.

The boy laughs, rocking his legs back and forth at the foot of the bed. The nurse takes his temperature and then reaches for his morning pills. He opens his mouth just enough for her to slip them in. With a bite, he shuts it before she can and runs off, laughing.

Time, along with many nurses and doctors, ends up having to chase him. Him and his bursts of rebellion. When they catch him, he always asks the nurse or the doctor to stay and play with him. They sigh, apologize, and say they have other patients to treat. He is the same with service workers who bring him his food. The service workers shake their heads daily, apologize, and say they have other patients to feed. The boy smiles and says he understands. Then he says hello to his plate, to his fork, to his cup, and he eats on his own.

I follow the boy after his morning medication round and his checkups. I am not curious about those parts of his life. I already understand what's *wrong* with him. I want to understand what he is. I want his in-between moments.

An explorer, he runs across the halls without care, asking questions, not to anyone in particular, but just to ask.

He has no care who is watching or where he is. He moves like he is a part of the hospital, a universal puzzle piece. He becomes, as I am, a background detail noticed but not questioned like the color of a wall or the weight of the front door.

However, for how constant the boy is to this place, he has no constants of his own.

No one ever visits him. Not parents, not family, not a soul. He has his usual nurses and doctors, but there is a barrier there, as there must be. He is one of their many patients. He is not their *one* anything. He is nobody's *one*.

That is a very lonely existence.

Little did time know, when it gave him to me, that I am lonely too . . .

I've never spoken to a patient before.

In fact, I've never spoken to anyone before.

At first, I hide. Then I observe the boy from the threshold of his room. He plays with tiny potted plants on the ground.

"Good morning," he says when he sees me peeking out, not the way you'd greet a stranger. I flinch, retreating almost fully out of view. He cocks his head to the side, laughing. "Are you shy?"

"I . . ." My voice is fresh, a muscle that's never been used. I swallow, stretch it, let my tongue move in my mouth, calibrating. "Hello."

"People aren't supposed to see me without a mask and gloves," he says, but his caution wavers with a shrug. "You can come in if you want, though. I don't mind."

I hesitate.

The problem is I know him. But he's never had a chance to know me. He is a painting I've been admiring for a long time without the courage to walk into it.

The boy looks up, taking me in as I do him. His clothes are well-kept, but his shoes are muddy. His hair is soft, ungroomed, but his gaze is full of curious edges.

"Have we met before?" he asks. "I feel like I know you."

"In . . ." I stutter, walking into the frame and brushstrokes. "In a way."

Sweetness and soil flood my nose. His walls are bland, but there are undeniable hints of him accenting the space. Some books on the night table, a string of lights behind the bed, the plants in his hands.

"You like them? I took these from the garden outside."

"Why did you take them?" I ask.

He makes an *I don't know* sort of noise.

"I thought they could be my friends." He picks them up in his arms, placing each with care on the windowsill. The sun caresses their leaves as it does when it wakes him.

"Do you live here too?" he asks.

I nod.

He hums in response. "Do you want to play with me?"

"I'm not sure how to play."

"That's all right. I'll teach you."

We walk out of his room together. He puts his hands in his pockets and looks at me with a smile back over his shoulder—a smile with teeth and shut eyes. A smile you feel rather than see.

"My name's Sam."

Sam.

Does Sam know he has suns in his eyes?

Sam and I are physically similar. I tried to model myself after him, but Sam's mind is mine's opposite. He is brave without having to try, animated by little things. He is mischievous, strolling into places he doesn't belong and speaking without care for his volume or who is around.

He leaps, he shrieks, he exists freely.

He questions so much about his world, yet he doesn't question me.

In his eyes, I am just another child. A playmate.

Sam teaches me a great many things. He teaches me about toys, wooden figures we assign voices, and story roles. Of tiles, where we jump in patterns for hopscotch, of nooks and closets where hiding from each other is a great game of suspense. I'm not very good at games, but Sam says it's okay.

He puts aside his routine, and he shows me his world. There are patients he knows and likes. An older woman who gives him bread, a mother who is waiting for her baby to be born, and so many more. He greets them through the doors with a wave, and only once he makes them smile does he move on to the next.

"Are you hungry?" Sam asks as the dark draws over the hospital.

"Do you want to eat in your room?" I ask.

"No." He smiles with that twinkle of mischief. "Let's go eat outside."

"Are we allowed outside?"

"Knights are allowed everywhere in their castle," Sam says.

"Knights?"

"Yes. I'm a knight. I'm the castle's protector. Like in fairy tales," he whispers, his face dropping when he realizes I don't understand. "You've never heard of fairy tales?"

I shake my head.

"Oh." Sam blinks for a while, his cheeks and lips puffed out. "Okay. I'll tell you some."

We tiptoe through the hall, Sam giggling under his breath the whole time, bread rolls stuffed up his sleeves. He runs once we're out of sight, up, up, up till we reach a stairwell.

Sam opens the window at the very top and ushers me through it. We emerge, and there, I meet the sky. It's cold and gray, the ground harsh, and the wind harsher.

"This is the roof," Sam says. I shiver, hunching and rubbing my hands up and down my arms. Sam seems to like it, though. He takes the bread rolls from his sleeves, gives me one, and sits.

"Look." He points up. Against a layer of darkness, the sky wears lights. They're faint, yet they flare like candle flames about to go out.

"Those are my stars," Sam whispers like it's a secret he trusts me to keep. "They're the most beautiful things in the world."

Stars, I think, the word playing voicelessly on my tongue.

"Are you a star?" I ask.

Sam's mouth opens, a surprised sound stuttering from his throat. Then, he laughs, the eruption crackly and full.

"You're silly," he says, and when his laughter ceases, "We can share my stars if you want."

It's a breath. A promise. The first promise he ever makes me.

I nod with a pleased hum.

We eat together, me in silence, him telling me his fairy tales. They're grand stories, ones with neat endings and no loose ends to tie. I ask him why stories in real life don't end that way. He tells me fairy tales end however we want them to. He says his nurse tells him that fairy tales are meant to teach people lessons, but he doesn't believe that. He thinks stories are meant to make people feel things.

I ask him what that's like. To feel.

The wind passes between us, stretching his grin.

He says I ask good questions.

Sam slides his hand across the stone on his last bite of bread.

"This is our castle," he says. "Will you protect it with me?"

I blink. The knights in all his fairy tales are brave. They conquer kingdoms and rescue those in danger. For all I am, I am not brave. I chew on my lip, chew on the question.

Sam senses my doubt.

"There's a lot of sick people here, you know," he says, creeping a little closer. It's the first time I notice how golden his eyes are, flares of yellow across a dark background. It's a detail you can only see from up close, not just by admiring a painting but by being a part of it.

Sam smiles. A smile you can feel. "We can protect them, you and I. Would you like that?"

I would. Even without bravery at my side. Already, from a single look, a single span of a day, I know so much about him.

Sam. A name, simple and warm, but at once musical in the right tone. Yellow. In his eyes, bright when he is happy, even brighter when he is sad. His voice is young and high yet comfortable no matter the listener. He holds himself like a character, a hero in a novel, a knight without a self-conscious bone in his body.

"I'll teach you how to be a knight, okay?" he says.

"Really?"

"Yes. I like playing with you." He looks at my face the way I look at his. Reading me. "What did you say your name was?"

"I don't have a name."

"You don't?"

"I am"—I begin—"I am not like the other broken things you know."

A name is relevant. Backgrounds don't need relevancy. That defeats their purpose.

Sam, with the sky illuminated at his back, thinks otherwise.

"We can share my name, then. Your name will be Sam too. I decided," he declares into the cool breeze, leaning closer to me. "Go ahead and try it. Say, *I'm Sam*."

My voice is small. Everything feels small compared to him.

His name feels anything but.

"I'm Sam," I say.

With glee, one of Sam's hands, soft and baby-like, grabs ahold of mine, and I become the stone beneath our feet. He is warm, the gold in his eyes traveling down his body, through his skin.

Fire flickers between our palms. It melts all the way to my bones.

I've never been touched before. I shudder from it, suddenly wondering if the fluttering in my heart is what they call *feeling*.

"I'm happy I met you, Sam," the boy says.

"Hap-py?" I whisper.

"Mhm." He doesn't let go of my hand. He plays with it, explores it.

"I like you," he says. His cheeks flush, gaze averted. "You're beautiful."

I've never been called beautiful. I've heard the words and watched them escape the lips of lovers. But many words, I find, aren't always truthfully spoken. People lie. Children lie. But children rarely lie about beauty.

"Will you play with me tomorrow?" Sam asks.

"Yes."

Yes, I say in my head again. *All my tomorrows are yours.*

"Thank you," Sam says. He kisses me on the cheek and climbs back inside, waving. "Good night, Sam. Have sweet dreams . . ."

The day I met him is a memory laced with the joy of its happening and the pain of its passing. Because even if I told you I have forgotten, you can't trust me.

You don't ever forget the first time you fall.

13
rain

SOME PEOPLE WEAR pain on their sleeve. Others let it lie beneath their clothes. The roof wears its pain plainly. Scratches in the stone, white like chalk, paired with black smudges of stomped-out smokes.

I look with half-open eyes and a half-there body. My knees bend into the cradle of my arms. My back is pressed up against the wall at the ledge. I look at the shadow of two children sharing bread and stories, staring at the sky. Beside them, another pair stands over a cardboard box full of books, their souls reaching across a palpable distance.

My hands come together like a lock and key. The heels of my palms, through the valleys of my fingers, all the places both of my suns set me afire.

Yellow dances in the wind. Time's shadow snuffs it out with rain. As clouds muster a storm above, the broken watch catches raindrops so I don't have to cry alone.

The door across from me is lodged open with a wooden wedge. A phantom creak is all that sounds as footsteps cautiously make their way up.

My friends walk into the downpour without cover.

"I'm sorry," I say, rain and tears pooling in my mouth. "I'm so sorry."

Their dreams of an outside world, chainless and free, were for nothing. And it's my fault.

Sony sits next to me, crisscrossing her legs.

"Our everything can wait. It's not going anywhere," she says. "You need us right now." She calms me like she would her cat or her kids with diligence. Her dirty white sneaker borders my shoe. The rain soaks the laces and tends to the sole's scuff marks. "Tell us what's wrong, Sammy."

I'm going to lose you, I think. *I'm going to lose you, and even if I knew all along, it still hurts to face it. It hurts so bad. I feel eaten from the inside out.*

"We're not upset with you," C says. He kneels as if I've only just fallen like I did a year ago, knocking into his chest. His forearm-length hand covers Sony's on my elbow. "Just tell us what happened."

I stutter over my breaths. "You always said that you were stealing to prove that you're still human, that your diseases don't own you. You said the escape was the final part of the heist. I thought it'd be okay because you'd be free, and that's all you've ever wanted, but—"

"But we're not free," C says like it's a fact he accepted long ago. His lips thin as he realizes why my fear was so all-consuming. The understanding passes contagiously. Sony's backpack shifts on her shoulders. Neo's fingers make a loop around his wrist. "You can't escape your own body."

The guilt twists in my stomach, wringing it like a towel. Their diseases robbed them of so many moments, and I robbed them of their greatest one. I scrunch my face and try to hide again.

"Sam," C says. "You got cold feet today. Everybody gets cold feet. Who cares? We can sneak out every day of the week, and if you get scared again, then we'll try the next day. It doesn't matter. We don't steal and escape as some big statement about how society perceives sick people." He presses his palm flat against his heart and shrugs. "We're just living."

If we were just living, we would have never met here. In C's dreams, I see us all sitting in the back row of that English classroom. We would get detention for stealing from teachers and pulling pranks. Sony would be the cool older girl who taught us how to not smoke and not drink in the most fashionable sense. She'd crane kick Neo's bullies senseless and pester me about my crush on Hikari. C and I would be quiet, onlooking, spacing out, and getting in trouble for it. After school, we'd escape, just the five of us every day. We'd have bikes to ride along roads and the hearts, lungs, and legs to ride them across the world.

"What about your Heaven?" I ask.

C smiles. His eyes meet mine, a warm, dark color you can sink in. I see that dream there. They're tired, but their essence is untouched. His eyes are as kind as they've always been.

"I don't need to go looking for something I already have," he whispers.

The rain starts to slow.

"I don't understand," I say.

C shakes his head. "You always overthink things." He taps my nose and catches a raindrop. "What do you need, Sam? Whatever it is, we'll help you get it."

"I—I don't understand."

"Oh, Sammy." Sony wraps herself around me as if she can feel me come undone and wants to keep me whole. "Why are you so afraid?"

"Because you lost someone."

I look up.

Neo is the only one left standing. He's soaked to the bone, but not a single shiver wracks through him.

He glares at me. "I'm right, aren't I? You lost someone and it hurt and you can't get over it so you're scared you're gonna lose us too?"

"Neo, don't," C warns over his shoulder.

"Who was it?" Neo's question is like a pinprick making me flinch. "No, don't look away from me. Tell me who it was."

"I don't remember," I say, covering my ears.

"You told me when we first met that you couldn't remember if you'd ever been in love. I knew you were lying then, and I know you're lying now. Tell me."

"I can't—"

"I don't care," Neo bites out. "Tell me."

Behind him, I see the little boy again, sitting in the middle of the rain, little potted plants between his legs. He looks up, welcomes me into his room, yellow flares in his gaze.

"He's not real anymore." I shake my head till he disappears. "He's dead."

"I know he's dead." Neo steps toward me. He grabs my arms and tears them off my face so that I have nowhere left to hide. "Tell me who he was."

"H-he was born without an immune system—"

"No, I don't give a shit about his disease. You didn't love his disease. You loved him. Tell me about *him*."

Neo doesn't relinquish his hold on me. He tightens it. His sleeves fall from his wrists to his elbows, old bruises rotting near the surface.

The sun stretches behind the clouds, a single streak of light pinched across the drizzles. It kisses Sony's hair, C's skin, and half of Neo's face. It plays with warmth, a crease in the rain, a strangely familiar permission to finally open the gates.

"I was so alone," I whisper. I see him there again, just over Neo's shoulder. He's exploring, snickering, interlacing our hands, his smile everlasting.

"I wasn't supposed to be alive. I was just the background of a play wherein people suffered." My breath hitches, the recollections like acid in my veins. Blood and screaming and death crawl through them, so dense they may as well be solid.

"I never understood why people had to die, and I thought that maybe *he* held the answer." A little boy who always said that things would be okay. A little boy who saw the good in everyone and everything. A little boy who lied to me.

"He taught me how to live even though I thought I wasn't meant to. He taught me about the world. He taught me how to dream."

Those memories flow with ease. They're soft in nature with hints of faraway noise. His shrieky laughter in the distance, his shy kiss on my cheek, the flushed skin on his face.

It's always like that. The pain-ridden seconds are eternal. The year's worth of joys are fleeting. Another one of time's tricks.

"He killed himself in a snowstorm."

C and Sony's faces fall. Neo doesn't react. The little boy behind them recedes into the shadows that stole him from me.

"It's not like people say it is," I say, wiping my face. "When he died, he didn't take a piece of me with him. He left a piece of himself behind. A hollowness. A reminder that I could never let myself love again without pain to follow. So after the storm passed, it was easier to just pretend it never snowed at all. I stopped asking questions. I stopped looking for reasons. I stopped caring about everyone. And somewhere along the line, I stopped trying to exist too." Because my stars couldn't compare to the one that faded into the dark.

"But it's okay," I admit. I smile up at my friends as if it will make any part of our story sound less despairing. "The narrator isn't supposed to sneak into the words and dream with the protagonists. Not living meant not suffering. Not wanting meant I had nothing to lose."

With the memories I buried that Hikari brought back, I see Neo three years ago. He flirts with the line between living and dying, yet he's grown. His face is that of a boy becoming a man. Sony is a woman. C, despite his heart, grows with them. For all the times I looked away from their dying, I forgot to notice that they were still alive. They *are* still alive.

"But I care about you," I say, the only rain left streaming down my cheeks. The sky turns back to a measly gray, no sun to shine through it. "I want to save you. I want you to be happy."

The truth of my existence settles.

Stale and as hard to accept as it always has been.

"But I couldn't save him." I sob, a noiseless, pathetic sound. "I can't save anyone."

"Sammy." Sony is squeezing me tightly, her breathing shallow. My cries pulse through my empty body. Cries I held in for the years since that blizzard.

Neo stands up and turns around. His feet clap gently against the water. They stop on the outskirts of a puddle, Hikari's broken watch at the center. Wet strands make a curtain as he looks down at it. Neo casts his hair back, making a noise that almost sounds like a scoff. A snort of derision. Something meant to mock me.

"You know, Sam, I never understood you," he says. He looks back at me over his shoulder, blank and impenetrable. "I mean,

I should've known. You were strange from the beginning. You
never had parents or family come around. I've never even seen
you leave the hospital for more than an hour." He walks back to
me, slower, but harder, the water cast aside in ripples.

"Neo, don't be cruel," Sony says, but he ignores her.

"You don't even have a personality," he snaps. "You're as stupid as a rock and as barren as a wall."

"Neo!" C yells at him, but Neo doesn't look away from me.

He stares me down like I disgust him. "All there is to you is
this insatiable curiosity that always gets you in trouble and some
cowardice to go with it." He's so close he may as well be spitting
in my face. Brutality blooms in his words. He's right. I know he's
right. I shut my eyes and bury myself in the cocoon of my elbows.

But then I hear Neo's shoes skid against the concrete. His
knees touch the ground. His hands reach from my jaw into my
hair, forcing me to look at him. "And you're the most caring person I've ever met."

At a glance, Neo seems the type not to care because it is easier
that way, but if you read him long enough, you eventually find
those poems italicized in his heart. For all the harshness he spouts,
there is a line soft and resounding at the end.

"You already saved me, you idiot," he says. "You saved all
of us."

I stare with a loose jaw and wide eyes.

"I don't understand."

"We're going to die," Neo says. "So what? Everyone dies,
and everything ends. Sometimes endings are abrupt. They hit
you in the face and it's too soon and it's unfair, but that doesn't
matter. The last page doesn't define the book. Time will cease,
disease will fester, and death will die. We promised we would kill
those bastards, remember? So get over yourself. Get over this

fear you have of existing and stop walking behind us. You're not just our narrator, you're a part of our story. You're my friend," he says, furious, as if my greatest sin was believing that I am a skull and not a soul.

"You have the right to live," he says, banishing any other notion. "You live by going after what you want. Tell us what you want, Sam."

Neo is a writer. His words ring true, give a certain chill. He has the power to make you fall into them. I take both his hands on my face and remember a time when he was the one on the ground, hollow and crying.

I wanted to comfort him. I wanted to be there for him. Just as I wanted to be there for Sony when her mother died. Just as I wanted to be there for C when he needed the courage to claim Neo's heart.

All I ever wanted was to understand. I wanted the people I came to see pass through these halls to survive. Now, looking at the sun kissing my friends with such adoration in the light, I know I want to see them not just survive, but live. And selfishly, at this exact moment, I want something for myself.

I decide to stand back up from my fall. I slosh through the puddles where the watch lies and pick it up from the ground, wiping the tears off the crystal.

"Hikari," I say, effortlessly, as if her name was always mine to speak.

The moments she touched this watch, the moments she gave me, and all the moments from here on that I want to give her seep from the stock-still hand. I turn back around and face my friends. My fist closes around the gift, renouncing the line it drew. What's left of the rain washes it away.

"I want to save her too."

14
real

M Y SHOES SMACK the tiles of the hallways twisting into each
other like an elaborate labyrinth. Awkward-bodied, I take
turns like a drifting car, C, Neo, and Sony on my tail. Sony cack-
les, breathless. C and Neo snicker at the doctors yelling at us to
stop. Weaving through this place is second nature. Only now do
I pay attention, not just to the finish line, but to the scenery of
the race.

I guess that's what happens when you let yourself live for the
first time. You notice the little details that used to be invisible
behind the blinders. And I may be a terrible runner, but there's
nothing like chasing the sun after a storm.

"Eric!" we all yell. "Eric!"

He flinches at his name, looking in our direction with abso-
lute terror.

"Hey! Slow down! Quit running!" We crowd him like dogs
jumping on an owner who's just come home, all speaking at the
same time, an incoherent mess of adrenaline. Sony and Neo
get grabbed by their shirt collars while C is stopped by an out-
stretched foot. "What's the problem?! Who's hurt?!"

Sony called Eric ten minutes ago, telling him it was urgent he come to the hospital at once.

"We need you to steal something!" Sony yells, grabbing the front of his shirt. Nurses from my old ship's hull overhear, their tasks slowing to a halt.

Eric's face contorts. "*That's* your emergency?!"

"Yes!" Sony breaks into a fit of giggles, her feet tapping. "Sam's in love with Hikari!"

"Didn't we already know that?!"

"Eric," I say. "Can you get something for me?"

"Oh, for God's sake, Sam."

"Eric, please—"

"No, no, no." He drops Neo and Sony, pointing an accusatory finger at me. "You're not dragging me into your weird Robin Hood–club extravaganza."

"What if we don't sneak in beer and cigarettes anymore?" C offers.

Eric frowns at him. "You still do that?"

C clears his throat and quickly pretends the ceiling is incredibly interesting. "No, sir."

"Yes, we do. But we'll stop," Neo says. "And we won't sneak out unless it's absolutely necessary."

"And I'll stop sneaking in animals, I swear it," Sony piles on, clasping her hands together.

Our promises are empty, Eric knows, but he doesn't care. He's in his own clothes, no scrubs, and bedheaded. He came because we needed him, not because it's his job, even if he'd like to play it off that way. Seeing the wishfulness in our whispering *please*s, Eric groans, pinching the bridge of his nose.

"Fine," he says. "But by tonight, if you haven't eaten dinner, taken your meds, and gone to bed, so help me, God—"

"We will, we will, we will," we all say at once, singing his praises, grabbing at his shirt, and jumping up and down.

"Sam," Eric says. He rubs his eyes and plants his hands on his hips, staring right at me. "What do you need?"

———

To my Hamlet,

I said your name for the first time today. It was an overdue heartbeat, a breath lying at the bottom of a single lung. It was a fear surmounted.

So.

To my Hikari,

I write to you with stolen stationery and an old pen on its last ink reserves. Where? In Neo's room. Headquarters. The place we always end up sitting a little too close, convicting bouquets of wrongful symbolism and nursing succulents back to health.

This is the place you told me you'd give me a dream.

On the notorious stepladder, Neo stands on his tiptoes, his skinny fingers perfect for tying thin threaded string lights to the ceiling.

C stands just below, a hair's breadth away from grabbing the ladder. "Are you gonna fall?"

"I'm not gonna fall."

"You sure?" C asks. "You look like you're gonna fall."

"Sony! Hand me those scissors so I can stab him," Neo yells, just as she walks into the room with so many random objects in her arms she has to open the door with her elbow.

"I got everything!" Sony says, dropping her stolen merchandise on Neo's bed. Her cat wobbles in behind her.

I quit my pacing and take inventory of the spoils. If you remember our first meeting, Hikari, you took me on an adventure to gather a measly pencil sharpener. Back then, I didn't realize the morbidity in that. Even if the ends were wrong, the means were a spark to our fire. It was the first time we stole together. The first time we shared our humanity with a bit of sin.

"Thank you," I say as Sony organizes the arts-and-crafts supplies she took from the library. A pair of scissors, markers, a little paint box, and colorful paper.

Eric lends us the Christmas lights. With them, we create our own finite constellations that cannot be overshadowed by clouds and the city's pollution. He even gets me a cardboard box, one identical to Neo's, from one of the maintenance closets.

"Will this work?" he asks. We exchange a knowing look, one with history behind it that holds a thank-you in the air like a light on a string. Then he gives me a light smack on the head. "Don't set anything on fire."

"Eric!" Sony jumps and wraps her arms around his neck. Eric groans, his chin settling on her shoulder.

"I'll see you tomorrow." He tucks her hair behind her ears. "No racing. You hear me?"

"Mhm," Sony hums and Eric holds her close for some time. Then he says his good nights to Neo and C, leaving me with a few parting words.

"Sam." I swear, Hikari, I'm not lying when I say he actually grins, tapping the doorknob a few times as he says, "Good luck to you and Hamlet."

Then he leaves us to our grand gesture.

"So, what are you going to say to her?" Sony asks me.

"I'm not sure yet."

The box grows with memorabilia. It's lined with a yellow

blanket. It carries a succulent I could never bear to leave alone, the hit list with its spiral spine coming off at the end, copies of *Wuthering Heights* and *Hamlet*, drawing supplies, and, of course, a watch only we know how to read.

"Urgh," Neo sounds, still on his ladder, using a screwdriver to mount the last of the string lights. "I can't stand romantics."

The stepladder shifts a bit beneath his feet when he turns.

"Be careful, please," C begs, holding on to it.

"Touch it again and I'll stick this in your eye." Neo squints his eyes and points the screwdriver at him.

"I'm not sure what to say," I tell Sony. "I want her to know I'm sorry. I pushed her away because I was afraid, but . . ." I graze my wrist.

"Sammy, you overthinking oaf!" Sony yells.

My head tilts. "Oaf?"

"A stupid, uncultured, clumsy person," Neo says, waving his screwdriver around like a teacher with a ruler.

"Oh," I say. "Yeah, that does seem accurate."

"You're making this so much harder than it needs to be." Sony flicks my forehead. "What is Hikari to you?"

"She's my Hamlet."

"Your what?"

"They read *Hamlet* together," Neo says. "Weirdos ruined the spine of my only copy."

"I want to tell her all the things I ever thought but lacked the courage to say. If I'm a stupid, uncultured, and clumsy person, then I want to be *her* stupid, uncultured, clumsy person, be-cause—"

I've never truly written. I'm like a cook who's never held a knife. A tailor who's never seen thread. So how am I meant to tell you, Hikari, that it's because "—she made me dream again."

The room buzzing with anticipating workers goes quiet. We're creating a safe haven. A place with beauty in the physical and metaphorical, but it seems even the furniture and memorabilia mull over what I have to say.

"You both care, Sam," he says. "You just have to show it."

An idea comes to mind then, and just as my pen begins its dance across the page, Hee limps over to the infamously sensitive stepladder. She nudges it with her paw, meowing for attention. It folds, collapsing instantly. Neo falls backward, arms flailing. C catches him, both of them stumbling onto the floor.

Sony and I laugh as smoke rises from Neo's head.

"Not one word," he grumbles, pink shading his face as C hugs him tight and chuckles into his neck.

Neo recovers quick, proud of his work with the string lights. C plugs them into the extension cord and the ceiling comes alive. All I can think of, Hikari, is the smile that'll light your lips when you see them.

"Is it okay?" I ask. Neo reads over the letter I wrote you. He hums every few lines, mumbling critiques to himself.

"You suck at structuring," he finally says, tossing it onto the box.

"I don't know what that means."

"Doesn't matter. It gets the point across. Even if it's boring," he says. "You really felt that way this whole time?"

I nod.

He rubs the back of his neck, then pats the butterfly rash on his face with a wet cloth, and nudges me with his fist. "Then it's a good thing we're here to make you go through with this."

"Sam! Sam!" C yells my name from outside the room, practically tripping over himself as he opens the door. "She's not in her room," he pants, elbows braced on the doorframe. "Her parents were there. They said her doctors had some news, but they don't know where she went. I checked the cafeteria already, but—"

"Did you check the roof?" Sony asks.

"I tried; the door's locked."

"The library maybe?" Sony tries to think.

I hold the box with one hand on the edge, the cardboard digging into the crease of my palm.

Where did you run to, my Hamlet? Your need to escape is what brought us together. The roof, the gardens, the library, ledges, and bridges—I search those places in my mind for you, but they come up empty.

"Guys," Neo says. "She never told us what it is she has. But if she's still here after this long, maybe the news her doctors gave her isn't what she wanted to hear."

You never told me who your killer is. I always knew it lived in your blood, but I was never quite sure just how determined it could be.

A dreaded sort of cloud settles over us.

"C," I say, swallowing on a rough throat. "What's in your hand?"

He unfolds it to reveal a small piece of paper with a torn outline, some smudged writing at the center. "It was on her bulletin board," he says, sliding his thumb across the promise. Tucking its edge between his thumb and forefinger, he opens the cardboard box and places it neatly beside the books.

It reads,

For our newcomer,
I'll steal you a broken thing

"I think," C says, "someone who loves broken things will do." Hee nuzzles against my leg. She purrs, her half ear creased backward. Sony's cat and my friends look to me for guidance, for where to go next.

I've always been a follower. I don't know how to lead. It was always you who pulled me from the backgrounds, from the edges of the frame. It's you who always knew how to read me. On an abandoned stretcher, in a nightly garden, on a ledge, in a place where broken hearts were once healed—

"I know where she is," I whisper.

"Where—"

I break into a run, hopping over Neo's bed and out the door.

"Sam!"

I have nothing in hand. Not our memorabilia, not my pen, not anything. There's a faint image in my peripheral vision of C grabbing the box, Sony and Neo pushing the door to follow me.

I get to the stairwell first and hurl myself down the steps.

I know where you are, Hikari. I know the places your soul finds solace because I know you and I do not need a letter to prove it.

You are compulsively readable. Your eyes, your glasses too big for your face, they never look too far ahead, so what you can't see, you touch. You feel with freedom in a way I both envy and adore.

Your mind is a palace greater than the one we live in. Within it, you hide secrets and the details of people's lives: The line of a song that made C sink into his seat with a peaceful sigh. Neo's favorite chair in the library, the one you always save for him. The candies Sony munches on and the properties she always buys in Monopoly.

Let it be said that you are a sun, but you are also a girl and you are flawed in the most smile-inducing ways. You're messy, clothes strewn about your floor, with no shelf empty of a plant. You never fail to get crumbs and chocolate on your face. You can be blunt and mean, but I know you don't mean to be. Your humor is cynical, but I've never met a person quite so willing to dream.

There are scary parts of you, the darker parts of you. The thoughts of self-hatred bite at your pride because you fell into a pit with a greedy animal. It convinced you to cut away at your skin till it became hilled with scars. It ate your joy, your pain, everything you had until all that was left was the shell of your body, but you survived. You crawled out of the pit and left the animal to starve while you quenched your hunger with books, risks, and a little wind. I promised to protect you from it, from all the shadows, and to never cower should I need to stand between you and their jaws.

I cowered in the face of you instead because I am weak. I am a cowardly creature who couldn't resist your warmth but was too afraid to let myself feel it.

You are warm. You are beautiful. You are kind. You are passionate. You are resilient. And you are lonely, just as I am.

I know you may not forgive me for shutting my eyes and saying I couldn't see your pain, but I am sorry. I'm sorry for letting my past keep me from appreciating the present you gave me.

I want to share it with you, Hikari. I want to show you, even in the darkness of a hall where hearts were once healed, that we can be more than victims of almost. And even if you can't forgive me, I promise to protect you from the shadows, anyway.

I push past two doctors who yell over their shoulders that I need to slow down.

For the first time since I can remember, my voice is alive, and it is for you.

"Hikari!"

The hall's personnel thins the farther I go. Past a corner I once stumbled in, past an old vending machine scuffed by crane kicks, past elevators that once witnessed a spilled tray. Eventually, in that old cardiology wing, my footsteps become the only sound to echo.

They halt once I see you.

Only now, the piano plays no melodies.

No winds dance in your company.

No yellow is left to catch the light.

———

Blood drips from her fingers like rain. It stains her bare legs, smudged teardrops painted red.

She sits against the wall, her shoulders slumped, arms cradling her knees, wearing an examination gown. Her hair, for the first time in weeks, is down. The yellow strands have dulled to a sullen color. And they've begun falling out at the roots.

Her hair tie is on her wrist, neighbored by thin, sloppy slashes. They bleed just above her veins, performed with an instrument sharp enough to cut, but too blunt to kill.

I grab the hem of my shirt and start tearing. The sound rips through the air.

Her eyes peek out just above her arms, but they don't see me. They're barren, sightless, the girl who pulled me from the road nowhere behind them.

"Hikari," I say, sinking to my knees. I take her hand, gently pry it from her legs, and wrap the cloth around her raw, inflamed wrist, a makeshift bandage. "It's okay. You'll be okay."

I bite down as the red seeps through the fabric.

I didn't see it till now. I didn't realize how pale she's become, how a sickly green underlines her jaw and trails the old scar from her collar. I didn't question why she put her hair up more and more. I didn't see that her hope was starting to thin, starting to fall strand by strand until I was the one who pulled it out at the roots.

"Hikari," I whimper. I press my hands to her frigid skin, then to her hair. Her breathing stutters as I touch the edges of the yellow in search of her.

"I thought . . ." Her voice may be faint, scratched at, but it's a lifeline. I listen to her, my eyes wide and reaching. She stares at her hair between my fingers. "I thought I would just go away with time."

"Sam?"

My friends still a few feet away. C's arms sag with the box's weight. Neo and Sony tread cautiously into the isolated corner of the hospital. She doesn't look up or react to any of them.

"Hikari," I say. "I was wrong. I'm so sorry. I was wrong about everything."

I see our enemies crawl onto her shoulders, beckoning her with poisonous promises. They whisper in her ear as viciously as time does in mine. They lull her to their side and they try to take the most precious piece of her.

"Hikari, please," I say. Her cheeks are soft, the weight of her head as much in my hands as on her neck. She doesn't look at me. She doesn't look at anything. She listens to the poison as I once did.

"I know you're hurting, my Hamlet," I whimper, our noses touching. "But don't leave me yet, I'm begging you."

My fingers reach into her hair, the brittle strands coming undone, limp like leaves falling from a tree.

I clench my eyes shut, my forehead falling against her chest. Her heart is slow, beating with lethargy. Her blood runs sluggishly. Her body acts like a cadaver waiting to be emptied.

"I should've been there for you," I whisper, regret hot at the backs of my eyes. "I shouldn't have run away."

"Sam." C tries to pull me away from her.

I twist out of C's grip, getting closer, afraid to be torn away. I remember all the times I should've let my touch travel to hers. All the times we stole together, read together, every moment she coaxed a little life from my bones.

"I'm here, Hikari. I'm here. I'm listening. I believe you," I whisper, my lips barely a breath from hers. I run my fingers to the back of her scalp, shielding it from the wall as I press my forehead against hers.

Hikari doesn't look at me. She doesn't say a thing. The numbness has taken her. The animal in the pit mauls at whatever pain or joy it can scrounge. I see its shadow folding over her, claiming ownership.

I won't let them.

Wiping away the smudge of red on Hikari's cheek, I feel the rim of her glasses against my fingers and the ridge of her nose. Then I cup her face and press my lips to hers.

They're soft yet chapped at the edges, full and evocative of her smiles, her smirks, and all her teasing. I kiss her, long and indulgent, like drawing a breath after drowning. Her glasses brush against my brow. Our noses don't quite fit. But it feels right. It feels pure. It feels like the warmth we shared in our past lives.

I part from her, caressing her face, letting the heat of my breathing keep her from the cold.

But Hikari doesn't look at me.

She doesn't say a thing.

Time's mocking laughter echoes at my back, telling me I am too late.

The cardboard box sits beside me, watching, on the threshold of our distance. Within it, I see all I should've appreciated while it was still mine. I hear the door creak to the roof, Hikari's light shining onto a gray rooftop. Her mischief escapes her lips as she parades her first stolen spoils, me her accomplice. She sits boyishly on Neo's windowsill, marking our tether with a potted plant, her first gift to me. She dances, holding her hands up to give me a sense of comfort, a yellow blanket on her bare legs. Her affection drifts tangibly, her gratitude following on its wing as she held *my* first gift to her heart.

I dig through the box, a pair of scissors at the bottom. I pick them up, all else blurred and muffled. Without method or rhythm or pattern, I start to cut away at my hair. I fist tufts of it, tearing and sliding the blades across like clearing grass from a field.

My friends panic. They all start to yell, grabbing at the scissors, then at my hands, my arms. I fight to get them back. Neo takes the scissors and throws them across the hall. Sony and C both push me to my knees, their terrified voices in my ear, telling me to calm down, to sit, to stop.

I don't really hear them. A familiar liquid, viscous and hot, trails down my forehead.

Pain and I had a neat arrangement. As long as I promised never to feel anything else, it stayed at bay. I broke the contract when I sealed my lips to Hikari's. I broke it when she pulled me from the road. Now it stings and ravages as it pleases.

"Sam." I flinch. Not away from the voice. Toward it.

Hikari stands over me. She kneels slowly till she's close enough to reach out and gather a drop of blood from the hook of my brow.

"You hurt yourself," she says.

I stare in wonder as I did the first time she walked into my life. Her yellow sings, still alive. The shadow recedes as she looks with worry at the red on her fingers that belongs to me.

"This body never felt like mine anyway."

Our eyes meet. Hikari's begin to well. She witnesses the carnage wrapped in my torn shirt and her hair still falling.

"I'm scared, Yorick," she cries. I take her in my arms. Her weight settles against my chest.

"It's okay. You're okay," I whisper. "Fear is just a large shadow with a little spine. I won't let it take you."

There are no string lights or stars or grand gestures to be had. Hikari's illness has not relinquished her, but she did not become it. I form a shield around her body, pulsing with cries as she lets herself feel the pain of it all.

"I don't want to die," she sobs. "I don't want to be alone."

I keep her close, the distance squandered to nothing. I don't look away. I pull her from the road, where she would've been swallowed by greedy souls. I give her back that hope she gave me.

"You're not alone, Hikari," I say. Sony hugs her around the back, interlacing her hand with mine. C pets what is left of her hair, he and Neo wrapping around us. "You're not alone . . ."

She is a part of our story now.

I have stolen her.

She is real.

Flesh and full and fallen and I will love her.

Even if in the end, on the very last page, I will lose her too.

15
before

SAM WAS BORN with a body unfit for the outside world. They say he was pulled from the womb with crumbling bones; blood oozing from his eyes, nose, and mouth; skin so thin it slipped from his flesh; wailing earsplitting cries and cursing all those who touched him.

Those stories aren't true. They're tales children who Sam isn't allowed to play with make up. They say he is separated from them, because he's dangerous, a beast, that he'll swallow them whole.

Disease likes to repulse, both mind and body, tying fear's nooses. Those children snicker into the backs of their hands and spread their story. Like a disease of its own, it takes hold of whoever will listen.

In reality, Sam is just a boy. He was born naked and crying his lungs out like all babies. His body was a bit small, his head was a bit large, but he was nothing monstrous, nothing like what some made him out to be.

His mother only held him once. She cared about him, I think, however much you can care for someone you don't want to know.

The doctors told her he would need constant attention, medication, and therapies, and that he might not grow up to be like other children. She spent the night on the edge of the cot, blood she refused to have cleaned between her legs. Sitting there, she pulled the hem of her dress over the red. She looked into the crib where her baby lay wheezing. Her knuckles caressed his cheek, and her lips laid a kiss on his forehead long enough for a goodbye. She left before the sun rose, and no one ever saw her again.

By his second day of life, Sam was alone.

The reason he can't play with the other children is simple. It is the same reason he can't interact with other patients except through a glass partition. It is why all who come into his room must wear masks and gloves.

Sam's body can't protect itself. It has no shields. A cold that would pass in a week could kill him in a day.

The hospital is all he knows. It is all he can feel without something in the way.

Sometimes, I gaze over while we play with his potted plants and wonder if he'd rather be elsewhere. Sam's fairy tales occur in magical kingdoms, places far less clinical and repetitive than a hospital. I ask him, "Sam, do you want a castle? Do you want enchanted forests and high seas like in your stories?"

Sam hums at my question, adjusting the pots on his windowsill.

"We already live in a castle," he says. "The forests are for our adventures." The adventures he wants to have with me. "And we don't need a sea. The sea is scary. I read a book about it. The sea has a giant whale."

"A giant whale?"

"A giant whale." He hops to my level. "In the book, it ate a whole boat and all the sailors too."

My face falls.

Sam laughs at me. "It's not real; don't feel bad. I couldn't read the book for real anyway. The words are too hard. Nurse Ella just told me the story."

I sigh in relief. Sam snickers. He's amused by me, always amused. We've been playing for a year now, and seldom does he ever not laugh at my misunderstandings.

Sam is allowed to play with me, no mask or gloves in the way.

He is kinetic. He is curious. He touches. When hair starts to grow on my arms, he runs his fingers over the prickles. He presses the joints in my shoulders, in my wrists and ankles, asking me if I've grown through the night. Collars, hems, and sleeves are his fidgets. He grabs and toys with the fabric, asking if he can feel me, the skin of my neck or my stomach.

Children explore physicality. It's part of how they become self-aware. But Sam's body is too medical. It's a vessel, a thing that takes his mind place to place. There are screws missing, its parts improperly put together. Sam says his body isn't *his* at all. It belongs to his disease. It is a problem for his doctors to solve and an engine for his nurses to keep running. Sam's relationship with his body is passive, but since we met, he says he's learning to accept it. I ask him why. He smiles and says without it he could not feel me.

In the mornings, Sam greets his broken things. He passes by all the rooms he can, waving to his sick people. I tag along. In the afternoons, we play together in his room. In the evenings we eat sweet bread and pudding on the roof, no matter the weather. Those are our in-between moments. The rest are for Sam's vessel and its repairs.

I spent so long watching Sam. Living with him is different. He talks and touches without inhibition. It's harder for me.

This body doesn't feel like mine. It is rebellious to exist too much with it. Touching him, interlacing our fingers, dragging my thumb across his palm, letting his pulse beat against my wrist; it feels like indulgence. Sam never thinks much of it. He accepts my touch, and we walk down the hall to witness the stories the hospital has to tell.

One day, in the midst of Sam's many lessons on how to be a knight, he pauses outside a particular room. Inside, a woman lies, feet wrapped in bandages. Pain pulls the strings, knitting her brows and scrunching her nose.

"Her killer is called diabetes," Sam whispers, on his tiptoes to look through the glass.

"Her killer?"

"Mhm," Sam hums. "She's the nice lady who gave us our sweet bread, remember?"

It takes me a moment, but I do. *The nice lady.* The first thing I noticed about her back then was that she stumbled when she walked and that she always drank so much water. What Sam noticed was her warmth and the time she took to stop by his room to gift him treats.

He takes my hand.

"Don't worry, my sweet Sam," he says. "She's strong. She'll make it."

My sweet Sam. That's what he calls me. *Sam* because we share the name. *Sweet* because he says I never leave him feeling bitter. And *my* because I am his. Those three words have become my beck and call, a source of comfort like his touch and the yellow flares in his eyes.

The memories of red smeared across skin and floors alike have not left me. Violence continues to seep into these walls. It finds new shapes to take. Disease does too, skillfully. I've watched

so many people succumb to them both, but Sam begs me to protect the castle and everyone in it anyway. He begs for us to do it
together.

All I want is to make him happy.

So I pretend.

I pretend for weeks, as the kind woman deteriorates, that I
believe Sam when he tells me it'll be okay, not to worry, that she's
strong, and that she'll make it. Sam doesn't ignore that she's becoming an outline of her skeleton fixed beneath the sheets. He
acknowledges she looks worse, but rather than give up, he brings
his potted plants and shows them to her through the window.
Barely able, she turns her cheek, a brief moment of joy interrupting her stillness.

Another few weeks pass, and every morning, Sam and I greet
our sick people, and every morning, we bring the woman bread.
She can't eat it. Sam doesn't know that, but I don't tell him. Since
he isn't allowed past the glass, I am the one who delivers the gifts.
The woman, hardly alive, tries to thank me. I nod and wish her
peace. Sam tells me she'll make it. I lie and say I believe him.

On the first day of summer, despite the agony and her killer's many attempts to pull her under, the nice lady who brings
Sam treats sits up. Color brightens her skin. She sees me passing
by, and with the strength that once battled to keep her alive, she
waves to me. I wave back.

I have to tell Sam.

I'm almost tempted to smile, to mimic the expression he'll
wear when I give him the news. He'll throw himself out of bed
to storm the halls, no matter who's in the way. He'll shriek. He
shrieks when he's excited. But when I reach Sam's room, he isn't
in his bed. He isn't in the room at all.

Down the hall, a noise jostles the air. Here, plenty of sounds are customary. The wheels and gears of a stretcher with a storm of footsteps. Codes, signals, machinery, chatter. This noise is different. This is a subtler sound. I run toward it, the weight of the unknown pressing on my throat. I hear it again, this time louder. It's coming from the supply closet, the large one that's usually locked.

When I push the door open with my entire body, a ruckus of laughs erupts. Laughter can be beautiful, spontaneous. It's one of my favorite things to hear because it is so *un*customary here. This laughter is anything but. It's premeditated, superior, and it falls from the mouths of children beating Sam.

He covers his head instinctively, his elbows beneath his chin, arms covering his ears. One of the taller boys without hair on his head steps on his shoulder. Sam whimpers unwillingly, his teeth stuck together, his muscles braced. The shelves cast shadows, the lack of light outlining shapes and blurred actions.

Nothing obstructs the boys' words as they spit cruel taunts. *Where are your horns and fangs?* They hit him again when he won't answer, prop him up against the wall, and hold him down. *Why do you get your own room? Why do you get special treatment?* A little boy, one even younger than Sam, watches. "Don't touch him," he says. He's smaller than the rest, trying to tug the older boys away, guilt on his tongue. "Don't touch him—he could kill us. It's dangerous. We could die." Sam flinches as if he's been hit again.

The boys aren't done with him. Any movement of life from him is enough to keep probing. Another tries to grab him by the collar. I grab his hand and push him away. He stumbles back into his herd, the other boys following.

I stand in front of Sam.

The children, two of them in hospital gowns, the rest in their own clothes, are all sick, just as he is. The oldest will die soon. The pale green of his skin is telling enough, and he's been here the longest. Another has more meat on his bones, but his wrist is shaky and his eyes bulge. His fist is damaged from hitting. He swallows hard, and though I can't tell you how I know for certain, I know he will pass away within the next few weeks. The rest will leave soon, patients of intermediation, small scars and treatments that the outside world can tolerate.

We've never spoken, but I know them. I've watched them.

They aren't cruel. They've let cruelty consume them. It quickly spits them back out at the sight of me. I don't frighten them. They don't know me. What frightens them is that, like everyone else, they feel like they've met me before.

My gaze, my silence, my unwillingness to move are deterrent enough. They disperse, running out of the room, almost knocking shelves over in the process. Their scurrying sends a shivering breath through Sam as if he's been holding it since they started on him.

Once they're out of sight, I kneel down, push aside his hair, and look at his wounds. He clings to his stomach, wincing when I go near it. His lip is split, a swelling pit gathering color on the side of his face.

"Don't move too much," I mutter. Sam nods, his tongue poking at his lip. The coppery taste makes him frown, and I'm almost too relieved that his biggest discomfort is the bitterness.

I start to carry him back to his room. We're roughly the same size, but for the bravery I lack, I'm stronger than I look. I feel an urge to squeeze him, to show my relief. Instead, I am tender. I hold him with care, the way you hold a box or a tray of food.

Sam whispers an apology into my shirt, saying thank you.

I tell him to be quiet.

He is for a few steps.

"Why do they hate me?" he finally asks.

"They don't hate you," I promise him.

"They hurt me." His voice cracks. "Why do they hurt me?"

"Because they're weak," I explain. "Hurting you gives them power. Or at least an illusion of it."

"They want power?" Sam asks. "Like evil kings and queens in fairy tales?"

"No." I shake my head. "More like . . . sailors," I say, turning into his room. "It's easier to pretend you, someone as small and weak as them, are the enemy when there's a whale circling the boat."

I place Sam gently back in his bed. I ask him if his stomach still hurts. He nods, wincing. I tell him I'll go get help. He whines when I try to leave, but it fades at the end. His eyes start to close, fluttering, his consciousness fading.

"Sam?" I call, but he doesn't hear me. He's gone, a fit over-taking him. He must've hit his head in the closet. A seizure scours his nerves, convulsing through him.

I yell for someone, anyone, propping Sam on his left side. I yell so hard my throat tears. And when the seizure ends, Sam's heart stops.

———

I can leave my body as I wish. That is how I can tell you things you think I shouldn't know. It is how I can be a narrator even for the scenes I am not a part of.

A body is merely something through which I can be per-ceived. All I have to do is be completely still, and then I travel. Into the wall, the ceiling, the windows, anywhere at all. I can spectate in any part of this place, not just the hospital, but the stretch of its influence.

In the simplest of terms, I am a soul like all those Sam likes to greet. I've always been able to watch, to see, but I've never lived. I don't have a life, as people do. I am a narrator. Narrators watch.

But I became greedy. I'd had far too many violent, bloody tales to tell. It was through Sam that I learned how to create peaceful ones.

It's been thirteen days since the woman I was sure would pass away got better, and it's been thirteen days since Sam fell unconscious.

The door creaks open, letting in a thin cut of light as the woman walks in. It gleams on Sam, bypassing my shadow in the chair next to him.

The woman wears sadness beneath her mask. With her gloves on, she hands me two sweet breads wrapped in wax paper. She tells me she made them for him, for when he wakes up.

The woman, in her kindness, made a mistake just now.

She said *when*. *When* Sam wakes up. That single word could hold such power if only it weren't a lie. I want to believe, looking at his shut eyes and quiet body, that he will wake. But time does not grant me a *when*. It is not that generous. It grants me an *if* . . .

Sometimes, in the middle of the night, I find myself crying. A tear, slow and soft, trails down my cheek and catches on my jaw. I hook it with my finger, feel the wetness, taste its salt. Then more tears well. They fall as I press myself against Sam's bed and lay my face on his pillow. I used to touch his hair, his nose, his hands, but I can't anymore. They're too limp, too empty of him. Instead, I beg silently through the dark,

"Wake up." Again, louder, "Wake up, please." Selfishly, "Wake up, Sam, for me."

He doesn't. He's elsewhere, in another castle, in an enchanted forest, swimming in a sea as the whale circles, circles, circles.

———

"Sweet Sam?" A voice. It's faint, raspy. The throat that bore it hasn't been used in some time. "My sweet Sam, wake up."

I open my eyes to a still, dark room. The ventilator hums on-ward, a machine of endlessness. But when I look up, the mask through which it breathed isn't on. Sam holds it away from his face.

He is awake. Sam is awake, eyes half-lidded but still brilliant, full of light and life and him.

I shudder, pushing myself out of the chair so hard it falls over.

"I'm here," I say, grasping the edge of his sheets, pulling the mask off entirely. It catches in his hair, making Sam wince. I smooth it down apologetically, but at the same time, I am re-lieved. I am relieved he can express anything, even if it's discom-fort. I am so relieved his face scrunches up, and his body jumps on reflex. I am relieved his chest rises and falls on its own, the sounds of the ventilator silenced by his breathing.

"My sweet Sam," he says again, a tired curve of his lips re-vealing a crooked row of happy teeth. "My sweet Sam, could you hold my hand? I don't feel my best."

"Yes," I say, although it's more a whisper. His palm meets mine, his fingers slow, his skin cold but radiating life. His cuts and bruises healed while he was asleep, but there is still a mark on his wrist, a scar.

"You're so warm," Sam says, and like water, his light flows through my veins.

"Look," I say, lifting our fingers, showing him our tether. "Our hands are kissing." Sam's bangs get in his eyes, so I cast them gently back. He sighs and follows my touch, falling into it.

"Are you in pain?" I ask.

"No," he says. "My knight is here."

He's lying. We both know, but neither one of us says it. He's been kept alive through various tubes, an IV for liquids, isotonic fluids to keep his blood balanced, and another for nutrients. The suddenness of waking up is shocking.

Sam vomits on the floor. I lift his upper body up and cradle it so he doesn't get any on himself. His stomach is empty, acid burning his throat and tongue.

Nurse Ella rushes in to care for him. Two doctors enter too. They waste no time flashing lights in Sam's eyes and asking too many questions at once. I stand back, against the wall. Sam looks at me the entire time he is examined.

"Thank you for protecting me," he rasps after the doctors have gone. I drag the pad of my finger over the scar on his wrist.

"I'll always protect you," I say, sitting in my chair now, staring at our hands.

"Did you go see our stars while I was asleep?" Sam asks. "They'll be sad if no one comes to say good night for too long."

"They aren't shining today," I tell him.

"That's okay," Sam says. "They'll shine tomorrow."

Tomorrow is already here. Dawn washes over the skyline in the distance, blacks becoming blues, easing into the day. I shake, thinking that this would've been the fourteenth tally in my head. That if he hadn't woken up, I would still be in that chair wondering if he ever would.

"Sam?" I say.

"Yes?"

"Could I—could I hold you?"

Sam nods, and when I climb into the bed, he wraps his arms around me. His touch runs down my back, kneading my shirt, feeling my skin, my spine, my flesh beneath.

"My sweet Sam, don't cry over me," he says as he feels my tears I don't know how to control fall to his shoulder. "I'm strong. I'll make it. We still have so many adventures to go on."

"How do you know?" I ask. "How do you know that you'll make it? How did you know the woman would make it?"

"I didn't know," Sam says, his chin on my shoulder. "I just hoped she would."

I wanted an answer. I wanted, as I have wanted since I was born, a solution, a way to defeat the three thieves who encroach upon my home and reap it of its life. But as Sam speaks, he gives me that one thing I can't fathom. He gives me another lock rather than a key.

"Hope?" The word tastes elder, a truth of the world, yet so young, like a secret.

"Mhm," Sam hums. "Hope is like . . ." He shifts, his chin against my ear now rather than my neck. "Hope is like waiting for the sun to rise," he says, looking through his window, greeting the sky. "We don't know if the stars will shine or if the sun will be here tomorrow, but I trust the stars. I trust the sun too."

"I don't understand," I breathe.

Sam's heart beats against mine. The rush of blood coursing through his neck, the pulse I can feel, calms me. His aliveness, his heat—it all feels so uncertain, but his heart, even if I fear it will stop, keeps going.

"I hoped for you, once," Sam says after a while. "I dreamt, with all my heart, for someone, anyone in the world, to be mine." He holds me tighter. His hand snakes through my hair, and a tear rolls down his face.

I can only think as he touches me that his hands are mine, as he kisses my cheek that his lips are mine, as he talks that his words are mine. That he is mine. My light, my reason. I wonder if my wish for answers came true. I wonder if we were each other's wishes.

"I don't understand."

"That's okay," Sam whispers. "It doesn't have to make sense."

We don't talk anymore after that.

He just kisses my face till the sun rises.

16
now

AUTUMN DESCENDS UPON our city. Jaded greens fade into tan oranges and sulky reds, tinges of yellow bloom in the cold.

I wrap my arms around Hikari's waist. Melodies like piano notes escape her in wavelets, a loose fabric dress fanning her bare legs. She folds Neo's freshly washed shirts and hoodies (most of which aren't his), dropping each item onto the windowsill.

Her sweater is all that covers the bandages trailing down her arms. We share a haircut, hers a thin shade of black, mine like infant stalks of grass. After I "terrorized" my scalp, as Eric said, he went to work with clippers.

That night, Hikari and I slept in her bed. I held her the whole night through. She told me she was okay, that if I wanted to go, I could. I shook my head and pulled her closer. The next morning, I woke to her fingers drawing patterns on my face as dawn slid through the blinds. She smiled. A smile like the sunrise after a rainstorm.

"Sam?" Hikari says.

"Yes?"

"You're doing it again."

I fumble with her fingers, observing how they intertwine with mine. The scent of her soap and the softness of her neck coax my chin to her shoulder.

I've found that touching Hikari is different from touching other people. A stranger may brush my side walking past. A nurse may graze my arm handing me something. But those are dull touches, intermediate touches. Touching Hikari for the first time was eclipsing, the birth of a star, but as time goes on, the eclipse becomes habitual. Comfortable. Ritualistic.

"You're distracting me." Hikari folds Neo's shirt and tosses it to the side, starting on another, her tongue between her teeth with focus.

I chuckle. "I'm not distracting. You're just messy."

"You *are* distracting. And rude."

"Not on purpose," I whine.

"Most definitely on purpose."

Absentmindedly, I splay my hands over her stomach. She's warm there. Her pulse thrums just above her hip bone.

"I like distracting you," I tease.

"I like when you keep your arms to yourself," she whispers, turning her head so our faces are but centimeters apart.

"What arms?" I whisper back.

"Rude."

"Messy."

"Disgusting!" Neo throws a pen at us. "Isn't it bad enough I have to see you engage in your cute couple crap? Now I have to hear it too?" He points to the nurse call button meant for emergencies. "I'll push that thing. Don't test me."

"Sorry, Neo." Hikari laughs. Neo rolls his eyes, pulling another pen out from its cup holder at the edge of the desk, getting back to work. The desk was Eric's gift to him for his birthday, so he could stop screwing up his back, Eric said. It was also a congratulatory present because Neo and Coeur are almost done writing their novel.

I can tell that makes Neo nervous.

He scratches his head where the hair has been reduced to a layer of fuzz. After Hikari and I shaved our heads, it became a unifying force. C's curls were already short, but he sat on the stool right after me, like a little boy giddy for a haircut. But it was Sony who was, by far, the most enthusiastic. Right after her hair was shaven to a thin coat of red, she practically tackled Hikari, begging her to draw them together.

It turned out there wasn't much time for that. After our failed escape, Sony's lung decided to strengthen a few races' worth. Since then, she's been living in Eric's apartment.

Outside Neo's room, I catch sight of her through the glass. Her animation captivates the child she talks to. The boy laughs, his cheeks curving up to his eyes. Sony pokes his nose and hugs him tight, her feet pitter-pattering as she does. When the boy's mother takes his hand, Sony adjusts his coat and the cap snug on his head. She tells him goodbye, a rendition of *I'll miss you* on her lips as he goes home.

"My fellow pirates, I've had an epiphany," Sony says, kicking Neo's door open, her backpack void of a tank or breathing tubes to adorn her face. Hee follows in before the door closes, meowing for attention and winding between my and Hikari's legs.

"I am a lazy waste of energy according to many"—Eric—"and I think it's due time I retire from my days of stealing."

"What do you mean?" Hikari asks. Like tragedy's just struck. She slaps my hands off of her, rushing to her fellow thief. "You don't want to steal anymore? Is the world ending?"

"Sadly, no," Sony says, waving at the air. "But I don't know, I thought maybe I could get a job or something."

"Sony," I say. She leans back on Neo's bed. "You want to work with your kids?"

"Yeah," she says. Thoughts of the children she plays with in the oncology wing widen her grin. "I'm happy here."

"Thank God," Hikari groans, falling on top of Sony. "I thought you were leaving me for some boring city job."

Sony snorts out a laugh. "Oh, please, no one would willingly hire me. I work hard to be this unbearable." She wraps her arms around Hikari and pecks her face all over. "I'm gonna make Eric get me the job. We have grouchy boys and grouchy nurses to annoy together. I'd never let you do it all on your own."

"You promise?" Hikari asks, pouting.

"Hell yeah—oh, Baby!" Both Hee and Neo startle at Sony's volume, hair at the backs of their necks standing on end.

"You're almost done!" she cheers, hopping to his desk. "Is that my sweatshirt?"

"It's mine," Neo says, possessively clutching the hoodie on his back. "What do you want?"

Sony fishes around in her backpack. She removes a handful of leaves from the front pocket, holding all the different colors out like playing cards.

"I brought you these from the park."

Neo frowns. "Why?"

Sony doesn't answer. She places them gently on his desk and violently swipes the entire top half of the manuscript into her arms.

"Hey!" Neo yells. Sony skips out of reach, jumping back-first into his bed and holding the papers over her head. "What do you think you're doing?"

"It's quid pro quo," I say.

Neo shoots me a glare. "Shut up, Sam."

"Hikari, you should draw the cover," Sony says.

"No one's drawing anything. It's not finished yet."

"I can't wait to see it on a shelf, Neo." Sony sighs, flipping through the pages as if the words are written in gold. "Then I get to tell everyone I was the first to read it."

A blush runs across Neo's cheeks.

"Whatever," he mutters. "Just don't lose it."

Neo's gained color since fall struck. His butterfly rashes and fits of pain have subsided. He hasn't spit out his pills or taken out his IVs since C got discharged. His anorexia remains an uphill battle. There are days he stares at his plate, picking it apart until it all seems like too much, and he has to push it away. The only time he comes close to finishing his meals is when we eat with him. And when C brings him apples.

C's been on bed rest, perpetually ignoring the fact that he's on bed rest. Given how close he lives to the hospital, he's *rarely* bed resting. If he is, it's next to Neo, sleeping with his mouth open and mumbling in his dreams. Otherwise, he acts as if all is right with the world. Like he isn't nearing the top of the transplant list. He goes for walks with Hikari, apologizing to local bakers when she steals a pastry and paying for her misdeeds. He paces while reading his and Neo's story, obsessing over every detail. He dances with the cat and plays board games with Sony, half here, half elsewhere.

His parents have tried everything. Locking his door. Taking his car keys. Lecturing. Ultimatums. Warnings. Nothing works. C always finds his way back to us.

"You all right, Sam?" Hikari asks.

I'm staring at her. I do that a lot.

Her skin has *lost* color. It's a thin gray, like parchment turning to ash. That's why I hold her this way. She's sick, and I'm not so blind anymore that I choose to ignore it. I worry during her coughing fits. During exhausting bouts that lull her to sleep for days on end.

"Can *we* read tonight?" I ask, dragging my thumb over Hikari's lower lip, admiring the fullness.

She smirks, mirroring my motions. "The lonely stretcher at six?"

Comfort works through me with her voice, for it's always been satin and coquettish, but it has never been mine till now.

"Mhm," I hum. I drag my touch over her arms, the slope of her bandages ending at her wrists. The animal in the pit hasn't dared to bite since that bloody night. When any other shadows try creeping into her head, they catch sight of me standing guard, and with spit slavering from their mouths, they slip back into the dark.

Neo's door opens then. Sony pitches herself upright. Hikari and Neo beam, expecting C to stride in, leaving a trail with his shoes, bag, and coat.

But it isn't C.

"Dad?" Neo breathes.

A man walks in with the posture of a soldier, adjusting his coat. His hair is cropped and neat, his face chiseled and wide. When he closes the door behind him, silence falls over the room.

I grasp Hikari's hand, a reflex, pulling her closer to me.

"Hello," Neo's dad says, pleasantly surprised by the number of people in the room. "You must be Neo's friends."

He wasn't supposed to be here today. His presence is a rustle in the bush, a snapping stick, our ears perked like deer sensing a wolf.

Sony stands up from the bed, holding the stack of papers at

her hip as if it belongs to her. Hikari says nothing. Her jaw is wound tight, and attention is drawn to the box of books in the corner.

"Good to meet you, sir—I'm Sony, this is Hikari," Sony says. Her church bell voice is tamed, shaking at the ends. She walks backward, the coyness a symptom of caution. "That's Sam."

"Sam, yes," Neo's father says. "You bring Neo his dinner."

"Dad," Neo whispers, his hands gripping the edges of the chair by his thighs.

"Don't be embarrassed. I'm happy to see you being social." He walks past Sony, rubbing his son's shoulder. Sony eyes his hand like it's a knife scraping the surface of Neo's skin.

Neo tenses from the touch. His gaze fixes on the lines in the tiles.

"I wasn't sure if Neo had any friends till now." His father pats his head like a pet but stills when he notices the change. "What'd you do to your hair?"

"Is Neo's mom coming?" I ask.

I'm buying time. Or at least bargaining with it.

The distraction seems to work. He looks my way, surprised, as if he remembers me being far more docile. Maybe I was. Interfering is a great sin because of what I am, but Neo is the one who told me to step into the pages.

"No," his father says. "I just got back from a business trip, and she had errands to run for Neo's cousins—"

Tension curls at the cutoff. Neo's father finally sees the work spread about the desk. The hundreds of handwritten pages in the far corner. The pen in Neo's lap.

He sighs, shoulders slacking, a hardness passing over his face as he draws his hand over his jaw and reads over a few exposed lines.

The silence cuts through Neo. He shuts his eyes like he's bracing for impact.

"Are Neo's cousins academics too?" Hikari asks. She stands without strain, her arms crossed, defiance like a glint in her tone. "Sony's thinking of getting a job here, helping out with the kids. Neo's been helping her with her writing skills for her application."

Hikari is a seasoned liar, but this man knows his son.

"He's always been smart, that's for sure," he says, looking straight at Hikari. Picking a fight with someone like him is dangerous. Baiting him is far worse. Hikari doesn't seem to care. She dares him with nothing but a look to try and see what happens if he challenges her.

"I don't mean to be rude." Neo's father doesn't care about the writing. "But would you mind giving us some privacy?" He cares about Neo's defiance, no matter its shape.

Sony's heart falls in her chest. She stutters over her next set of words, stepping beside Neo's chair. "Um, well—"

Neo grabs her sleeve so hard he shakes. He chews on the inside of his cheek, slowly looking up at her out of the corner of his eye. A silent message passes between them, a signal that can only mean one thing.

Sony doesn't want to leave. None of us does. But it's Neo's decision.

"All right," she whispers. She squeezes Neo's hand over the material of her sweatshirt, biting her tongue as she begrudgingly walks away.

Hikari doesn't ask before grabbing the cardboard box in the far corner full of Neo's books.

"Sony, don't forget your papers," she says, clearing Neo's desk with one swipe of her arm. The papers collapse into the box, safeguarded.

"Right," Sony says, helping her gather any straggling sheets.

I haven't moved from where I stand. I stare at Neo's father, recollections playing back like film frames. Every memory I can scrounge of Neo smiling has been followed by that man and his transgressions. It's almost as if he can feel Neo's happiness in the air. And if it doesn't stem from him, he finds an excuse to destroy it.

"Sam," Hikari says, motioning for me to follow them out.

There's only one person I can possibly think of who could challenge Neo's pride, and I'd recognize his footsteps anywhere.

Hikari whispers, "Sam——"

"Wait just a second."

When the door opens a second time, it's to a whistling tune. Wearing a scarf made of earbud wires and a high school varsity jacket, C strolls in, humming a string of music notes.

"Neo, I got my essay back. Still didn't get an A, but I finally understand what a semicolon is. Sort of. I think." He kicks off his shoes, balancing himself against the doorframe. "Sorry I'm late, by the way. My parents were home, so I had to sneak out through my window and take my dad's tru——"

C stops in the center of the room. The thunder in his chest becomes practically audible.

"Coeur," Neo says. He tries to swallow his fear, playing it off. "Go. I'll come to find you later."

"Coeur," Neo's dad repeats, like he remembers hearing a similar name but can't quite place it. He notices the jacket, a curt smile on his lips. "You go to Neo's school. Are you an athlete?"

C takes a moment to find his speech.

"I was," he says. "I'm not anymore."

Neo's father must've seen C's name in the papers, must've heard about the boy who nearly drowned and was told he could never swim again. He quickly recognizes him, clearing his throat awkwardly.

"That's right. I'm sorry."

"Don't be," C says. "Turns out I'm more of a reader, anyway."

"Coeur," Neo says, practically shaking in his chair. "I'll be right out. Go."

One thing C and I have always related to is the point of our elsewheres. Mine is traveling through inanimates. C's is in the mind. He retires there with half his consciousness because it's a peaceful place where reality can be what he wants it to be. It's a world where lies turn into truths, and C can tell himself whatever stories fit a comfortable narrative.

I can see it going through his head. Those little lies.

That day he walked past a seemingly innocent scene. Neo and the boys from his team by the lockers. The bevy of bruises he's found on Neo's body, the subtle ones, the aggravated ones, every single odd hue. Every occurrence when he walked into his lamb's pen to find the same shadow of a wolf against the wall and did nothing.

C closes his hand around the shoulder strap of his bag, and now all of him is present.

"No, I think I'll wait here," he says, turning around and grabbing the extra chair by the bed, putting it next to the desk.

"Um, Coeur." Neo's dad clears his throat. "Neo and I have some things to discuss, if you don't mind—"

"I don't mind," C says. He mimics the same polite, flat tone Neo's father uses. Taking a notebook out of his bag along with his phone to plug his earbuds into, he pretends to work on homework, tapping his ear. "My hearing's faulty, anyway."

"C, c'mon—" Hikari says, grabbing his shoulder.

"Young man—"

"Yes?"

"Listen to your friend." Neo's dad's voice drops. "Before I get security involved."

C's voice drops lower. "I'm not leaving him alone with you."

Neo's dad looks to his son.

"What have you been saying?"

"Nothing," Neo says, panicking. "I didn't say anything."

"He didn't need to say anything," C says, leaning back in his chair. "The second you slip up and leave the blinds open or put one of those bruises somewhere more visible, *I'll* be the one calling security."

C's never been bold. And as he pointed out, he isn't an athlete anymore. His heart is on its last legs, and his skin bruises with a flick.

"Dad?" Neo is familiar with the look of rage clouding his father's vision. He swings his arm past Neo, pulling C up by his collar.

"Dad, no! Please!" Neo begs, whimpering. Sony and Hikari try to step forward, but C waves them away.

"Please don't hurt him," Neo cries. He grabs at the hem of his father's coat, his fingers trembling. "Dad, take my books, take everything, just leave him alone, please—"

"Quiet!" Neo's dad yells, the arm that isn't holding C raised, like an ax threatening to fall. Neo flinches hard, hiding his face.

"Touch him again," C bites, reaching for breath. "Do it. Give me a reason."

Neo's dad turns around, presumably to grab Neo and show C exactly who's in charge. Hikari and Sony let out a second's scream when he does. Because instead of grabbing Neo, he's met with me.

On reflex, Neo's dad grabs my shoulder to push me aside, but I don't budge.

The room goes silent. Neo's father suddenly looks uncertain.

"I know, it's odd. I'm stronger than I look," I say, holding the chair's back behind me.

Neo's dad looks at me the way everyone does when they get that funny feeling in their gut. That they know me. That they've met me before. That I somehow have more power than I seem to from afar.

I can feel his lungs. I can feel his heart racing as the stunned look on his face gradually turns back into anger.

"I understand why you do what you do," I say. He wants control, and when it slips away, he uses violence to get it back. The pattern is common. A rule that men have turned a blind eye to for centuries. Because none of them can get their heads around the fact that: "Control doesn't exist, sir. Only uncertainty does." It dawns on me that he doesn't realize how serious I'm being. That none of this is mockery, and all of it is truth. "And unless you leave right now, I'm not certain you'll leave this room without an escort."

I hold up the nurse call button connected to the wall. It blinks red. Neo's dad looks out of the corner of his eye. The blinds are barely drawn, but even through the thin lines, you can see Eric at his station, noting a chart and checking his pager.

Neo's father lets me go. He rubs his hand over his face, much like he did when he entered. He straightens his jacket, looking down at Neo, who's staring at the ground, squeezing his wrist so hard his hand could fall dead from the joint.

"It was my mistake letting your doctors keep you here this long," he says. "I should've handled your tantrums myself." He leaves with a threat of his own, the kind that drives a final prick of fear through Neo's chest. "I'll be back with your mother."

The moment the door shuts, we all exhale audibly, like a tense muscle finally released from flexion.

"Are you okay?" Hikari wraps her arms around me.

Neo shudders in his chair, his hand curled into a fist against his mouth. He pushes the bile back down his throat, petrified.

The only reason his father didn't drag Neo out of here by his hair is because he *needs* Neo's mom. She's the one who signed everything when Neo was admitted for his anorexia, and his doctors will only recommend he can go home when his weight is over a certain point and he's eating regularly.

"Neo, it's okay, you're okay," C says, falling to his knees beside the chair. He takes Neo's hand away from his lips.

Sony presses her palm against Neo's spine.

"We'll call your mom," she says. "She'll calm him down. She'll take care of you."

"No, no, my mom's too scared of him," Neo whimpers.

C's anger fulminates, like if he was physically capable he'd chase down Neo's father and finish what he started. "Screw that. We'll tell Eric; we have proof—"

"No, he'll kill me, he's going to kill me," Neo says, and what breaks me is it sounds like he truly believes that.

"He's not laying a finger on you," C growls. "Not while I'm breathing."

The cozy colors ease back into the room, the tension Neo's father brought to it draining from it drop by drop. Sony, Hikari, and C try to comfort Neo, but he's stuck. Stuck in a perpetual loop of wondering what pain his father's return will hold.

The large window that was looking forward to welcoming him glimmers, as if the sun is looking through a lens. I turn to it, the expanse of our city reaching across the bridge.

The waters rage in the fall, overflowing from end-of-summer rains. It's in the winter that they calm to a black stillness. I can practically hear the cascades, the drowning force of that one crossover that never failed to reject me.

Today, I find myself unafraid to stare it down. The dread that twists my stomach like a rag upon seeing it never comes. Instead, I can see past it, a semblance of what C and Neo call Heaven taking shape in a possibility *I* used to reject.

"We can run away," I say.

C makes a noise. "Sam, this isn't the time—"

"I'm serious." I turn around to face my friends. "We never did have that escape, did we?"

"Sam." Hikari looks at me through her glasses, concerned. "Are you sure about this?"

"It's what you all wanted, right?" I ask. "Do you still want to?"

They look at one another, like they're checking to make sure I'm not insane. Neo comes back to reality, looking me in the face. He knows I want to save him. He knows, more than that, that I want to stand beside him.

"C," I call. "You have your dad's truck?"

"Yeah," he says, the keys jingling in his pocket.

Eric's key card is still in mine. I take it out, flipping it once the way Sony flips a pack of cigarettes.

Sony smirks. She looks to Neo for a final say. "Now?"

Neo thinks it over. But whether in wheelchair, on crutches, or feet, he's never been able to escape the impetus of our missions. He stands, his legs wobbly like his desk's, staring at the story we salvaged.

"Now."

17
tears of joy

"RACE YOU TO the car!"

"Sony, stop running!" I yell.

Her laughter vibrates down her body like chills, dirty white sneakers smacking against the sidewalk. The back exit isn't busy this time of day. We manage to make it through without anyone stopping us and asking where the hell we think we're going.

Neo's hood hides his face as he scurries with his papers nestled against his chest. C is right behind him, fumbling with the car keys.

"Crap—crap—crap—" he curses under his breath, finally managing to unlock the doors. Neo climbs into the truck's front seat while Sony throws herself in the back.

Hikari ran back inside, to get something important, she said. I keep looking over my shoulder, waiting for her to come running back out.

"You can drive, right?" Neo asks.

"Sure," C says.

"Sure?"

"I can drive."

"But you have your license, right?"

"I took my driver's test."

"And *passed*, right?"

"Neo, it's rude to ask about grades."

"It's rude to get us killed in a car accident."

"There's Hikari!" Sony yells, pointing out the window.

Sundress swaying around her legs and sprinting back to us, Hikari throws an arm up in the air, a prize in hand. The metal spirals catch the light, the front page torn off. Hikari smiles at me through the glass. Victorious smile. Contagious smile.

C starts the car.

Hikari doesn't bother opening the door. She throws herself through the open window, flipping over, her legs landing on my lap. We all shriek at the same time. Hikari's glasses almost fly off her face.

"The hit list!" Sony yells.

"*Our* hit list," Hikari pants, reaching across me to kiss her face. "Let's go, C!" she yells.

Neo huffs out a breath, bracing. "Put on your seat belts."

"Put on some music!" Sony throws both arms up, bouncing in her seat. C turns on the radio, the engine rumbling as he drives it out of the parking space and onto the road. The turn is a tad dramatic, more of a swerve, really. The visitor pass on the dashboard flies to the opposite end. Neo hits an imaginary brake with his foot, holding on to the door and seat for dear life.

"Wanna hold my hand?" C asks.

"I want your hands on the wheel. Look where you're going! Coeur!" Neo tries to protest, but before he can, C interlaces their fingers and brings Neo's knuckles to his lips. He gives him a side-eye, a crooked grin playing on his face. "Let's go have that sixteenth-century heartbreak on a beach," he whispers.

Neo doesn't blush like you'd think he would. Instead, he looks directly at C's profile, unspoken gratitude in his gaze.

As we pull out on the street, the hospital shrinks in the rear-view mirror.

I look over my shoulder again, this time at the buildings swallowing my home's image. A nervous flutter runs through me. The farther we get, the more I think maybe we're making a mistake.

I can hear the water, the bridge we near with every ticking second. I can hear the snow, the shadows, all of it whispering that I am violating a law of nature, that I'm spreading myself thin across my world, straying too far from my palace.

We near the bridge, my entire body tensing. C turns into another lane. I brace for impact as we drive into the tunnel that takes us to the other side of the river.

I grab Hikari's hand hard and press my face against her sternum. My instinct to shield her from the dark overtakes me. I hear the echoes of what has been and what will be. Then my eyes shut, and the shadows envelop us.

"Sam," Hikari whispers, her lips against my ear. "Sam, look."

When I do, I realize no one is in the tunnel but us. C's truck is lonesome, trekking the road. And above us, light streaks in stripes across the ceiling, moving so quickly you can barely catch them.

C drives on, dragging his thumb back and forth over Neo's knuckles on the gearshift. Neo lets the cool air caress his face, leaning back against the headrest with closed eyes. Sony chuckles, reaching out the window like she could grab freedom by the hand.

Hikari holds me, leaning her head all the way back on the door and staring up at the cavernous lights. She has no hair to flow behind her. Even so, the wind hasn't lost its infatuation. It takes to her as it did on that rooftop on our very first night.

"You're beautiful," I breathe.

Hikari slowly raises her head, still rocking to the music. She links her wrists behind my neck.

"So are you, my beautiful set of bones," she whispers back.

"Not bones anymore," I say, leaning into her when she tries to lean away. "You brought me to life."

"And I'm only just beginning," Hikari says. She kisses me on the nose, quick and briefly connecting. "I've yet to make you dream, Yorick."

We emerge from the tunnel, on the other side of the river.

We have no provisions, no stolen apples, no safety nets. Our only possessions are made of ink and paper and the clothes on our backs. We are aimless, but aimless adventures become the greatest stories.

This is it, I think, *this is our escape.*

————

Our first stop is unprompted. We were driving along to classic rock stations when C said he was hungry. Neo reminds him he has about five dollars in his wallet. Hikari then says she has ten. Sony says she has ninety cents. (Sony is a natural freeloader, as thieves must be. Those ninety cents came from a fountain she decided to swim in the other day for no particular reason.)

C drives the truck to a parking lot with a variety of stores and restaurants all stuck to one another.

I've never been this far from the hospital before. As such, I've never had the luck of smelling a fast-food restaurant. The scent of the french fries is ethereal, like palpable heat and salt. We eat them in the car.

Hikari gets ketchup on her face. I mock her, and she stuffs fries in my mouth to shut me up. Sony plays I Spy with Neo. He ends up eating about half his portion and giving her the rest. She eats like a starving animal, her mouth a veritable black hole for hamburgers.

Just as Sony finishes chewing a bite the size of a tennis ball, she screams.

"Are you okay?!" C asks.

Hikari instinctively reaches under the front seat. We brought an oxygen tank just in case.

"What the hell is wrong with you?!" Neo yells.

"Look!" Sony's greasy hands press against the glass as she points to the building adjacent to our restaurant.

————

"Hi. Can I help you?" The attendant behind the desk has a single nose piercing and trails of ink mapping his neck from jaw to collar. He sits with a magazine on a crossed leg, his attention diverted to the five nearly hairless people who just walked into his parlor.

"We would like five tattoos, please!" Sony exclaims.

"Um, okay," the front desk man says, looking between all of us like he isn't sure whether we're in a cult or just think military cuts are in season. "Do you have any designs in mind? The cost—"

"Oh no, we don't have any money," Sony says.

The man opens his mouth, and nothing comes out for a moment.

"But you want tattoos?" he asks.

"Yes!" Sony says. "We are tragically ill. Neo, this sickly young chap here, he'll probably drop dead tomorrow!"

Neo nods his chin. "'Sup."

"Uh, hi, boss! I need help up here!"

Emerging from behind another wall, a man considerably balder than we are marches out of his office.

"What the fuck do you want, Carl?"

Carl points at us cluelessly. "They don't have money."

Bald Boss cocks a brow at us. "You don't have money?"

"We have fifteen dollars and ninety cents," C says.

Sony snickers. "Hah, nice."

"Get out," Bald Boss says, then turns back to Carl. "There. Was that so hard?"

"But—they're tragically ill," Carl says.

"So?" Bald Boss smacks the back of his head in a very Eric sort of way. "We don't take pity cases."

Sony clears her throat. At this point in time, the other tattoo artists in the parlor have already started looking in our general direction.

C bends down to our fearless leader's level. "Sony, before you open your mouth, please remember that I've never been beaten up before, and I don't know how well I'd handle it."

Neo holds his manuscript against his chest, nudging C with his elbow. "It's fine. I'll teach you."

"Sir! A moment of your attention," Sony calls.

Hikari looks at me. "She's gonna get us arrested, isn't she?"

"We may not have a method of payment, but money itself is a scheme!" Sony begins, quite theatrically, for that matter. "A story is worth more than a crumpled bill. Money is an illusion of security. And yeah, yeah, money can't buy happiness, but more important, money can't *replace* happiness. It can't replace a memory of dancing on a rooftop or the adrenaline you felt running away with your friends.

"So we all agree that the crumpled bill is worth something to society. Do you know what conforming to society is, sir? It's cowardly! I mean, look at us! Sure, our diseases don't make us who we are, but diseases are like pets. When you're out with one in public, some people are repulsed, some are intrigued, but everyone is watching. It's all they can see. And death may as well be a pet leashed to our wrists.

"My point is that we don't have the luxury of being cowards. We're like everybody else. We're like you, even. We just know the value of today is infinitely greater than the value of tomorrow.

"So take a risk! Make a lousy investment and tattoo some people with missing body parts, prosperity be damned! Because you know in your heart that sharing this story and a few laughs will have more value than making a few bucks ever will.

"Now. Are you going to take the pity cases or not? 'Cause I'm about to faint from lack of air here, so I could really use somewhere to sit."

Sony's voice falters at the end as she lays her upper body weight on the counter. Hikari helps her remain upright from behind while Bald Boss stares in bewilderment. He blinks a few times, his lips slightly parted.

Then eventually, he marches back into his office, grabs a coat, and starts to leave.

"You. Sit in that chair," he says to Sony. "Carl, you take them."

"Boss?"

"I'm going out for a drink."

"Sony has that effect on people," Neo says.

Hikari and I look at each other and shrug. None of us are really shocked at Sony's bullshitting abilities. We're just impressed they worked.

Carl leads us to one of the hydraulic chairs. Sony plops herself down, shimmying in excitement. Carl puts on his gloves, gathering his supplies.

"Um, that was amazing, by the way," he says.

Sony looks at him blankly. "What was?"

Carl points back to the front desk. "What you said."

"Oh, that?" Sony's teeth gleam. "I stole it from a book."

"Everything's stolen from books anyway," Carl says.

"Everything's stolen," Sony rebuts, poking his nose ring as if he's a close friend and not some stranger, although Carl doesn't seem to mind. "Or it will be. By us. We're killer thieves."

Carl smirks. "Where do you want the ink, honey?"

"Right here. In the middle," Sony says, taking off her sweatshirt and pointing under the crest of her collarbones, the peak of her sternum.

Carl nods and explains the process to her, says it might sting a little bit and if she's on any medications, she should tell him before he starts.

Sony and C listen attentively. Neo, for a change, half here, half in his own head. He props his chin on the manuscript against his chest, swallowing once.

Sony looks at him out of the corner of her eye, then she glances at the pocket of her sweatshirt, the one Neo is wearing. One of her mischievous little grins lights her face.

She grabs Carl midspeech and pulls him closer to her. Carl stutters over his words, and deftly shuts up when Sony whispers in his ear, "It has to say this—psst, come 'ere." I don't hear the rest, but Carl looks up as she talks, as if memorizing her words.

"All right." He nods once she's done. "You want a design with it or just the phrase?"

"A design?" Sony cocks her head to the side, her knees up, dirty white sneakers tapping on the chair's seat.

Our first meeting flashes in my memory. The same shoes forever on her feet, the same temper and bravery no matter how much breath she can draw. The same careless, joyful, passionate attitude she's always had, the spirit of a child in the body of a thief.

"I have an idea," I say.

Sony beams at me. "Okay! Don't tell me, though! I want it to be a surprise! It better not be Eric's face."

"It's not," I promise.

I whisper my idea in Carl's ear. He pulls out a little notepad and draws a simple version of my request. I tell him it looks right, and he prints the stencil.

"Remember, it's gonna hurt a little, okay?" he says.

"Go for it! I fear nothing."

Carl laughs. "I don't doubt that. Try not to move, honey."

Sony hums at the endearment.

While Carl gets to work, Hikari and I explore the graffiti-rampant parlor. Bold colors pop against the dark walls, drawings like I've never seen all over them. Hikari takes my hand in hers and points to her favorite designs. I ask her what kind of god tattoo artists are in her bohemian religion. She smirks over her shoulder, lips twisting as if she's trying to rein in her amusement. She doesn't answer me. Her arms are more devious. They sneak and interlink around my back as she recommends I get definitions tattooed on my hand. For the sake of remembering pretentious Latin words. I tell her she should get her drawings tattooed on her so they live forever. She tells me sometimes I am more considerate than her teasing allows.

"How are you doing, Sony?" C asks.

"I'm great!" Sony yells. We are only privy to the finished product, she said, so we listen from the other side of the shop. Sony chuckles. "It feels like a spicy ultrasound."

"So what do you do? You a college student?" Carl asks her.

"Nah. I just take care of kids. Most of them are in oncology or the daycare center. It's gonna be my job soon."

"That sounds fun."

"It's so fun! Kids are great. I mean, they can be jerks sometimes, but they're honest and funny and a little crazy. It's never boring."

"I get what you mean. I have four younger siblings. They're monsters, but I love 'em."

"Those are my four little monsters right over there," Sony says. I see her finger pointing at us.

"Yeah?"

"Yeah," Sony says. "They're my family."

Carl and Sony continue their conversation over the pen's buzzing. Hikari tells me Carl is smitten. I ask how she's able to tell. She says he has the same look I did when we met on the roof. I remind her that I was equally terrified as I was smitten. She says Sony is equally terrifying as she is beautiful.

C agrees. He flips through outdated magazines, one earbud blasting in his ear, his natural state of being.

Neo, on the other hand, still isn't with us. He's in his hospital room, fixed to his chair, his father's figure looming over him. His only sign of life past staring out the window is a methodical thumb and forefinger looping around his wrist.

"Neo?" C draws a hand over Neo's knee. "Where are you?"

"My dad's gonna be angry about this. He's gonna look for me. You know that, right?" Neo asks, holding his papers so close that the stack's edges crease.

"Hey," C says. "What'd I tell you? No one's gonna get through us."

"I don't care what he does to me," Neo bites out.

C stands, towering over Neo, taking the same care of him as he has since Neo was at the mercy of crutches and wheelchairs.

"He can't hurt any of us. Not here."

C grabs Neo's face in his hands. Neo's face is so small compared to his palms. They practically envelop him. C smiles as he does this, poking Neo's cheeks. Even if Neo is in the process of creating wrinkles between his brows, you can tell this calms him.

"You're getting one too, right?" C asks.

Neo's lip lifts in disgust. "A tattoo?"

"Yeah. When you're a big famous author, and you're being rude to all your fans at signings, you're gonna need something to remember us by."

C's words crank a lever, winding up Neo's face. He pulls C's hands off his face and turns around.

"You're an idiot," he says under his breath.

C gets defensive. "Tattoos aren't that reckless, Neo—"

"You're an idiot to think I could forget you," Neo snarls, offended. "And don't act like you're not going to be bothering me at signings, anyway. It's our book, remember. Not mine."

Neo and his words are in a forbidden affair. A stolen passion. Language and his craft are furiously in love. You can feel their bond radiate from every drop of ink that ever was and will be.

"We're all done, guys," Carl calls.

Hikari and I are the first to see the tattoo. Sony sits up, admiring the mirror Carl holds up, so that she may take in the subtle beauty of a symbol that will live as long as she.

"Neo," C says, making room for our poet to see. "Look."

Beneath the crown of Sony's collarbones, etched onto the meeting place of her heart and lung, a pair of wings spread above words of promise.

time will cease   disease will fester   death will die

Neo's jaw slackens, his eyes gone soft.

"It's for you," Sony says. "It was the first thing you ever

wrote in our hit list." She meets Neo's gaze. In it, every single gasp, fit of snorty laughter, and tear shed that Sony gave Neo's stories lives. "You always said you wanted just a little piece of you to be immortal."

Neo's hands shake around his stories. His babies that have been torn, taken for granted, mistreated, thrown like corpses in his face—he remembers them all. Because his sea is thick with suffering, and we are who he chose to row with.

Neo drops his story into C's arms, stifling a sob. He covers his mouth with a bony hand, and, without hesitation, he hugs Sony.

"Silly crybaby," she whispers, embracing Neo as he cries on her shoulder. Sony reaches into his (or really her) sweatshirt pocket, removing a crinkled piece of torn paper. "I promised I'd get you happy tears, remember?" she says. "I've been telling you from the beginning that you're a pillar. Did you think I was just teasing?"

"You're a stupid idiot," Neo blubbers, his tears soaking her shirt.

Sony hugs him back, pressing kisses to his head.

"I love you too, Baby."

————

"Hikari, hold my hand." C huffs out a breath. He braces in the hydraulic chair, much like Neo does when C operates a vehicle.

"Deep breaths, bud," Hikari teases, abiding by his request.

"Don't laugh at me," C warns.

"I'm not laughing."

"You're laughing."

"You're a funny guy."

"You ready?" Carl asks.

C squeaks. "No. Can you count down from three?"

"He's ready!" Sony says, hopping up and down, using Carl's shoulders as a pogo stick.

C took his shirt off for the process, baring the circuitry of his body. Along the faint memory of muscles, his heart pulses beneath the branching outlines of his veins. Thunder and lightning arisen from a gentle organ.

C sighs, throwing his head back. Sony tries to distract him from the spicy ultrasound with dramatic readings of Neo's manuscript.

During a particularly grueling passage, audible reactions over the quiet buzz echo through the room. Unbeknownst, Neo looks around and realizes the whole shop is listening in, artists too. He swallows down disbelief, suppressing a smile I never knew could grace him with such brilliance.

C gets a rendition of Neo's quote in the same spot as Sony and a pair of earbuds over the text. Neo goes next, same quote, an open book crowning the words.

Hikari and I watch from a distance. She removes her sweater to go next. Self-consciousness pulls at her bandages and tucks her forearms behind her back. I take her hands in mine, tangling our fingers together. Standing at an angle, I conceal her arms between us so no one can see.

"You never told me what this scar is from," I whisper, tracing the thick, jagged line crossing from shoulder to the apex of her breasts.

"When I was little, I had imaginary friends," she begins. "I chased them all around the forest in my backyard. I climbed the boulders, the trees, all of it. One day, I climbed a little too close to the sun and . . ." Hikari blows up her cheeks, flicking the length of her white line. "When I got older, I had real friends, but they didn't *feel* real. I felt closer to my imaginary teddy bear. I never connected with anyone, or I guess, no one ever connected with me. Anyway, it was clear that I was the problem, so for every person I met, I acted a little different each time."

As if identity should be rewritten to the whims of others. A thing to be solved rather than nurtured.

"Over time, I realized that creating a new personality for every friendship has a temporary effect. You can pretend, but you always revert back to who you really are." Hikari licks her lips. Her fingers fidget with a piece of lint on my shirt. Her eyes stray from the present, sadness not unlike the kind that took her the night she told me of her childhood ghosting over her face. "So I just started acting like myself. A lot of people thought I was weird, but I liked just being me for a while. I reopened this scar climbing the same exact tree." Hikari tries to laugh, but the joyful memory is tainted with sourness, a little bit of a lie stitched over the truth.

"It grew a branch," she says. Her joy fades. Her eyes unfocus, drifting behind me to the sight of our friends.

Regret coils in her gaze, originating from the ravines beneath her bandages. All the other little branches that riddle her body send pinpricks up her spine.

"You know I don't *like* hurting myself, right, Sam?" she whispers.

"I know," I say.

"It's like a release," she goes on. "Like everything becomes too much, and I can transfer the pain somewhere else and . . ." She looks down at her hands as if the blood of another pools between her fingertips rather than her own.

"They're only scars," I say, kissing the edge of her wrist. "Like the essential parts of us kept only for the gazes of mirrors and lovers."

She blinks, returning to me, gradually, then completely. I

bring my forehead to hers, wondering how there was ever a time I had the strength to stay away.

"Are you my lover?" Hikari asks.

"You're my mirror." I poke the bridge of her glasses, making her laugh.

"I never knew you liked my glasses."

"Maybe I need a pair of my own."

"You did tell me that hope is nearsighted."

"Am I your hope, Hikari?"

"Am I your despair, Sam?" She smiles. A comforting smile reaches my face as she runs her thumb across the curve.

"I'll draw it for us," she whispers.

"Draw what?"

Her lips meet mine, the parting like light admiring darkness.

"The moment despair fell in love with hope."

18
before

S AM MAKES REPETITION feel new. He makes years pass in seconds.

"The sun never rises quite the same," he tells me as the sun curves over the earth like a halo. Silhouettes of construction workers play with their orchestras of metal and machinery outside Sam's window.

Every day, they build, till our little town becomes a city. The process is gradual, but it feels instantaneous. It feels the same when I realize Sam is growing as fast as our home.

Lanky and pale, he begins to fill out. His bones stretch furiously overnight. Those honey eyes settle on thinning cheekbones. His voice starts to crack, and his shoulders broaden. His temper becomes unpredictable, foul, and moody too.

But for all that's changed, Sam is still a child. In the mornings, he wakes me with tickles up and down my sides. His breakfast goes untouched unless sweet bread and pudding sit on the plate. He lies about little things like brushing his teeth or doing his lesson work. And his curiosity is as insatiable as it always was.

"Sweet Sam," he whispers. "Sweet Sam, wake up."

My eyes flutter open. Sam's face casts a shadow on mine, blocking out the sun. The summer heat turns him dopey and half-lidded. He leans in, voice cool on my chin, lips a breath from my nose.

"You're so beautiful."

"What does that mean?" I ask.

"It means I like looking at you," Sam says. He scoots closer, sighing and stretching his limbs like a cat. "I like being with you." His fingers trace my shirt collar, up my neck, poking my features.

Sam is still unable to touch other people. Other people are not allowed to touch him. I am the only exception. Most of the day, he is confined to his room. He calls it his bubble, his chamber, and, on sadder days, his cage. He spent so long staring through its glass partitions, I think he started to resent it. It was easier to pretend that room was the world when he wasn't tall enough to see outside of it.

"I like being with you too," I say.

Sam hums in pleased, tired tones.

Nurse Ella explained Sam's disease to me a long time ago. She said it was simple, yet it wasn't. She said he was normal cognitively, physically, in every way but one. She said his body couldn't protect itself. She said that job fell onto our shoulders.

"If I see a single scuff on those pants, I'll make you wash them in the river, young man!" she yells, sitting on the park bench as Sam and I run together across the field.

Nurse Ella is a harsh, disciplined woman. She wears her hair in a tight bun at the back of her neck. Her white uniform is neat, pressed, stainless. I'm convinced her back does not bend, and her hands are made of iron.

"Old hag," Sam whispers, laughing, sticking his tongue out at her, and tugging me along.

Nurse Ella opens her newspaper with a displeased grunt.

Sam is under Ella's care. When he was little and rambunctious, no other nurses could handle him. Nurse Ella was not deterred. She washed her hands vigorously and marched to wherever Sam had run off. She grabbed the collar of his shirt, dragged him back to his room, and warned him that little boys who don't take their medicine cannot grow into strong knights. She told Sam that if he wanted his pudding and his sweet bread, he would keep himself clean, tidy his room, and do as he was told.

Nurse Ella is good at bargaining.

She is good at keeping Sam safe.

She told Sam all the fairy tales she knew. She reads to him and smacks his arm with the cover if he interrupts. She sewed him a mask, told him not to lose it, and to always wear it over his nose and mouth. She scolds him frequently. She makes him sit and think about his actions.

Almost daily, Sam tells Nurse Ella that she is boring and mean and an old hag. Nurse Ella reminds him that she doesn't care.

She does care, though, I think, as much as I do.

For someone in Sam's position, not living is a precaution, she once told me, looking at Sam past the glass as his doctors made him lie on his side and examined his body. *That's what those foolish men in white coats tell me.* She made her signature displeased grunt. *Pessimists. The lot of them, keeping a child cooped up here forever. That won't do. He must live. Once you're my age, living is unpleasant. Come along.*

Where are we going? I asked.

Nurse Ella never answered my questions. She just told me to hurry up and follow.

She takes Sam and me outside every Saturday, no matter the weather. She makes sure Sam is wearing his mask and gloves. She tells us to hold hands as we cross the street. She takes us to the bakery, to the newspaper stands, and to the park.

Sam feigns deathly injury when I poke my stick between his ribs. He retaliates, his sword swinging at my leg. I jump over it, landing off-balance and falling in the grass.

Sam laughs at me. He says I look like a rag doll. Then he throws his stick aside and sits next to me, trying to catch his breath. Heat swelters beneath his mask on days like this. Sweat trickles from his brow, and his lungs beg for cooler air. Sam is careful not to touch his face despite that. He doesn't take off the mask or fidget with it. Instead, he closes his eyes and lets the trees' shady patches cool him and distant construction sounds obscure his hard breathing.

Nurse Ella sits on the bench, back straight and iron-handed, giving us the occasional glance. All around her, people exist in a world I seldom see.

The park is full today, of color and birds and people passing through, on bikes, on foot, in couples, with pets, and with joy.

A woman dressed in far too many layers throws bread crumbs in the path, pigeons gathering in a flock around her. An old man wipes his grandson's crumb-ridden mouth with a handkerchief. Girls, in a hurry, canter with their arms interlaced and schoolbags bouncing on their backs.

Just behind them, a couple holds hands, the two leaning on each other, whispering endearments, and smiling all the while. A girl spins in her dress, the boy twirling her by the hand. They don't pay any mind to the park or the world around them. The path is merely a dirt road, and the civilians around them are merely background to their play.

The wind blows, leaves rustling overhead. The boy takes the girl's face in his hands. Their noses brush. She presses a kiss to his lips. Pink dusts the boy's cheeks.

It makes me smile that the girl gives him color.

I wonder if Sam feels the same way. Only Sam isn't smiling at the sight. His mask conceals his mouth, but his eyes are lightless.

The woman throwing bread crumbs glances at him, staring at the mask and gloves. She shivers, quickly turning back to her flock. The old man holds his grandson's hand. He picks up the pace, passing Sam, leaving more room than he would with any other stranger. The running schoolgirls pause to look, their canter slowed to a trot as they whisper to each other and stare.

Sam quickly turns away from the path. He hooks his elbows around his knees, hiding his face, making fists to conceal the gloves behind his pant legs. After a second's fidgeting, he grabs me by the wrist and pulls me upright, dragging me into a hiding place behind the bushes.

"Sam?" I call. "What's wrong?"

"People are looking at me," he whispers. His thumb slips over the scar on his wrist, the one he was given years ago in the dim corner of a closet. "They all think I'm different."

They. The children in his past? Some are dead; some have gone home. What they left behind is greater than a little white line on his wrist.

Sam lets me go, breathless, too aware of himself. Even beneath the shade, behind a cluster of hedges, he hunches, makes himself smaller. Like he doesn't want to exist.

"You *are* different," I say. Sam's gaze drifts from the ground to me. I smile, just as the girl did looking at her partner. "No one else has suns in their eyes."

Sam blinks. The sun sifts through the leaves, casting shadows that flutter with the breeze as if to prove my point. They play on his face the same way rays of light kiss him in the mornings.

"You're beautiful," I say, my fingers dragging up to his face, trailing the jaw that's become sharper the older he grows. "People like looking at you."

The passersby going on with their days are left only with an empty space of grass. I wonder how blind they must be. To not notice all the joy that exists under Sam's mask.

"Do you mean that?" he asks. The bush crams us together. Our knees brush, his hip nudging mine. He looks down at me as if all the people on the other side aren't there anymore.

"Of course I do."

Sam doesn't smile. The skin around his eyes doesn't crease. Instead, he smooths his touch down my arm, his pupils expanding. His curiosity explores more freely than before. The shame he used to wear when accidentally grazing my chest or my back or anywhere that clothes cover skin dissipates. His inhibition fades with it.

Sam pulls down his mask.

I panic, reaching to put it back on, but he stops me. He takes both my wrists and bends down so our foreheads kiss.

"Sam, you'll get sick—"

"I don't care," he whispers. His eyes close. He breathes me in, releasing my hands and cupping my face. His movements are awkward, unsure, but at the same time impatient.

I plant my hands on his chest. His pulse thrums fast and hard. It quickens as he leans in, so close that our noses touch and his lips just barely sweep across mine.

"Sam! Get out of there this instant!" Nurse Ella's voice rings like a church bell. If church bells were terrifying, that is.

Sam pulls away, tugging the mask back over his face. He grabs me by the arm again, dragging me into a run.

"C'mon, c'mon, let's go!" he screeches. We almost trip over each other and the twigs, somehow making it out in one piece.

Together we sprint, Nurse Ella marching on after us. Sam laughs all the while, jumping over the paths, through the trees, making sure I'm still with him.

The two of us skid to a stop right before falling into a puddle of mud, but the wind has other ideas. We lose our balance and fall together. The mud sloshes around us, seeping into our clothes. Sam sits up to make sure I'm all right. Once he sees that we're both only breathless and covered in mud, that smile finally curves his face, creasing the skin around his eyes.

He looks so happy. Even if it is brief, a cursory tick of a hand on a watch, the moment ebbs with rays of light. It makes the times Sam is lost in his own head, cooped up, staring through glass, seem insignificant.

"Oh, you filthy little animals!" Nurse Ella yells, stomping over to the edge of the mud bath. She plants her hands on her hips. "At this rate, I'll have to hose you off like dogs! Out! Now!"

Sam and I obey, trudging out of the water, side-eyeing each other in the process, snickering under our breaths.

Nurse Ella drags us back home by our ears, all the while spouting lecture after lecture. She drops us right outside the door, telling us to wait for her unless we want to eat nothing but spinach for the rest of the week. She comes back with buckets of water and pours them over our heads. Sam and I squeal and shiver. Nurse Ella takes to scrubbing our heads with what looks like a small broom.

Once our skin is raw, and we smell of soap, Nurse Ella grunts. "Silly children."

"I'm not a child anymore, Nurse Ella," Sam says, rocking back and forth. "I'll be taller than you soon."

"Yes, well, until you've learned not to play in the mud, you'll be a child in my eyes," Nurse Ella says. She drops towels on our heads. Tells us to come back inside once we're dry. Before she goes, she takes Sam's temperature, releasing a heavy exhale when it comes back normal.

She's a good person, I think.

Good and mean, but good all the same.

"Sam," I say. "Do you think we could have more adventures like this?"

He looks out into the horizon, past the park and the bakery and the newspaper stands. Past the construction miles in the sky and all the noise with it.

"We could run away together," he says. "Just you and me. No one else. What do you think?"

I swallow hard, the hospital's walls and all the people inside tugging. I think of everything I'd be leaving behind, running away. But then I think of Sam's face as we hid in the brush. I think of his laughter in the mud, of his lips so close to stealing mine.

"Will that make you happy?" I ask.

"Yes," he says.

"Promise?"

"Promise." Sam grabs me around the waist, tucking his head in the crook of my neck, stretching his limbs like a cat on a rooftop. He kisses my cheek, whispering, "You make me so happy, my sweet Sam."

19
heaven

THE OUTSKIRTS OF the city trail the shoreline. The sea mingles with eroded cliffsides, birds flying in arrowheads, matching the rhythm of the waves. Driving the road fringing an open bay, I gaze out at a world I've never seen with my own eyes.

"That's the ocean?" I ask, leaning over Sony, hands against the window.

"Is it as beautiful as you imagined?" Hikari asks.

A half-moon crests her skin above our binding line of promise. On mine, a half-sun mirrors hers.

We left the parlor thanking Carl for his hard work. Carl thanked us for the story. Then, timidly, he tapped Sony's shoulder and asked if she'd give him a call sometime.

Sony smirked, as devils do. She grabbed Carl by the face and kissed him with such force he stumbled back into the front desk. Freedom comes in degrees, and Sony basks in whatever heat of freedom she chooses. Once she was done with him, she wrote her phone number on his palm and followed us out.

The ocean graces us with tart, salty scents. We grace it with our scream-singing voices and poor renditions of beloved classic rock songs. Windows down. Music blasting. Not a care for what we leave behind.

With our remaining fifteen dollars and ninety cents, we park the truck beside the boardwalk and convince a short woman with a white hat and a cart to sell us ice cream for half the price. She calls us damn kids and shoves the cones into our hands.

Hikari points to the ocean reaching for shore, foaming white. On the beach, parties hold on to their end-of-season zeal. People dance beside bars with the familiar smell of actual cigarettes and alcohol.

After lapping at the ice cream, Sony gives her remaining cone to Neo. She flings her dirty white sneakers off, leaving them on the boardwalk and hopping down to the sand. Effortlessly, she blends into the crowd of end-of-summer deniers.

Strangers look twice, caught by that brutal beauty. The roan layer of hair and the dancing constellation across her nose. C hops down with Neo on his arm. Strangers look twice as strength's tiny body moves in sync with compassion's gentle beat. I take Hikari and her sundress into the scene. She stumbles, but I catch her, interlacing our fingers, dancing the only way I know, with her leading my hand. Strangers look twice, not for any indication of lost time, repulsing illness or death. They look twice at kids lost in the moment and in each other.

We race across the beach all the way to a stretch uninhabited by anyone but the gulls diving for fish and the critters in the sand.

The wind is ferocious here. Sony shrieks into it, stretching her arms out to either side. I run with her, shivering as we dip our feet in the water. She declares this beach, from the grassy dunes to the depths of the sea, to be ours.

The waves we gifted with our messy dancing and lack of hair urge us on. C takes off his pants and shirt shamelessly, letting the sea take him. His chest and the plastic protecting his tattoo stay above the surface as he drifts with his old friend, cupping the sea in his palms and splashing it onto his face with a sigh.

Seashells weigh down Sony's pockets as she and Hikari fish into the shallow end like fishermen in a canal. They're soaked from the waist down, but neither of them seems to care. Sony wrings out the material of Hikari's dress and rolls up her pants before they sit in the sand, dirty and giddy as they sort their spoils.

Chased mercilessly by me and C, Neo throws his hoodie over his head, leaving his shirt and pants on. He pretends to be angry when we tackle him into the water. Once his lower half is submerged by the waves, a violent tremble runs up his body. He wraps his arms around C's neck for warmth, the two beaming at each other. C twirls in the water as he did on the beach, smiling into Neo's neck.

I bring Hikari back stones. They shine, some with a single white line encircling them like rope. I also bring her a tiny crab missing a claw that was stuck in a shell. Together we bring it back to the ocean, watching it scurry into the sea.

Later, on a pile of our dry clothes on the dunes, Sony, C, and I make out the shapes of offshore islands, giving names to lonely ships in the far distance. Neo and Hikari write and draw in the hit list. They mark each stone, shell, island, and ship. The wind weighs in on our conversation, flipping pages in disagreement and tickling our noses when it is pleased.

My friends laugh, filling page after page, not a dull moment between them. They smile, hug, kiss, run, speak, sing, shout, swim, play, create, and love without constraint.

With a pencil between her teeth, Hikari walks me to the foamy edges of the shore and hands me a drawing. Three kids dance together among a nameless crowd. Their expressions are their own, but they are real. I stare at the drawing, ghostly fingers dragging over my friends' faces. It is a single moment, but through her gift, it is engraved in eternity.

I smile. Because it is a single moment that cannot be stolen.

When Hikari turns toward the sea, the breeze flirts with her figure. Her dress catches on her curves; the wet fabric sticks to her legs. My hands roam to her hips, pulling her to me, paper in hand.

I trace the lines of her face. She bites her blue lips and inhales the newborn air that very well could've been carried from across the earth. I mimic her. Our new tattoos touch, a spark of electricity exchanged by our hearts.

"Hikari," I breathe.

She runs her fingers up my scalp, the watch on her wrist carrying grains of sand against my neck.

"Yes, Sam," she whispers, and surrounded by the people we care about, I realize that this is what it was always supposed to feel like.

~~Our enemies have no claim~~ to this place.

They have no claim to this day.

In Hikari's arms, I forget what I am and where I am from. The idea of home no longer has gravity. I have flown off my orbit, chosen to follow meteors with no aim but to roam.

I am not afraid of what constitutes life or mere existence. I watch and yet I smile, hug, kiss, run, speak, sing, shout, swim, play, create, and love all the same.

This place—this exact spot where land and sea meet—is where the world was born. It is where time ceases, disease festers, and death dies.

Because the world was built for kids who dreamt of life and were raptured by loss. It is theirs, and it is mine. It is ours to claim, and it is ours to reap. In this place, freedom takes us by the hand, and we dance to its rhythm in coarse, cool sand and wild, welcoming waters.

In the book of our lives, upon a single page dedicated to its creation, we name it Heaven.

————

When night falls, we retire to C's dad's pickup. The clouds dissipate with the dark, revealing a sky rendered black by a layer of stars. Fortunately for us, C's thieving grants us yellow blankets to warm our soaked skin.

We lie in the truck's bed like poorly laid out sardines. We are tangled together, a mass of bodies huddled, shivering, and laughing. Sony is at the center, Hikari and Neo clinging to her like babies while C and I make the outsides.

Our stories flow between us. Some are old humorous tales that get interrupted by cackling because we already know how they end. It's like a joke that doesn't need a punch line. A communal store of memories that make way for new stories.

"I can't believe you kissed Carl," Neo says.

Sony smiles in that way you know she's thinking about doing it again just for the fun.

"Carl's nice," C says, arms crossed behind his head, acting as a pillow.

I'm about to add that Carl is also very skilled at his job, but then Hikari says, "He's cute too," and now I'm less eager to say anything.

I look down at her, propped up on my elbow with a frown. She rolls her eyes at me and squishes my face.

"We should bring Eric out here," C says.

Hikari giggles. "He'd scold the fish for swimming too close to shore and curse the seagulls for flying too close to the sand."

"He'd curse the sand for being sand," Neo says.

Sony taps their foreheads. "Oh, shush, he'd secretly like it."

"He'd like it because we do," I say, the only fish sitting up in the bunch, listening to the waves that never sleep as the tide pulls in. I imagine Eric at the center of the nocturnal beach, watching us play as the gulls fly overhead, the salt sprays on our tongues, and the music plays from the boardwalk.

"Ever thought of turning your heartbeat into a song?" Neo whispers, tucked against C's chest, his ear pressed against the hollowed valley.

"Would you write the lyrics?" C asks.

Neo shrugs. "We can write them together."

"I'd like that," C whispers.

"After our story?"

"Yeah, after our story."

Sony stretches her limbs with a yawn.

"Neo," she says, nudging his shoulder, "let's read more of your manuscript. I want to know what happens next." But when Sony looks, C puts a finger to his lips, revealing a sound-asleep poet. He shifts in C's arms, turning so as to be in Sony's as well.

"Tomorrow, then," she whispers, and kisses his forehead. C wraps them both in his embrace, squeezing my hand and Hikari's arm once before they all fade into sleep.

"Look, Sam," Hikari says, wide awake. She looks up at the sprinkled dusting of the galaxy, a painting that is ours. "Your stars are shining."

They are. And their brilliance is reflected in her.

I tuck the yellow blanket over her shoulders, dragging my touch down her covered body to make sure she stays warm. Her drowsy gaze finds mine. The joy of today floats in the color, a liquid that cannot be dissolved by time's passing.

"What's on your mind, Yorick?" she asks.

"That you and I were created for each other."

"Were we?"

"No."

She laughs.

"You're a prince, and I'm only the skull of a nameless jester," I remind her.

"Nothing is nameless," she says. "Not even bones."

"Hamlet wouldn't say that."

"What would Hamlet say?"

"He would call the skull a fool for wanting him. For thinking it was any more than a skull at all."

"Hamlet would never say that to his friend."

"What does Hamlet know? He's friends with a skull."

She laughs again, dragging her fingertips across my face. I'm tempted to wrap myself around her, to breathe in the scent at the crook of her neck and simply be so close that the idea of distance is forgotten.

"Hikari," I whisper, the drawing of our friends still tucked in my pocket. "If you could go back and keep yourself from climbing that tree or going to that lake or from whatever unlikely steps led you to this place . . ." I hold the same hand that saved me from that road and reminded me that to be alive is to feel as I do now. "Would you?"

"No," Hikari says, without a second's hesitation, shaking her head. "No, I'm happy here. With them. With you." She looks at the stars again, then at me, no shadows left in the night.

"I'm happy," she says again.

It fills the void in me, and what was once an empty shell, an outline of a person, is full. I take her glasses off, placing them neatly on her chest. Now there is nothing in the way, not even a mirror. I fantasize about kissing her lips just to taste the words.

"What is it?" Hikari whispers, mimicking me, her finger caressing my cheekbone.

"Do you remember the night in the garden that we stole a race? You asked me what I thought of life." I want to tell her that what I have has never felt like a life. But I also want to tell her that if this is living, then a life with her is all I want.

"I have to tell you something, Hikari," I say. "About myself."

Hikari blinks, waiting for me to speak, but somehow my words lose their shape before I can find them. I stare at her longingly. Her affection is measured in teasing glances, gifts only we know the meaning of, and nights peering over books. I cannot find the strength to squander all that. Not yet.

"There's a dream in your eyes, my Yorick," she says, and I decide I will tell her the truth later. The now does not need renditions of the past, and the future does not need foretelling.

We have time.

I take the hand always so keen on exploring and kiss Hikari's knuckles, the heel of her palm, her wrist, and all the little scars healing above.

"I dream of this life," I whisper. "Us. Together. For all tomorrows to come."

Hikari kisses me, pulling me down to the bed of the truck. I kiss her back, my arms on either side of her head. As her promise went on that little piece of torn paper, she says, between our affections, "Then all my tomorrows are yours."

———

I don't wake to the sun.

I wake to the sounds of struggle and choked gasps.

Someone is trying to breathe, desperately so, but the breath cannot be caught. It is interrupted, stuck in a coughing fit.

Air is a necessary medium of exchange between a body and its environment. It is not an infinite resource, and those who no longer have the means to collect have only one place to go.

That is what I wake to when the dream is over.

I wake to Sony drowning from the inside out.

"Sony?" Hikari, C, and Neo wake simultaneously, a herd hearing the faint cries of a wounded member in the night.

"Oh my God, Sony!" Hikari yells.

Sony is on her back, her eyes wide and afraid, her nails digging into the bed of the truck, her chest caved in. Spots swell on her right side as blood spurts from her throat and stains her chin.

"C, get her in the back seat. Neo, start the car," I order, and everyone moves quickly, like doctors running down a hall when a code sounds on the intercom.

Hikari whimpers. C rushes to pick Sony up. I open the back door and fumble for the tank under the seat and the oxygen mask.

C sits Sony down so that her back leans against my front. Hikari is crying in fear, her hands shaking as she helps me put the mask on Sony's face.

The engine rumbles, and the headlights stretch into the empty lot, Neo turning the key in the ignition. He moves into the passenger seat over the console to make room for C. He reaches behind the middle compartment, grasping for Sony's hand or knee or anything he can hold on to, not bothering with his seat belt.

"Sam-my," Sony tries to speak. Her vocal cords are submerged. Her body is weak and cold, yet still laboring. A body has automated responses to keep itself alive. Sony's one lung will keep rising and falling till it doesn't have the means, no matter what ravages it.

"Squeeze our hands, Sony. Take deep breaths," I say, holding her neck straight, keeping the pathway for her lung as open as I can.

It's the middle of the night, and the roads are empty. C slams his foot on the gas, remembering the fastest route to the hospital.

Sony spits up more blood and pus. She doesn't have the strength to tilt her head, so the mess ends up in her lap. Hikari tries to clean her up the best she can with her sweater. Panic trembles through her hands and her voice alike.

"Hikari?" Sony rasps.

"I'm here, Sony. Just hold on, okay?"

Sony smiles deliriously, her body going completely limp in my arms.

"You're always so warm," she says.

"Sony? Sony, stay awake! Sony!" Hikari yells, but Sony's eyes have already slipped back into her head.

20
wings

REALITY ISN'T KIND to those who deny it. It thrusts itself back upon you, not with a knife in the back, but through the lung, staring down at you distastefully for leaving it behind.

A metronome is all reality leaves behind with its blade scraping the ground. It pulses in the form of a heart monitor, drawing a steady string of green mountains on the screen.

We cling to it, to the beat that slows with each passing hour, afraid that if we let go, it will become lax, and the beat will turn into an infernal, constant ring.

I sit up in my chair, careful not to make noise. The ICU is loud outside this room, but with the door shut, you could hear a feather drop. Neo, C, and Hikari sleep in three chairs on the wall facing the bed. They fell asleep when the doctors left.

The harsh acceleration of the truck, the horror-stricken yelling, Sony's choking—it's all there, in their dreams, haunting them. We arrived at the hospital with Sony fading in and out of consciousness. They rolled out a stretcher and took her from C's arms.

Despite Hikari's inability to handle the fear and the panic, she managed to calm down enough to call Eric in the truck. He was waiting in the ER, and when they wheeled in Sony, he did something I'd never seen him do.

He froze.

He saw the blood and heard Sony's struggles, and he just stopped moving.

A mass of people surrounded her. They stuck a hole in her chest, a geyser of liquid spurting out. Then they took her away, yelling one code after another, sticking her with needles, and disappearing with our Sony, still unable to breathe.

We shook. Hikari buried her face in my chest, hands fisting my shirt as I held her against me.

Eric tried to run to where they treated her, yelling over nurses and doctors who didn't know Sony, about her history, her treatments, everything.

They had to kick him out of the room. Neo, C, and Eric stared at the hall entryway to the ICU and we waited an infernal set of infernal minutes until a doctor came out.

Now Sony lies in a room I can only describe as blue. A path of tubes works under her nose. Her chest is a mess of medical work. It must've been an infection, working slyly without symptoms until it pulled the drain and flooded the battleground.

"We got caught, huh?"

I look up to a grating voice. It's weak, rocks scraping the back of her throat. But it carries a melody I know. Sony is there, behind those half-lidded eyes. A flame burning low, but still burning.

I rush for her hand, nearly disrupting the fragile systems all connected to her.

"We always get caught," I whisper, squeezing it.

She doesn't squeeze back. I don't think she can. She can't sit up or move. She can barely turn her head.

"They didn't ruin my wings, did they?" she asks.

The tattoo isn't visible beneath the bandages, but her wings were too young to undergo so much. All that's left are ink feathers plucked and fallen beneath the crown of her collarbones.

"No," I say. "They didn't."

"Good." Sony smiles. "I've always wanted wings."

I nod, coursing my touch back and forth over her knuckles.

"You said that to me the night we met, you remember?"

"Of course I do," she rasps. "You'd never had chocolate before, you little stranger."

"You introduced me to candy and ice cream and fries too."

"Gosh, I'm a bad influence."

I chuckle. She wants to laugh too, just to join me, but I think that is also one of the things she can't do right now.

Sony realizes the sadness it brings me. She tries her hardest to close her fingers over mine. They shake, unable to apply any pressure, but her smile outweighs their weakness.

"It was a good day, wasn't it, Sammy?" she whispers.

"Yeah, it was."

I wish I could tell you that her skin still smells of salt and her cheeks retain sun blush. I wish I could tell you that people retain who they are in these moments, but they don't.

Sony has reached the point of sickness where she no longer looks like herself. Her freckles are faint, her skin pale and laced with sweat. Any animation, any dimple that could've led you to believe she was a smiler, is gone. Her limbs lie limp from deoxygenation. All that is left to fight is that half of her chest rising and falling, over and over, never giving up the game.

"How long have you known, Sony?" I ask.

She swallows, but it hurts, like a letter opener across the tonsils.

"The day you fell in the road, I had a tickle in my throat. The chest pain came next. Then, when I stumbled, I knew," she says. "I don't know how, but I just knew."

She gives me an apologetic sort of look, the kind you give when you've been keeping a secret as monumental as this.

"You never said anything—"

"There was nothing to say." She speaks as if the subject is moot. As if any preventative measure would've been useless, and she would've ended up here, anyway.

"Sammy, the night we met, I told you I'd had a hiking accident, do you remember?" Sony's words overlap, slurring a bit from the drugs, but I can make them out. She attempts to move her arm, to move closer to me. Tears well in her eyes as she struggles, not from this pain, but from another, older kind. "I lied to you. I'm sorry."

"You don't have to be sorry," I whisper, catching beads of sweat on her forehead with my sleeve.

"I am, though. I'm so, so sorry. I was young, and I didn't know what to do," she cries. Neo, C, and Hikari stir, but they don't wake.

"Sony, it's all right," I whisper.

"I got pregnant," she says. And then I remember more clearly. The bruises on her legs and the butterfly-stitched cuts on her face. The anger. The way she kept touching her belly.

Sony's breath hitches, saliva dripping down her chin. I wipe it with my sleeve again, but Sony keeps on talking, trying to spit it all out like a nauseating bite of food. "My mom would've understood. She would've helped me raise the baby, but I couldn't do it. I couldn't tell her. The night I met you, I took the car, and I drove until I wasn't on the road anymore."

The night we met, Sony had scans done. Scans that showed trauma to her left lung. The lung they had to remove.

"Sony." My voice shakes. "Why?"

Sony's escapades, the ones where she fled from Eric's watchful eye, they never seemed purposeful, but they were. She never stole for herself. She stole for her kids. She spent her time with them. Not because they were sick, but because that's who Sony is. Like a child, she is curious and fiery, and brutally beautiful. She lives for the races, the thrills, and the games. She rescued a broken cat and gave it to a place where broken people come to heal simply because it is her nature.

"Did you see the toll it took on my mom?" she asks. "Having to see me gradually become half of who I used to be?"

"Your mother adored you." I shake my head. "Every part of you."

"I couldn't do it," Sony says. The materials keeping her alive that are strapped to her chest blur in her periphery. "I couldn't take the risk knowing the child might end up like me. It wouldn't be fair to it."

Sony cherishes children. It isn't till now that I understand just how much she cherished the child she never had.

Every fantasy I ever had of Sony as a woman starts to fade, an old photograph I never got to take withering. I saw her, somewhere in a distant future that doesn't exist. I saw her with a lover and a child in her arms. She blew endless kisses, nuzzling a baby with its mother's wild red hair and little freckles that danced when it laughed.

Tears stream down Sony's jaw as she catches that picture in me. Then they stream down mine.

"It'd only be a chance," I whisper.

Sony smiles. A smile of acceptance marred by sadness.

She knows it'd only be a chance.

But a chance is enough.

"I wanted to tell you," she says. "I wanted to tell you that even if I have regrets, the last two years with you don't hold any of them." She squeezes my hand harder this time. Then she looks beyond me, at our friends.

"You're my second-in-command. You have to keep them in line, okay?" Sony says. "Oh, don't cry, Sammy." She lifts her arm. I help her, bearing the weight as she rests her palm on my cheek. "It was a good day."

I choke on a breath, wetness gathering at the back of my throat.

Today is worth infinitely more than tomorrow. But Sony's tomorrow held a career, the end of Neo's manuscript, a look in the mirror at a new tattoo, and a sparkling infinity of futures that rightfully belong to her.

I knew that there would come a day of no tomorrows.

I knew, and I cry, anyway.

We're lucky, I think. *Today was a good day.*

Sony and I hold each other's gaze as I whisper, "I just wish I could've given you more."

Eric comes back a few minutes later with Hee in his arms. He's panting, quickly laying the cat down by Sony's legs. He checks all of Sony's vitals, muttering to himself, obsessing over every tiny detail.

Sony is only half-conscious. He strokes her head, asking her all sorts of questions in a soft voice. Neo, C, and Hikari wake up, each careful not to crowd her.

I stand to give them room as they gather around their friend.

Time, in a turn of kindness, slows. It stands beside me, watching, as it has since I was born. It whispers no cruelties or taunts. It drags a hand down my back and slows the metronome, holding it off until that inevitable flat note rings.

"Sony?" Hikari cries. "No, no, Sony!"

Eric yells at all of us to leave. Sony's doctors flood the room.

Hikari is so distraught I need to carry her out. C cries, following us, covering his face.

Neo is the last to leave. He shuts his eyes to the yelling and kisses Sony's face. When he's ushered out of the room, he takes Hee with him.

We cry together in the empty hallway, huddled from the blue and the cold. When we sink to the floor, there is the inevitable weight of something missing, like a limb cut clean from our bodies.

From outside the checkered windows, I watch with blurred vision as Sony takes her last breath. Once her eyes close, they don't open again.

————

Death isn't playful.

Death is sudden.

It has no taste for irony or reason.

It is a taker, plain, direct, no tricks up its sleeve.

But at least,

This time,

Death was kind enough to wait for goodbye.

21
before

SHE'S THE SIZE of a stick of butter. Nurse Ella calls her Butter Baby. She was born six weeks ago, six weeks too early. Today is the day she was *supposed* to be born.

Her mother is a nurse too. Unlike Ella, her face is satin. Her belly fills out her dress, her arms and legs are heavy. She takes Sam's vitals when Nurse Ella is home, a much gentler creature who bribes with lullabies rather than lectures.

Her baby takes after her softness.

"She's so small," I whisper.

"Be careful. That's it, cradle her just like that," her mother says. She twiddles with the braid cascading down her shoulder.

I've never held a baby. I've met so many, seen them swaddled in blankets and fed at their mother's breast, but I've never had the responsibility of carrying one.

I adjust the cloth cap more securely over her head, supporting her neck in the crook of my elbow. She coos. Her pudgy little hands close around my finger.

What an incredible creature she is. A new life that knows only how to breathe and suckle encased in a body fragile as porcelain.

I lay her back in her crib, but she's a greedy thing. She pulls my hair, squealing out her laughter, little fat legs kicking.

"She likes you." Her mother giggles. She presses a chaste kiss on my cheek. "Come see her anytime, all right?"

"Goodbye, Butter Baby," I whisper. I bow my head, and even once I leave the room, the baby grins toothlessly over her mother's shoulder till I'm gone.

————

"Bam! Another win!"

Henry is a regular, Nurse Ella says. He lives in a cabin neighboring the river. No children or family to speak of. So when his eightieth year struck with a leg infection, he had nowhere to stay but with us.

I like Henry. His hair is gray, like pale smoke rising from the pipe that dangles between his lips. That thing is an extension of his body, another limb. He's never without it. All its ashes nearly fall from the tobacco chamber when he laughs at his own jokes.

"You damn old man," Sam says, tossing his cards down on the table between them.

This is the nurses' break room. Technically, patients aren't allowed in. However, Sam and Henry are the resident troublemakers, me, their right hand. Where else could they gamble uninterrupted but where their nurses would never expect them to be?

Henry shimmies his shoulders back and forth, a victor's chuckle wafting smoke in Sam's face.

"Luck of the draw, my boy. Luck of the draw," he sings.

"Yeah, right." Sam throws one arm over the back of his chair. "You were hiding that king in your wrinkles, admit it."

"Uh-oh." Henry takes a drag from his pipe, gathering the cards. "Looks like we have a sore loser in our midst. Quick! Get him some ice. The boy's getting absolutely flamed."

Sam tries not to laugh.

He likes Henry too. One night, Sam was walking past his room, mask and gloves handy, when he heard a series of angry mumbles through the wall. Sam peeked in to find an old man staring at nothing, just talking to the air, two wooden crutches tucked under his armpits.

"You there!" he yelled, using one to point at Sam. "Come in here at once; this is an emergency."

"Are you hurt?" Sam asked, rushing in to help him. "Do you need a doctor?"

"A doctor? Are you trying to get me killed? No, no, boy, this is much worse than mere injury. I am bored. Dreadfully bored. If I have to be in this room one more second without something interesting to do, I might just drop dead."

"Well." Sam scratched the back of his neck, exhaling in part relief, part amusement. "We can't have that."

"We cannot!" Henry tapped his crutch's end on the ground. He removed a pile of coins from his pocket. "Do you like cards, boy?"

"Sure, sir."

"Excellent!" Not bothering to count the change, he dropped the money in Sam's open palm. "Go buy us some; that witch of a nurse took my last deck. Buy yourself some sweets while you're at it."

Sam was never one to turn down running an errand. He didn't ask Nurse Ella. He simply hauled me along, feasting on any excuse to feel the wind on his face and run a race down the street. We came back with a fresh deck of cards from the corner store. When Sam tried to give Henry the change, he waved him off, said Sam ought to use it for something useful, like gambling.

Although Henry, like Sam, never really left the hospital.

Bodies strengthen with age, then they wither, return to their state of weakness when they were as little as butter sticks. Henry disagrees with this view of existence. He is all mind and all memory. Beneath the pipe and the gray, he's as young as they come, a boy still in his prime, ready to dance, party, and gamble with the best of them.

"Sweet child," he says, waving me over. "Come shuffle for us; my arthritis is acting up."

"No, no, don't come over here," Sam says. "I don't want you to see me getting humiliated."

But I do anyway. Sam eyes me over his mask as I shuffle the cards. Yellow shines in the flares like amber. The only language that light knows is mischief. He winks at me, sliding a hand beneath the table and running it up and down the back of my thigh.

"I've barely put a dent in you, boy," Henry says. "You should've seen me during the war. We played blackjack for whiskey flasks. Even my sergeant couldn't beat the likes of me."

"Yeah?" Sam teases. "How'd a great player like you end up in a place like this?"

"Oh, time is a rotten old friend and crafty card player. Only gambler that could ever best me, that one."

I give Henry back the cards. A few spill through my fingers.

"Hah, a clumsy dealer. Thank you, dear." Henry's constant laughter falters for a moment. He thins his eyes, tilting my chin gently to get a better look at my face.

"Have we met before?" he asks, searching.

I smile at him as I did at my butter baby, shaking my head. "I don't think so, sir."

"Ah, that's too bad." Henry pats my cheek. "Such a pretty face."

Henry's said that to me before. He's asked me that question

before too. Because in a sense, he and I *have* met, a long time ago.

Henry is dear to me. His stories of army days and the war are echoes of memories we share. After all, Henry didn't buy that pipe; he stole it from a friend. A friend he lost on a bloody day, along with all the flesh and bone below his right knee.

"Another game!" Henry orders, pushing his chair in, tapping his one leg.

"All right." Sam sighs. "But only one."

"What are ya?" Henry teases, tossing him a hand. "Scared?"

"Scared of losing all my change."

Sam and Henry play another game. All the while, Henry hums old songs, smoking, talking to himself. At times, I'll catch him having entire muttered conversations with the air. I wonder if that is a habit one develops living alone. I wonder if he's talking to someone in particular, a ghost with which he shares that pipe.

"Hah!" he cheers, raising his arms over his head as high as they'll go. "I've still got it."

"He's cheating," Sam says, throwing himself back in his chair. "Isn't he? He's got to be cheating."

"I think you're just a lousy card player," I tease.

Sam reaches under the table and pinches the back of my knee. I flinch, smacking him away. He runs a hand through his hair, the locks unruly, spilling over his forehead.

Sam's gained a boyish confidence. He still acts the kid, only now with strut in his step. His doctors and nurses call him hand-some, a soon-to-be heartbreaker. He's become confident from the praise, and the deviousness of his childhood has turned fatal.

"Hooligan!" Of course, Nurse Ella doesn't take days off. She marches into the room, fists at her sides, steps quick and ill-tempered. "Did I not tell you to leave him alone?"

"Sorry, Nurse Ella," Sam says. "We'll go soon."

"She was talking to me." Henry beams.

"Shut up, you old pest. You have to wear a mask around him, you hear me? Put that wretched thing out." Nurse Ella flips a needle out from her apron, flicking it with her middle finger. "Take your medicine." She sterilizes a spot on his arm, finding a vein with machinelike efficiency.

"Such a demanding woman," Henry says, not so much as wincing from the injection. He cranes his head back, taking in Ella's stony features. "I should marry you."

Ella's displeased grunt sounds. "As if I'd ever marry a gambler."

"Everything in life is a gamble, my dear, even love itself." Henry sighs. He reaches for something on his other side. His crutches lean against the chair's back. His pipe is in his mouth.

I kneel, his empty hand settling in mine.

"Would you like to play another game tomorrow, sir?" I ask.

"You're a sweet child," Henry says, patting my face again. "Aren't they, Sam?"

My knight and I exchange a glance.

A proud look flickers in his yellow.

"Yes," he says. "They are."

———

I walk Sam back to his room when the sky grows dark. Henry hassled Nurse Ella to let us stay a little longer. She agreed so long as we promised to go to bed without argument afterward. Henry told us his stories, his adventures, the kind of fairy tales with a touch of reality that held Sam's attention the whole way through.

"I'll see you in the morning?" I ask as we reach Sam's room.

Sam and I are rarely apart. From sunup to sundown we're

eating, playing games, doing lesson work with the other kids, sitting through treatments and exams together, going outside when we aren't supposed to, getting scolded, visiting other patients, and gambling with Henry. The nurses say we're joined at the hip.

When Sam heads to sleep, he demands attention beforehand. He wraps his arms around me, pressing me into him. At times, he'll hold me for a few minutes, murmuring silly things—that I smell nice, that he wants to bite me through his mask for no reason at all, that I should sneak into his room so we could sleep in the same bed like we did as little kids.

Tonight, Sam doesn't embrace or murmur. He tells me to be quiet, grabs me by the wrist, and drags me with tiptoeing silence down the hall.

"Sam?" I stumble into the nurses' rest break room after him. "What are we doing?"

"Shh," he whispers. It's completely dark. Sam maneuvers blindly till he reaches for a doorknob to what I always thought was a closet.

"Where are we going?" I ask.

"Henry told me about this exit. It's a surprise," he says.

He unlocks the door, which, miraculously, opens to the outside world. The night casts a blue shadow. Sam closes his hand around my wrist like a baby would around my finger, the skin around his eyes so creased I know he's smiling with an open mouth beneath his mask. "C'mon."

Sam's shoes beat against the water on the empty sidewalk. Streetlamps lay gold halos on the concrete, making the puddles seem like a sheen of oil. Sam tows me through them, hopping to avoid the ones we could sink into.

His legs are long, thin, but powerful. His muscles stretch like rubber bands to accommodate the impatience of his bones. They carry him and me down the street and into a clearing, the grass wet with fresh rain.

A few years ago, Sam couldn't run long distances, but Sam has grown like any other boy would. Now he helps Henry out of bed in the mornings. He carries boxes from the back doors to the front desk. He carries me sometimes, says he remembers the days I was the one who used to carry him.

The clearing ceases just beside a building that resembles our hospital. Adorned with bricks, a few stories high, and checkered windows. Only, rather than stretches of city at its front doors, this place folds out into a courtyard, one with string lights, tents, and a hundred adolescents dressed in evening wear.

Sam brings me to the edge marked by a fence and a short line of saplings. The band's music travels to us, voices and instruments faded by the distance.

"What is this?" I ask, some aftermath of adrenaline shaking in my voice.

"A school dance," Sam says, amused by my amazement. "I heard some girls talking about it at the park the other day. I know we can't go in, but I thought—"

Sam swallows. The party wanes at the fence line. It illuminates his clothes, which I didn't notice earlier: slacks Nurse Ella just got him and a dress shirt buttoned to the crest of his collarbones. The boys out there are wearing suits, ties, clothes Sam's never even touched the likes of. He mutters curses like he's done something wrong and tries to fix his sleeves.

"Sam," I say, taking his hands, stilling them. He stares at the gloves, the separation it marks. I slip my fingers beneath them at his wrists. "What did you think?"

"Um—" he stutters, and the sound rouses warmth in my chest. His newfound confidence sometimes falters. Sometimes, his childish bouts of shame return with rosy shades on his cheeks.

I have the urge to tease him for a change.

"Do you want to dance with me?" I ask, taking a single step forward, mimicking the scene we've trespassed upon. Sam blushes harder, the heat solid. I move his hands to my waist and hold his shoulders.

"We've never danced properly before," he says, his breath catching on the air as I start to sway.

"Yes, we have."

Nurse Ella used to leave the radio on for us. Sam rocked his head to the beat. He jumped on the bed. He pulled at Ella's skirt, asking her to dance with us. When she shooed him off with her newspaper, he taught me little moves he'd read about in his fairy tales, said we were knights in a great ballroom.

"Did you forget?" I ask.

"No, I just . . ." Sam's fingers flex, like he wants to touch me more, like there's still too much between us. "Hold on."

He takes off his gloves, shoving them in his back pocket.

"Sam, we're outside," I warn, my fingers closing around his shirt collar.

"Shhh—we'll get caught if you keep talking." He smiles. He sighs in relief, feeling my jaw, my neck, sliding his hands back down to my waist and pulling me into him. He re-creates a memory from a few years ago when he was a tad smaller but just as mischievous. One where we hid in the bushes from our jailer and leering onlookers.

"You're silly," I whisper. Sam moves me with the music, a gentle rhythm we follow together.

"You're bad at this," he teases.

"So are you," I tease back.

We dance and banter for a few songs. Needless chattering and clinking glasses don't distract us. Even if Sam and I are rarely apart, we are rarely alone too. We take advantage of the time and the dark.

"Sweet Sam," he whispers.

"Yes?"

His touch runs up my spine, his eyes soft and melting. "Let's run away together like we talked about," he says. "Just you and me."

My body tenses.

"All those kids over there, I don't envy them," Sam keeps talking, his voice in my ear, his mask rubbing against my temple. "I don't need anything ordinary. Henry ran away with his friend to join the army when he was only a little older than us. I don't need anyone but you. So let's just run away. We can dance every single night, we can raise the little plants you like and share a bed and see the world. Let's run away, my love. Like this, but forever."

"What about our castle?" I whisper. My limbs feel stuck in a loop with the music. But I'm no longer there. I'm spreading through the ground, the hospital's body, its bricks, its concrete, its souls pulling me back. "We have to protect our patients, remember?"

Sam doesn't respond. His breath gains another kind of quality, a quieter sort of disappointment that sags against my shoulder.

I bury my face in his neck. I breathe in his scent, the comforting notes of our home embedded in his skin. We sneak out, we trail the outskirts, but we've never strayed forever. Sam *can't* stray forever. Even with barriers, his mask, his gloves, he can't survive without his medicine.

He can't be like the people on the other side of the fence.

"You're right," Sam says, rubbing his hands up and down my sides. "We'll wait till we're older, till I've gotten stronger."

"Are you sad?" I ask, peering.

"No." He presses my palm to his masked cheek.

"Promise?"

"Promise."

"I want you to be happy," I say, desperation behind it. "We can still go on adventures," I say, like I'm trying to make up for the regret on Sam's face. "We can eat sweet bread and pudding every day and—and play card games. We'll sunbathe every morning and play in the park and—"

"Sweet Sam," he interrupts.

"Yes?"

Sam leans in till our foreheads touch. The air is humid, thick, and cool. Sam breathes it in, slipping the mask below his chin. I shudder, but I know better than to stop him. His eyes become half-lidded, like suns setting beneath a hill.

"Can I kiss you?" he asks.

The couples dancing across the line hold one another close. They lose themselves in the music. They might even peck one another's cheeks and let their noses brush.

But none look at one another the way Sam looks at me.

"Yes," I say. And Sam doesn't hesitate.

He's sloppy at first, hungry, but his tenderness doesn't waver. He hooks his arm around my back, the other cradling the back of my neck. I slip my fingers into his locks, the heat traveling through us like steam. The talking, the dancing, the singing—the noise of anything that isn't us—disperse till we're convinced no one else exists.

Sam's never kissed before. Neither have I. Yet it isn't what either of us imagined it would be. Like all things between us, it is electric at first, grand and revelatory, a flame settling in a comfortable fire. Soon enough, Sam is smiling, his eyes rolling on a high.

"You're bad at this," he teases.

"I'm sorry."

"I'm joking." He picks me off the ground, purposefully falling backward into the wet grass. I shriek against his mouth, his chuckles vibrating through his chest beneath me.

"Wow," he sighs, kissing me again, kneading the flesh of my legs and sides.

"What is it?"

"Nothing, keep kissing me," he orders, pecking my face like a bird. On my brow, my cheekbone, my chin, my nose, my eyelids.

When he lies down, he keeps me with him, our sated hearts beating together.

"Look," I whisper, pointing at the sky. "Our stars are out."

"Yes, sweet Sam," he whispers. He stretches his limbs like a cat on a rooftop and kisses my cheek. "Our stars are out."

22
broken things

HIKARI IS VOMITING. I rub her back as the acid burns her throat and her body pulses with coughs. Her head hangs in the aftermath.

"I'm sorry," I say, making sure she rinses her mouth with water and swallows her medicine, no matter how painful.

"Don't apologize," Hikari rasps. I walk her to bed and she tries to smirk at me. "You're more nurse than lover now."

"That mischief never leaves you, does it?" I tease.

She lifts her arms, allowing me to take her shirt off. She's lost weight. Her ribs cast skeletal shadows. I throw the dirty shirt into her hamper and pick one from her pile of clean clothes. She shakes her head, so I pick up another. She nods for my third choice, a black long-sleeve that'll conceal unhealed marks.

Helping her put it on, I also smooth down her pant legs and put on her shoes. She can do it herself, as she's told me many times, but the perpetual swelling in her legs makes it difficult to stand or walk for long periods of time.

I can list the symptoms all day like a rendition of Hikari's chart. Taking care of her is a part of my day. Before that night in the old cardiology wing, I enjoyed passivities. I enjoyed listening, watching, being beside her. After that night, I enjoyed being *with* her. Physically, mentally, emotionally, to a level that transcends nearness. This is a part of it. Like eating or sleeping, it is a necessity I appreciate.

"What is that?" Hikari asks, pointing to her side table. On it rests a potted plant with red bulbs blooming from the leaves that I stole from the gardens. I lay it in her hand, let her take it in through drowsy eyes.

"To add to your collection."

Hikari smiles. A weak smile, but at least she is trying.

"I'd kiss you if I weren't gross right now," she whispers. I put my hands on her knees and peck her lips, taking the succulent from her and setting it next to all the others on the windowsill.

"Is it time?" she asks, looking at her shoes. I kneel before her and tie them, catching the sorrow in her gaze.

"I'll ask Eric if we can go tomorrow."

"No." She shakes her head, standing up. "No, let's do it."

"Are you sure?"

"Yes," she says, and so I lead her out of the room.

———

Sony passed away six days ago.

The first three nights, Hikari cried. It was the violent sort, the kind where loss thrashed in steady waves of sobbing through her body. Then it died into silence and her tears fell without a voice behind them.

The last three have been dry, but there are moments Hikari falters. Because you don't lose someone once. You lose them hearing a song that reminds you of their smile. Passing an old landmark. Laughing at a joke they would've liked. You lose them infinitely.

I hold Hikari's hand as we pass C's room. Through the wall, you can hear his parents speaking in French. Their anger at C for stealing his dad's truck and running off didn't survive long once they heard about Sony. What did is their concern. It bleeds through the language.

"*Cœur, t'es pas censé te promener, allonge-toi, je t'en supplie,*" his mother says.

He's near the top of the transplant list now. He isn't meant to be standing up, much less overexerting himself. But the moment he sees the time on the clock, C tears out his IVs and gets out of bed.

He grabs his jacket and starts putting it on as his mother grabs him by the shoulders, begging him to sit.

"*Je vais chercher Neo. Tu peux être au téléphone avec lui. Je comprends que tu sois en deuil, mais tu dois rester ici maintenant—*"

"She's my friend, Maman. You can come with me or you can stay, but I'm going."

C's father watches from the chair in the corner of the room, hands on his face. He doesn't rush to stop his son or help his wife. I think he and she are at different stages of acceptance. C's mother still has faith in medicine, in the possibility of the transplant. C's father sees his son withering to a weaker version of who he used to be with each passing day.

"Coeur!" his mother yells.

"*Chèrie, laisse-le,*" his father says. He stands, grabbing both their coats. "Coeur, you can go, but let us come with you."

"*Merci,* Papa," C says. He opens the door to Hikari and me.

"You ready?" he asks.

"Yeah."

He nods, a bit disconnected.

"Where's Neo?"

Neo's parents haven't contacted him since our escape. When Sony died, he was escorted back to his room and hasn't emerged since. Hikari and I have tried to visit him, but he never answers the door. C hasn't had the chance to so much as leave his room till now.

He doesn't waste time knocking. He barges into Neo's room without forewarning.

"Neo?" he calls. "We have to go now. I——"

Neo's bed is empty. Instead, there is a boy crawling on the ground, looking *under* the bed, around it, searching every crevice in the room with a frantic look in his eye.

C stalls. "What are you doing?"

Neo doesn't bother with formalities. He doesn't even acknowledge us.

"Hee," Neo says, moving his bedsheets around.

"What?"

"The cat," he says.

I notice now, his hair is uncombed and it doesn't look like he's changed clothes in a long time. The sweatshirt he wore the night of Sony's episode is in the corner of his room, folded but unwashed, blood staining the seams.

"She was just here," Neo mutters to himself, searching the same spaces over and over again as if Hee will appear in one of them if he looks enough times. "I need to find her."

"Neo, we'll find her later," C says. "We have to go now."

But C isn't the only one who's disconnected. Upon C's words, Neo finally looks up.

"I'm not allowed to leave," he says.

C frowns. "What? Why not?"

"I haven't eaten."

Neo's head droops, not in shame but in preoccupation. C notices, then, the pills and food tray that have gone untouched on the side table, and he isn't tender as he usually is.

"Then eat," he orders.

Neo stares at C, a glaze over his eyes, fingers forming a loop around his wrist. He becomes a statue, untouchable. He looks like if you touch him, he will combust, the tightly wound knots of his muscles will snap, and he will come undone.

"I need to find Hee," he whispers. Then he goes back to searching the same places yet again.

"Neo," C says. "This is important."

"It won't make a difference. I can't leave. We went too far this time, and I can't go. There's nothing I can do— Hee, where are you? Come out."

"Neo—"

"I have to find her!" Neo's voice cracks. He spins around to face us, his breaths short and fast, the marble of his statue cracking. A glossy layer of tears pools at his waterline.

"Neo." Hikari.

C and I both turn to see her standing at the door, picking a wobbly cat up in her arms.

"Neo, she's right here. Look," she says.

Neo comes to a frenzied stop.

"Hee," he whispers, wiping his eyes with his sleeve. Hikari hands him the cat. Neo huffs with relief, his brows arching as his lip trembles.

"I'm sorry for being mean," he says, swaddling her. "I'm sorry. Don't run away again."

Hee meows at him.

Neo sniffles, checking her chipped ear, the stump where her fourth leg should be. His feet give out from under him, as if they've been carrying a weight so heavy they can no longer bear him.

"Neo—" C tries to keep him upright, but Hikari is the one who catches him, like a doorframe he can lean on as he descends to the floor.

"It doesn't feel real," he says, his voice muffled in Hee's fur. "It feels like a joke. It feels like another one of her jokes." He inhales as if drowning. "She left me her cat. A lawyer came and put papers on the desk. She left me her clothes too. She left me her stupid cat and her clothes and her sneakers. She knew she was going to die and I was mean to her and it doesn't feel real."

"It's all right," Hikari whispers, hugging him.

"I just keep pretending she's off somewhere stealing from a toy store or racing a homeless person or something. And then, *this*, and—" He motions with one arm to where an unopened suitcase and dirty white sneakers fill the dank corner. "Her kids asked me when she's coming back. Because she hasn't finished reading them their story, and they looked up at me, and they asked when is Miss Sony coming back." He looks at Hikari, guilty tears rolling down his cheeks.

"She didn't finish the story," he repeats, tucking his face into Hikari's shoulder. "She never got to know the ending."

"It's okay," Hikari says again. She rubs his back up and down. "It's okay. She's with her mom. She has her mom now; she's not alone."

"Hey." Eric. He walks in wearing his own clothes, a wrinkled shirt, an old jacket, and sleeplessness in his eyes. He pats down his matted hair and clears his throat. We stare at the box sitting in his arms.

He looks at Neo. "I called your mom." A short word of approval. Locking and unlocking his jaw, he motions to the hall. "Let's go."

The drive is silent. Not like our last car ride. Beyond my window, the ocean gleams the same as it did the first time I saw it. Gulls fly their paths, the wind trekking the waves.

For how monumental death can be, the sea doesn't stop to notice. Too many of her sailors met their end in her arms.

But Sony adored the sea. I like to believe that the sea is angry for her. Why else would she crash against the cliffsides and crawl with foamy fingers to land if not to search for the passion that's been stolen from the world?

Eric parks the car, C's parents right behind. The walk to the beach is akin to the drive.

Our bare feet press into the sand. The salt spray and tart taste give us a glimpse into the near past. Farther down the stretch of land, I can make out shapes of people dipping into the ocean, running across the bank, and sitting in the dunes.

Eric carries Sony's ashes to the threshold between land and sea. He doesn't bother adjusting his clothes. The water soaks through his pants above his knees.

C's parents wait onshore. With Neo and Hikari's help on either side, C walks into the water. It's cold, icy stones and shells in the silt.

Eric asks us if we'd like to say a few words. We do, each of us saying a little something to the empty expanse. Logically, we know Sony can't hear us, but this isn't really for Sony at all.

Eric caresses the surface of the box. He presses his forehead to it and closes his eyes. A moment passes, and I remember those days Sony fell asleep hooked up to a ventilator. I remember how he used to cry and choke it all down so she wouldn't wake. I remember the whispers I could never make out every night after tucking her in. It's only now, as I hear it up close, that I realize they weren't renditions of good nights or little reminders to stay alive or anything so confined to a nurse-patient relationship.

They were a father's *I love you*s.

Eric opens the box.

"Good night, Sony," he whispers. "I hope you find your everything."

Her ashes spring free in the shape of wings. Wind carries the sheer gray cloud into the sky, dusted rain settling on the waves that give it passage to other worlds.

I take hold of Eric's hand as he lets the box sink into the water. He wipes his face and looks out as far as the horizon stretches, watching Sony take the shape of water.

When the cold begins numbing his limbs, Eric retires to the beach. He sits in the sand, Neo and C joining him.

Hikari lingers a little longer in the shallows. I stay with her, helping her return the seashells in her pockets to their home. The only one she keeps is the black stone I gave her. She traces the white band with her finger.

"Is it always like this?" she asks. "It just happens, and we get no say in it?"

Laughter sounds in the far distance. Hikari catches the silhouettes of those strangers playing on the shore. They run into the water, shrieking from the temperature. One hugs another, splashing and spinning. Their laughter is like a song playing too far away, a story too far to read.

"I didn't even know her very long," Hikari says, tucking the stone back into her pocket. "It feels like I started to love her and never got to finish."

Love isn't a thing that's ever finished, I want to tell her. It's not a chronological feat. Her love for Sony is based on gentle affections, loud adventures, and the little pieces of friendship people tend to overlook. It does not end simply because we had to say goodbye.

Hikari sighs. When she does, she feels lighter somehow, not quite as full as before.

Grief can be destructive, a parasite that needs expulsion, water flowing over a dam, but like most terrible, necessary things, it can be shared. Time is kind with grief. It takes it from you, piece by piece, till the sorrow is a song you remember the beat of but no longer hear.

I take Hikari by the wrist, coaxing it from her pocket. The stone is still in her palm. I snake my hand down her arm and intertwine our fingers so that the gem can be cradled rather than clutched.

"Look, Sam," she breathes. With our joined hands, she points at the evening turning to night. The sky kisses our angry sea with gold and red tints, breaking through the clouds to caress the ripples.

"The sea's on fire."

———

Before we leave the beach, C has a panic attack.

He cries, the sunset's light casting shadows on his face. He shields himself with a hand, the other holding Neo. It's the sort of crying that trembles through his jaw. The kind of crying that tightens in his chest and he chooses to fight rather than allow escape.

"Here, sit down," Neo says. He guides C to the grassy area by the parking lot. C stumbles when he walks, his legs shaking. He falls onto his seat bones, nearly taking Neo down with him.

"Stay here," Neo says. "I'll get your mom."

"No, don't go," C begs. He grabs Neo by his pants and wraps his arms around his legs, tucking his face to Neo's stomach, eyes shut tight.

Neo lets him, cupping his shoulders.

"What's wrong?"

"I can't do it," C says. "I can't go back."

"What are you talking about?"

"I don't want to give it up, Neo." C's words become humid, his forehead wrinkling with every breath. He shakes his head, choking on the air, the voice of a child running from a nightmare in his throat. "I want to keep my heart."

That word is practically a curse spoken from C's mouth. Neo's hands stroking C's head and back, trying to comfort him, still at the sound of it.

"Coeur," he says.

"I want to keep it." C grasps Neo tighter. "I don't want another."

Neo tries to pull C off of him to no avail.

"Coeur, stop."

"I'm not doing it." C shakes his head, suffocating himself in Neo's hoodie. "I won't go through with it. I can't."

"Coeur." Neo struggles, pushing and squirming. "You're not thinking straight—"

"I can't, Neo."

"Coeu—"

"I can't—"

"Coeur, you'll die! Are you listening to me? You'll die." Neo shoves C back by the shoulders, holding him there. "Your heart can't keep up with your body anymore, and you can't just pretend that nothing is wrong, waiting for it to stop beating."

"No, no—this heart is what makes me *me*," C says, pointing at his chest. He meets Neo's gaze, affection and fear mingling in the mix. "My heart beats with thunder and lightning, and I know it's weak, but it's the one I gave you."

Neo clenches his fists in C's jacket and shakes his head.

"You don't get to do this."

"I'm scared, Neo."

"I know you're scared! I'm scared too, but you're not allowed to give up!"

"What if this fear means something? What if the transplant doesn't work?" C's trembling travels down his body. He puts his hands over Neo's, staring into his eyes as if he never quite got a chance to look at him long enough before now.

"I want to be with you," C says. "You're all I've ever wanted. What if I don't get the chance?"

Neo, like the rock he is, isn't shaken by such words. He would've said in the past that choosing between what-ifs is not a luxury for people like them. He would say that the world is fundamentally unfair and chances are illusions of choices time takes for itself.

But Neo is not imprisoned by the past. He is the strongest of all of us, but he is also the most willing to be weak. He doesn't put up a fight, not for himself. The only people he will fight for are the ones with him now.

Neo wipes C's tears with his thumbs and cups his face. "Then I'll spread your ashes in the sea and walk into the waves."

C blinks, his hands falling on Neo's.

"You really are a writer," he whispers. "You'll read to me tonight?"

"Yes."

"And you'll stay with me after I fall asleep?"

As Coeur tidies up Neo's collar and wipes his shirt of any sand, Neo hugs C around the neck and presses his nose into his hair.

"*Si Dieu me laisse, on sera ensemble pour toujours,*" he says, and though it is broken and perhaps not said completely right, C hugs him.

"Your accent is terrible."

They laugh together, and when C finds the strength, he walks back to the car holding Neo's hand.

We go home, all of us in the car's back seat, uncomfortable, with wet pants and sandy shoes, huddled under a single blanket, letting the wind kiss us goodbye through the windows as the bomb on C's wrist goes tick, tick, tick—

23
music

C OEUR NEVER KNEW what he liked. People asked him what his favorite color was. They asked him if he preferred playing at the park or in his backyard. Coeur was quite indecisive on the matter, and as a four-year-old, he spent an inordinate amount of time thinking of answers to these questions. But why did he have to choose? Both the playground and backyard were fun, and if any color went missing from the world, Coeur would miss it.

With these indecisive philosophies and his relatively quiet nature, Coeur became a passive child compared to his rowdy older brothers. He was the kind that just went along with what others did and liked. As Coeur grew up, however, he found that this lack of personality made him feel hollow. The kids on the playground had their favorite games. Some had insatiable energy and capricious attitudes, while others were tender-voiced and lethargic. Coeur, for the life of him, could not figure out what he was, so he must've been missing a part of himself, right?

That's what Coeur believed the pain was. The muscles between his ribs ached. His teeth were sore. His hearing faded in and out by the time he was ten. Coeur never said a thing about any of it. He believed it was merely a symptom of being empty.

When he graduated into adolescence, Coeur found his peers liked him. Girls called him a pretty boy, and boys respected his size and athleticism. Questions of personality became irrelevant in the face of popularity.

To maintain his image, Coeur took up swimming. Not because he liked it, but because being good at it made him like himself.

His hollowness felt momentarily breached, filled with the pool's water when he swam. Winning race after race kept the dam full as people clapped.

The dam, he found, leaked rather fast.

When Coeur's father drove him home from a tournament, saying they'd have no more room for trophies, he clasped Coeur's shoulder and said he was proud of his son. Coeur found the age-old question sitting at the back of his mind like the hook on a drain.

Why?

Coeur didn't try very hard at swimming. He was just good at it because he was tall and naturally muscled. He looked at his dad from the passenger seat. Then he turned back around to face the road, too afraid to ask.

Coeur did find distractions from the hollowness. He found peace in an old record player his mother gave him for his birthday. Not much of a talker, he listened to music all day long because even if he had nothing to say, he always had something to sing. His habit worsened when he got earbuds and a phone. Music became his constant companion.

It was hardly enough, though. One can't live their entire life lost in diversions. There were only so many songs that sounded out Coeur's desire to feel complete.

A girl once took it upon herself to kiss him.

Coeur was poor at academics. Numbers were difficult for him to wrap his head around, and words were far worse. A girl in his class offered to help him study. At her house, about twenty minutes in, she pressed her lips to his.

Coeur was startled. He'd never kissed or been kissed, and the concept of kissing had only crossed his mind as something people did because they were in relationships or because they were bored.

Coeur was bored most of his life, but he'd never resorted to anything sexual to cure it. Like everything else, he wasn't sure if he liked girls or boys or anyone at all, so it was easier to ignore the choices. But it felt good *being* liked. It filled his hollowness as she got on top of him, and they kissed till their mouths were sore.

"Why are you doing this?" Coeur finally asked.

"Because I like you," she said, kissing his jaw.

"But . . ." Coeur pushed her away gently. "Why?"

It took the girl a moment. Her eyes flickered about as if the answer lay somewhere around her bedroom. Then she said what Coeur feared.

"I don't know." She shrugged. "You're cute, and you're nice," she said, smiling, reaching for him again. Coeur held her arms, stopping her midway. He swallowed and asked if they could just go back to studying.

Coeur didn't go to anyone's house after that. He soon figured out that his quiet friendliness signaled one of two things when he was alone with people. They either took it as an invitation to be physical, or they found it off-putting.

People called him aloof, in the clouds, half there, but in reality, Coeur was almost always paying attention. What he was ignoring were his own problems.

He didn't have chest pains that sometimes got so bad he felt like he was dying. He wasn't lonely to the point of crying at night. He didn't look at his ceiling, listening to his music, wondering if he was just an outline, someone who was secretly made of glass without a center. A hollow beast with a bleeding heart.

Then, on a day that his heart ached more than most, Coeur met his match in a skinny, short boy with a temper from Hell and a face to fit.

Coeur sat next to him in literature class, got his books, and in return, Neo helped him answer questions.

Neo was a savant of silence. He did it with substance rather than insecurity.

There was something strange and compelling about him, Coeur thought. He was pretty in an unconventional sense. He had high cheekbones, messy hair, pale skin, a button nose, hard eyes, and lips Coeur swore had never smiled a day in their life. He was a cute yet elegant album cover in Coeur's eyes, but his music was something to get used to.

Neo was mean and impatient. A brisk tempo with harsh orchestra strokes.

"Sorry, I'm stupid," Coeur would say, messing up on a sentence.

And Neo would say, "Could you not apologize every two seconds? It's annoying."

Or:

"Neo, am I doing this right?"

"I already said you're fine, Coeur. Quit asking, would you?"

Neo had a habit of calling Coeur by his full name. Everyone called him C. Even his teachers. But not Neo. He said it in full. And especially when he was being mean.

"Coeur." He flicked his forehead. "Pay attention."

"Coeur." He dropped a paperback on his head. "Don't fall asleep."

But like all musical pieces, Neo revealed subtly softer pieces of himself, like strings of a piano's melody.

"Hey." He poked Coeur's finger, the one tracing a line on the book's page. "Don't get frustrated. We have time. Just try again."

Then:

"Coeur, wait." Neo'd pull him back when they were walking out of class and tuck the tag back into his shirt.

Neo was also funny in a way that wasn't trying to be funny: a brass instrument with a quiet but sudden and sharp entrance.

"In *The Picture of Dorian Gray*, there's a character named Lord Henry who says that being in love is the privilege of the boring," Neo said, while he and Coeur sat in detention for talking too much in class.

Neo read. Coeur watched him read. And occasionally, Neo would say something, and Coeur would smile and listen. "He says that people resort to love because they have nothing better to do."

Coeur looked over his shoulder at their sleeping teacher, then back at Neo's pouty face as he flipped through the novel. He propped his chin on his arms with a crooked smile and asked in return, "What if the greatest adventure of *my* life is being in love?"

"Then you're boring."

Coeur laughed. Neo was the smartest person he'd ever met, yet at once, the worst hint taker in the history of hint taking. Not that that bothered Coeur in the slightest.

For the first time in his life, he knew what he liked. He knew what he wanted. He was aware that he was aloof, up in the clouds, half there, and wholly infatuated with his mean, smart classmate.

Love does not require reason. But Neo gave Coeur the simplest one. He looked into Coeur rather than at him. He sought past the surface, wading into the deep end of the pool.

So one day in detention, when the teacher had once again fallen asleep—

"Neo," Coeur whispered. "Why do you like me?"

"I don't like you. You're annoying."

"You tolerate me."

"Marginally."

"Why do you tolerate me, then?"

Neo looked up from his book. His gaze didn't flicker or search. Such a question didn't have an answer sitting in some corner of the classroom. Instead, it lay in Coeur. In that center he was so sure was missing.

"You're kind," Neo said. "Not the normal kindness that people throw around. It's a real type of kindness, the raw, thoughtful kind that comes from the heart."

A sudden shyness overtook Neo, pink hues marking his cheeks as he met Coeur's gaze. "You didn't grab a book for someone because they asked. You grabbed it because you saw they couldn't reach." Neo shrugged then, wiping at his face. "Also, you're only partially annoying, I guess."

"What part of me is annoying?" Coeur whispered, smiling like an idiot.

"For one, you're attractive. It draws too much attention."

"That's cute. Did you steal that from *Pride and Prejudice*?"

"Do the homework, Coeur," Neo said, standing up and putting his backpack on as the bell rang. "Or I'll stab you in the eye with my pen."

"Which eye?"

Neo smiled, a little laugh made of mostly breath escaping his lips.

That was the day Coeur decided he would tell Neo how he felt.

"This is for a girl you like?" Coeur's mother asked later that night, reading over her son's shoulder as he wrote a letter, a letter he'd been writing and rewriting for hours in the dim corner of his room.

Coeur shook his head. "It's for a boy."

"Oh."

"But I do like him."

"Yes, *chérie*, I gathered that." She chuckled, bringing Coeur's dinner to his room and then kissing her son's cheek. "I look forward to meeting him."

Coeur finished his letter, not completely satisfied, but then he never would be. There is no perfect way to describe what finding love for the first time in your life feels like, except, maybe, to explain how comfortable you are with them and how passionately you are thinking of them.

Coeur fell asleep, hours later, staring at the ceiling, holding the letter to his chest restlessly, not thinking of loneliness, hollowness, or his heart.

He thought of Neo.

But Neo wasn't in class the next morning. Coeur waited in his seat, peeking at the door with every click of the doorknob, disappointment settling in his stomach when it was someone else.

He'd never asked for Neo's number or anything because the one time he brought it up it made Neo tense. He said his father was a bit of a helicopter when it came to technology, so he'd rather not hand it out.

So when excruciatingly long days followed and Neo didn't come into school for a full week, Coeur walked, letter in hand, to his teacher's desk after the bell rang and class was dismissed.

"Excuse me, sir?" Coeur cleared his throat. "Do you know where Neo's been?"

"Neo? Oh, he'll be out for the foreseeable future, I believe," his teacher said. "Poor kid's back in the hospital now."

Coeur took a moment to process the words, thought he'd misheard. Then, if a bit brokenly, he asked, "What?"

His teacher looked up at him through his glasses, curious now. He must've noticed Coeur's distress, the slight tremble in his hand, because he visibly softened, facing his student head-on and removing his lenses.

"I'm sorry, C. I assumed you two were close," he began. "Neo's been ill for a few years now. That's why he's out of school so often."

Coeur had always just assumed Neo had prior engagements— a club he didn't talk about, some sort of excuse to skip class half the week—not . . . not something like this.

The teacher sighed. "He had an accident with some boys last week. I'm surprised you didn't hear about it. It's been buzzing all over the school. He was hurt quite badly."

An accident. With some boys.

Coeur thought back to the morning after detention when he walked into school. He'd just told his coach he was going to quit swimming, to which his coach had yelled and flailed his arms. Coeur didn't remember much else except agreeing to do one last tournament, and then he'd be done.

He remembered walking past Neo in the hall, past teammates who he hadn't really spoken to outside practices. They practically surrounded him, but Coeur didn't see it that way at the time.

He saw his old perceivers, the ones who thought him nice, athletic, a good-looking picture to decorate the scene. He saw them gathered around the picture of his happiness, the person he perhaps didn't *look* right with but felt right with.

Coeur had a choice. He could walk over and grab Neo by the arm. He could tear him away from the danger his classmates might pose or even just ask his "friends" what they were doing. He could've done any number of things. But Coeur always had an affinity for avoiding decisions.

"Don't let it shake you up," his teacher said, but Coeur was already lost replaying the scene over and over again as if thinking of the past would somehow change it. "Why don't you go visit him? I'm sure he'd appreciate seeing a friend."

Coeur nodded and left, the guilt spreading through his body like a virus. It ate at him for the following weeks until the hollowness Neo had filled became a cave with raw, wounded walls.

Coeur cried silently the first night. He felt bad, yes, but more so, he missed Neo. Although that wasn't entirely correct either.

In French, you do not say you miss someone. You say they are missing from you.

Tu me manques, Coeur said, inside his head, mouthing it, as if Neo could hear.

Every night Coeur wrote Neo letters till he was surrounded by dozens of them. Every night, Coeur repeated the same line over and over again, *Tu me manques tellement que même mon coeur souffre*, until little by little, his heart adopted the words as its own.

Waking up in the hospital was a stroke of fate. Coeur was sure of it. His parents were up to their necks in worry, not knowing what was wrong with their child.

Coeur didn't care.

He was mildly aware that his health was in trouble, but his mind was on other things.

Was Neo in the building somewhere? Was he reading and delivering pretentious opinions with wry little insults to other sick children? Was he all right? Had he forgiven Coeur? Coeur struggled with that question the most. He fidgeted on the bed, an anxious dog waiting to be taken off its leash.

When the doctors diagnosed Coeur's disease and how fast and aggressively it had progressed, they gave his heart an expiration date. As if it were a fruit slowly rotting.

A year, they said. A year and then Coeur would need another. Even then, he was at risk of a multitude of attacks, infections, and other things Coeur had no interest in knowing about. What *he* heard was that he'd have to remain in the hospital for observation for a while, which made him smile—morbidly, from his doctors' perspectives.

"Can I go now?" he'd ask, over and over.

Eventually, his father told him to just go on and take a walk if his doctors thought it was fine. He roamed with purpose, searching the halls, sneaking into an elevator he had no right to access, and working floor by floor, until finally, he collided with a strange, running creature.

"Oh my God!" he yelled. "I'm so sorry!"

The first thing Coeur ever gave me was an apology.

The second was a story to unveil.

He spent the rest of that day in a turmoil of emotions. Neo *hadn't* forgiven him. He wouldn't for some time. But when Coeur was finally able to confront his own ignorance, time and friendship wove their paths back together.

Coeur kept his letters. He kept them in his possession along with his story for an entire year. Because, as it turned out, Neo didn't need a grand confession. He didn't need to be swept off his feet or entangled in a forbidden romance.

Tonight, Coeur has all the animation of a corpse. He lies in his bed hooked to an ECMO machine. An eternal pump keeps his blood flowing. His senses are dulled by medicine. He cannot walk or stand or eat, yet he is content.

Neo lies beside him, his head on Coeur's shoulder. They read books they've read before, listening to songs they know by heart. Neo points to certain passages that make him laugh, humming to the tunes.

When Neo writes, Coeur shuts his eyes, pressing his nose into Neo's messy hair. He hugs him around the waist. The melodic pen strokes bring him peace.

Their story is almost finished. Given the state of things, Neo reads Coeur the full manuscript in a day. Coeur's eyes never leave Neo's face as he does.

"What do you think?" Neo whispers.

"I think the world is going to weep for every word you write."

"That doesn't sound like a compliment."

"It's your first review."

"It's my only review."

"You should quote me on the inside of the cover."

"'To my Coeur,'" Neo mocks, "'for making fun of this manuscript before it was even finished.'"

"Perfect."

"Good. I'm keeping it. You sappy Frenchman."

"I've been meaning to ask, did you secretly learn to speak French for me?"

"No." Neo frowns. "I secretly learned French so you and your mom couldn't talk behind my back anymore."

"My mom likes you more than me." Coeur laughs.

"Well, I know that *now*."

Neo's head dips, their laughter mixing. Coeur sits up and cups Neo's face so that he can keep looking at it. They touch noses, their chuckles fading.

"Our story's just begun, Neo," Coeur whispers.

"Don't start."

"It's just the beginning. It is," Coeur presses on. "You have so many stories left to read and so many left to tell."

Coeur slips one of his letters into Neo's lap, the first one. The one that is too long, riddled with mistakes, and so utterly imperfect that Coeur cannot fathom a truer confession of love. Neo unwraps it with care, smoothing down the paper. He reads it aloud, at times stopping to gather himself as his jaw aches.

Kindness and resilience were born in the bodies of two broken boys, and all they ever wished for was more time to be together.

They are not a tragedy.

They are a story of love and loss.

When Neo finishes the last sentence, Coeur smiles. Their silhouettes connect in the dark. Coeur caresses Neo's high cheekbones, his perched nose, and his lips, which have smiled for him more times than he can count. He admires his favorite color pooling in Neo's eyes, and he cannot imagine that he would want to be anywhere else.

———

The surgeon described the procedure to Coeur's parents multiple times. Coeur's mother is talking to him now as they inject Coeur with sedatives for the operation.

Neo, Hikari, and I aren't allowed in, so we wait outside. Right now, Coeur's brothers are each taking turns talking to him. His father holds up his old varsity swimming jacket, talking about something or other as Coeur falls under the medication's spell.

His mother is the last to see him off before his stretcher is led into the hall. When they tell her it's time, she struggles to let him go. Coeur is her youngest. Her baby. And she must relinquish him to strangers to have his chest cut open and his heart replaced.

Once they wheel Coeur into the hall, Neo stands. He approaches the stretcher.

Eric asks the nurse to give them a minute.

"Neo," Coeur says, a bit too loudly. He smiles deliriously as Neo leans over him, taking his hand.

"Hello, my Coeur," he whispers. "How are you feeling?"

"So great," Coeur says. "Drugs are so great."

"Are they?"

"So great. But don't try them, they're bad for you."

"If you insist."

Coeur continues smiling, his eyes closing for a few seconds, then opening again, his head lolling to the side, then back.

"You said you'd steal me a heart, you remember that? Was this you? Did you get it for me?" Coeur asks in a whisper, his pupils expanding the longer they remain on Neo.

Neo's lips thin, his eyes glossing as he remembers the slip of paper. The promise.

For Coeur,
I'll give you a heart.

That piece of paper is still wedged in the hit list like a bookmark. Coeur wanted to keep it somewhere they wouldn't lose it.

"No, I didn't," Neo says, dragging his thumb back and forth over Coeur's knuckles. "But you know you've always had mine."

Coeur cannot sanely take in the words, but he can see the sentiment on Neo's face. He looks at him as long as he can with a certain kind of joy only simple pleasures offer. Holding his hand. Hearing him. Seeing him. Being with him.

"Neo, Neo, Neo," Coeur whispers, as if to himself.

"Yes, Coeur."

"I love your name so much. It's my favorite name," Coeur says.

Neo attempts to keep his composure. He swallows hard, his exhales shaky and frail. His palm presses to the center of Coeur's chest over the gown. The thunder and lightning rumble just beneath.

Neo drags his fingertips over Coeur's face. He leans down and presses his lips to his. It is slow and gentle. Coeur kisses him back, as much as he can, the two of them parting with flushed smiles.

"You better kiss me like that when I wake up," Coeur whispers.

Neo laughs a breath, a tear rolling down his cheek.

"I will."

The nurse gently tells Neo that she needs to take Coeur to the operating room now. Neo nods in agreement, holding Coeur's hand until he is taken down the hall.

"Neo? Are you coming?" Coeur calls, although the calling fades into whispers. "Neo, Neo, my Neo."

Hikari holds Neo's hand. He doesn't wipe the tear. He lets it hang from his jaw and watches as Coeur disappears into limbo.

I've told you before that I am not tied to my body. Similarly, my body is not tied to common perceptions. Normal people aren't allowed in operating rooms, but you've probably gathered by now that I am neither normal nor a person.

"Sam."

"Yes, Coeur," I say, standing at the head of the operating table. Around me, nurses and techs gather their supplies. Two surgeons get ready to scrub in. One nurse places each tool that shall soon be used to tinker with Coeur's organs on a tray while the anesthesiologist prepares.

All can see me, I think. *They simply do not think my presence is unnatural. They accept it like the sound of a scalpel against a metal tray and the brightness of the surgeon's light.*

"Sam," Coeur says again, eyes half-lidded, yet on the verge of panic. "You have to take care of him while I'm under, okay?"

I caress his hand, the one that Neo had to let go.

"Okay."

"You need to make him take his medicine. He—he has—has one round in the evening and two in the mornings. He won't eat if he's alone either, all right? Sit and—and eat with him, that way he'll have a little at least. And—and you have to offer to do something with him, otherwise he won't get out of bed. Take him to the library or the gardens, but—but don't let him sit too close to the hedge, his skin gets itchy. And he says he hates hugs, but he doesn't, he needs them. Hug him tonight, all right? Just hold him whenever he's sad or scared. And . . ." Coeur stops, breathing in as if he's trying not to cry.

"Sam, if his dad comes, you have to protect him. I—I know you don't intervene—I know that's one of your rules—but you have to keep him safe for me."

"I will," I say, and Coeur knows I mean it.

"Thank you, Sam." He smiles and my hand slips from his. "You really are a strange, beautiful creature."

The anesthesiologist stands over Coeur and places a mask on his nose and mouth. "Count down for me, sweetheart, okay?"

"Will you count with me, Sam?" Coeur breathes.

I nod.

Memories twist into one another, not like film strips, more like a book's flipping pages melting into one another. That's all a person is in the end, isn't it? Bones and blood and beauty spliced to memories.

Four.

Coeur does not think of that as he descends into the depths of an ocean so deep he cannot see the surface. He does not remember the things he did or didn't do.

Three.

He remembers Sony cheating at Monopoly, Hikari's jokes and drawings, Eric flicking him, the long drives with his father, the sports games on TV he watched with his brothers, his mother chuckling and bringing him his dinner late at night.

Two.

He does not think of loneliness, hollowness, or hearts. He thinks of Neo's lips and the laughs he breathed against his neck and his cold yet gentle hands, and his little smiles, and the tear that rolled down his cheek the last time he saw him.

One.

Coeur sinks into the dark.

And his love for Neo sinks with him.

24
before

I DON'T KNOW WHAT love is.

Some say it has two forms. It can be roaring and passionate. It swallows you, consumes you, the other person a source of breathing. Like a violent flame that burns out in a single night.

Love can also be gentle, subtle. A wave washing into shore on a quiet afternoon. It settles over you till you become comfortable with the tide.

Sam has taken to calling me *my love*. It started as a phrase of endearment, the kind he would whisper when we kissed in closets or under tables.

Kissing Sam is addictive. For someone who feels like an intruder in their own body, it is connection given an act. It makes me feel like I belong. Like I belong with him.

"My love, tell me things," he says.

"What kind of things?" I ask.

"Anything. I want to hear you."

"You taste like medicine," I say, and he smiles, his teeth against my lips. It is, perhaps, my favorite feeling in the world.

Sam and I sleep in his bed. His legs tangle with mine as

the dark rolls over the light. His head rests against my chest, drowsiness humming through him, the sheets tucked right up to his chin. Before he falls asleep, he traces my cheekbone with two fingers and asks, "What do you dream of, my love?"

"I don't think I can dream," I tell him.

"Everyone dreams," he says. "I dream of you and me sailing across the ocean, and seeing the world."

"The whole world?" I ask.

"Every corner of it." The sheets rustle as he shifts. "What do you dream of, my sweet Sam?"

I think, reveling in the feeling of Sam's lips laying affections on my neck.

"I dream of this," I say. Sam's curiosity looks at me through his lashes. "I dream of you and I like this, together, tomorrow, and every tomorrow after that."

"My love," Sam says like it's a statement of its own, a kiss that's spoken rather than had. "All my tomorrows are yours."

———————

Sam stretches his neck back against the table, blowing out his breath as the doctors untie his gown. He lies horizontally, an object of examination. Sam has marks on his body, patches that rise above the skin. They crack and bleed in the cold. They become sore and raw when he bathes.

The men surrounding him talk to each other as if Sam isn't there. They are his mechanics, and his engine needs tending to. Their hands run over his screws and bolts, picking out inconsistencies and mulling over how to remedy them.

I sit across the room. The doctors obstruct my view of him, like a kettle of white vultures. His face is all that's visible, or rather, a disconnected version of it. Like I do, Sam attempts to look at himself from another point of view. The ceiling, the walls, some inanimate part of the room he used to give a soul.

Being naked, poked, and prodded at—none of it is strange to Sam. He's undergone the routine since he was little. It's the norm. But the shame never goes away, he says. It isn't a logical thing to feel, yet he does. He feels exposed, leered at, vulnerable.

Working on a swallow, Sam eventually looks to me. I smile as if it could make any of this easier for him. Sam sticks his tongue out. I frown. He holds in a laugh, his lips twisting.

Once the exam is over, he sits up and covers himself, muscles shaky.

I run to his side.

"Are you okay?" I ask.

"Yes, my love," he says. He kisses my nose. "I'm in the mood for a laugh, aren't you? Let's go play cards with Henry."

"Okay," I agree, helping him off the table and back into his clothes.

————

Children who experience illness can harden. It isn't a response to pain, it's a response to their life feeling stretched, thinned into a cycle. Memories blur into each other. A year in a hospital can feel like ten. Maybe that's why so many patients have the wisdom of an old man and the temper of a child.

Henry tells me that war is a lot like being sick. There's a sense of *Will I make it out of this or won't I?* A lot of pain, a lot of boredom, and camaraderie among the hurt and bored.

Henry tells me he remembers the exact weight of his rifle and how odd it felt in his arms as he ran with a bouncing pack on his back. The air was nearly black, he says, full of smog so thick you could feel the tar in your lungs. The sirens and ammunition shot through his eardrums about as harshly as the blood stank.

He turns to me, his head limp on the pillow. Then he asks if that's what dying feels like. Running into the dark, not knowing whether light exists on the other side.

Henry faces his pipe again. He caresses the mouthpiece, looking across the room as if another cot sits beside his, a neighboring soul under the covers.

He speaks to the air, to that little ghost he keeps handy. He mumbles things I can't quite make out, something about *I remember*, and *almost*, and *I'll be there soon*.

I wait till Henry is asleep before I go see Sam. He's reading a book, one of his hands in a fist as blood slowly drains from his arm and into a bag.

The patches on his skin sting against the cold air, cracking and bleeding, making him wince. Gray and purple hues shroud his eyes. I crawl into the bed with him and ask about his day.

He kisses my head and talks to me, drawing his sentences out, using more words than he has to, because he knows his voice calms me.

I ask Sam if he feels trapped by his body as Henry feels trapped in his.

Sam asks why I would think that. I tell him that he's sick. He says you don't have to be sick to feel stuck. I ask again if that's how he feels. Sam says *trapped* isn't the right word. He says he feels grounded because his mind can go anywhere it wants, but his body always brings him home.

He plays with my hair as I trace the healthy skin around the mounds of rawness.

He asks me if I'm okay.

I say I wish I could listen more without understanding less.

Henry dies a few days later.

We're in the middle of a card game when a wave of exhaustion hits him. Sam asks if he's feeling all right and if he wants some water. Henry says he just needs a moment, a little nap before the next game. But when Sam and I leave the room, his heart stops beating. He tries to draw breath but can't.

Nurses flood the room, Ella at the head. She flattens his cot, hurried codes and orders flying back and forth. Their loud, brutal efficiency is overshadowed by Henry's gasping.

Sam tries to pull me out of the room.

"Wait," I plead. Henry opens his eyes, turning his head on the pillow, a single arm reaching past his pipe. He tries to speak, no air to create words left in his throat. Then his body goes limp. His eyes glaze over till nothing—no one—exists behind them.

"Wait—"

"You don't have to see this," Sam whispers, pushing me down the hall. There isn't time to calm me down, so he opens the door to the old supply closet and leads me in.

"He was doing so much better," I whisper, walking backward, trying not to replay the scene in my head.

"I know. I know, it's not fair," Sam says, hugging me tight, but I know he's crying too. "It'll be okay. It'll be fine." His breath huffs as he speaks, the heat blowing on my hair, his voice muffled. "It'll be okay. Don't lose hope."

"He was so strong," I say. "Why did he die?"

"I don't know," Sam whispers. "I don't know, my love."

"He just wanted to be with his friend."

"What?"

"Henry," I say, my chest all tight. "When he lost his leg in the war, his friend died next to him. He cried. He screamed. He just wanted to be with him."

"He told you that?"

"No." I shake my head, and the blood of that day may as well be spilled on the floor. I can smell it, feel it. "No, I saw it."

"My love, Henry lost his leg over sixty years ago," Sam says. "You wouldn't have been born yet."

My existence is difficult to phrase and even harder to explain. No one has ever questioned it. No one has ever wondered. As such, when Sam's confused gaze meets mine, I'm not sure how to say it.

"I . . ." I swallow. "I am not like the other broken things you know."

Sam's arms fall slowly, his hands settling on my wrists, the scar he bears brushing against my skin. He frowns, confused.

"I don't understand."

"This place," I say, "this is where I belong. This is who I am." I bring my hands up to Sam's face, tracing the curvature, the way it's changed yet stayed the same in so many ways.

"I was so lonely," I say like I'm apologizing. "I wanted to know why the people I'm meant to protect always slip through my fingers." I want to cry. I want to cry and bring Henry and his friend both back. I want them to hug like Sam and I hug and smoke their pipes and live together in that little cabin by the river.

I stutter over a sob. "Why do people have to die?"

Sam doesn't know what to say. This has always been my one search for a reason despite the fact that I condemn reason.

And Sam has no answer.

He bites down and makes a frustrated noise. He holds on to my wrists, his forehead against mine.

"We can leave," he says, a little whisper behind it.

I blink. "What?"

"We can get away from all this," he says. "All this sadness and death. We can get away from this place so barren of story and adventure."

"Sam—"

"We'll take vials of my medicine. I'll be careful. I can get a job. I'll take care of us," he whispers, urgency in his voice as if he's ready to run and pull me with him like we're just children in a park. "We can go see the world, my love. We can experience all the things we never got to feel. We can finally be free and watch the sunrise without glass in the way."

Everything is moving so fast. Sam's grip is iron. His words are fluid, drowning me. I feel like air stuck underwater.

"I can't," I whisper.

"Yes, you can," Sam says. "I know it's scary, but we'll have each other, and—"

"I can't leave, Sam." I slide out of his hold, walking backward till we're disconnected. "Not forever," I say, dragging my sleeve across my mouth as if my words could take up less space if I muffled them. "Not like you want me to."

"What do you mean, not forever?" Sam asks, all softness evaporated.

"I—"

"Don't you want to be with me?" Not a question. An accusation. A reach for a lifeline, like Henry searching for his ghost. "Don't you love me?"

Sam and I stare at each other, the closet so dimly lit I can only make out his face and his outline. The longer I take to answer, the more he tenses.

I want him to be happy.

I want him to be happy with me.

I want him, and he wants the world.

So for the first time, I'm not sure that I'm enough.

Sam's body sags slowly. The tears that belonged to Henry dry. He wipes them from his cheeks, his jaw flexed. He looks as he does when he is being examined, vulnerable, shame behind the echo of his breaths.

He rubs his face up and down. Then a hardness I don't know comes over him, like a knight putting up a shield.

"All right," he whispers. He turns around, reaching for the doorknob.

"Sam?" I call. "Sam, don't leave, please," I beg. I try to grab the back of his shirt, but he's already opened the door and shut it behind him. "Sam!"

The room goes completely dark.

Like a smog-ridden battleground.

I wonder, as I cry, if Henry got an answer to his question about what happens after people die. I wonder if he ran through the black and came out on the other side. I wonder if, in the light, his friend was waiting for him, smoking a pipe, smiling with open arms.

And then I wonder if Henry is still running. I wonder if he will run through the dark only to learn there is nothing on the other side.

25
the in-between moments

Dad,

My first memory is of you.

You kiss my face, laughing when it contorts, gentle hands on my back. Mom is beside you, her hands tickling my belly. Your eyes are warm. Your words are tender. My world is a crib, and your love is the weather.

I'm not certain how much reality that memory holds, but I don't waste time questioning it.

Funny how memory works, isn't it? You remember what is strange more than what is normal. The normal days blend together, but the in-between moments stand out.

I wonder what it says about my life——that I remember more vividly the moments of your kindness than I do your hatred.

I wasn't aware of it when I was younger. The hatred, I mean. I didn't know that it was abnormal for your dad to scream and slam the table because you accidentally broke a plate. I didn't know that it was odd to be stripped naked and thrown into an ice-cold bath because you asked why boys couldn't kiss other boys.

Mom was the one who cleaned up the shattered remains and

dried me off as I shivered. It made me sad when she turned the other cheek, but unlike you, her kindness was constant. She never once hurt me.

One night, when you were away on business, she slept in my bed. She cried when she thought I was asleep. The next morning I saw the bruise on her cheek. Streams of wine color caught in a patch of putrid greens and yellows.

That was when I decided I wouldn't hate her.

Of course, I couldn't hate you either. You were all I knew.

You taught me right from wrong. You guided me through the beginnings of life. And every time I went the wrong way, acting a little too weak or a little too curious, you said:

God will forgive you.

I was stupid back then. I was a little boy who thought kindness lay in a clenched fist and that my existence was something to apologize for.

But you forgot, Dad, that the more a child grows, the bigger the world gets. My crib became a house and our house became a town and little by little, I came to know what kindness really looks like.

There was a day you took me to the park to play catch. I had just gotten my first-ever report card. I had good grades, so customarily, you smiled, but you were bothered beneath it. Kids are intuitive. They pick up on those things.

I knew, even then, when I was barely at your knee, that it bothered you when my teachers called me reserved rather than outgoing. It bothered you that I should've been at your hip by that age, that I never spoke, and that I couldn't catch.

So when the baseball hit me in the head as a symptom of your frustration, I let it happen. I let the blood seep over my eye, and I let you carry me back to the car, kissing apologies on my forehead.

That was the first time other people had witnessed you hurt me. I remember mothers with their toddlers by the slide and swing set putting a hand to their mouths in shock.

I wanted to tell them that it was okay. That it was an accident. That you cared about me and you only hurt Mommy and me some of the time.

That night you washed my hair and bandaged up my head. You kissed me good night and said you would teach me and that it would all be okay.

Though I didn't cry when you turned off the light, I felt this intense emptiness. Mom and I were a quiet pair. The house itself had more to say to us than we did to each other. I had no friends or siblings to talk to either.

I was lonely.

I wanted your kindness, and for that, I was willing to learn how to catch. I was willing to pretend to be someone I am not to please you.

It worked for a while.

Your anger grew rarer. There was the occasional frustrated bout where you screamed at me or called me names or pushed me, but you always caught yourself and apologized.

There was this one habit you had.

You'd grab me. Nothing else. You'd just grab my arm. You'd watch your hand practically swallow it. Then, after a moment, you'd laugh, let it go, ruffle my hair, and tell me I should eat more.

You liked seeing the fear in my eyes. You liked the momentary high it gave you—knowing that you could break the bone in two and there wouldn't be a thing I could do about it. You liked that no matter what I did, it was all in your hands. You were the one who decided what was right and wrong, and you had the power to shape me into whatever you wanted me to be . . .

Or maybe that was in my head.

Maybe you were just being playful, so I kept on trying to please you. I kept on closing my eyes at night and asking God to forgive me.

But there were things I couldn't change for you, parts of me you could not alter to your liking.

You'd say things . . .

Neo, eat some more. I can see your bones through your shirt.

You should build some muscle, you've got sticks for arms.

Neo, don't make that face, you look like a girl.

Looks like you won't be riding a roller coaster anytime soon.

Don't be pouty, I'm just teasing you.

You have hips like a woman, you know that?

I became keenly attuned to the pitch of my voice and the size of my body. I felt guilty for being too short, too skinny, too feminine.

I hated myself.

My loneliness festered. It ate at me. I was a patch of soil, a feeding ground for weeds of shame to grow and flourish till I turned to nothing.

I wanted to kill myself before that happened.

At nine years old, I dreamt of falling asleep in Mom's arms when you were away on a trip and never waking up. Maybe I would meet God, I thought. Then he would tell me I was forgiven. That I didn't need to be hit or frightened anymore. I dreamt of taking Mom with me too.

The next morning, I planned to walk into the road and let the bus run me over. I kept imagining myself flattened on the road, *my skull cracked open, blood and brain oozing from my head.*

But when I sat down, I found something. A book that'd been left at the bus stop. It had Great Expectations *written on the front. I stole it without a thought. The words were too difficult for me to make out, but I tried anyway. The road could wait.*

My teacher saw me struggling and gave me other books to start with that would be easier. I was determined to read the book, so I took her advice and read all the easier ones first.

That's when I fell in love with stories.

Stories gave me an out, a loophole in life's weaving.

It turned out I didn't have to be me. I could be anyone. I learned to live through pages, ink, and writing. I guess I have you to thank for that. Without the shame and the loneliness, I would've never found my raison d'être.

Mom encouraged me while you were away on your business trips. She read to me before bed and gave me a pencil and a notebook whenever I asked.

The shame and loneliness slowly began to wilt. I shed them like skin on paper, and I wrote till I became good at it.

I think this bothered you too. Because I became less reliant on you. I became consumed, intensely avoidant of reality through literature. I began to learn and formulate opinions that weren't yours.

I started becoming someone.

Neo, come spend some time outside with me.

Don't you have any friends you want to play with?

Put the pen down, c'mon.

Don't buy that book, it'll put poison in your head.

Neo! Put that stuff away. Let's go.

Don't read that gay shit. Fucking hell.

Give that to me! Where did you get this?! What kind of faggot gave you this?! Tell me!

One night, I came home from school with a smile on my face. A boy sat next to me on the bus and called me pretty. He kissed my cheek and told me to keep it a secret and I felt something so new: butterflies in my stomach, jitters, the good kind, an excitement that could not be stolen.

Or so I thought.

I wrote a story about the boy and me and you ripped it out of my hands and read it in full.

Then you took off your belt and whipped me with it. You locked me in the closet for over a day and a half. Mom cried, screaming at you to let me out. Finally, when you left, she ran upstairs. You'd hit her too. Her lip was split and she couldn't open one of her eyes. She let me out and collected me in her arms. I'd pissed myself, and I was shaking, but Mom didn't care. She hugged me and apologized.

She bathed me, washed my clothes, and in an oddly intimate way, we patched each other up. I dabbed her lip with a cotton ball and she put ointment on the lash marks.

I'm glad you weren't there to apologize. It was your apologies that were the cruelest. Because you meant them. You knew you were hurting us every time, and you continued to do it anyway.

I know you remember these moments, Dad.

But I want you to relive them.

I want you to know that your wife and your son found each other in the wake of your violence. I want you to know that even after that night, I still didn't hate you.

I chose to pretend that the bruises, the hitting, the yelling, those were all just fever dreams. What was real was the kindness.

I held on to the memory I have as a baby, to the smiles you shared with me, to the jokes we made together, to the times you'd pick me up and make airplane noises, to the good-night kisses, *to the movies we watched together, and every bump in a road.*

The night I decided to hate you, you didn't even hurt me.

You came home from a business trip.

I was reading in my room. I'd taken to hiding my books and writing in boxes in the attic since you never went up there. That night, I heard your voice gradually get louder and louder through the walls. I peeked out of my door and I heard the sound of a lamp breaking against the wall, a dish against the tiles.

I didn't want Mom to get hurt, so I walked down the stairs, thinking you'd stop if you knew I was there.

But you didn't.

You took what was left of her sanity and you raped her right in front of me.

I didn't care what the reason was. I didn't even care if there was a reason. I wanted to kill you. I fantasized about getting a knife from the kitchen drawer and driving it into your back.

Mom didn't even realize I saw it happen. She'd bitten through her arm to keep from making noise and tried to clean up before she caught sight of me.

Mom.

Oh, Neo, *she said, smiling, pretending there weren't tears streaming down her face.*

It's okay, honey, just go back to bed.

Your face is bleeding, *I said.*

Is it? *She touched her cheek and hissed.* I'm so clumsy these days, aren't I?

Mom?

Yes?

Can you sleep in my room tonight?

She sniffled and nodded.

Yes, *she said.* Yes, of course I can.

————

C couldn't live without his heart.

I think I always knew that. Sorrow isn't the first thing that hits when the surgeons emerge into the waiting room. It's the realization that what I've been waiting for is here, like I've reached the end of a path I knew was a dead end.

You really are a strange, beautiful creature, he'd said.

That is the last thing he ever gave me.

Hikari and Neo hold hands, leaning on each other. I sit on Hikari's side, my eyes closed, my consciousness traveling through the walls so that I can watch the surgery.

When C rejected the new heart, dread leaked into the room, submerging his doctors in difficult decisions.

They did everything they could. They always do.

C's mother is the first to burst into tears when the surgeons give her the news. His father cries too, hugging his wife, C's brothers, each falling into their own version of misery and frustration. Two of them stand, storming off. Another presses his hands to his face, shaking. The last surround their parents as if holding one another up will lessen the blow.

Hikari sits there in disbelief. She is crying, but it is noiseless. In her hand, the tangled earbuds C gave her for safekeeping sit. She looks down at them, not sure what to do. I gather her in my arms, kissing the side of her face, salty and wet. She hides in the crook of my neck.

Neo is tearless.

He does not cry or fall to the floor. His hands are neatly folded in his lap, C's phone loose in one, the promise he made crumpled in the other. Calmly, he stands up after the surgeons and their condolences have gone. He walks to C's family, stopping at his mother.

"Madam," he says.

C's mother lifts her face from her hands, sobbing breaths stalled into quieter cries. Neo kneels in front of her.

"*C'était là où il gardait toutes ses chansons préférées,*" he says, handing her the phone. Then, in the softest voice he knows, "*Je suis désolé pour votre perte.*"

Neo leaves after a few minutes. He asks Hikari and me if he can be alone for a little while. He walks back to his room the way he would on any other day, greeted by a shut door.

He opens it to his father sitting at his desk with Neo's letter to him folded over his lap.

Neo meets his gaze, apathetic, no change in his body. He regards his father like you regard a new, uninteresting piece of wall art and proceeds inside without much more care than that.

"You've been gone awhile," Neo says, shutting the door behind him. His father folds the letter neatly and clears his throat.

"Your mother convinced me to give you space," he says.

Neo doesn't fail to notice the state of his knuckles. He imagines what he must've done to his mother for them to retain such bloody coloring. He wonders if he is capable of killing her, if he already has. He laughs a little then, thinking of the odds that his mother and his heart died on the same day.

"Are we going to talk about this?" his father asks, holding up the pieces of paper.

"There's nothing to talk about," Neo says.

He traces his stacks of books, reaching under his bed to take out a single cardboard box and, one by one, putting them in it.

"You went and found some bravery after running off?" Neo's

father asks, although it isn't aggressive or scornful. Pride flows through his tone, hooked on the corner of his mouth. He's happy, Neo realizes. His son, rather than stay pitiful, weak, and afraid in the hospital, actually took his shot at escaping.

"I'm not brave," Neo says, spines running down the cardboard and thumping to the bottom. "I never have been. I know you're disappointed by that." He stares his father in the face. "But at least I can acknowledge that I'm weak."

Neo's father sighs. It's a sigh that preludes the violence Neo knows all too well. On instinct, Neo stands up, his breathing racking an unsteady rhythm. He backs off as his dad makes his way to him.

"That doesn't matter because—" Neo is interrupted by a rough grab of his forearm, but he doesn't fall into his resentful quiet. He speaks louder. "Because I'm a good writer!" he yells. "I'm smart, and I learned infinitely more from books you deem immoral and the people within these walls than I ever have from you."

Neo makes fists with his hands, tensing. He focuses on the smell of crisp pages and the pinching vise grip around his flesh. He waits, breathing with his mouth open, for his father to hit him. He waits for the stinging sensation, a nail to nick his lip, or the numbing heat.

When Neo looks into his father's eyes, he finds the frustration, the restraint, the desire to hurt him that is as old as the day he threw a baseball straight at Neo's skull.

Neo laughs. He laughs so hard tears run down his face and drip onto the papers on the floor.

"There was a part of me that always believed you could change," he says. His limp wrist rises to his eyes, blanketing them. "When I got sick, when I got beaten up, when I was in a fucking wheelchair—all those times I thought, *Maybe he'll change.*"

Neo's father doesn't relinquish his hold. He doesn't move to strike or shove or startle him. He knows it's futile. Neo is not hurt by those things anymore. In fact, it hurts more when his father tries to show concern for him. It hurts that after all this time, he can still show him affection.

Neo laughs again, practically wailing. Pain in its purest form rips him apart from core to skin. It infects all echoes of C. It claims him as a casualty of the past and reminds Neo with every fleeting memory they share that from here on, there will be no more.

Neo throws his head back against the wall, his crazed laughter becoming a long sigh. "I wonder, Dad, would you change now?" he asks. "If you knew that the boy I love just died? Would you hug me and tell me it'll all be okay?"

Frozen, Neo's father cannot so much as open his mouth, let alone answer.

"No, you don't care enough for that," Neo says. "You care enough to feel sorry for me, I think, but your values are stronger. I mean, you knew all along, right?" He smiles with a whisper. "Your hatred always had a name. We just never spoke it."

"I'm sorry about the boy," his father says quickly, sitting down on the bed. He doesn't let him go. "I can't blame you for being confused. When we go home—"

"I'm not going home with you." Neo stares at his stories, the ink dissolving in his tears like paint.

His father pulls him by the arm in the slightest, a warning.

"Neo—"

"You may want to be careful when you touch me now," Neo says. "You're not the only person I wrote a letter to."

The door opens abruptly. Eric stands at the threshold. He practically crushes the doorknob, hair frazzled, scrubs rumpled, and dark under-eyes at the ready.

"Neo, is everything okay?" he asks.

"It's all right, I'm his father—"

Eric's eyes flick from the irritated red and creased skin on Neo's forearm to the wet trails down his face.

"Get your hand off him."

"Excuse me?"

"You're hurting him, sir," he says, urgency in the tone. "I'm telling you to get your hand off him."

Neo's father tries to reason with Eric, calm and collected like a true businessman. Neo rolls his eyes at the age-old tactic that always seemed to work when he slipped up and raised his voice or grabbed Neo too roughly in public.

"Oh, for God's sake, do you ever shut up?"

His father's head snaps in Neo's direction.

"What'd you say?" His hand goes from vise to branding iron, squeezing so hard that Neo cringes.

Eric snaps, "Security!"

Neo watches as panic stirs in his father's eyes, a satisfaction dulled by guilt settling in his stomach.

"Neo." He takes Neo by the shoulders as gently as he can, the way he did when he kissed tenderly worded apologies. "Tell him you lied, that you're confused."

Neo does nothing of the sort. Instead, he smiles again.

"I'll always love you for the in-between moments, Dad," he says. "But I don't forgive you for the rest of them."

The head security guard rushes into the room and escorts Neo's father out. The commotion catches attention from the whole floor, but Neo retains his calmness.

Eric lets Hikari and me into the room, telling Neo he'll be right back, that he's okay now.

"Neo," Hikari calls, Hee cuddled in her sweater. The cat hops up on Neo's bed, nuzzling onto his lap.

"I'm fine," Neo says. She stares at his arm with crescent-shaped cuts dripping onto the sheets. Neo runs his touch around Hikari's neck and pulls her into an embrace. "Don't cry, stupid. I'm fine."

Neo decides to stop packing his things then. Instead, he leaves the room as it is, our headquarters. He imagines Sony lying supine on the windowsill, playing with Hee, while Coeur sits tapping his thighs with the rhythm of his earbuds.

His and Coeur's manuscript sits in the corner.

He tells himself he will finish it another day.

"I want to lie down in the sun for a while, don't you?" he whispers. Hikari agrees and we make our way to the garden together, careful not to sit too close to the hedge. Neo lies flat in the grass, wearing C's varsity jacket, inhaling his scent and his warmth, pretending that it is C's arms holding him rather than empty fabric. I lie beside him, Hikari and Hee too. Lonely, sun-kissed survivors.

I wonder what Neo's father thought of his son's letter. I wonder if he'll ever read the rest of it. Although as Neo stares upward to Heaven with peace, I know that it doesn't matter.

Dad,

Two weeks after you raped my mother, I came down with an infection. You said it was nothing, remember? A symptom of my tantrums and my refusal to eat. Then, a week after that, I was hospitalized. My disease is so rare for boys my age that it took them a year to get the diagnosis right.

I didn't think that was funny, but it made me laugh when the doctors asked if I played sports. With the bruises I had, I should've. I knew CPS would take me if I said anything, so I just told them I roughhoused with my friends and I was clumsy and they believed it.

Either way, I was overjoyed.

A lifelong illness, they said.

I was so happy, Dad. I don't think I'd ever been happier.

For the last three years, I've been gifted an escape. A place you can't hurt me past a little bruise here and there. A place where I am free of your control.

I read and write so much here, it's euphoric. I made friends. Strange, beautiful, funny, kind friends that you have no claim to. Friends who have taught me what it feels like to belong. To be happy and to be appreciated.

I realize now, you were as happy to have a son as I was to be sick.

I just wasn't the son you wanted.

You molded me into an image of someone I am not, and if I diverted by an inch, you felt threatened. It was never me you were attached to, nor your authority. It was that image. That idea. That person who doesn't actually exist.

That's why I don't blame you, Dad.

But my last memories will not be yours.

They will be of my mom and the nights we healed each other. The nights she read to me and encouraged me to be who I want to be.

They will be of a beautiful, loud girl I stole clothes and a cat from—of a witty girl with optimism to reach the stars and jokes that made my belly shake—of a strange friend who coaxed my nightmares away and never once left my side—of a boy with more heart than most. My last memory will be of his lips, his joy, his beauty, his optimism, and his everlasting kindness.

This letter is not for you, Dad, it is for me.

Because I have nothing to be sorry for. I do not need to be forgiven for who I choose to be and even less for who I choose to love.

So thank you, Sony, Hikari, Sam . . .

Thank you, Coeur . . .

For teaching me to love myself.

26
great expectations

DON'T REMEMBER WAKING up or falling asleep. I phase into another world, another shape. It's as if I spaced out, focused on a particular grain of sand or a low-hanging cloud, and all of a sudden remembered where I am.

Wildflowers and tall grasses sprawl across the land, not a speck of concrete jungle encroaching upon the field. Birds sing, small animals scavenge, and trees frame the pasture. The sky meets mountains at the edge of the canvas, and all else are the splendors of nature.

"Oh, good." The wind accompanies a voice. I turn around to an ocean's scent and umber blues foaming at a shoreline. "You're awake."

Sitting next to me, staring at different scenery, a boy cups a tiny potted plant with the sleeves of a stolen sweatshirt.

"Is this a dream?" I ask.

He nods.

"I've never been in someone's dream before."

"I don't think it's *my* dream," he says. "I think it's yours too. Like two paintings intersecting past their frames."

I stare back at the field, the life and the light within it, then I turn back to his endless sea, its tart scent, and its clouds brewing in the far distance.

"I want to bring Coeur here," he says. "It's secluded and, other than the waves, completely silent." He points to the undisturbed waters and dark sand. I look instead at his face as he speaks. His mouth parts slightly, the corners lifting at the thought of C walking along the sand with him hand in hand.

"He'd adore the beaches in France too," he says. "He's never been there, I know, but his parents have, obviously, so they could take us. People can be spacey in Europe, just like him. There's this library in Paris I want to show him. He'd take pictures of it like a tourist." A bit of amusement plays in his tone. He fidgets with the succulent, placing it delicately between us as if it contains a soul with which to watch the tide drawing in.

"Neo," I say, breaking him out of his daydreams. "Where are we?"

He hugs his knees to his chest, and thinks for a moment.

"My dad used to bring me here when I was little," he says. "It was another world. A place I wrote and my mom read on towels while he skipped stones."

False figures made of shadow and wind mingle with his memory. Flashes of a pencil's stroke and a flat-edged rock clapping against the waves. A father playfully lifts his son up in the air as his mother watches. The memory fades back into his mind, and reality inclines to pull us from it.

"Where are we really?" I ask.

He bites his lip, dragging a finger across blades of grass gently fading into stones.

"Child Protective Services came to see me a few hours ago," he says. "Coeur's parents offered to take me in, whatever hap-

pens. My doctors haven't discharged me, though, 'cause, well—"
he tries to be lighthearted, for my sake, but it comes out dry, an
ironic detail that completes a dark picture—"'cause I'm lying
with a feeding tube in my stomach while you and Hikari sleep at
my bedside."

I shudder thinking of his bony body eating itself in more ways
than one. He notices. "It doesn't hurt, not here."

As the air cools around us, his stare hardens upon his ocean. It
becomes transfixed, so much that my side of the dream does not
exist to him anymore.

Something akin to fear and affection tied to a stone works its
way up my throat. It waits in the silence.

"Neo," I say. "Are you going to die tonight?"

He lets the question flow past him like a gust of wind.

The clouds above us sink, whales dipping below water and
resurfacing for air. They draw patterns, shadowing us before letting the light seep through again.

"Life is so full of shadows." He sighs, removing a book from
under the hoodie. The spine is damaged. The pages are thin and
pale but overflowing with text. "It's easy to forget that some people prefer the dark."

The book mimics the sea in a sense, gray and blue and rather
daunting. He flips through it, each word like a cell, each sentence
a line of muscle.

"On the surface, this story's about the value of affection over
social class, but at its roots, like most things, it's simpler," he says.
"It's about guiltless affection that is unasked for and expects nothing in return. It's about not letting that sort of bond pass you by."

Then, with a disdainful snort, he throws his legs out and lies
down, holding the novel over his head. "I hate this book."

I can't help the smile. "Do you?"

"Yeah. Pip's an idiot." He puts a hand out like a mocking actor. "'I love her against reason and against all discouragement that could be.' He sounds like you." He says it to make me laugh, and though it works, the two of us remember quickly where we are. The water and the wind serve as gentle reminders that our time here is limited. It will end, and when it does—

"I think that part of Pip lives in all of us," he says. "We're similar in the end—people, I mean. We all want a little piece of extraordinary. Unfortunately, most lives go by without anything extraordinary happening, and even if it does, it's the ordinary moments that we should've appreciated."

There is no regret in his voice. No resentment of an unfair, uneventful existence. As if his life has just begun and he is declaring that he will not let it pass him by.

But I have learned enough to know it is the opposite.

"People have this delusion of inherent purpose as if fate is written in stone, when really the pen has always been in our hands." His fingers close around the pages, crinkling the edges. Then he lets it go, sitting up and letting the book sit with him. "We are all passive protagonists until we learn how to write."

"Then what are we when we put the pen down?"

"Then we've reached the end of our story."

"And is this what you always intended?" I raise my voice, my fists clenched. He glances my way as I glance his. "When you created a sea of inked pages and wrote till your fingers bled, did you want to never reach the end?"

"Sam—"

"You can still live, Neo," I say, and the words echo, but I don't think he truly hears them. He hears his illnesses, whispering like sirens in his ear.

You must've seen it.

From the very beginning, you must've known.

When Neo caressed his bandage on the rooftop, when he turned the other cheek to treatments. His subtle frustration whenever someone pointed out that he was getting better. Every single thought that ran through his head, a narrative that twisted his disease into a fantasy.

Whatever it is in this world that hurts Neo, he lets it.

The great abuser of Neo's life was not his father, but the sickness in his veins. It was a bond Neo forged, unasked, expectant of flesh and sanity, but for all the pain it caused him, it never came close to the pain of pretending to be someone else.

So he fell in love with it.

"You were making yourself sick all these years, weren't you?"

He doesn't answer me, because I already know the answer. For every meal Neo left uneaten and every pill he faked swallowing, he counted the days it would add to his sentence in the hospital. Every episode, every flare-up, every instance he came close to death was just an indication of what he chose.

"What about your story?" I ask, trembling at the thought of him asleep with a tube taped to his mouth, at the thought that he is okay with dying in such a way. "What about all the stories you have to tell?"

"Only one matters," he says, taking my hand, stilling it. "And I trust my narrator will finish it well."

"Neo, please—"

"Life is made of so many goodbyes welded together." He squeezes, his touch as tangible as the day I first felt it. "So dread the endings. Cry and rage and curse them." A sad smile plays on his lips. "Just don't forget to cherish the beginnings and all that comes in between."

"I don't understand."

"You've always adored love stories, Sam, so go after yours," he whispers. "Love her. Love her. Love her. And against all discouragement that could be, let her love you too."

I choke on a cry, wishing Hikari were here.

I hold his hands, the cold, thin, artful instruments that learned to be held rather than roughly grasped. I bring them to my face, memorizing all the times they handed me books and held me close in fits of laughter, tears, and everything in between.

"Is there nothing I can do to change your mind?" I ask.

He leans in, twiddling his fingers like loose screws. They travel down my arms, holding them as they did on the days I helped him learn to stand again.

"You know you never wanted us to be happy, Sam. Happiness is a brittle, fleeting thing," he says, looking into my eyes, I think, so that I can see he is not sad. He is not in pain, nor is he regretful, resentful, or anything other than at peace. "You wanted us to feel loved, and we did."

Looking out at the sea, his gaze reaches across its endlessness. He picks up his book, fidgeting with the strings of his stolen sweatshirt.

Then he stands up on his own. He walks across the tether of our dreams and roams toward the ocean. *Great Expectations* soaks up the sea and sinks, its ink dissolving into nothing.

He climbs into that rowboat of his, pushing it from the muck with one foot below settling in its center. As he begins his journey, I stand, and though I cannot follow him into the dark, I cry and realize he was never in love with being sick. He was in love with the home we gave him. He sails to the heart of that home through waves and storms and a layer of darkness so thick it can be breathed.

On the other side, I like to imagine that he finds a shore. There, the shapes of a boy and a girl draw in the sand with sticks and seashells.

He cannot contain his joy. He jumps from the rowboat, swimming the remainder of the way. He trips in the shallows, the mud to his ankles, yelling their names. He runs up the beach, overcome with rejoicing laughter.

Coeur hears his voice and turns around. Heaven casts light upon him till the only shadow that remains is that of Neo jumping into his arms and kissing him just as he promised.

27
before

I HAVEN'T SEEN SAM since the night Henry died. Well, I have *seen* him. He reads in his bed most of the day, finishing books as quickly as he picks them up. He doesn't sleep often. When he does, I look at him just a little longer as I pass his room, wishing I could crawl into the bed and apologize.

I feel half-gone without him, like I'm missing a part of myself.

Without Sam, I follow Nurse Ella. She calls me her shadow. We care for patients together. Or at least she does. I mostly watch. Babies and infants, people who have yet to become people, are what bring me joy. Nurse Ella says I stare at the little creatures too much. I tell her that once you are her age, living is unpleasant and I must enjoy the pleasure of looking at babies while I still can. Rightfully so, she smacks the back of my head.

"Is Sam doing all right?" I ask. She scribbles on a sheet of paper. I have no interest in what. Paperwork in hospitals requires whole forests for production. Paperwork is like violence. Overly abundant and often useless.

"He's been a ripe old pain in the arse," Nurse Ella says. "You two haven't been causing much trouble now that I think about it. What happened?"

"I upset him," I tell her.

"What ever for?"

"I didn't *mean* to upset him."

Nurse Ella grunts, displeased. "Sam is becoming a man. You should learn while you're young, men are an emotional lot. God knows who let them be in charge of things. Is this why you've been sulking like a hound?"

"Hound?" I ask, unfamiliar with the term.

"Stupid child." Nurse Ella throws her papers down and wipes off her apron. "Come along."

"Where are we going?"

Nurse Ella never answers my questions.

She merely leads and I follow.

Sam's room is dark. He has a single lamp in the far corner, his blinds drawn. The potted plants on his windowsill that have grown into vines and shrubbery for the past decade withered away in the blue overglow.

Nurse Ella marches in without so much as a knock or a greeting. Sam looks up from the lesson work propped on his knees, brows knitted.

"Nurse Ella?"

"Get up," she says, rounding his bed and snapping her fingers.

"What?"

"Up," she says again, taking the work from his hands and tossing it aside.

Sam frowns. "No."

"I'm sorry, did I preface that command with *if it please your knighthood?*"

"Hag."

"Up. Now!" She claps her hands. "And you! In here. Sit."

Once Sam and I are both at the edge of his cot, Nurse Ella plants her hands on her hips, scanning us like prisoners deserving of a baton.

"In my entire career, I have never encountered such pains. Since you were at my knee, you've been wreaking havoc together. By God, the headaches I've suffered taming you *beasts* of children." Nurse Ella makes a masterpiece of her scoldings. She is theatrical, inhaling strength as she pauses.

"That being said, when you are apart, you are even worse. You." She waves her arm at me. "Becoming a mopey babe clinging to my skirt at all hours. And you." She flicks Sam's forehead, I assume in an attempt to rid him of the wrinkles he's forming from that scowl. "Losing your temper every hour of the day because you got your feelings hurt. Did I raise you to be so pathetic? I am not a patient woman. I have better things to attend to than your squabbling. So make up! And do so promptly."

Walking out, Nurse Ella continues muttering about our various crimes against her sanity. The door shuts behind her, and a draft cuts through the room with heavy, ugly silence.

Sam and I don't look at each other. In fact, we don't look at anything until he speaks.

"You told on me?"

"No," I say. "I think she was smart enough to piece it together."

Sam pushes off the bed and wanders to the window. He doesn't open the blinds. Instead, he crushes browning leaves, listening to the crackling like a fire. His sleeve falls as he does, revealing the patches on his skin. Shades of pink rise from his skin like plateaus, raw and scabbed over.

They've spread.

"Sam, your skin." I hurry across the room and try to touch him, but he tugs away. Not on reflex. Willfully.

My fingers curl, arms falling back to my side. "You're still angry at me."

"Really?" Sam scoffs. "What tipped you off?"

"I don't understand."

"No, of course you don't. I'm surprised you understand how to tie your shoes."

"You're being cruel."

"And you're stupid."

"I'm not stupid," I say, my voice tight.

"Really? Do you even understand why I'm angry with you?"

"You're angry because I don't want to leave."

"No." Sam takes my face in his hands, the way he does when he wants to embrace me. Only now, he doesn't want to kiss. He doesn't laugh or press our foreheads together. He holds me so that I'm all he sees.

"I'm mad because you're the only thing I live for," he whispers. "And you can't even tell me who you are. You can't even say you love me."

He lets me go gently, the way you'd release a fish back into the sea. Without regard for where it ends up, so long as it is alive and not in the boat.

His footing is unsteady as he returns to his bed. He's thinner than I remember too, a sicker shade graying his face. He gathers his lesson work and settles back atop the covers as if this discussion is anywhere near finished.

"Did you know the sun kisses you in the mornings?" I call. "It reaches across worlds, just to greet you. It has since you were a baby." Sam pretends not to listen. He continues to scribble away as if he is writing anything but meaningless lines of gibberish.

I step closer. "Pink shrouds your face when the light lingers. There are other shades: the shades that emit heat when you're laughing or when we kiss. Your hands are like that too. They're gentle. I remember when you were little, and they cradled your plants."

The closer I get, the more Sam's face twitches, as if I am pricking him with a pin with every word I utter.

"You always made such silly noises when you couldn't contain your excitement and you were so quick to pout when you didn't get your way, you still are," I say. "You eat like a baby. Pudding always ends up on some corner of your face. We used to eat our cups in the park, do you remember? You like that one shady corner beneath the willow tree. We talked about bringing Henry and Ella and playing his card games in the grass while he told us stories."

I sit on the bed across from him. Anger slowly falls from Sam's face, a mask of dust withering away into nothing, like a crackling leaf.

"I don't know why you're telling me all this."

"You said this place is barren of story, Sam, but you're wrong. It's full of it," I say. "It's full of people trying to survive just like you. But most of them don't, and I want to know why."

Sam stares at me now, his childish curiosity seated beside a hunger to understand and a grudge he's trying to keep.

"I want to know why the people who find refuge in this place have to suffer. I want to know why so many of their lives end unfinished. I want to learn how to fend off my enemies. I want to save everyone, as is my purpose." I tremble. My voice was only ever his, but my existence is my own. It is an enigma. Difficult to phrase. Even harder to say aloud.

Sam softens when he realizes what I'm trying to say.

"You've never questioned where I came from nor who I am nor why I'm here. No one ever does, because I'm a part of this place. Like the color of a wall or the heft of a door." A ghost of sadness crawls over me. It is dry and worn, familiar and faded. The pain of being perpetually alone.

"I was so lonely when we met, Sam," I nearly cry. "No matter who I came to know, they all left me one way or another, but you never did. My curse made a mistake the day that you were born. We were both alone, but it gave us each other. I've never lied to you, and I won't start today. I don't know what love is, but I never would've tried to understand it if it weren't for you."

Sam throws his papers and pencil aside. They fall to the floor. He rises to his knees and collects me in his arms.

"Sweet Sam," he whispers, crushing me to him.

"I love you," I say. "I want you to heal and be safe and have the life you want. I want you to be happy. If that's what love is, I've loved you longer than I can remember."

"I want the same for you; you know that. I was just—I was so upset when you couldn't say it back," he says. He breathes me in, falling on top of me, propping his weight on his elbows. Then we are kissing. Apologetically. Hungrily. To steal back some passion that time tried to sneak away while we were apart.

"I'll go with you," I finally say. I push Sam back onto his haunches so that I am the one holding him upright. "Once you get better, we'll go. Just you and I."

"But—what you said—"

"I *do* belong here, but"—I stop to reconsider that the rules of my existence can be broken. I have never ventured too far outside these walls, but—"I'm still searching for those answers," I tell him. "I want to search with you."

"You mean that?"

"Yes." I kiss him again. I kiss the corners of his mouth, his nose, his eyelids. Then I ask, treading a fine line, tiptoeing around my secret. A chest to be opened with a lock only I carry.

"Then . . . do you want to know who I am?"

Sam smiles.

"I know who you are," he says. "You're a caring friend." He kisses my lips. "You're a meticulous nurse." He kisses me again, sliding his hands under my shirt. "You're a lousy card player." His lips travel to my neck. "You're a brave knight." He grabs my waist. "You're a loving dancer. And all your tomorrows are mine."

———————

Sam's doctors identify his mysterious new sickness a few days later. There is no way to know exactly how the disease was transmitted, but given Sam's immunocompromised state, the prognosis isn't promising.

Sam tells me it doesn't matter. He tells me he's survived everything since he was born. He tells me to hold on, that we'll go on our adventure once he heals.

But as time passes, Sam's condition doesn't improve. I never leave his side; as such, even the littlest changes matter. If he walks straighter, if he spends a whole night without succumbing to coughs, if he can eat without nausea—they're all minute instances of hope.

But hope is fragile. It isn't infinite.

My butter baby dies in her third month of life. Sam chases me into the street, saves me from getting run over, holds me, shushes me, telling me it'll be okay.

More people arrive at the hospital. More people I come to know and care for. More who wither into skeletons and ash. Every time, I return to Sam, whose skin becomes grayer and whose strength wilts come fall. He holds me in the night. He shushes me, telling me it'll be okay, telling me not to lose hope.

I wonder, in his arms, how something as intangible as hope is lost. It cannot be misplaced. It cannot be thrown aside. That means it must be forgotten.

Forgetting is an essential part of grief.

28
soul bared to paper

*The broken heart. You think you
will die, but you just keep on living
day after terrible day.*

LONELINESS IS A soft-spoken abuser, singing lullabies, *you are
alone, you are nothing, you are empty.*

Hikari lies in my arms, and though I vowed to protect her
from small spined shadows, she has never felt lighter.

The blinds are drawn, thin lines of light drawn across the hills
of our legs under the covers. I speak to her, tell her things, ask
her things, but she rarely replies. She is cold no matter how close
I hug her. Sickly purples ghost her under-eyes, no matter how
many kisses I cast on her lids.

Her parents come to see her as much as they can. They've
both taken a leave from work, but Hikari doesn't talk to them.
She doesn't speak to her doctors or to anyone else.

She speaks to me, I assume because she thinks I am the only
one who understands. Because I am a prisoner of this place as she
is a prisoner of her reliance on me.

I see it when she picks up the knife to cut her food and gazes at herself in the reflective plastic.

"Hikari," I say. "Can you eat something, please?"

She no longer recognizes the reflection, but she knows it is still her. Her fist squeezes the handle. The knife shakes.

I draw patterns over her knuckles when she loses herself in those thoughts. I ask her to talk to me. Sometimes she does, shakes her head, and puts the knife down. Others, she grips it harder, falls further, and tries to slash at her wrists.

She struggles as I stop her, her breaths huffed from her nose, her jaw clenched. I take the knife and throw it on the ground so she can't get it back. Then I hug her, cupping the back of her head as she fists my clothes and pushes me away.

She hits me in the chest, the strikes dwindling with her strength. Then, once she is still and quiet, I loosen. She slowly parts from me, muttering an apology.

Later, once she's finished eating what she can muster and thrown it up, I help her wash herself. I re-dress her and apply ointment to her scars. Then we lie together in her bed, beneath the covers.

"Did you ever find the answer?" she asks, her voice this hoarse, sad thing. "Did you ever find out why people have to die?"

I shift on the bed so that my mouth is against her neck as she faces away from me.

"No," I whisper, caressing her hands, touching the leather and crystal of the watch on her wrist.

"Maybe there isn't one," she says. "Maybe death is as pointless as life."

The dream I shared with Neo denounces that, but I can't tell her. She needs to be heard, not fought. So I wrap myself around her, pressing my forehead to her back, trying not to focus on the prominence of her bones or her words. I focus on her breathing, her heartbeat, any sign that she is not a corpse.

"Do you love me, Sam?" she asks. "Or are you just taking care of me because you feel bad?"

"Of course I love you," I whisper harshly, holding her tighter. "Do you love me?"

"Yes," she says. The sheets rustle. She wriggles from my embrace and sits up on the edge of the bed. "It'd just be so much easier if I didn't."

Her bare feet meet the tiles as she unhooks her IV bag and hangs it on a wheeled stand.

"Where are you going?" I ask.

"I want to see Neo," she says.

The stand serves as her support as she exits the room.

———

Neo killed himself by starvation. His heart failed.

Hikari saw his body. She was holding his hand and woke when the life had already drained out of him. It felt cold, stiff, like a rock filled with icy liquid, she said. She talked about it without any emotion, as if she hadn't processed what happened. I just remember her saying he shouldn't have died like that, with a tube taped to the side of his mouth, his body nothing but a gray skeleton, and a butterfly rash on his cheekbones. She said he should've died somewhere surrounded by his books, at peace with his own ideas and his own creations.

I told her that Neo died in the way he wanted. I tell her he sailed his ocean, and he emerged with the people he loves on the other side.

She told me I don't know that.

Since then, Hikari has entered a state of regression. She mutters to herself sometimes, as if speaking to someone in the room who isn't me.

She tells me, *I want to see Sony*, and then walks to the gardens. She sits in the grass and stares at the clouds, talking, about what, I can't hear. She tells me, *I want to see Coeur, I want to see Neo*, and she goes to Neo's room and reads his stories. She puts the sleeves of C's jacket around her shoulders as if his arms could wrap around her. She remains a part of old settings, only brought back when she sees me.

Maybe that's why she resents me. I understand the pain, but I also remind her of it. I understand what it's like to finally find who you think you belong with and have them ripped away.

I walk behind Hikari by a hall's length, the same way I did the first night I ever beheld her. The difference is stunning, an insult. Her yellow dimpled dress is replaced by a dull hospital gown. Her lively, curious steps are now slow, her breaths focused on the next. She does not explore, or steal anything, not even a glance. Her silhouette is bent and broken and it limps behind that of her past.

She doesn't want me to follow, but I do. I need to. For her. For my peace of mind.

When we reach Neo's room, she halts before reaching the door. It's open for some reason, held by a wedge. Neo's mother stands outside with her back against the wall. Upon the sight of us, she tenses. I don't understand until I hear the shuffling of papers and see the packing clutter coming from inside the room.

"Hikari," I say, standing in her way so that she can't see. "Let's go see Sony or C, okay? I can carry you, come on—"

"What are they doing?" She squints, looking over my shoulder, trying to make out the people moving things around in Neo's room.

I don't know who the other two men are. Perhaps his cousins, perhaps some other extended family that was always so fond of sending bouquets instead of showing up. In their midst, Neo's father neatly collects every single sheet of paper in the room, every notebook, every novel, every pen, and he places them, with all the care in the world, into a cardboard box with a lighter right next to it.

"What . . ." Hikari is at a loss for words. She tries to walk into the room. "What are you doing?"

Neo's father hears her. He looks up, his eyes raw and red and sensitive. He doesn't acknowledge her or me. He wipes at his tears and picks up the last of the papers: Neo's manuscript. And an old spiral notebook with the front torn off.

"Wait." Hikari pushes against my front, but I block her path. "Wait. Stop."

"Hikari—"

"That isn't yours. You can't take it," she says. Neo's father throws the lighter atop the stack and picks up the box.

"No, no, please!" Hikari tries to grab him past me as he walks out of the room. Like a child reaching for a book on a too-high shelf, she fights with what physical strength she has left.

"Please!" Hikari cries, clawing at me, at him, ripping her own IV out just to reach. "Please! That's all we have left of him!"

She grabs the box just over my shoulder, but Neo's father tugs it away, a disgusted, almost frightened look knitting his brows.

I feel the urge to hurt him, to pry the box from his arms and shove him against the wall just for looking at Hikari that way, but I don't.

I hold Hikari back as her voice breaks and she sinks to her knees. "No, no, please, you can't take them away," she sobs, her fists clenching my shirt, her face pressed into my chest. "You can't take them away, you can't, please."

I don't know what's come over me. A streak of protectiveness maybe. Anger at my inability to act.

Eric appears beside me, waving off the other two nurses trying to take Hikari from my arms.

All I can do—all I ever can do—is be there. Be there as what is important to her is taken away. Be there as she is too sick to even fight it. Be there as the person I love cries and suffers and loses her right to grieve.

"Sam," Eric says. "We have to take her to her room—"

"I have her," I interrupt, my voice hardened.

"Sam, just let us—"

"I have her!" I yell.

I pick Hikari up off the floor and, not knowing where to go, I walk, cradling her like an infant, to wherever loneliness and hurt cannot touch us. All the while, I think of Neo's mother tightening her fist around her necklace the way you tighten a loop around the wrist.

I don't know if there is a God.

I've seen too many be manipulated, exploited, and cheated by those claiming to know God's will, to know for certain. I think God can be a good thing, a good idea. God is the greatest provider of hope among those who cannot find it in themselves.

God has never spoken to me himself, herself, themself, whatever God may be. The closest I have ever come to it is the hospital's chapel. It's a rather run-down room with a cross hanging on the far wall and benches sitting in rows for worship.

I gaze up at the cross in the center, the podium backlit by faux-stained-glass windows, and I wonder if time and disease and death are his accomplices or if they are his enemies too.

I know one thing for certain.

If God has ever spoken, it is through the yellow flares in Hikari's eyes. The yellow flares in Sam's eyes. The affection so strong in my core that I am willing to challenge the curse God placed on me when I was born.

But today, Hikari's eyes are dull and God is silent.

"You warned me," she says. I lay her down on the bench farthest from the door. She stares at the ceiling—no—past it, her tears trailing down her temples without sound. "You told me hope was useless. I should've listened."

"No." I shake my head. "No, I was wrong back then. I was just angry at the past. You know that."

"How are you like this, then?" she asks, as if she's accusing me. "How do you *choose* to feel nothing so easily?"

"I do feel. I've been through this before, and it's tearing me apart. I'm just—I love you. I need to be here for you." I take her hand, the one hanging limp off the side of the bench, dragging my thumb over her pulse point. "I love them too, and I hold on to that—"

"Loved," she corrects.

"Hikari. Love doesn't fade when people do." I reach across her chest, to the black pattern of a moon crested as a partner to mine. "Time will stop, disease will fester, and death will die."

"They're dead, Sam!" she yells, throwing my hand off of her. She shakes, pulling herself upright by the bench's back to put space between us. To create distance. As if the mere touch of my skin will burn through her like paper.

"Our enemies won. They took them, and they're gone now." Hikari's hands are curled around the edge of her seat, her eyes wide and downcast.

"Coeur and Neo will never get to finish their story," she says. "Neo will never get to run his fingers over a cover with his name on the spine. Coeur will never get to wrap his arms around him and smile into his neck while he does. Sony will never be there to give them her sweatshirts, and she'll never get to bring those stories back to her kids."

Her words beckon shadows I banished. They creep past the threshold of what is meant to be a sacred place. They infest it, patient predators that have been waiting for this moment. They crawl past Hikari. They already view her as something of theirs. They set their sights on me.

"They'll never grow old," Hikari says, but she is so empty her voice is only air. "They'll never get married. They'll never have children. They'll never see the world or live the lives they were meant to have, and they'll never leave this place."

Hikari looks at me as if I am one of the shadows, as if I belong with all the little-spined monsters that reap us of our lives. She looks at me as if I am seated among them, and just as much to blame.

"They're gone. We didn't save them. It's over, Yorick," she whispers. "People die, disease spreads, and time goes on."

Her eyes draw to the tattoo peeking from beneath the crown of my collar as they draw to her knife during meals. She rejects the reflection as a thing of the past. And this time, when she stands to leave, I know I cannot follow . . .

Am I a shadow, God? I ask once she is gone. *Am I loneliness and fear foolish enough to believe I am light?*

I wait for an answer, but without Hikari, my loneliness coils around me. Don't misconstrue. I do not care for Hikari because she is a body to fill a space. I am not afraid of being alone. I am afraid of being alone without her.

"I won't tell you again. Give that back to me."

"Are you going to hit me? Here, of all places?"

"You're grieving. You're not thinking straight. Just let me handle all this—"

"No. No, I'm not letting you *eradicate* him like this—"

Just outside the chapel, a man and a woman argue. When the man raises his voice, I stand up. He's been escorted out by security for harming a patient before. Whether that patient was his child or not is irrelevant. If he isn't careful, he'll get forcibly removed, and this time for good.

Neo's mother knows that. She uses it to her advantage as her footsteps clap against the chapel floor and her husband, muttering things under his breath, storms off down the hall.

She walks in with panic, her body practically shaking all over. Her hair is down, a short cut the same color as Neo's. While she tries to re-collect herself, I notice that dark violet cups her jaw and cheekbone.

"Ma'am?"

She jumps at my voice, mildly recognizing me. She's holding something in her arms. Papers, I think.

"Hello, um . . ." She stops in her tracks, a submissive edge to her voice. I know from the look on her face that she can't tell if I'm a girl or a boy. The existence of anything in between doesn't make sense to her, so she waits for me to fill in the gaps.

"My name is Sam," I say.

Her face lights up.

"Sam," she repeats. "He talked about you. When he came back for his treatments, I didn't understand what the doctors were saying. He said to me that it was all right, that he wouldn't be alone, that Sam would be here for him." She recounts the story with fondness, then with a hint of sorrow.

"Did you read his—um, Neo's writing?" she asks.

"I did."

She nods at that, licking her lips. "Since he was a boy, he was so quiet. He rarely smiled, but he was so happy when I read to him," she says. "I wish I'd kept doing that, despite everything . . . You were his friend, weren't you?"

"Yes," I say.

"Was he happy here?" she asks. "Did he smile?"

I think of Neo the day I met him. It doesn't feel like three years ago. It feels like I've known him his whole life. I remember his scowls and his complaints and his constant need to be negative about everything under the sun. I remember how those scowls softened, how treasured his little acts of compassion here and there were, how his trust in me was something I never understood the worth of till now.

I owe it to him to tell the truth. I owe it to the smile he gave me before walking into the ocean.

"Every day."

His mother stutters over her next breath, her arms hugging the papers as if they carry Neo in them.

"Thank you," she says, embracing me, smiling as she cries. "Thank you, Sam."

Neo's mother places the pieces of paper she managed to salvage in my hands. Though they are wrinkled, they are intact and overflowing with ink. Neo's father will burn the rest, I'm sure, but at the very least, beneath those stray sheets, the words *Hit List* stare back at me. Metal spirals catch the light, little notes in the margins with time stamps shown off as if the notebook itself is telling me it has not been stolen just yet.

The last of the survivors is a single envelope that Neo's mother keeps for herself.

I'm not sure what Neo wrote to his mom. I am not sure if he has forgiven her or condemned her, or simply said his goodbyes. I am not sure if she will ever read it. I only know that she walks out of the chapel, holding it against her heart rather than toying with her cross, and when she leaves, whatever direction her husband took, she goes the opposite.

"Hikari!" I run into her room. It's dark, night drawn over the city, but she isn't in bed. I unfurl the hit list, not bothering with the light switch. "Hikari, look. Neo's mom, she . . ."

I stop, catching my breath, realizing she isn't here. Her dinner tray is on her bed, but none of the food has been disturbed. Instead, all that's missing is the knife.

"Hikari?" I ask, more cautiously, waiting for a noise of some kind, an answer, anything to know where she is. Out of the corner of my eye, I notice the door to her bathroom is open. Inside, a girl bears her weight down on the sink, her head hanging between her shoulders. Her figure fades with the dark blue background, like watercolors. The glint of teeth on a blade trembles in her fist.

"Hikari," I breathe, afraid to take so much as a step. "Hikari, put it down, please."

She doesn't answer or even turn to look at me. She shuts her eyes tight, and I know the moment I run at her, she will cut herself. A plastic knife takes time to reach blood, but she has the motive to dig.

"Please," I beg, not moving, feeling the heat at the backs of my eyes swelter and form a glossy layer of water.

Hikari lets loose a whimper.

It would be so much easier if she didn't love me, she said. But at least she loves me enough to throw the knife in the sink. The moment it clinks against the ceramic, I run to her, pulling her into me.

"Don't touch me," she says. "No, no, stop it. Stop it. Don't touch me!"

Hikari starts hitting me in the chest, in the stomach, trying to push me away, but she's become so weak. If I let her go, she'll collapse again. I cup the back of her head and wrap my other arm around her back. She hits my shoulders with her fists, crying. It stings, but I'd rather she hurt me than herself.

"I'm sorry," she cries, her pain-fueled violence fading into defeat. "I'm sorry I'm like this."

"It's okay," I whisper, kissing her hair. "I'm not angry. I'm right here. Do you want to read some Shakespeare with me?" I ask. "We can draw together if you want."

Hikari hasn't opened a book or a sketch pad since Sony passed on. She shakes her head, so I carry her to bed, and before laying the covers over her, I reach one more time.

"Hikari," I whisper, caressing the cool, weightless ridges of her hand. "Do you want to go see our stars?"

She doesn't answer me. Instead, she stares at the dying plants on her windowsill. I try to water them every day, but without Hikari's care, they wither anyway.

"Sam," she says, breaking the silence.

"Yes?"

"At the beach. You said you had to tell me something. What was it?"

Settling back on the bed, I can't help but think that our grief has become cyclic. She clings to things of the past, objects, moments, and places, as if she could crawl into time's body and tear it apart from the inside if only to emerge where her friends are still alive.

So she feels her pain, her loneliness, the excruciating feeling that she is dying, but at the same time not dying soon enough. She grapples with her guilt and her fear and her love for me. They torture her until she can no longer bear it and must feel the pain with blood. When I stop her, she resents me. She resents me for keeping her alive. Then it begins again, till all that's left of her to torture is her mind thinning away with her body.

"It can wait," I say, lying under the covers with her.

As Hikari falls into sleep, a selfish fantasy of mine rears its head. I dream that Hikari and I become one person. I dream of being so utterly close that we melt into each other. That way, I could take all this pain she has, every drop of this misery, and nurse on it. I could rid her of the shadows. I could bear every single suffering note till her smiles and her mischief and her curiosity and all the things that are hers return.

I beg the possible to gift me this one impossibility. I beg as I once begged the dead to haunt and wallow in the silence. Because if she and I were one, then I could never lose her.

"I know you're hurting, my Hamlet," I whisper, trembling. I hold her so tight. "But please hold on. Just hold on for me." I kiss her again. I kiss her till I realize she has already become as empty as I used to be. I kiss her till it feels like my fantasy could come true and even if she dies tonight, I will pretend I have died with her. I will crawl beneath the ground as soil is spread onto our bodies and the dark submerges us. I will hold her as she decays to bone and then to ash, and I will love her till time takes the world away and my curse is vanquished by its end.

"Please, Hikari." I kiss her like it's the last time. "Please don't leave me yet."

29
I understand

"**I**S THIS HOW you felt when Sony was dying?" I ask. I sit in a rolling chair at the nurses' station, holding the hit list as I watch Hikari's room from afar.

Winter is here, and her mom has quit her job. She spends her days at the hospital to stay with her daughter while her husband continues to work to pay off medical bills.

"Did you think, *This is it?*" I ask again. "*This may be the day I lose her?*"

Eric either doesn't hear my question, or he ignores it. Rummaging through charts, he handles paperwork with efficiency, as always, only now with an added edge. After we spread Sony's ashes, he went back to work as if nothing had happened. He was offered leave, which he didn't take, but all of his colleagues tiptoe around him still.

I don't think Eric likes that.

I don't think he's ever liked me either, but I've known him since he first began clinical rotations fresh out of school. When he first saw me, he reacted the same way all others do. He felt he knew me fundamentally, a face from his past, but he didn't question it. It was a natural ignorance. He saw me as a detail. A stethoscope around a doctor's neck or the sound of shoes against the tiles.

It doesn't dawn on him that I don't look like I've aged a day since then. People don't question background details unless prompted. They accept them as they are. Sometimes, though, I wonder if, like Hikari, Eric wonders what I am. I wonder if he *does* notice all those peculiarities. I wonder if he ignores them because, for all he doesn't like about me, he likes that I am constant. I don't bend and tiptoe for him. I don't offer what I would not have offered him before.

People need that sometimes. They need things to stay the same to make room for what has changed.

"I think I'll lose her every day," I say, standing up and laying the hit list on the counter next to whatever Eric scribbles on. "Every night once her mother goes home, I lie with her and I beg her not to leave me."

Hikari is no longer tempted by blades of any kind. She barely has the will to be fed by others, let alone the will to feed herself. In the absence of knives, she becomes vegetative. She doesn't leave her bed unless forced. She can't be awake more than a few hours at a time. She vomits after every meal. She loses strands of hair before they have a chance to grow.

"Neo's mother gave me this," I say, caressing the front page and title of our glorious little notebook. "It's everything we ever stole." It's everything they never got to steal.

"She thanked me," I say, my voice weakening. I didn't save Neo. I didn't save any of them. And yet . . . "Why did she thank me?"

Eric continues to go through his charts, letting them fall loudly back into their trays as if to accentuate he has no answers to offer me.

The cat that has made a home on this floor hops onto the counter.

Eric ignores her too. With a hooked paw, she plays with his ID badge clipped on the breast pocket of his scrubs. If I thought she was capable, I'd say Hee was trying to cheer him up. At another time, maybe if Sony were still alive, Eric might've actually smiled for her.

He doesn't. He grabs another chart and gets back to work, only now his pen is fresh out of ink. He gets frustrated and scribbles so hard that the tip breaks through the page. His eyes become heavy, as if the pen itself has committed a great offense by not working. He tosses it aside and knocks the chart off the table entirely. It clatters, and Eric plants his elbows, pulling at his own hair.

"Eric?"

"Do you know where the word *patient* comes from?" he asks. "It means the one who suffers. *Hospital* comes from the word *hospes*, which means *stranger*. Or *guest*, depending on how you interpret the Latin. I learned that in college. I was on my eighth cup of coffee alone in the medical section of the old library. I sat in a crummy chair praying that I'd pass my finals, and right there, in the midst of my privileged struggle, I realized that a newborn baby and a dying old man are both *suffering strangers*." His hands descend to his face, forming a prayer bind around his nose. "I realized that I was starting a career in a place where people begin and end their lives."

Hee meows again, propping herself up on her hind leg to press her paws against Eric's chest. She nuzzles under his jaw, scratching her head against his stubble.

Eric sighs and pets her.

"I could lie to you, Sam," he says. "I could tell you that it's important to be grateful, like Neo's mom, but I'm not. I'm angry. I'm angry that their doctors didn't do more. I'm angry that *I* didn't do more. I'm angry that *kids* have to go through this sheer amount of pain, and I'm angry they died."

His voice thickens. But rather than throw a pen or capsize a chart or hit something or yell, he crumbles. He takes Sony's cat into an embrace and stifles a cry into her fur. When she gives a little mewl of protest at his clinginess, his cry turns into a laugh.

"You were all so happy that day on the roof, dancing together," Eric whispers. He smiles against his hand at the thought. "You have no idea how comforting it was getting your phone calls, catching you sneaking out, stealing, being stupid, and just . . . being kids."

I remember the night we all fell asleep under blankets like little yellow hills on the rooftop. Eric must've come to tell us to come back inside, but when he saw us in the midst of music and frost, he let us just be.

I used to have an estranged concept of love. I think I tried to give it a face the way I give faces to all things I don't understand. But from the look on Eric's face as he remembers Sony dancing, I know for certain that it cannot be stolen.

"Your purpose isn't *saving* suffering strangers, Sam." Eric wipes his eyes. He hugs me and pats my hair, and smiles the way you smile at an old friend. "I hope you know it's so much more than that."

Eric doesn't say anything else. He picks up the chart and pen, putting them neatly back into place. He straightens his ID card and smooths his wrinkled scrubs down. As he turns to get back to work, a group of toddlers runs into his legs. The little gowned creatures huddle around him like herding dogs. One of them holds up a picture book, the rest jumping up and down, shrieking and giggling.

"Hey! Slow down! What did I say about running?! Sebastian, stop picking at your mask. Caitlin, Nora, didn't we already read you this book last week? You didn't steal it, did you? Hey! Sawyer, quit kissing Hazel. You're going to eat her cheek if you keep at it! C'mon, I'm not reading unless everyone takes their medicine *without* complaining— Did you hear me, Nora? Don't walk away from me, you little pest. I see you."

Eric picks up one of the children, bouncing her in his arms once and adjusting the breathing tubes over her cheek and ear.

I smile for Eric. I know he is hurting, but as he leaves to care for his new little band of thieves and doesn't look back, I know he is content too.

A stale, burrowing sadness lies heavy in my chest when I gaze back at the lonely notebook on the counter. Eric boxed and took home Sony's clothes and her dirty white sneakers. Coeur's parents emptied his room and took home his records and tangled earbuds. Neo's father burned his manuscript and all of his books.

The hit list is all I have left of them.

I slowly flip to the first page and read the dedication, the raging declaration of war against all those who committed injustices against us. I can feel Neo's skinny fingers writing out the words and hear C's voice orating. I see Sony's tapping feet as she spins in circles around the notebook, the wind catching her hair and splaying it red against the gray.

I flip to the next page. The words are jumping ship, uneven, scribbled about, with note after note in the margins and a list of things stolen so long it should be kept from the police at all costs.

I smile to myself, remembering when Sony said that once. I flip more pages, reading them all. I laugh at center entries, the time-stamped ones Neo wrote with such vigor, the rather funny entries made by Sony, the rather odd ones made by C.

The last header stares back at me in bold: **Our Escape**.

In the end, they didn't escape with all they took.

They didn't get away with it.

They didn't find their everything.

And their only Heaven left to reach was in death.

I don't realize I am crying until a teardrop hits the page. It soaks into the white and smudged tint of blue and black. I clench my fists over the counter, shutting my eyes so hard they hurt.

Is this it?

Is this what their lives amounted to? Is this the unfair ending that I was told to cry and rage and curse? Is that single day full of tattoos and beaches the in-between I am meant to cherish? Did they live only to die? Is love pointless? Is even the only thing that cannot be stolen destined to be lost? Is there anyone, anyone in the world, whether they be human, shadow, enemy, or God, who could answer me?!

I cry silently, staring down at the empty page. I miss them so much it carves through me. I miss Hikari and all the things that make up her soul. I miss being able to fall and knowing I would be cushioned. I miss the moment we caught her and our embrace on the cold floors of the old cardiology wing that kept out the world.

Hee meows in my face then. I try to pet her, but she shakes me off. She meows again, running across the hit list, knocking it over and tearing the page with her claws.

"Hee! Careful!" I yell.

I grab the notebook as tenderly as I can, placing it back on the counter like a crying baby in need of attention. I wipe it off and look through the ripped piece. Only, after the torn, tear-ridden page of **Our Escape**, there aren't the empty pages I expected . . .

A sad string of piano notes plays as it begins to snow outside the window. All else becomes blurred. Muffled. Lost to another world. White spots sink in a gray, foggy evening. They cast their light through the glass on a glossy photograph taped to the page.

It's a Polaroid.

Taken by Sony on a sunny day with shrubbery as a background. She extends her arm with a toothy grin, showcasing herself, Neo rolling his eyes beside her, C holding Neo's hand, and me on the very edge, awkward and stiff. Beneath, it reads:

Spring.

There is a paragraph under the caption, a messy, albeit legible, marker-written account of what we did that day.

I'm confused at first, my crying stalled. But when I turn the page, there is another.

There is one of Neo and me asleep in the library together. There is another of C trying Sony's oxygen therapy, the tubes sticking out of his nose as she giggles when he says it feels funny. There is a photo of Neo's first day in a wheelchair. There's a photo of his last. There is a picture of C getting an ultrasound of his heart, his tongue sticking out. There is one of Sony hugging me on her first day without oxygen therapy. And there are so many more.

There are song lyrics and book passages and movie lines. There is a leaf, brown and crumpled, taped down. There are little drawings and doodles I recognize as Hikari's. There are excerpts from Neo's stories, the ones I always said were my favorites. There are depictions of the bad days and the good days. There are moments we laughed and moments we cried.

I reach the last page with a trembling hand.

Here, there is no writing. There are no artifacts or lyrics.

There is only a photo of a beautiful girl in a sundress kissing her ordinary lover on a shore. Tucked beneath is the final picture Hikari drew of our friends. And on the other side, just before the notebook shuts, there is a message.

Sam,

Your garden grew and flourished and it was beautiful for a time.

It fell ill and died and its beauty lasts only in memory.

But without you,

Those flowers might've never known light.

So to our narrator and dearest friend, thank you

For the memories.

For the goodbyes.

For the Heaven.

The snow continues to fall with the slow rhythm of a sad song. I close our lonely notebook and gaze out with blurry vision at the city I watched grow from the time it was a wilderness.

My tears flow, and yet I smile.

I smile and crush the hit list to my chest.

I think to myself how lucky I am.

To have known a boy, foulmouthed and resilient, with poetry in his heart. A girl, brave and brusque and passionate. A heartful beast, gentle, musical, elsewhere, and, above all, kind. An illtempered nurse with a sense of duty and care beyond anyone. A girl whose soul I already knew.

She walked into my life through that door, a creaky, loud entrance, bright yellow crowding the darkness of her roots and glasses, too big, too round, perched on the bridge of her nose. When she gave me her everything, and I gave her mine, I fell again.

Although when I look out the window a second time, in the middle of a brewing storm, the empty streets carry a single traveler. A girl whose soul I already know walking across a bridge in nothing but a coat, a hospital gown, and bare feet to mark the snow.

30
before

WHEN A PERSON dies, we say they have passed on. As if they've traveled from their body into another world the living can't perceive. We say that we've lost them. Then we argue what it is exactly we lost them to.

What shape does death take after it's taken?

Compelling in the hypothetical and terrorizing in the tangible.

Because what if there is nothing? What if death is the explosion of countless synapses, a light going out, and that's it? What if Henry and all soldiers trudge through the dark, only for there not to be another side?

Human beings are selfish. They don't accept this because they cannot fathom a world without their existence. As such, there must be an eternal life of some kind. Whether it is found in spirituality, in delusion, or in God, there must be an after. A Heaven.

There is affection in that belief too. When nurses close their patients' eyes, their sadness is coupled with gratitude. If there's something everyone can agree on, it is that there is no pain in death. Only an eternal sort of peace.

I know that Sam is not the eternal being I make him out to be.

One day, he will die, and when he does, I will lie beside him in the ground. I will put this stolen body to rest in his embrace.

Selfishly, like a human, I'm reluctant to accept that he will die. He still has so much life to live. He is just a boy, and if time has any charity in its heart, it will gift him more.

His medicine will work. He will heal. Even if he can't stay here forever, he will live his life out there in the world, and despite the laws by which I live, I will go with him . . .

You must know by now that I am not normal. My flesh and blood are fabrications created to quell my aloneness.

I am not a person. I cannot die. I will never fear death. It cannot touch me. Neither can disease or time. All they can do is take from me.

Now you understand why it is so dangerous for me to live? Everyone wonders what comes after death, but none can grasp the cruelty of being kept alive forever.

In the end, my curse is simple.

I will remember those I love longer than I had a chance to know them.

———

Nurse Ella dies at the peak of spring. Breast cancer. She was fifty-two years old.

Flowers surface where she is buried. Her headstone arches from the ground surrounded by them, as if the buds bloomed to read her name.

Sam sits against the unchiseled side, facing the trees. He twirls stalks of grass, pulling them out. A single finger digs at the soil.

"Sam," I say, crouched in front of him.

He opens his eyes, his mask shrouding the bags and ugly color beneath them. I hold out a newspaper I stole from the dispenser.

"Do you want to read to her?" I ask.

Sam shakes his head, moving aside and patting the ground next to him.

"You read it," he says, his throat sore and tired.

"All right."

I sit against Ella's headstone, a cold and tough thing. It feels like Ella holds us this way. A ghost of her. Grunting in displeasure that we'll get green stains on our pants and that no sweaters shield our shoulders.

I open the paper and start reading the first headline about the recently constructed bridge uniting the river that split the city in two.

Sam drops his head to my shoulder. He listens till he falls asleep, silent tears streaming down his cheeks.

———

The coming warmth alleviates Sam's sorrow as time passes.

But not his sickness.

He and I sleep in the same bed every night. Before nightfall, I always tune the radio to his favorite station. I stand on the cot, humming and nudging till Sam stands up. A smile slowly curves his lips and we dance together like we used to.

I tell Sam about the other patients I see when I bring our breakfast to his room. He smiles obediently and kisses me, as is our routine. I ask, as we eat, how he's feeling. He says he's all right, but he hardly eats a thing. I ask if he'd like to go on that escape soon, the one we've been planning. He says maybe tomorrow as he has been for a lot of yesterdays.

Sam gets bad coughs at night. He spits up blood, gripping his throat. I rub his back and fetch him warm water till the fits ease.

The medicine he's been pumped full of is meant to keep him

alive, but it has the added effect of dulling his senses. When I kiss him, he gains no color. When he eats, his boyish grin never comes.

The simple pleasures he used to rely on for sanity are no longer pleasures. His passion begins to starve the longer this sickness grips him.

He looks out the window for hours on end. He closes his books before finishing them. His smiles are fewer. His kisses are lighter. He doesn't ask about other patients anymore.

I suggest that we go to the park, to the bakery, to see our stars, or go read Ella the newspaper. Sam says he is tired. He says maybe tomorrow.

A few weeks pass, and Sam weakens considerably.

He thins. His cheeks become hollow ravines. His legs shake when he walks, frailness in each step. The raw, bleeding patches grow, like countries on a map overtaking a sea of healthy skin. He can no longer bathe without hissing at the pain.

I ask him if there's anything I can do, but it is a cruel question. Like asking a person holding on to a ledge what you can do from the ground below.

I never leave his side.

When the pain is too much to bear, I read to him, sing to him, talk to him. I tell him I love him. I tell him I will always be here. I tell him all my tomorrows are his.

Late at night, when he thinks I am asleep, Sam cries. He holds me, whispering to himself over and over, "Stay alive. Just stay alive."

More tears fall, and he chokes down a suffering sob at the risk of waking me.

"Just be strong. Just live through this."

He drags his hands up and down my spine. He kisses my hair, holding in whimpers.

"Just stay alive," he says again, and even if I cannot die with him, I want to tell him that it's okay. I want to share a final kiss and tell him that it's okay to let go. That I will be with him till he fades from his body and his soul passes to another world we cannot share.

But I don't. For all the human I am not, I am selfish, and I don't want to live without him. So I pretend to be asleep and hold Sam tighter to me till he falls too.

———

Some doctors like to call unlikely remissions *miracles*. I find this a tad insulting. It isn't called fighting a disease for nothing. Henry was right when he called it a war.

When Sam wins against the illness, he isn't left unscathed. His skin is permanently scarred, blotted in dark, freckled blemishes. His face is sallow, the upturned lines of past smiles sunken. He will never walk the same again. His organs will never function as well as they did.

The pain is gone, Sam assures me. I smile at that, close to tears with relief. Sam, however, isn't overjoyed by his victory. His boyish grins and playful manner that fell into hibernation do not wake with him.

Together, we phase into winter, the months gradual, the days long. I spend them all caring for Sam. Our routine is as it always has been. Every day, I ask Sam if he is ready for our escape.

Every day, he says maybe tomorrow.

———

Winter is here. The first day of it shivers in with the wind's cool breathing and extra blankets for all. I spend the day going to every room, ensuring that patients are being kept warm. Nurse

Ella used to do that every first day of winter, albeit in a harsher, more scrupulous way.

When I finish, it's nearly nightfall. The old dirt roads are now cobblestone. They freeze over outside. The bakery across the street closes early. Civilians are scarce. All disappear back into their homes, nested with their families for the coming cold.

"Good evening, Sam."

I walk into his room. The curtains are drawn, the light kept out, unable to kiss its little gardener or the potted plants on the sill.

Sam sits up on the edge of his bed, looking at the ground rather than the window. I undo the curtains and press a passing kiss to the side of his face.

"Everyone gets extra blankets today and no pudding, but I got us sweet bread." I lay down the treats wrapped in wax paper on the side table.

"Do you want to go outside tomorrow? I've never been outside in the winter," I say. Sam hasn't either. The air is too dry, and pathogens search for a home in bodies this time of year. But now that he's recovered, if he wears his mask and gloves and I am with him, we can share the adventure, no matter how slight.

"Sam?" I call. He doesn't respond. He doesn't react to me. "Sam, are you all right?"

"Do you think the sun rises because it fell?" he asks. He looks through the glass now, at the colors fanning across the sky, each darker than the last.

"Maybe," I say. "But I trust the sun to rise no matter what."

"Do you think it ever gets tired?" Sam asks. He talks the way he breathes. As if he is exhausted by it. "Do you think once the sun sets, it wishes it could set forever?"

"I don't know," I admit, gazing out at the same colors. Only their fading makes me turn away, while it entrances Sam all the more.

I kneel before him, pressing my hands on his knees, smiling the way he's always done for me. "I think the sun knows that without it, we'd be lost forever," I say. "I think it keeps rising for us."

A conflict brews on Sam's face. He bites down, and his brows knit as if his nerves have been pulled like threads stuck in a needle.

"I'm so sorry, my sweet Sam," he whispers.

A sneaking sort of worry stirs through me then.

"Don't apologize to me; you haven't done anything wrong," I say. "You're getting lost in your head again. Let's play cards and go get some dinner. We can pack your things tomorrow and go on that trip. It can be as short or as long as you want it to be. What do you say?"

I stand up, tidy myself, patting Sam's legs. I take his hand in mine, only when I try to lead him, he doesn't move. My body is jerked back to where he sits.

He swallows once, forcing himself to mimic past expressions. A crooked smirk, a little glint of yellow clinging to life like a dying bulb in his eye.

"I never deserved you, did I?" he breathes.

"I don't understand."

"I'm sorry, my love. I can't do this anymore."

I still completely, a sudden sense of dread pooling in my stomach.

Sam was born during a storm. His mother left him when he was a baby. He grew up without the protection people need to survive. I tried to shield him, protect him myself like armor.

At first, Sam's life was like any other child's. His home was what he made of it. The hospital was our palace, we its knights. But the taller Sam got, the more he saw of what lay outside. The more he saw what he was missing.

I remember the look on Sam's face when he took me to the

school dance. He peered at the kids on the other side, reminded that he would never have what they had. He told me it was okay. Because he had happy years with our patients, with Henry, Ella, and me. But I see the look on his face now, and I know.

It's spelled out between us.

The only reason Sam fought this hard to survive is that he wanted to live for me. For all the memories we share, they are also full of his suffering. From the way Sam stands, and guilt runs across his face, it's clear that I am no longer enough to overshadow it . . .

Our palace is a ruin.

Ghosts haunt its halls.

And Sam is too tired to keep pretending his cage is the world.

He holds my hands, waiting for me to say something.

"B-but you're better now. You healed. You're okay," I say in disbelief. "I know it was hard, and I'm so sorry I couldn't do more, but you're okay now. We can escape together like you wanted. We can go. Let's just go, Sam. Anywhere you want, please."

"I'm never going to be better. I'm never going to heal. You know that." Sam doesn't push me away. Not physically. His words do it for him. "I've always been sick, and I always will be, and not even love can change that."

"No." I shake my head. "Please don't do this. Not after everything. You told me to hold on. You told me not to lose hope."

"You were my hope, my sweet Sam," he says. His warmth, which once bled into me with nothing but our connection, is cooling. Instead, the light is drained. He kisses my hairline. "I just can't wait for any more sunrises."

I cry a quiet wail, the kind that lingers like toxic air in your lungs. I don't want to lose him. Not when we've been through this much, not after he fought so hard to survive. He's no longer hanging from a ledge—he got back up, he made it. And now he wants to jump.

"Please," I whimper. "You don't even know who I am."

"Yes, I do," Sam whispers. He takes both my hands, holding them against his heart. "You're my first and only love, and that's enough," he says. "Even if it can't be forever, it's enough that all those years ago, you answered a little boy's prayer and made his wish come true."

Night falls.

He parts from me.

He walks out into the cold.

I follow him onto the bridge above still, black water.

I tell him who I am.

But I cannot sway him.

I cannot stop him.

Sometimes hope just isn't enough.

It isn't meant to save people.

The dark swallows him, and I watch him die.

I realize, as my tears fall, that I always wondered if the suns in his eyes would suit the moons in mine till they shut forever and every night left to come, it rained.

31
a rhyming line
in my history

SHOULD'VE NEVER let them.

I sprint through the front doors and onto the gray street layered by mist. Snow falls, not a single car on the road or person on the sidewalk disturbing its blanket, all but one who leaves a path of footprints in her wake.

I'm out of breath, running as I did all those years ago, yelling a different name with the same fervor.

Hikari looks out at the rushing river, her body gravitating toward it. Reddened fingertips slip atop the metal railing, her breath made of steam. In nothing but a hospital gown and a coat falling from her shoulders, her chin lifts to the sky.

The darkness creeps up behind her. It wraps its arms around her waist and lays its chin on her shoulder. Then it pushes ever so slowly till her head hangs from her shoulders, and in her mind, there is nothing left to do but let her body fall to the water's embrace.

"Hikari!" I yell so hard that my throat hurts. The line I swore to never breach, the bridge I swore to never cross—I push past them. I climb the stone steps, and I run, and I don't stop.

Hikari blinks. With frailness, she looks away from the river, and when her eyes find me, the shadow at her back clenches its fists.

I'm almost there, and once I have her, I won't let go. I won't let the shadow whisper that it is better to end her life than to endure the minute painful part of it. I won't let it throw her to the cold and laugh as her corpse cascades downriver.

"Hikari!"

A car's headlights breach the fog turning onto the bridge's road.

"Sam?" Hikari's voice travels, reaching for me as mine reaches for her. She turns away from the edge, toward me, like a magnet that has no choice in its direction. She takes one step after the other, her bare legs red and her bare feet raw. She uses the railing as a crutch, but the moment she pushes off of it, she trips from the curb.

A honk blares, and the car swerves, its wheels screeching against the ice. Hikari's eyes shut, her arm shielding them from the light. The tail end of the car veers off course, and Hikari braces. The shadow reaches out a hand, but it only knows how to scare, how to watch, how to push.

Maybe I am a shadow too, but I know what it's like to fall.

I grab Hikari by the arm and pull her body onto the sidewalk, sending us both tumbling back on the pavement. Hikari lands on top of me, then beneath me. I shield her, my hand on the top of her head.

When I look back at the road, the car has already gone, driving out beyond the fog, not even its taillights left to be seen.

Hikari is breathless, the panic in her veins returning to something more familiar. All of a sudden, as she sees my face hovering over hers, everything I mean and everything I am comes back to haunt her. She struggles, tears welling in her eyes at the sight of me.

Up close, she sees her friends sick, herself sick, her friends dying, herself dying. She shuts her eyes tight, shaking her head against the concrete, pushing at my chest.

"Hikari—"

"No, no—" She whimpers, as if I am poisonous, as if I have cursed her. I keep her down, because I know if I let her stand, she will walk into the fog, across the bridge, down the river, and into the dark.

"Hikari, please—"

"No, I can't—I can't—" She fights me, the scars on her arms throbbing, the one on her neck raw from the cold. The shadow is here, standing over us, and whether its name is suicide, self-harm, fear, depression, abuse, or hate, it will not take her hand. Not this time.

"Hikari, it will end!" I yell, pinning down her arms. She stills, her chest pulsing. I hold on to her wrists, our weight making indents in the snow. Hikari's lower lip trembles, her skin cold beneath my palms. It heats as emotions find her face again, as the shadow that looms over her takes a step back.

"It will end," I whisper, shaking my head. "Everything dies, and everything ends, even your pain. Don't die for it, my Hamlet. Don't give it the satisfaction. I promise you it will end."

"Even if it d-does . . ." Hikari stutters, her breaths broken and wet. "Even if it does, I don't want to live for what comes after."

"Yes, you do."

"No, I can't. I'm always going to be sick, Sam. For the rest of my life. I'm not strong enough."

"Then I'll give you my strength," I tell her. She cries for the night we lay exactly like this. When waves rather than a river were our background and stars rather than snow were our light.

"I know you miss them," I say, wiping her tears with my thumb and cupping her face. "I know it feels like they were ripped from us by the roots, and I know it hurts, but this torture you feel, this intense feeling that it will never get better, *it will end*."

I smile a sad smile that I know she will not catch, but that I know she will understand.

"One day," I whisper, "you'll look back on your time here, and you will cry, but you'll smile too. You'll smile thinking of Sony's snorty laugh and Coeur's tangents about music and Neo's rare hugs. You'll remember our nights dancing and kissing with Shakespeare and every moment in between. You'll survive and feel your scars and remember that even if it was the hardest thing imaginable, you lived through it. You lived through it, and you met three beautiful people, and you loved them as long and as much as you could."

"Sam," she cries.

"Hikari." I press my forehead to hers as I did the night the shadows ripped out her hair and her dreams. When I part from her, she looks at me with the same pleading I once did to her in another life.

"Why do people have to die?" she asks, and all of her hurt escapes in those few words.

There is no cure for grief. It is the most tangible yet intangible of pains because only one thing can make it livable. Forgetting is not an essential part of it.

Time is.

Time stands beside me now, its own shadow. My enemy that has also been my companion. It bends down and casts a gentle palm over the thin layer of Hikari's hair. It does not promise a future, but it promises a past that cannot be stolen. It promises that it will go on for her.

"I don't know," I say, because it is the only truth I have. "We will look for a reason till even the sun and moon are gone because we believe that an answer will balance the tragedy." Hikari stares up at me with desperation glimmering in her tears. I wipe them away as mine fall with hers.

"There is no reason for tragedy," I say. "One day, the universe will collapse, death will have no one left to claim, disease will have no one to infect, and time will come to an end, but even then, it will not have been for nothing. Because if we chose to only love what we couldn't lose, then we would never love at all."

I take her face in both my hands and even if it hurts, I remember each and every moment I held her this way. I remember every moment I held Sam too.

"Love is not a choice," I say, smiling with all the gratitude in the world that I am the pitiful creature she chose. "And even if it were, I would choose you every time."

"Sam."

"Hikari."

Every memory I locked away on this bridge breaks from its confines. They fly from their glass caskets and I let them all live within me as they deserve to. The snow continues in a haze around them. Hikari's arms wrap around me, her head tucked to my chest to shield her from the brewing storm until she finally lets the snowflakes kiss her face.

"The stars are falling," she whispers.

"My love," I cry. "They already fell."

The thing about hope is that it is a fearful reaction. We are hopeful because we are afraid. Because we think on some level we are owed. But this story was never about the hope that arises in catastrophic moments. That hope is passive, not a being but a state of being.

There is another kind of hope. The kind that is eternal, a scenery you don't quite notice until you glance a second time. It is not a wish, it is an appreciation, a grateful desire for life as it is.

Everything has a soul. Even books, broken things, and hope have souls.

Hope chased despair down the street that day. It caught her by the waist, and it saved her just as she had saved it from the unbearable brightness of their own making. After all, suns cannot see their own light.

So hope and despair held each other close until the shadows were gone.

32
after

IT TAKES TIME.

But over the course of winter's coldest months, Hikari begins to heal. Her body, and, thanks to time's grace, her mind too.

Her parents agreed to go to therapy with her, a recommendation from her doctors. They learn to listen as Hikari learns to communicate. I see her mom hugging her more often, and reading with her. Her father looks at her drawings and talks to her about them. Their relationships, however wounded, mend with every subtle, contagious smile.

Every day, when the broken clock above the door should strike noon, Hikari takes me by the hand, her notebook in the other, and together we make our way to the library, the garden, all of our places. She begins to meet other patients close to her age. At first, Hikari is reserved, afraid, as she was in the past. But with me beside her, she regains her confidence. Those that appreciate Hikari's creativity, brazenness, and little strokes of mischief become friendly with her. After a few weeks of encouragement, every chance she gets, Hikari gifts a little bit of her time, a little bit of her kindness, and a little bit of herself to someone new. She learns, as she did with our three thieves, that there are people who understand her, and more than that, people who will try even if they don't.

And us?

We are us.

We go through the hit list together sometimes, reminding each other of good days as her worst ones begin to better. We steal apples and share them in the night over books. We dance like actors and sing like playwrights to the voices of Shakespeare.

I consider myself the luckiest creature in the world to be graced by her. Hearing the laughter that reddens her cheeks and thins her eyes, feeling her hands mirror and meet mine, and all the little moments. The everything moments.

Hikari has come to terms that there will never be a time she is not haunted by shadows. She will live with her depression and her disease for the rest of her life.

Chronic illnesses are just that. Chronic. Reoccurring. Forever. They are not annoying, occasional pains to get rid of with a pill. They are persistent in their pursuit of your sanity.

Their symptoms accumulate, and their severity fluctuates. They stack up like dominoes falling with random patterns. They can be deadly as they were in Sony and Coeur. They can be deadly in other ways as they were in Neo.

A chronic illness is not difficult to live with because it is endless. It is difficult to live with because it is unpredictable. But like grief, every flare ends, and though the looming threat is constant, you learn to live beside it. A shadow of mixed blessings. It does not heal as wounds do, but it teaches you of your own strength till you can wear it like a battle scar.

Hikari knows that better than anyone.

She will be discharged tomorrow. She will go home with color to her skin and wounds licked clean. Her older features, those full cheeks and her ever-humorous grin, return with every passing day. Her emptiness fills with the support of those around her till she is full enough to stand and walk and touch and be.

The day those yellow flecks in her eyes shine like they did the first day I saw her, a bittersweet relief rushes through me.

"You're so affectionate," Hikari says as I sigh into our embrace.

"Why shouldn't I be?" I ask, her scent filling me. My face settles in the crook of her neck, her hands playing up and down my back.

"At the beginning, you were so afraid to touch me, remember?" she whispers. "You were scared I'd burn you."

"I was scared you'd burn away into nothing," I tell her. When I raise my head to meet her gaze, my jaw grazes against the same eclipsing heat that now warms my heart. "I wanted to save you."

"Did you?"

"No."

Hikari laughs.

"You didn't need to be saved," I say, kissing her nose just below the bridge of her glasses. "You just needed to be reminded that you aren't fighting alone." I press my lips to her shoulder as the elevator rises.

"In the end," I whisper into her hair, "you eradicated my loneliness."

"Because you eradicated mine."

"With my rude, affectionate arms?"

"With your tomorrows."

I want to savor this moment. This little blip in time when she is mine, and I am hers, and the rest of the world outside of us may as well not exist.

"Are you all right, my Yorick?" Hikari asks, dragging her fingers tenderly down my face.

"I have something to give you."

The elevator doors open with a ding. I take Hikari's hand in mine, walking her up our stale concrete stairwell.

"Another grand gesture?" she asks.

I glance over my shoulder at her. "Not quite."

A creak and a gust of wind welcome us to the rooftop, our meeting place, our graveyard, and our ledge. Only it isn't barren and gray tonight.

Tonight, string lights adorn the walls, a yellow blanket at the center set up like a picnic. Atop it, a familiar cardboard box with memorabilia sits, its crown a little succulent that no longer needs my care.

Hikari marvels at the scene, the light reflected in the crystal of the watch on her wrist. She fidgets with it, smiling as her feet border the blanket.

"Is this a going-away party?"

"You hate parties," I remind her, a pastry bag rustling as I pick it up from behind the cardboard.

"I like food, though." She tries to take it from me, but I hold it over my head.

"And grand gestures?"

"Sam," she begs, laughing as I take a bite of the chocolate buttery thing she can never get enough of. Rather than scold me or steal away the pastry, she kisses me hard on the mouth, getting a taste for herself.

"Here." I hand her the bag, and it takes all of two bites for the chocolate to stain her face.

"Thank you for all this," she says as I wipe her bottom lip with my thumb. "I'm sorry I didn't get to appreciate it the first time."

The first time, I would've handed her a letter under false stars. Tonight, I give her my words under real ones. I think she is happier with that. That makes me happy too. My universal puzzle piece that could fit in any landscape is a natural part of this painting and, at once, the most striking color in it.

"What is it?" she asks, her head cocked to the side, her dark, smooth hair long enough to move with her.

"You're beautiful," I say.

She purses her lips, narrowing her eyes at me. "That's my line."

I bow dramatically with attempted elegance, as much as an oaf can have. Hikari laughs and plays along, allowing me a kiss to her knuckles when she takes my hand.

"In whatever form you grace me, my Hamlet, you never fail to infatuate my heart."

"So poetic tonight, Yorick," she kids. "This isn't you saying goodbye, is it?"

She's joking. Teasing me. But the nervous end to that question isn't helped by the silence that follows. Hikari looks at the box, then back at me, waiting expectantly for me to say something else, to give her the denial she wants to hear.

You wouldn't be able to tell from the smile I wear for her, but even as I admire her words, her touch, her everything, every day, there is a reason I am trying to memorize them.

"You've healed, my Hamlet," I say, my voice gone faint. "You're ready to leave me now."

"Hey." Hikari puts the bag down, walking to me with concern knit on her brow. "I'll come visit you. Every day. You know I will. Until you get better, I'll be here—"

"Do you remember that night at the shore?" I ask. "I said I had something to tell you about myself."

Hikari blinks after a moment, nodding, like she's anxious for what will follow.

I grasp both her hands, trying to work up the courage to finally explain. "Ha-have you ever noticed that I am not quite the same as everyone else? That I have no parents or family to speak of or even a room of my own?"

Hikari looks confused. Sam wore the same expression when I told him. It's like trying to force someone to question gravity. Their feet are on the ground, and so it's so difficult for them to look twice at something that feels so simple.

Hikari swallows, shaking her head. "You're—you're just—"

"I'm not sick," I say. "You just see me that way because that's how you want to see me."

"I don't understand."

"You've called me strange since you first saw me, remember?"

"Yes," Hikari says, stepping closer. She runs her thumbs over my knuckles. "You're my familiar stranger."

"I'm familiar because we've met before, my love," I say. "We met in a past life when you had the same yellow flares in your eyes and the same soul."

"Sam, what are you saying?"

Hikari's hair was once yellow. Not golden or flaxen, *yellow*. Like dandelions and lemons. The color crowded the darkness of her roots, framing her face with big, round glasses perched on her nose.

Sam's eyes were once yellow, bright when he was happy, even brighter when he was sad. His voice was young and high, yet comfortable no matter the listener. He held himself like a character, a hero in a novel, a knight without a self-conscious bone in his body.

And together, across different planes of time, they are the reasons I am here.

"What if I told you that hope has a soul?" I say. "What if hope wanted to know why the strangers it cared for slipped through its fingers? What if it was so desperate for answers that it created a body and decided to walk among the living in order to find them?"

"I don't understand what you're saying—"

"Everything has a soul, Hikari, even those without a name. And I never had a name until someone gave me theirs."

Hikari frowns in her thinking, connecting lines she never saw could intersect before now. It only starts to make sense when she remembers that no one has ever described me. No one has ever claimed to see me in any way other than myself. No one has ever questioned me.

"Sam." Hikari's eyes go wide, pinned on mine as gravity comes undone. "You're hope's soul?"

I shake my head. "What you see as a hope is a last resort. I am more than that, I think. I am the soul of an unfulfilled wish. I am what arises to keep people afloat when it seems so comfortable to sink."

I am not a woman or a man, a boy or a girl, a child or an adult. I am not of any race or origin. I am not fat or thin or tall or short or anything in between. Yet, at once, I am all those things. I am whatever you need me to be. Whatever face you give to the shadow you need when the sun sets.

"I was born when this hospital was. When there was more suffering than sense," I tell her, remembering when this body was of conditional existence, and my true frame was inanimate.

"People needed me, so I cared for them, and then they died. But it took a long time to understand that even if I am cursed to remember people longer than I had a chance to know them, I was blessed with meeting a lot of souls I wouldn't have had the chance to know."

Wise elders, beautiful children, kind nurses, trying doctors, friends who showed me other worlds, loves who showed me how to live in my own.

Hikari presses her hand to her mouth, in disbelief, in shock, in sadness, in all the things I mirror now.

"Hikari." I try to coax her back to me. "If I weren't cursed, I never would've met you."

She shakes her head, trembling. "You aren't real."

"I am."

I am as real as any person you can see and touch and hear. I am simply different, younger yet older at the same time, stronger and weaker, an illusion, a narrator who transcended its purposes and chose to crawl into the pages of the story.

I shed the same single tear Hikari cries. "I'm just not real in the way you need me to be."

"But—but you can leave this place," she says, clinging to my existence as she knows it, not because it breaks some kind of narrative, but because she is slowly creeping toward the same realization I did when I put her life ahead of my own. "You escaped with us. You—"

"I can stretch as far as the hospital's influence goes. As far as any patient goes," I tell her. "But I can only stretch so far until I must come home."

"Sam." Her voice thins, pinched to a whimper.

What I give her tonight isn't just the truth of who I am. It is the truth of our relative impossibility. I clung to it with Sam as I cling to it with her. This dream of becoming one being together forever.

I knew that there would come a day of no tomorrows.

I knew, and I cry anyway.

"I love you," Hikari says, my hands clutched in hers like a plea of their own. "I don't want to live without you."

I pull her into me again, the weight of her body, the ridges of her bones, and the plushness of her flesh all burned into my memory. Forever is an impossible dream, but it's what makes you hold on this way. It's the hope of it that binds you to the other person with memories of all the extraordinary and all the mundane moments you spent together.

"You will have so many loves, Hikari," I whisper. "You will have a life that's far more than me."

I see her with the friends she's made, going to a beach and letting the sea soak her sundress. Her laughter rings as she watches a movie with her parents, drawing her favorite characters on random surfaces. She will find boys and girls who excite her, who make her stomach rise with butterflies, and who treat her as if she is the most precious thing in the world because she is. She will have a family of her own choosing. She will see the world and read and write for it, listening to our old favorite songs with tangled earbuds.

She will think of me on the lonely days, grazing her fingers over a spine with Shakespeare's name. She will ask me to haunt her, and I will in memory and in vision. She will have hard days she doesn't feel like standing back up, but she will anyhow. She will take long car rides with rock music blasting through open windows as the breeze flirts with her hair.

I crush her to me, shuddering against the heat of her skin.

She will have a life far more than me. "And I am so glad that you held on for it."

"What about you?" Hikari cries. "What about your life?"

The wind passes between us, reminding us of its existence. It travels from the first floor all the way up to here, where we touch the sky. Through its carry, I feel every person in the hospital's walls, and I remember that even if I will never be alone, "You know that you're the only life I ever needed."

Hikari's eyes well, the yellow glossing like suns reflecting the moon. She touches the tattoo on my chest.

"If what you say is true, then no matter how many lives I lead, you'll lose me every time."

"Yes," I say, crying with her, moving aside her collar to catch the arrowhead edges of her half-sun. "But it also means that I will always find you first."

Two lonely souls across different boundaries sharing a single universe cannot be kept apart by anything. They cannot be stolen from each other. And as long as I am here, I will never break my promise again.

"All my tomorrows are yours, Hikari," I say, our noses brushing, the salt of our goodbye meeting in a stream.

Her breath hitches against my lips. Tucking her hair behind her ears, I kiss her, every kiss we've ever shared held in it. I've had my life with her, and I could not be more grateful for the time we were given. It stands behind me, ready to lead my body away as the wish that Hikari and I could become one comes apart at the seams.

"Will you come back, my love?" I ask. "When you've lived this life and had your loves, and you're ready, will you come back to me one last time?"

I slip a torn piece of paper into her hand, stolen stationery. I bared my heart on the night we first kissed in the old cardiology wing. On it, another dream sits, ready for the taking, another promise. Hikari reads the words as her tears trickle onto the paper. One last time, she graces me with her contagious smile, and even if it is bittersweet, it will be that smile I cling to when she is gone.

"Yes," Hikari breathes. Her palms slip from my face till all they hold is the shape of wind. "I'll come back to you."

The body I created decades ago fades till it is nothing but an idea resting in peace. I spread through my greater home, my soul tethered to the place it was born in.

The parting hurts. It feels like a part of me is severing as I bleed out onto the stone, and when Hikari leaves, I know she will cry for me as I cry for her.

But she knows.

She knows that when she returns decades from now, I will hold her in my arms and keep her close as the shadows close in and death takes her gently into another realm. And if time is willing, it will give more than just goodbye.

"I promise."

33
Hikari

TWO CENTURIES AGO, a hospital was born. Men built it of stone, lumber, and faith that could move mountains. Within it, something came to life past the realm of understanding. A creature of sorts, a soul made of the dreams the people who built the hospital held on to. That soul gave me this story, and now I pass it on to you.

The hospital's infancy was long. It was difficult to care for, to keep up. As it grew and evolved, it became a place everyone knew. It became a place people came to be saved.

Mine workers and tailors with cuts and broken fingers arrived, patched up within an hour's time. They left sore but grateful. Though it was but a bit of space with no human body of its own, that soul within the hospital saw joy in their expressions as they waved goodbye. Others came in need of help. Some were too withered to survive, so that lonely soul held their hands till their breathing ceased. It always made the creature sad having to say goodbye that way.

Soon, though, it met children. Children were the most beautiful of them all. They were loud, colorful, and attracted to all things they did not know. Children, it learned, suffered from curiosity just as it did. They laughed at anything and ran across its halls to play, pure and kind and hopeful to the bone.

It loved them all, that creature. It loved the babies whose fists curled around fingers and who cooed in their parents' arms under its roof. It loved their sleepy breaths, jaws slack, dreams amok in their wild, untamed minds.

Time went on. Children grew. They became people. And if the soul was lucky, they lived long, happy lives and returned to it with babies of their own.

Of course, that luck had to run out.

Disease never came before or after. Disease was a staple of forever, but disease undoubtedly carried out a coup with violence. Disease took the children with its bare hands. Disease murdered babies in their cribs before they'd had a chance to catch light in their eyes. It murdered miners, tailors, nurses, and doctors too.

They were all taken away, given to death, a whale with a wide-open maw, never satisfied. It swallowed the hospital's people. Its children. Its babies. And all it could do was watch as the years went by under time's control.

The older that hospital grew, the more tears stained its floors. Mothers' tears, fathers' tears, lovers' tears. It became a place of last resort. A place where people come to lose those they love. Their bodies were given to the ground and their memories to grief.

It remembered every suffering stranger, but decades went by. Then a century. There came so much pain that it forced itself to forget. It tried not to feel at all. No pain, no warmth, no joy. Only morbid curiosity forever searching for a reason for all that carnage.

It was that way till a child, unlike the rest, emerged.

He was an eternal being given by God, but he was also just

a boy. A lonely boy who reached for hope's hand when it was lonely too. As they found solace in each other, that soul, that creature, *hope*, gave itself a means of being with him.

No matter how many died, no matter how many lives it couldn't save, hope had Sam. It created a body made of flesh and bone. It made itself tangible, real, becoming a part of the world it'd spent so long watching.

Sam was its first love. In one way or another, all first loves are lost.

Sometimes death is more merciful than life, and he chose its mercy over mine, it said.

Although it didn't just lose him. It lost everything attributed to him. Everything they shared. So it cried atop the pain of memories buried in snow. It fell in love with Sam because it thought they'd be together forever.

Forever is an illusion for mortal things, but time felt sorry for me, it said. *Time patched up my wounds, dried my tears, and did the best it could simply by passing.*

Time let it forget, but that soul kept Sam's name. It kept its curious body. It walked through its greater frame, the one made of wood and stone, and it searched for answers in those who came through its doors. It chose not to feel as it chose not to suffer, and it chose not to want as it chose not to lose.

It never let love in again.

Of course, you can't control that. Whether you're a human, a book, a cat, or hope itself, love is not a choice.

It was just like falling.

It fell in love with resilience.

Resilience is tough, skinned with taut language made of iron. He was forged by hate, dented but never broken. Beneath the impenetrable, fragile bones built his body. He was small, not broad as a shield should be. None of that mattered, though. Resilience is in the mind. He was made of poetry and broken things. Of stubbornness and dry humor. Of memories written not as proof of survival, but as proof that he lived.

It fell in love with kindness.

Kindness was always meant for a brittle, bleeding heart. Perhaps not very bright, nor very ambitious, kindness grew, never decorative, but always present. He knew, carrying resilience in his arms, hugging passion around the belly, and caressing hope's missing color, that he was needed. The melodies he shared drew smiles greater than artists ever could.

It fell in love with passion.

Passion was a goddess. She ebbed and flowed in the sea, her waves carving cliffsides. Her humor alone could take over the world. Grinning ear to ear, she spouted foul words, pretty words, all the words she wanted. Shame cowered in fear of her. Passion gave kindness friendship on which to lean, resilience a reason to laugh, and hope a fellow flame to dance with.

And hope. Hope is the bittersweet companion of loneliness. It lives in creatures of the forever, a caring home with more curiosity than sense. It tells little white lies and steals here and there. It gets lost. Lost in those who need it. Hope tastes like a day at the sea and holds your hand with a bruising grip. It is deep and afraid and hollow and brave.

Hope is the dirty white sneakers on otherwise ever-bare feet. The sweatshirts we share. The promise poems torn at the edges. The headphones with always-knotted wires and the dances on cold rooftops. The boring, comfortable hum of machines and the cool, thrilling beaches. The shadows against a protruding spine caressed by your lover. The heat of a kiss and icy fingertips against reddened cheekbones.

The little moments.

The everything moments.

The moments before the sun chooses to rise.

Though some shadows may ruin the world, there are people, people like them, who survive and crawl from the wreckage. The people who created this home, the people who continue to study and roam and practice to save one another. They are more than hollow shells to sate death's hunger. They are full of passion, of resilience, of kindness, and of immeasurable hope.

My hope, *my* love, was born from that wish.

It was born so that suffering strangers have a place to belong. To keep the night and the mirrors away. To let artists storm the halls and sketch as many smiles as they can. To make time feel endless. To make the despair that lives in us feel just a little less alone.

Walking out into the street, I blend into the crowd of new strangers and see the possibilities in each and every one of their faces. They do not know your names, my friends, and despite the world's greatest efforts, it will not remember you.

But I will.

I do not leave you behind. I take you with me into this new chapter of life beyond the pages. I will tell all my loves of you. I will tell my children of you. I will die, and before I do, I will read this story once more and remember that your names and your stories are immortal.

And to my love, to my Sam, before my last breath, I will look up at the stars and remember your letter.

To my eternal sun,
  My love for you did not begin.
  It did not end.

What we share is not a chronological feat.

It is a promise of its own.

It is the most basic form of trust.

It can be broken and rebuilt.

It can fade and reignite.

But it cannot be stolen.

Not even by death.

We were an eclipse.

A moment the sun and moon met.

A flash of light wherein hope reached for despair and they embraced, whether it be for a single moment or eternity.

Tonight, I will climb to the rooftop thinking of you. My ghosts roam beside me, a missing lung, a missing heart, and a missing mind returned by the night.

I will see you step out into the streets, yellow blending into the crowds, and I will reach for you with only one dream. If in your next life, you decide to find me again, with another name, in another body, I will give you a home. I will abide by my promise.

I will fall in love with you every time . . .

So will I, my love.
So will I.

Endword

H E SAID I'D make a good doctor.

In retrospect, I know he said that to make me happy the same way I told him while he was confined to a wheelchair that he'd make an excellent horseback rider. We made fun of each other like that, although even on the phone, he could never do it with a straight face and he could never not follow it with an *I'm joking*. It's rare to find people so inherently nice who've suffered that kind of pain. Pain is a nasty animal of the body's own creation, just like an autoimmune disease. It tends to destroy, but whatever it destroyed in him, it was not his kindness.

When he died, it blindsided me.

At first, it felt somewhat unreal, and then it graduated into a physical pain I couldn't stand. I remember lying on the floor, wanting to scream every time I thought of his smile.

My kindness, what fickle pieces of it were left standing, was pulled out by the roots. For years after, I plunged into a streak of cynicism and meanness and the general belief that life was a sort of sick joke and not worth the absolution of compassion.

I kept him a secret from everyone, save my mother. Somehow, that made it feel like I was preserving him. I tended to lie to people who asked about my past because that's what children do when they're hogging something. He was my first true experience with death, and he was my first experience with love, and I wanted him to remain something of mine. With my adolescence, that compulsion faded, as grief tends to. My aggressiveness and pessimism were replaced by a general coldness, which I find is just an inherent part of me that I must accept. I retain my ability to laugh, my ability to empathize, and, more important, I learned how to be kind.

Our real story—the thousands of emails we shared, the phone calls, the moments of laughter, and the stories we wrote each other—does remain mine. He and I inspired this story, but ours will always belong to the past, and to my memory of it, as it should.

To the boy who smiled and encouraged me to write, not for the world, but for myself, you will forever be a part of me. This story and the characters I described to you over the sound of a heart monitor and distant workings of the hospital all those years ago have finally found life. My heart beats with thunder and lightning, and even if it is weak, it is the one I gave you. It and this story are forever yours as much as they are mine.

To the reader who endured these sometimes heavy pages, my gratitude is not empty. Whatever you take with you, even if it is a single line, just know I appreciate the gift you've given me.

In the end, mean or kind, the world is full of people who are all similar. We are bone and blood, and some consciousness tied to it. So don't give your enemies the satisfaction of watching life go by, and whether it be a passion, a place, a person, or just a lonely friend bound to ink and paper, love as hard and as long as you can.

Thank you.